MOOCHIE'S PLACE

by

Jim Murdock

INFINITY
PUBLISHING

ISBN 978-0-7414-6746-1 Paperback
ISBN 978-0-7414-6859-8 Hardcover
ISBN 978-0-7414-9510-4 eBook

Library of Congress Control Number: 2011932831

Printed in the United States of America

Published October 2012

INFINITY PUBLISHING
1094 New DeHaven Street, Suite 100
West Conshohocken, PA 19428-2713
Toll-free (877) BUY BOOK
Local Phone (610) 941-9999
Fax (610) 941-9959
Info@buybooksontheweb.com
www.buybooksontheweb.com

To Mike and Matt

and

To Those with the Courage
to reach beyond their limits

Courage consists not in hazarding without fear,
but being resolutely minded in a just cause.
- Plutarch

Acknowledgements

While writing is a pleasure, it requires a lot of time and patience as you wait for your characters to develop and reveal to you what they want to say to the readers. I'm thankful to the following people who helped with encouragement and suggestions along the way.

God, for inspiring my thoughts.

My family for their loving support.

My writing group for their wisdom and advice:
Genie Bernstein, Dac Crossley and Pat Bell-Scott.

Marion Milford for her advice and especially her kind words.

Jay Tibble whose kind and gentle spirit has been an inspiration to me.

CHAPTER ONE

You are reading about the fabulous life of Moochie Dunlop and the man who saw the beauty of her soul. Both have survived their winter of darkness, but not yet found their spring of hope. Can they survive in this find-your-own-soup-bone world?

It was a pleasant Georgia evening in the spring of two-thousand-eight. They sat in foldable lounge chairs, purchased from Wal-Mart, next to their recently assembled, above-ground pool. Moochie Dunlop's over-doctored coffee and William Arrington the Third's Bud Light, sat on a plastic table between them. An empty chocolate-covered praline wrapper lay on the ground.

Moochie thought of her mother and father, both dead now, and wondered what in the world they were thinking when they begot me, or were they thinking at all? Why didn't they plan more carefully and have a normal baby, not one who was fat right from the beginning? Someone who could have been popular in school, maybe even a cheerleader or majorette? Life would have been easier and I wouldn't have had to decide whether to give up, or not care and move on.

Reading the "Police-Blotter" section of the local newspaper, she said, "Listen to this, honey. 'Local restaurant vandalized. The Coffee Cup Café was broken into last night. Unknown assailants did major damage to the furniture and equipment, and sprayed life-threatening graffiti on the walls. Police said there was no indication this crime was gang-related. When officers arrived, they found the elderly owner screaming incoherent threats against a local business man. The distraught man was rushed to Athens Regional where he was sedated. Police will interview him later to determine a possible motive or suspects.' Lord-a-mercy, if that don't beat all. Seems like no body's safe anymore."

William, simply known as Bud, faced the back of their three-bedroom ranch house, with a good view of the broken screen door, ancient York air conditioner and shaggy grass. He looked at Moochie and said, "You're right about that. Being in the food business is hard enough without something like that happening."

They fell silent, Bud thinking about his days as a short-order cook. Finally, he said, "Well, love, here we are, married, living on my check as a shipping foreman and your baby-sitting income. Is this it? I mean, have we arrived or what?" He closed his eyes and leaned back, not really expecting an answer.

"I've been thinking about that myself," said Moochie. "I've been put down all my life, mainly because of my weight. If you can't control your weight, especially if you're a woman, folks tend to think you're lacking in character, that you just don't have what it takes to make a go of anything."

Bud opened one eye. "Is that what you believe, Moochie?"

"Hell, no. I don't believe that and never will. I know this old world is what it is, and people are the way they are, but if they expect me to just sit here and take it without fighting back, they better reset their gyroscope. I resent folks when they judge me or someone else because of our appearance. They don't know what's inside me, honey. I mean to have my own business and be successful enough to help other people. That's what drives me and gives me pleasure, helping others. Don't you feel that way, honey?" Moochie turned to face Bud.

"Yeah, but so far, I've been too busy trying to survive, dragging myself from job to job, drinking myself silly, feeling sorry for myself because of my mama and daddy. I aim to be my own boss, hold my head up in the community. About all I've done up to this point is learn how to cook."

Moochie propped her chin on her hand and wrinkled her brow. Then, she smiled and reached over and took Bud's hand. "Honey, let's make a pact right now to have our own place. Let's be successful so we can help others and gain respect for who we are. What do you say, Bud? Are you with me?"

"I'm with you, love, whatever we do, but it won't be easy. I'll even give up my drinking if that's what it takes."

Moochie was so surprised to hear that Bud would give up his favorite pastime, she made a pledge herself. "And, I promise to not eat a praline before I get out of bed each morning, and only one Twinkie Twin Pack before going to sleep at night. How's that?"

"Sounds like we got us a deal," said Bud. He leaned back in his chair and drained the last of his beer. "That's it, babe. I'm done."

A breeze filled with the smell of sweet gardenias swept away the aroma of coffee and the dank smell of beer, just as their old lives would soon be caught up in the swirling currents of an uncertain economy and the desperate greed of those who worship money.

*****

The next evening Moochie and Bud drove to downtown Athens and found a parking spot on the south side of Broad Street, not far from the Arches, main entrance to the University of Georgia, which dominates and in many ways sets the tone for the city. They strolled around the original north quadrangle, which is heavily influenced by the architectural design of Yale University. They found peace among the beautiful, old brick buildings which stand proudly, surrounding a manicured square, gently shaded by ancient oaks which not only block the harsh southern sun, but also the fast-paced world they live in. Tonight they sat on one of the benches, soaking in the peace and love that seems to flow from the wise old trees. The scent of fluttering red Azaleas and other spring flowers filled them with assurance that all is well in God's world.

Moochie remarked to Bud, "You know, sweetie, just being here makes me feel smarter."

Bud replied, "In that case, love, we better bring a tent and stay a couple of weeks."

She grabbed his hand, "Okay, wise guy. Come on, let's take a walk before I slap your jaws."

Bud grinned and jumped to his feet. They walked along Broad Street, watching the assortment of people, nodding here and there if someone made eye contact. They created quite a stir wherever they went because of their disparate size.

As Moochie carried her five-feet-eleven-inch, three hundred pound frame along the sidewalk, most people voluntarily yielded space, rather than being bounced off like ping pong balls. She was cautious of young children and the elderly, often stopping to share a praline from her ever-present bag of goodies.

Bud, forty-five, was five years older than Moochie. At five-feet-eight, one hundred-forty-five pounds, he could either walk beside Moochie and add to the sidewalk congestion, or walk behind and not worry about the collateral damage. At times, he walked in front of Moochie because the view was more diverse.

Moochie first met Bud at a funeral, and Bud was fortunate to walk away without meeting his own fate. She'd grabbed him in one of her soon-to-be famous bear hugs, smashing his face and chest against her ample bosom and neck. Totally unprepared, Bud was unable to breathe and almost succumbed before being rescued by Rube Winters, his future employer. When she let go, Bud sank to his knees and almost lost consciousness; but to him, it was a romantic experience.

They were married within six months. Moochie insisted on keeping her own name. "Who ever heard of a Moochie

Arrington, honey? It just don't sound right. You know what I mean?"

Tonight, they turned left on College Avenue, walked one block and turned right on Clayton. In the middle of the second block they noticed a For Sale sign taped to the window of a closed restaurant. Above the door was a pitifully small sign reading Coffee Cup, which could have been easily ignored except for the spray-painted, red X across its' face. They stopped, and shielding their eyes from the bright street light, peered through the plate glass window, seeing "Get out or die," and "We'll get your wife" on the walls.

"This is it, honey! Remember the place I read about yesterday?"

"Yeah. I wonder if they found out who did it."

"I hope so and they put them under the jail."

Moochie thought for a minute and said, "You know, sweetie, I've always wanted my own restaurant, just like the one my mama used to have. That restaurant will always have a place in my heart because that's where I learned to eat. That's been my dream ever since I was thrown out of high school and not allowed to graduate. Ours could serve real, mouth-watering, down to earth food, cooked with plenty of fat and salt to give it flavor. See what I mean, sweetie?"

Bud looked up at Moochie with his presently downcast eyes for a moment to see if she was serious. "Yeah, sweets, I know exactly what you mean. You just don't find that kind of food anymore. But, what if someone did this to us?"

"Oh, the police will find those hoodlums. Besides, we've not done anything to anybody to get them mad at us. We'll just mind our own business."

Moochie grabbed Bud by the shoulder and pulled him close to her side. She loved the sweet smell of the Edge After Shave she bought him right after they got married. "I have an idea, Buddy Boy. Since you like to cook, and I like to eat, why don't we start our own restaurant? Huh? Why not?"

"Now hold on there. Just a minute. Since when did we become millionaires? Where in the world would we ever get the money to buy a place like this? I love you, sweets, but you're dreaming." Bud used a hand to sweep dark brown strands of hair over his left ear. His narrow nose angled meagerly to the left from a long forgotten bar fight.

Moochie squeezed him. "Now, don't be throwing a wet blanket so fast, Buddy Boy. There must be a bank somewhere that would lend a couple of upstanding citizens like us some money."

"Moochie, I hate to bring it up again, but you're a disabled baby-sitter, and I'm in charge of the shipping department at Health From the Source. That don't carry too much weight with the money boys."

Moochie thought for a moment, then her eyes brightened. "Hey, speaking of money boys, what about our good friend, Rube Winters? Hell, he's like a brother to me, and his son, Sam, is like my own. He knows you're a good worker. He's always looking for good causes to support. What could be a better cause than us?"

They mulled it over as they turned and walked, arm in arm, along Clayton and hung a left on Jackson Street. As they approached Broad Street again, Moochie said, "My feet are killing me. Why don't we stop in this coffee shop, rest and get something to eat before I waste away like one of them fancy models?"

They sat outside under a Bradford Pear tree, waiting for their coffee to cool. Moochie took a mirror from her purse and examined her short, curly hair, framing a fair, round face. Her pale blue eyes sparkled with amusement most of the time, but could be piercing when she was angry. The evening was pleasant, with a slight breeze that ruffled the branches that formed an umbrella of shade over them. Moochie reached into her bag for a praline; she also carried Twinkie Twin Packs.

Bud declined, "No thank you, honey bunch, I'm watching my weight."

Moochie replied, "Well, I'm watching your weight too, honey. And, I ain't seen it going up any. One of these days your gonna slip through one of these storm drain grates and float on into the Oconee River before I can fish you out."

Bud grinned to one side, took out a pinch of tobacco and stuffed it in his jaw. He leaned back, warming one hand on the coffee cup, waiting for the nicotine to work its' magic.

Moochie sipped her coffee with three creams and four sugars, while she stripped the cellophane wrap from the praline. She eyed her man, his brown hair sprinkled with gray and combed straight back, knowing that he was a kind and gentle soul. During their fourth date he had spoken to her of his love and his desire to marry her. Moochie had already given up on marriage, never thinking it would be a part of her life. She knew he had been born and raised in Mississippi, but he had never told her the details of his sordid life.

Bud liked that about her; she didn't pry and he didn't lie.

*****

Moochie called Rube's office the next morning. A new receptionist answered the phone, "Yes, Mrs. Dunlop. I'm sorry, Dr Winters is very busy. Would you like to make an appointment?"

"No, honey, would you do me a favor and go stick your sweet little head in his door and tell him Moochie is on the line?"

Shortly Rube came on the phone, "Hey, Moochie, how's my sweetheart?" His health care business was very successful, but he always had time for her. They had seen each other through difficult times, and there was no one he believed in or trusted more. She had practically raised Sam, his son. In fact, she had helped Rube deliver him on the kitchen floor.

"Hi, Rube. You better tell that sweet young thing you've hired who ole Moochie is," she cackled. "Tell her I've got a direct line to the company president."

Rube laughed. "Don't worry, Moochie, it just takes them a while to learn who the real boss is in these parts."

Moochie said, "Rube, me and Bud need to talk to you about a business we're thinking of going into. When can we meet?"

"A business! What kind of business?"

"I'd rather tell you when we see you, so I can explain. Is that all right?"

"Suit yourself. How would this afternoon at one o'clock be?"

"That should work just fine, honey. That'll give me time to get the information I need. Bud will have to take a little time off work. Is that okay?"

"No problem," said Rube. "See you then."

*****

Moochie and Bud parked on Washington Street in front of the yellow-brick, two-story building that Rube had bought and remodeled several years ago to serve as headquarters for his healthcare business. He offered seminars for doctors throughout the world, sold nutritional products and published a health magazine.

Bud worked in the shipping department located in the rear of the building and rarely saw the main offices.

They stepped into a large reception area. Straight ahead and to the right were glassed-in offices with people shuffling paper, some with telephone headsets. To the left was a fitness room with treadmills, weightlifting equipment and a mirror covering one wall. A few people worked out, straining to regain the health and beauty of youth.

The receptionist behind a large desk in the center of the room greeted them warmly and led them to Dr. Winters' waiting room. His secretary remembered the telephone call and smiled shyly when Moochie introduced herself.

Moochie and Bud were waiting when Rube returned from lunch. They hugged and shook hands. Rube was careful to use the techniques he and Bud had learned about how to survive a Moochie hug.

Moochie didn't see Rube in his business mode much. "Lord-a-mercy, Rube, you're as handsome as ever with your blond hair and all, but when did you start wearing them white shirts and fancy red ties with a big diamond stuck in the middle of it? Looks like you been working out, too. Your waist is getting too thin. You need to start eating more food; put a little weight on yourself."

Rube laughed. "Thanks for the advice, but my doctor says my weight is perfect for my six-two height. Would you call him and tell him to allow more desserts?"

"I sure will, honey. You doctors think you know everything, but good food is one of the great pleasures of life. It makes people happy, and this old world needs all the happiness it can get, don't you think?"

"Well, yes, but..." Then, Rube laughed out loud, realizing that an explanation would do no good. "Come on in and have a seat."

In Rube's office, Moochie came directly to the point, "Rube, me and Bud want to start up a restaurant."

"A restaurant! Moochie, I had no idea either you or Bud were interested in something like that."

"Well, honey, that's always been one of my secret desires, and Bud is a great cook---real down home cooking, if you know what I mean. As you know, he has cooked in several restaurants before." Moochie frowned, "But, since I talked to you, I found out how much the place would cost and I just don't see how we could do it."

"Where is it, and how much are you talking about?" asked Rube.

Moochie reached over and took Bud's hand, "Why it's only a leap and two short hops from here, over on Clayton Street. But, like I say, it's way too much money---."

Rube leaned back in his chair, waiting for the other praline to drop.

"I hate to even say it, Rube---five hundred thousand."

Rube didn't flinch, but Bud's stooped shoulders slumped another two inches. "Say what?" He leaned forward, not believing his ears. His brown eyes searched out Moochie's blues.

Moochie squeezed his hand, "Five hundred thousand, sweetie." Her gaze shifted to Rube.

Rube put his hand over his eyes, "Let's see, you're probably talking about payments of two to three thousand a month. Then, you would have to think about the equipment and food. And, you would have to hire help. Then, there are taxes, a license fee, et cetera."

Moochie stood up and grabbed Bud by the arm. "Come on, sweetie, we just went bankrupt, even before we started."

Rube said, "Now, wait a minute, Moochie," holding his arm up. "Please---have a seat. Let's talk this out. There may be a way to do it. Buying that property may be a good investment for this company. I could buy it and lease it to you with a long-term option to buy. That way, when you're ready, all of your monthly payments would go toward the purchase."

Bud and Moochie eased back into their seats. Bud said, "I don't know, Rube, we'd still have all the other costs." Moochie's brow furrowed and her eyes squinted. A sweat bead meandered down her back.

Rube said, "All right. Now, let's just sit tight on this for a while. I'm going to have my accountant contact the real estate people---see if that price is firm. And, they can look at other ways this might be done. Let's wait and see what they say."

He got up and gave hugs. "I love you both, and if there's any way, I'll make this happen."

Moochie turned and guided Bud, whose head was still reeling, toward the door. There was a flicker of hope and thankfulness in her eyes as she turned and waved goodbye. Rube cared about her for who she was, which contradicted all that she had experienced up to this point in her life. Her shoulders and arms trembled briefly until she was able to re-establish her persona of not caring what others thought. That had always been her safety net and she couldn't let it go. Not now.

CHAPTER TWO

Rube phoned on Monday morning. "Moochie, good news, the owner of the old restaurant is retiring, wants to get out and will sell all of the equipment along with the building. And, here's the best news, he'll let it all go for four-hundred and fifty thousand."

"Well, honey, four-hundred and fifty is better than five-hundred any day. Why was he willing to come down so much?"

"Just said he couldn't take the long hours, and he was tired of fighting with the restaurant owner across the street."

"Oh," said Moochie. "Who's across the street?"

"The realtor says it's a man by the name of Lumkin, Wilson Lumkin. He and his father own several buildings in Athens. Has a lot of influence," said Rube.

"Shouldn't be any problem," said Moochie. "I haven't seen many people that ole Moochie couldn't get along with."

Rube said, "The only other problem is the place is a mess. It will take a lot of cleaning and repair."

Moochie sighed, "Well, I don't mind cleaning, and Bud fancies himself a handyman. We've seen it through the front window and you're right, it's a mess."

"I had an appraisal done and they say it's worth what he's asking. Also, I had an inspection of the building and it's structurally sound. The owner will correct a few electrical and plumbing problems. The heating and air system is only five years old."

"That's good," said Moochie. "We couldn't afford to do all that."

"Say, Moochie, if you're really serious about this, I'll buy the building and lease it to you and Bud. My accountant tells me if I charge $2,500 per month I'll just about break even."

"It's a big risk, Rube, what if we don't make it?"

"I have faith in you, my good friend. If I didn't, I wouldn't make the offer. Besides, if you don't make it, I'll just sell the building or rent it to someone else."

"Well, I love you, honey. And, I trust your judgment. Let's go for it. I'll break it to Bud tonight."

"Okay. There are just two problems. One is Sam. I know he's fourteen years old, but he still needs someone to watch out for him."

"No problem, honey. I'll just run by the school and bring him to the restaurant if it's all right with your ex. Kristy can pick him up there. In fact, I might even put him to work. What do you think?"

There was a pause, then, "You know, that is a good idea; give him a little worldly experience. But, don't tell Kristy I had anything to do with it."

Moochie laughed, her azure blue eyes sparkling with amusement. "I understand, Rube. What's the other problem?"

"Well, Mooch, it's a small matter of me losing the best shipping foreman I've ever had," said Rube.

"Oh," said Moochie. "I didn't think about that. Buddy Boy might just have to work two jobs for a while, until you can find a replacement."

"Okay, I'm sure everything will work out. I'll have the agent arrange for the closing. Make sure Bud is sitting down when you tell him. I'll be in touch."

CHAPTER THREE

Bud opened the door for Moochie and they stepped inside. The mouth of his perpetually sad face curved down. He reached for Moochie's trembling hand and said, "I ain't never been a proprietor before, love. I thought that was only for rich people."

He felt convulsions running down Moochie's arm and turned to see his big woman falling apart. Tears flowed down the round face, framed by curly, blonde hair. He had never seen her cry before. He reached around her as far as he could and pulled her close. "Don't worry, sweetie, we'll be able to make it."

"Oh, I ain't worried about that, Bud. You just set me off, saying you ain't never been a proprietor and all. Shoot, I ain't never had anything myself. I've always been told I was too fat and too ugly to amount to anything. But, I've always believed that I would be somebody, someday. Anyway, this is a dream come true. These are tears of joy."

Bud kissed her on the cheek. "I love you, Moochie, and you're the most beautiful woman in the world to me."

They embraced and cried together for a time, trying to fathom just what they had done and where it would lead.

Bud reached over and flipped the light switch. They walked around the old restaurant with their mouths open. Moochie said, "Lord-a-mercy, honey, I ain't never seen anything like it. Call the weather bureau and see if there's been a tornado through this part of town."

When Bud walked into the kitchen , he recoiled from the stench of decaying food and rat droppings. "There ain't nothing that don't need fixing or cleaning," he said.

*****

The next two weeks went by faster than a down-hill skier. They set the opening date for April fourteenth which gave them two weeks. Bud worked every night the first week, before Rube found someone to take his place. He joined Moochie at four-thirty in the afternoon and they worked until ten at night. He remarked to Moochie one night, "If I still had my head in the bottle, I wouldn't be able to keep this pace."

Moochie patted him on the shoulder and said, "That's right, Buddy Boy. Now, if you could stop chewing, we'd have to put a damper on you to slow you down."

Bud was very good at whatever task he did, but he was very deliberate, some would even say slow. And, he liked to have a cup of coffee now and then, especially when he was deliberating about how he should do something. He would look, think and sip until finally Moochie would explode. "Lord-a-mercy, Bud, if you were getting paid by the hour, we'd be rich by now. The people of Athens are going to starve to death, and the rats are going to regain the lead if you don't hurry up and fix that counter."

Bud would grin on the side of his mouth not stuffed with tobacco, take another sip of coffee and get back to work. He loved to get a rise out of Moochie.

Rube came by one day and saw what they were up against. He said, "Bud, what you gonna do about painting the walls?"

"Well, I been pondering on that. I reckon I'll have to put that on my list."

Rube crossed his arms and looked around for a minute. "You know, I've been thinking. These are my walls and I'm the one who ought to do something about it. I'll have a crew in here tomorrow or the next day to paint."

As word got around Rube's company, others started showing up after work to help out. Even Uncle Billy, Rube's uncle and honorary chairman of his publicity department, came by several times to help.

Moochie tried a booth, but had to hold her breath and squeeze her way in. "My Lord, Bud, the owners before us must've had the skinniest customers in the country. They had to be puny to fit in one of these death traps."

"Don't worry, love. I'll get Uncle Billy to help me build one that'll suit you just fine. We'll re-build this one on the end and push the others up a little bit."

Uncle Billy tried to help Bud, but his shaky hands didn't allow him to do much. He and Bud stood around sipping coffee, puzzling over how to build the booth big enough and strong enough to hold Moochie. Bud said, "I think I'm gonna have to go to two by sixes instead of two by fours, so my bride won't fall on her tush."

Uncle Billy replied, "I think that would be wonderful, just wonderful." Everything was wonderful to the eighty-one year old veteran of World War II who had finally given up wearing his straw hat in favor of a Texas Ranger baseball cap. Like Bud, he was a recovering alcoholic.

Moochie who was scouring the kitchen sink, yelled, "Why don't you two coffee junkies just rent a crane and put a steel girder in there? You two beat all I've ever seen."

Uncle Billy leaned on the counter and slapped his thigh. "I just love your Moochie, she's just wonderful."

"She is a sight, ain't she?" grinned Bud.

*****

A friend in Monroe told Bud of an old jukebox for sale. Bud asked Uncle Billy to go with him and have a look. They took Bud's Ford pickup in case they bought it. When they arrived at the address, they found a metal barn packed to the ceiling with only a trail down the center. They were met by an older woman wearing high cut tennis shoes, a dress too big for her and a worn sweater buttoned all the way to the top. Her leathery face was highlighted by a large wart in the middle of her forehead.

"The name's Mildred. My friends call me Precious. What can I do for ye gents?" she squeaked.

"Heard you have a jukebox," said Bud.

"Sure do, and she's a beaut' too. Like to look her over?"

Bud said, "If you don't mind, ma'am."

The old lady scrambled for the cord and plugged it in. When it came to life, Bud was fascinated by the multicolored design featuring a cowboy standing by his horse, fingering a six string. He pushed a quarter in and selected number twenty-five. The metal arm rose to a vertical position, reached in and grabbed the platter and brought it to the turntable. The needle dropped into place and Bud heard, "I was country----when country wasn't cool----." He fell in love with the nickelodeon, and if alone would have grabbed the machine and kissed it.

While Bud looked the jukebox over, Uncle Billy talked to the Precious. He was mesmerized by the wart.

She said, "I see you're attracted to my wart. That don't surprise me none. All men are taken by it. You remember how them movie stars used to be proud of their moles? Beauty marks they called 'em. Well, I never did like them moles. They 'as ugly, I thought. But, now, a wart---that's different. It ain't black like them moles. And, I'm a lucky woman. My wart is right smack in the middle. If it was a quarter inch to one side or the other, it wouldn't be as purdy. It would cause a man to lose his balance, if you get my point?"

Uncle Billy stepped back and blinked. "Yes'am, I see exactly what you mean. It could throw a person off his stride."

Bud tried, unsuccessfully, to hide his enthusiasm. He said, "Ma'am, I like it, but I don't know where in the world I'd find records for it."

"That ain't a problem," she chortled. "Look in that box next to your feet."

He found hundreds of 45 rpm records, mostly popular and country. "How much are these?" he asked.

"Why them's part of the deal. I been collecting them for years."

"How much are you asking?" Bud didn't have much ready cash.

"The whole shebang is a hundred dollars, cash on the barrelhead. I hate to part with it, but for you fine gentlemen, I'll do it." She winked at Uncle Billy and pointed at the wart.

Bud flinched as he felt in his pocket. "I've only got seventy-five, ma'am."

Uncle Billy musing over the wart, said, "Don't worry, Pal, I'll make up the difference." The deal was struck, and there weren't even any corporate lawyers present.

As they walked back to the front to get a cart, Precious said to Uncle Billy, "You're probably wondering why I wear my sweater buttoned all the way to the top."

"Why I hadn't thought---," said Uncle Billy as he pushed his baseball cap back.

"Well, it's just like you being attracted by my wart. I don't want to lead anyone on, if you see my point. A girl's got to protect herself nowadays."

Uncle Billy said, "But, Miss Precious, I had no intention---I---," as Bud turned his head and snickered, then coughed to cover it up.

*****

Moochie or Bud picked up Sam at the middle school each day and he worked until Kristy came for him. Sam, tall for his age with thick, unruly blond hair like his daddy, and a broad nose that turns up slightly at the tip. His blue-gray eyes are large, but turn to a squint when he smiles. He loves to read and is a good student. His favorite sport is basketball. He often tries to sneak up behind Moochie, give her a hug and a kiss on the neck before she knows he is there. She says, "Lord-a-mercy, child, you about scared me to death." But, she loves every minute of it. Sam, Rube and Bud are the only three people who have ever loved her unconditionally. That makes life worth living for the big woman who has been scorned most of her life.

Even Kristy, Sam's mother and Rube's first wife, came in on Saturday and worked all day. She wore her long, blond hair in a ponytail most of the time. Her turned up nose made her seem younger than her thirty-four years. She loved Moochie to, but had never been able to say it. Moochie knew.

Rube and Amy, his present wife, worked two days during the second week when the schedule was getting close. Amy's auburn hair framed a perfectly made up face with her almond eyes and sensuous lips. Moochie called them her two love birds because they were always looking at or touching each other. Amy was a live wire and flitted from one job to another. She was Sam's stepmother and she and Moochie got along very well. It was a balancing act to arrange it so that Amy and Kristy were not there at the same time.

*****

On Thursday afternoon, the day before the grand opening, Bud, Moochie and Sam were there alone. Bud was putting the last of his food supplies away while Sam and Moochie hung pictures.

When Bud finished in the kitchen, he came and helped with the pictures.

Finally, they stepped back and looked at their handiwork. They stood by the front door which opened into the center of the room. There was a plate glass window on each side of the door. To the left, the counter, extended by Bud, ran the full length of the restaurant. It glistened with new light blue Formica and matching cushioned bar stools. On the other side, the dark blue booths had been cleaned and patched. They stretched from the back wall to the front window. The last one on the right had a deeper seat and more belly room. It became known as Moochie's office. Bud had removed the middle booth to give a place of prominence to the jukebox. Moochie wasn't sure about the wisdom of it, but conceded because Bud was enamored with the music machine.

The walls were a not too practical off white, but that's what Moochie wanted.

Rube said, "What the heck, if they get dirty I'll just have them painted again."

The blue curtains on the front windows matched the counter and stools. The tables and chairs were painted dark blue to go with the booths, then covered with light blue, dark blue, and white checkered tablecloths. In the center of each table was a single white, plastic rose, new salt and pepper shakers, extra napkins and a laminated menu.

The tile floor had once been white, but was now faded, especially in the traffic areas. It was a good thing it had cleaned up nicely because they just couldn't afford new.

"Ain't it a beautiful sight?" said Moochie, tears glistening in her blue eyes. Bud and Sam walked her to the counter so she could sit. They stood on each side with their arms around her. All three gazed up at the blown up picture of Moochie and Bud on the far wall, above the jukebox. Bud stood on Moochie's right with an upraised spatula in his hand. They smiled broadly.

"There we are, love---proprietors at last," said Bud.

"Yeah," said Moochie with a perplexed look on her round face. "I don't know what it is my sweet little man, but something's missing. It just feels like there's an empty space that needs to be filled. Know what I mean, Buddy Boy?"

*****

Kristy opened the front door, there to pick up Sam. Her usually perfect facial features seemed worried about something.

"What's wrong?" asked Moochie.

"Well, I've been meaning to ask you all about something, but I don't know if you'll approve."

Moochie said, "Go ahead, girl, ask us anything you want."

"Okay---well---as you know, Pretty Boy, my parrot was raised in my parents bedroom, and he learned some embarrassing things there. Since he moved in with us, he watches television all day long and has picked up all kinds of sayings. We never know what he's going to say. I know you and Pretty Boy are not on speaking terms since he bombed you at Rube's and my wedding, but I've got a little problem. I don't know if Sam told you, but I'm dating a real nice man, and, well, it's just embarrassing when he comes over and there's Pretty Boy saying things like, 'Gawk, let's make love.' It just sets a bad tone. See? Anyway, I was wondering if you and Bud would be willing to take Pretty Boy and keep him here at the restaurant. Sam would take care of him, wouldn't you, Sam?"

"Yes, ma'am. I guess so."

Moochie glanced at Bud, then back at Kristy. "Why, Lord-a-mercy, that dirty bird pooped all over my head and ear at your wedding---some even landed in my praline bag. I'd 'a' killed him for sure if I could've got my hands on his feathery ass. I just don't know---what do you think, Bud?"

Bud took out his tobacco pouch and peered across it at Kristy. "You know---some people like parrots---as for me, I've never been around one." He put a pinch between his cheek and gum.

"All right, already," said Moochie, exasperated.

"I'm thinking, love, I'm thinking. It might be an attraction to people, a way to bring customers in. Maybe we ought to give him a try."

"Okay, if we give him a try, do you two boys promise to take care of him?" asked Moochie.

Bud and Sam nodded. Bud said, "Well, I guess that empty space has been filled."

Kristy grabbed Sam's hand and started out the door, "We'll be right back with your new bird."

CHAPTER FOUR

It was Bud's idea to name it Moochie's Place. "The name needs to be short and memorable so people will pass it on. It's one of them principles of mass communication I been reading about," he insisted.

Moochie laughed and laid her hand on his shoulder. "Well, my little man, tell me what you can do with mass communication."

Bud stuttered, "Why--I can use a calculator with the best of 'em. Besides, it ain't what you can do, it's what you know in your brain. I may not have much schooling, but I keep up with the goings on in this old world."

"I know you do, sweetie, and that's just one of the reasons I'm proud of you. I'm tickled that you want to name our place after me."

*****

They arrived at five o'clock on April fourteenth, opening day, after getting little sleep the night before. Bud worried about having enough food, and whether he and Brad, the graduate student he had hired, could keep up with the orders. Moochie was just nervous. She wondered if anyone would show up. She had her blonde hair permed the day before and used a lot of spray to control her curly ringlets. Using well-placed rouge she had created cheekbones for her round face. Even though there was a smile on her face, her blue eyes showed sadness, but also determination which made her attractive to those she met. People wanted to listen to what she had to say.

Moochie paused to admire the sign above the door, painted by Garcia Rose, Rube's publicity man, while Bud unlocked the door. The large, blue letters on the wooden sign that said Moochie's Place, could be seen from down the street. When they stepped in the door, Bud lifted the cover from Pretty Boy's cage. The bird chattered and strutted around, "Gawk! Good morning to you---Good morning to you!"

Moochie said, "Oh, shut up, Birdbrain."

Pretty Boy, nonplussed, shot back, "Gawk! Let's make love."

Moochie said, "I declare, all that bird ever thinks about is sex. Hush, before I wash your mouth out with soap." She grinned as she brushed by the cage.

Bud got the parrot's food from behind the counter and dumped some in the feeder. "Now, Pretty Boy, you've got to be nice to our customers. Just say, 'Welcome to Moochie's Place.' Come on, now, say it, 'Welcome to Moochie's Place." But Pretty Boy was too busy pecking at his food.

Bud enjoyed watching his multi-colored friend. The top of his head, wings and part of his tail were iridescent silver. The black beak and neck were surrounded by a white face with black streaks. Bright yellow feathers began behind his eyes, ran and expanded to cover his chest and underside of his tail. Bud thought there must be a God to create something that pretty.

"I'll clean the cage after he eats," said Bud as he hustled across the room to turn the juke box on.

Moochie said, "You know, I think we should start putting Dirty Bird in the back room at night, it'll be like having a watch birddog back there, if you get my point. It would be easy for a burglar to break in that back door. We sure as hell can't drag his sorry ass back and forth to home every day."

Pretty Boy's feathers stood on end, "Gawk! In your face, punk."

Ignoring the remark, Bud said, "That would be okay, I guess. Up here he can watch people and traffic go by. We'd have to put a television back there to keep him company. You know how he likes movies."

"Gawk! A man must have his mate," Pretty Boy persisted.

"Lord-a-mercy!" Moochie threw her hands in the air. "Now, featherhead wants us to put a harem back there for him."

Bud smiled on the nontobacco side of his face, using his fingers to push his thinning, brown hair around each ear.

Moochie started the coffee, then, cloth in hand, went in search of specks of dust on the counter. Bud went to the kitchen to rearrange his cooking utensils for the hundredth time.

At six-thirty, April Southgate knocked on the front door. She was hired a few days ago to be in charge of the counter, under Moochie's supervision of course. April was an attractive twenty-four year old. She wore her bleached blond hair short, straight and combed back on the sides. Her green eyes danced when she smiled or giggled, which was most of the time. She was a little overweight, but not by Moochie's standards. Her breasts were large and she carried them proudly.

Moochie could tell April was nervous. "Hey, April. Now, don't you worry none. I know you've never worked in a restaurant before, but you'll do just fine. Hell, it's been years since I worked in Mama's place. Just watch ole Moochie and we'll learn together."

While Moochie and April reviewed how they would run the counter, Peola Rae and Brad Leaptrott arrived. Peola was a tall, skinny black girl who had graduated from high school a year ago. Moochie was determined to put some weight on her bones. Peola wore cornrows on each side of her head and long, loose hair in the back which she combed straight down. Her beautiful caramel-colored complexion was marred only by a dark birthmark two inches below her right ear. She would handle the tables and booths. Depending on the flow of traffic, Peola and April would help each other out.

Peola stood in the middle of the dining area without saying a word. Moochie walked over and stood in front of her. "What's wrong, child, cat got your tongue?"

Peola pointed to her throat and spread her hands, eyes flashing wildly.

Moochie, sensing fear, put both arms around her and spoke soothingly, "Relax, honey. There's nothing to be afraid of. We're all here to have fun and enjoy ourselves. Now, give me a little smile and relax."

Peola grinned sheepishly and in a high pitched voice said, "I'll be okay. Sometimes I can't talk when I'm nervous. Sorry about that."

"That's all right, sugar. Seems like we're all a little jittery today. We'll be fine as soon as we handle that first customer." Moochie walked her around and explained the procedure for taking orders.

Brad, assistant cook and handyman, headed for the kitchen and helped Bud re-arrange the utensils once more. He had been hired because, as Bud told Moochie, "We seem to hit it off somehow." Brad had graduated near the top of his class in entomology, couldn't find a job and was now in graduate school. Bud joked with him, "We ought to get along just fine because I've been around bugs all my life: bedbugs, fleas, cockroaches, lice, and Mississippi mosquitoes big enough to stand flat-footed and screw a turkey."

Brad was from Swainsboro, a small town in South Georgia where he grew up on a farm. A strapping fellow with dark red, unruly hair and midnight blue eyes, he was not afraid of hard work. He filled Bud's need for someone to handle heavy boxes of food and supplies.

At five minutes to seven Moochie unlocked the front door. She stepped outside to see if there was anyone she might invite in for a cup of coffee. Rube and Amy were coming down the sidewalk with a large basket of flowers. A big smile splashed across Rube's face. "Congratulations, Moochie. Welcome to the free enterprise system."

Moochie teared up as Amy put an arm around her. Amy was a strikingly beautiful woman with golden skin and perfectly styled auburn hair with reddish highlights; full, shiny red lips and arched brown eyebrows. She wore a lemon drop, linen shirt over a white, lacey tank top and matching three-quarter length pants.

Clutching the flowers, Moochie dragged them through the front door. "Wait 'til you see the place. Thanks to you and the rest of our friends, it's just beautiful."

"Gawk, just beautiful," Pretty Boy chimed in.

"Where's the other proprietor of this wonderful establishment?" asked Rube.

Bud burst through the kitchen door with a full-face smile that lit up the room. "Hey, Rube and Amy. Welcome to Moochie's." He glanced at Pretty Boy to see if he got the message. "You're our first customers. What can I get you to eat: eggs, bacon, sausage? You name it---it's on the house."

"Oh, no it's not, my friend. Amy and I are going to have a full breakfast of eggs, bacon, biscuits, grits, gravy and coffee. We're gonna splurge this morning."

Bud turned on his heel and went to alert Brad.

Soon, others from Rube's business began filtering in: Rube's Uncle Billy and Aunt Lucille, Garcia Rose, their secretaries, and several from the shipping department.

A couple of sleepy-eyed University of Georgia students straggled in, hoping to grab a bite before class. Final exams were around the corner.

*****

Later in the morning, Moochie was standing behind the counter chatting with Uncle Billy and Aunt Lucille. Lucille's grandmotherly smile seemed to cancel the deep wrinkles around her eyes and mouth. Her pure white hair was parted in the middle and combed back on each side. Their heads turned when a surly-looking man about forty-five with short black hair parted down the middle strode in the front door. His gaze started with Moochie and slowly moved around the room until he was staring into Pretty Boy's face. He blinked and stepped back, holding his nose. "Phewey," he grunted as he turned and walked toward the counter.

"Gawk. Here's trouble," warned Pretty Boy.

The man's eyes gathered every detail as he plopped his stocky body down on a stool and swiveled to face the counter. He wore a dark blue, business suit, white shirt and pale blue tie. He was not overweight and was handsome in a rugged sort of way, except for the menacing scowl on his face. He pulled a black book from his pocket and began jotting notes. He glanced up at the menu on the wall and smirked with unconcealed derision.

Moochie waddled along the counter until she stood directly in front of him, "Good morning, sir. How can I help you?"

"I doubt if you can help me, madam. I just stopped by to introduce myself. My name is Wilson Lumkin. I own the upscale restaurant across the street. We don't cotton to lower class eating places like this. It's a blemish on the reputation of Athens." He lazered Moochie with his cold stare, the corners of his mouth curled up in a devilish grin, expecting her to back away. She didn't flinch.

Moochie had seen the lighted sign across the street, Lumkin Café, with Fine Dining underneath, and she couldn't help but notice the billboard advertisements throughout Clarke and Oconee Counties. From what she could tell from the sidewalk, it was a pretty fancy inside---not a likely place for her and Bud. Rumor had it that the prices were a notch above unreasonable.

Moochie leaned across the counter, propped on her elbows, her face two inches from his nose, blue eyes blazing. In a low voice she spit out, "Listen, Mr. Lumphead, you smart ass, people like you are not welcome in Moochie's Place. We only cater to real people, so why don't you slither on your belly back across the street where you belong before I drop one of our rats down the front of your pants so he'll starve to death." She raised up, eyes steady and unblinking.

Anne Murray sang, "Put a Little Love in Your Heart," from the Nickelodeon.

Lumkin's face flushed, and his hand flew up and slapped Moochie. "Damn---" he started. Before he could finish, Moochie's big hand caught his left jaw and open mouth, sending saliva and unspoken words flying. His startled look flashed by each time the stool whirled round and round.

Lumkin grabbed onto the counter and shook his head to re-focus his vision, slid off the stool and reeled toward the door. "You'll be hearing from me," he blurted over his shoulder.

"Gawk! Looord have meeercy," squawked Pretty Boy. Lumkin flipped Pretty Boy the bird.

Bud stepped through the kitchen door in time to see his bride glaring holes through Lumkin's back. "Who was that giving my bird the bird?" he asked.

"Gawk! I love you," said Pretty Boy.

"That was the snake across the street who doesn't believe in the free enterprise system," said Moochie.

"Why that dirty son-of-a-bitch, I ought to go over there and---."

"Don't worry, Buddy Boy, I already gave him what for."

Uncle Billy smiled and held up a high five for Moochie. "You handled it just right, Moochie. It was wonderful, just wonderful. Bud, you would have been mighty proud."

"She's a sight, ain't she?" said Bud. He rubbed his chin. "That guy's gonna bring more trouble."

*****

The lunch crowd was not bad, considering it was their first day. Bud and Brad dashed here and there in the kitchen, keeping up with the orders. When they developed a system, it would become easier. They prepared the vegetables and several kinds of chili ahead of time (beef and chicken, both medium and hot). Bud said, "We might have to send out a fire extinguisher with each bowl." But salads had to be thrown together, and the Moochieburgers had to be cooked, along with the fries.

The smell of Bud's good cooking drifted teasingly throughout the restaurant. Customers were fascinated by the old juke box. They fed it a steady diet of quarters and chose a variety of songs: "Make the World go Away," by Elvis; "Precious Memories," by Jimmy Dean; and, "Blue Hawaii," by Don Ho.

Moochie broke away to pick up Sam at three o'clock. After a grudging session of homework at the end of Moochie's counter, he happily helped clean the kitchen and prep for the evening meal. Only ten couples showed up for supper. Most of them ordered a slab of ribs, slathered with Bud's special, secret sauce, and baked beans. As expected, most of their business would come at breakfast and lunch. Bud and Moochie were pleased with their first day, but arrived home exhausted. After quick showers, they fell into bed. For the first time, Bud saw Moochie go without her evening snack of two pralines and two Twinkie Twin Packs.

They fell asleep holding hands. Moochie, still shaken by the encounter with Lumkin, dreamed of her expulsion from high school during her senior year. Bud woke up running--- trying to find a man, someone he had never met. It was the old, familiar dream about his boyhood.

CHAPTER FIVE

The next morning after the initial breakfast rush, Moochie was idling at the counter, talking to a customer, when out of the corner of her eye, she saw a man peek through the front window, then duck back. Curious, she waited. A few minutes later, the man walked casually to the front door, all the time looking toward the street. He wore transition lens glasses that were straight across the top and drooped down on each side of his nose giving him a hound-dog appearance. Both shoulders were lifted and rolled forward. He paused at the door for a long minute, then swiftly opened it and walked in. He glanced at Moochie, and quickly looked away as he made his way to the counter. He sat on a stool but faced away from the counter, hands on knees. A kind smile rested on his lips, but his face was pale, as though he had seen a ghost, and his whole body quivered.

Moochie sensed his pain and said kindly, "Good morning, sir. May I help you?"

The man turned slowly and rested his shaking hands on the counter. He said, "Well, ma'am, I hate to bother you, but that coffee smells mighty good. Would you be kind enough to bring me a cup?"

Moochie returned and set a steaming cup in front of him. "Here's some cream and the sugar's on the counter." She gave him her brightest smile, and said, "I'm Moochie. May I ask your name?"

"Yes, ma'am, my name is M.D. Slocum. I own the little store, two doors down from here. We sell magazines, newspapers, soft drinks and a variety of things." He lifted his right hand to the side of his face and began tapping.

Rodgers and Hammerstein's "You'll Never Walk Alone," by Frank Patterson floated from the jukebox.

Moochie could feel the sadness oozing from this man. She rested her hand over his on the counter. "Now, don't you worry none, honey. Everything's going to be all right."

He was surprised. Then, tears formed in his faded green eyes. "Thank you, ma'am. Thank you."

Moochie smiled and came around the counter. "In fact, Mr. Slocum, you look like you could use a healing hug from ole Moochie. Stand up here. Now, since this is your first time, I'm going to take it easy on you, but you got to keep your head up and squeeze back as hard as you can. Got it?" Everyone in the place had their eyes riveted on the unlikely pair.

"Yes, ma'am, I guess so," said Slocum

When Moochie grabbed him, his heels left the floor and everyone in the place heard the air rushing from his lungs.

Pretty Boy squawked, "Gawk! Call a medic!"

Moochie let go and Slocum staggered, reaching for the counter to steady himself. She said, "There now, don't that feel better? Makes you forget all your troubles. It's good for what ails you."

Slocum caught his breath as he slumped back onto his stool. He coughed, then said, "Yes, ma'am, I feel a whole heap better. I can't remember what I was so worried about now."

The place exploded with applause, "All right! Way to go, Moochie!"

Others called out from the tables and booths, "Hey Moochie, how about a hug for me?"

"All right," she laughed. "Everyone who wants a hug line up right here, and I'll give you a squeeze. And don't worry, honey, I know just how hard to squeeze. Children, the frail and weak are safe with me. Sometimes it feels like I'm just gonna bust with love for people. Hugging just gives me a way to pass it on. That's all."

*****

Soon, rumors or flights of wishful thinking spread through Athens: "I was hugged by Moochie and my lumbago cleared up; I had a hug just before my trigonometry final, and aced it; My asthma is a lot better since I had my hug; I won a hundred dollars in the lottery the next day."

Moochie's hugs became the hottest topic in the area. Everyone wanted to see, and maybe even get a hug from Moochie Dunlop. The place was packed every day, especially at lunch time. Bud claimed it was because of his food. "People can't get enough of it," he bragged. "It's the secret way we prepare it, and my special sauces."

Moochie agreed and patted him on the back.

She didn't want to worry Bud about her run-in with Mr. Lumkin, but the hate in his eyes still played in the back of her mind. She thought, I'll never forgive that jerk as long as I live.

*****

A small group of football players began gathering at Moochie's. Bud's good food and large portions were the main attraction at first. As word spread, their numbers increased until they filled two large tables as well as a booth. Peola always waited on them, and they took an immediate liking to her. She was shy at first, but soon caught on to their gentle kidding, and began to open up to them. Peola stood sideways when she took orders, so the birthmark under her right ear wouldn't be so obvious. Each player gave their impression of what the birthmark looked like: the Easter bunny, a four-leaf clover, a panther, a hunkered down Georgia lineman, etc. Soon, everyone wanted to see the mark. Pleased by the attention of the players, she finally stopped being self-conscious about it.

When orders backed up and Peola became tense, they discovered that her voice began to rise in octaves, ending up in a screech barely audible to the human ear.

During the lunch hour rush, April came from behind the counter to help Peola. Her reaction to pressure was nervous laughter, culminating in a loud snort. The players weren't happy until they had Peola screeching at the top of her voice and April laughing and snorting with every breath.

Mama Moochie as they called her, frequently reminded the student athletes of the time. "Lord-a-mercy, honey, you all sit around here like there ain't no such thing as a university and classes. Now, get on outta here before ole Moochie puts a tackle on you that you won't forget." Those who had to make class, grabbed their books, gave Moochie a thumbs up or peck on the cheek and headed for the door.

Most of the time Pretty Boy had a comment from the 'trash talk' he had picked up from the players as they left: "Gawk! Your mama wears combat boots," or "Gawk! Go home to mama."

Bud, nearing half a century old, still considered himself strong, and he was for his size. He hovered between one hundred forty-five and one hundred fifty pounds. Most of these "kids" as he called the players could bench press two or even three times his weight. They playfully called him Papa Bud, Bud, the wimp or just plain wimpy. One day, Bud said, "Okay, all you mama's boys, I challenge anyone of you to an arm wrestling contest. If I lose, which I won't, you get a free Moochieburger and Coke. The thought of a free burger caused Winslow Harris, a two-hundred eighty-five pound lineman's hand to shoot into the air. He was immediately embarrassed, but couldn't back down.

The starting quarterback, Taylor Damato, jumped up. "0kay, let's clear this table off and get ready for the battle of the titans. Charles, you be Winslow's coach, and I'll coach Wimpey."

Taylor explained the rules, then stood behind Bud. He waved to Winslow and Charles, then winked. They nodded slightly and an amused smile touched their lips before transforming into a menacing look.

Taylor said, "All right, contestants take your position."

"Just a minute," said Bud. He reached into his pocket for his tobacco and tucked a pinch between his cheek and gum. "Okay, now I'm ready to take on this young whippersnapper."

To others sitting around the restaurant, it appeared to be an epic struggle. Winslow was a much better actor than Taylor thought possible. He grimaced a lot, grabbed the edge of the table, wrapped his leg around the table leg, and even broke a sweat. Finally, Bud's persistence appeared to payoff. Winslow's arm gradually weakened and finally flopped down with a thump. Winslow laid his head down in shame. Bud jumped up and raised his arm in triumph. "That'll show you kids who's boss around here," he said. Shania Twain confirmed it with "You're Still the One" on the juke box.

Bud, feeling benevolent while reveling in the flush of victory said, "Hey, April, bring this lad a Moochieburger and Coke. I'm afraid I was a little hard on him. After all, he's only a kid." The mention of food lifted Winslow from his funk. He laughed with his friends and slapped Bud on the back causing him to cough and sputter.

Pretty Boy said, "Looord have meercy!"

CHAPTER SIX

M.D. Slocum had always wanted to be his own boss; have his own business. That would be easier, he thought, than being responsible to someone else. He had been beat down by bosses during his life time, starting with his mother.

His earliest memory was getting slapped across the face by his mother after he wet his pants. That was her way of punishing him if he did something wrong. It became a systematic thing as he grew older. If it was a minor offense, he received a light tap on the jaw. If it was more bothersome, there was a moderate slap. A major mistake would cost him a head turning blow, and a really bad violation, like a D on his report card, brought a double head turner. It made sense to M.D. It was logical, and something he could count on. You do something wrong, you get a slap. It was as sure as chiggers in a blackberry patch.

M.D. went away to Georgia Southern University in Statesboro. He missed his mama and daddy, especially his mama. Not only did he love her, but he missed the certainty of her discipline. In his mind her love and slaps had become intertwined. When he made mistakes, as all freshmen do, there was no one there to slap his jaw. It was a lonely feeling, like no one cared.

He thought about asking his roommate to do it, but that would be foolish since his roommate was making the same mistakes. He had no other choice. He had to do it himself. After all, he had heard that you must first love yourself before you can love others. It began with a light tap on the jaw if he made a mistake on a math problem. Soon, he fell into the same pattern his mother had used, gradually increasing the force to fit the crime.

When he graduated and went to work for an accounting firm in Athens, he was not about to ask his boss to slap him in front of all the other accountants and employees. He thought about going to a psychiatrist, but had heard that all they do is talk to you, or allow you to talk to them. That wouldn't serve the same purpose as a good, hard slap.

M.D. was a good looking man, some would even say handsome. He parted his medium brown hair on the right side and swooped it down over his forehead. He used a leave on conditioner to help hold it in place, and even resorted to spray net at times. His ears were large, but laid close to his head and drew no unusual attention. His thin nose flared at the bottom, much like his mother's.

He met Carly, a young secretary at the firm. She reminded him of his mother, having a strong bent toward discipline and fairness. They were married within a year and bought a small house in an old, established neighborhood. One evening before bed, M.D. thought of a major blunder he had made at work. In fact, Carly had been the one who caught the mistake.

"Honey, I want to ask you to do something for me," he said as he pretended to ramble in a dresser drawer.

"What's that, dear?"

"Remember the mistake I made today on the budget for Rodan Industries?"

"What about it?"

"You should give me a good slap for that. It was a stupid mistake."

"What do you mean, give you a slap? What are you talking about?" Carly had a puzzled look on her face.

"I feel so dumb about doing that, I thought I'd feel better if you gave me a hard slap."

"M.D., have you lost your mind? I'm not going to slap you or anybody else. If I went around slapping everyone who made a mistake in that office, I'd be fired, if not locked up. Quit talking crazy. Get over it, for God's sake!"

From that point on, M.D. knew it was in his hands alone to mete out punishment.

*****

Still seeking his dream of being his own boss, M.D. spotted a for sale ad in the *Athens Banner-Herald* for a small retail business. He checked on it without Carly's knowledge, and found the price to be very reasonable, not suspecting why. He thought, this is your big chance to be free. Don't blow it. I would hate to slap my self silly if I don't take this opportunity.

The owner put pressure on him to decide, and he finally had to tell his wife. She held her hand over her eyes, and began crying. "M.D., why are you doing this to us? We both have good jobs, making good money with health insurance and even a retirement plan. Don't you know that a large percentage of small businesses fail in the first year?"

"Don't be mad, honey. I've always wanted to have my own business. The payment is low, and I'll work night and day if I have to. We can make it, I know we can."

Little did M.D. know that having your own business is just another form of slavery.

CHAPTER SEVEN

Wilson Lumkin hated it when there was something un-resolved in his life. In this case it started long before he was born. It fact it was before his father was born. In 1897 his great grandfather, Steven Wilson Lumkin, and his great grandmother, Loretta, had marital problems over Steven's attraction to one of the secretaries at his bank, Peoples First of Athens. He liked her so much he wanted to teach her everything he knew about the banking business and monkey business as well.

Loretta took exception. Even though she was pregnant with their fifth child, she filed for divorce. She was certain that she and the children would be well taken care of since her husband owned a bank. He also had half interest in a construction business.

She knew that Steven, even though, or perhaps because he was a banker, kept a lot of cash. After he had collected a desk drawer full, he took it to the padlocked trunk in the attic. He did this for years, and Loretta knew, but never questioned it because she was given everything she asked for. She thought perhaps he was saving for the children's education.

Loretta informed her lawyer of Steven's assets, including the stash in the attic. When he subpoenaed the bank records, he found that a recent audit showed embezzlement as well as other improprieties. Files from the construction company revealed similar problems.

Alarmed by the attorney's report, Loretta went to the attic. She found an unlocked and empty trunk. When she confronted

Steven, he said, "I have no idea what you're talking about. I'm not crazy enough to keep cash money around the house."

Two days later Steven died of a heart attack while teaching his secretary some new tricks.

The bank assets were seized and finally liquidated. After many months, Loretta received $5,000. The construction company finished the buildings on Clayton Street which Steven had been supervising, but a short time later went bankrupt. The court eventually split what was left among the creditors. The family got nothing.

Loretta knew beyond a doubt that the cash was somewhere. She passed that on to the children. Visitors to her home expected to find some part of the house or grounds torn up where Loretta had been searching for the cash. When she died, the children agreed to never sell the old home place, thinking that someday they would find the money.

From that time on, through the generations, there was never a Lumkin who did not spend at least part of their time looking for the treasure. It came up at every family reunion. What did he do with it? Where could it be? Did he give it to his lover? All ideas were followed up by at least one member of the family, but all led to a dead end.

There was never a Lumkin born who was not stubborn and persistent. Now, that persistence had focus. Money. Anyone or anything that stood between a Lumkin and money was fair game. Most would consider these traits undesirable, but no one questioned their effectiveness. Charles, Wilson's father, was very wealthy and probably the most influential man in Athens.

All of these traits were passed down to and personified in Wilson. He was ruthless toward those he perceived to stand in his way. His dark good looks and stout body oozed power. There were very few who could stand up to the penetrating stare of his cold, unforgiving eyes.

The only one who held sway over Wilson was his father. Charles always expected his son to be the best in everything and if he wasn't, there was hell to pay. He turned over control of the Lumkin Café, considered by many to be the finest eating place in North Georgia outside of Atlanta, to Wilson. Deeply disappointed by the declining revenue from the restaurant, and unwilling to accept Wilson's excuse of competition from the chains, hardly a day went by that he didn't tongue-lash Wilson or walk around the place shaking his head.

The only trait Wilson inherited from his father was his piercing blue eyes that seemed to cut like a razor through those who disagreed with him. He had always been told that he favored his mother who was short and stocky for a woman, and wondered if that was why his father didn't like him.

Disturbed by not being able to please his father, Wilson took it out on others including his wife, Delores, and their son, Billy, a twenty-two year old senior at the university. Without telling his wife, he began taking anti-depressant drugs hoping to escape the fear of his father's disapproval.

CHAPTER EIGHT

The early morning crowd had left, and Moochie was standing behind the counter talking to Uncle Billy.

"I appreciate your friendship with Bud. It's been a real comfort to him, having someone who's fighting the same demon," said Moochie.

Uncle Billy was having his usual glazed donut with black coffee. Being from the old school, he always took his Texas Ranger hat off when he came inside. It rested on the counter. Eighty-four years old but still spry, he refused to wear his glasses except when driving, claiming they made him look his age.

"Believe me, Moochie, it's been a blessing to me; getting to know Bud, and you too. You have both been a big help. If someone had told me a year ago that I could lay the bottle down, I would have thought they were crazy. My doctor said to me, 'Billy, I'm going to be honest with you. If you don't quit drinking, you may as well sell your boots and saddle because you won't be riding much farther.' I went home and told Lucille that very day that I was quitting. She didn't believe me, but I did it and she helped me through the rough spots like she always has. I love her with all my heart, but I don't deserve her. It's like you and Bud. You're good for each other. I'm lucky to have friends like you."

Moochie patted him on the hand and said, "Uncle Billy you're a special man. We love you and you're always in our prayers."

She could smell the mixed aroma of vegetables, cornbread and chili filtering through the swinging doors from the kitchen. At the other end of the counter April was talking to a dark complexioned man wearing a black silk shirt. Moochie guessed his age around forty. He smiled easily as April chattered away, cleaning the counter, laughing and snorting at the same time. She was blessed with a contagious laugh, but when it finally ended and she sucked in a breath, there was a snorting sound audible throughout the room. At first people were startled, then amused and finally captivated by it. The guys, especially, told jokes and made comments to coax a laugh so they could hear her snort.

Moochie moved toward them, curious about this dark and handsome man. Even as he smiled there was a melancholy look about him, like his thoughts were somewhere else.

"Hello, I'm Moochie Dunlop, part owner of this down home eatery. I don't think I've met you."

"Hi, Moochie. Antonio Colosimo. Tony to my friends."

"Nice to meet you, Tony. I appreciate your business. Say, I was just about to have my morning coffee and a little snack. Would you like to see my office?" She squeezed around the end of the counter. "Bring your coffee with you, honey."

They settled into Moochie's special booth. April brought the current morning snack for her boss: a large mug of coffee, a small pitcher of cream and three donuts. The sugar was on the table. Tony declined the offer of a donut.

"Well, Tony, you're obviously not from around here. You seem a little sad. Is there any way ole Moochie can help?"

He was far away from home and desperate for someone to confide in. First he swore Moochie to secrecy, then told her a bizarre story of the mob in New York City; said he had quit the La Cosa Nostra and straightened his life out. Moochie wondered, but didn't ask why he came to Athens.

"Moochie, I have a wife and three children in New York, and I miss them terribly. I can't go back there or even call them because it would not only put my life in danger, but theirs as well."

"All right, honey. Your secret is safe with me, and I'm glad you're doing the right thing now. You hang in there 'til things die down in Gotham City. Eventually, you'll be able to get back with your family."

"There's something else, Miss Moochie that I've never told anyone about." Surprised at himself for bringing it up, he continued, "I have an ex-wife and son in Louisiana that I haven't seen in several years."

"Why, gracious sakes alive, why haven't you seen them?"

"We were young, Moochie, and madly in love, at least I was. When the baby came, he looked nothing like me. He was blond and light skinned. Made me wonder. I got scared and just left; came back to New York. Got married to my present wife. I'm still confused about the whole thing and don't know if I did the right thing."

"Well, honey, life is a mystery sometimes. You may never know the answer to that. One thing's for sure, it's not going to help to keep worrying about it. You've got to forget it and move on with your life. If Our Maker wants you to know that son, he'll come back into your life."

Tony, feeling like an elephant had been lifted off his back, thought for a minute, then said, "You're right, Moochie. Thanks for listening."

*****

At ten-thirty Moochie saw a familiar face peek through the front window. Almost every day when she walked by Mr. Slocum's store she saw him alone inside, slapping himself. She waited, listening to "A Boy Named Sue" by Johnny Cash. M.D. walked swiftly to the front door, came in and headed for his usual stool. Moochie had his coffee waiting. She smiled. "Well, hello, sunshine. Why the gloomy look? Did your hug wear off?"

M.D. was wringing his hands. "Miss Moochie, may I talk to you for a few minutes?"

"Sure, honey. Grab your coffee and come on into my office. Hey, April, bring Slapper---." She paused, embarrassed. "I'm sorry. Is it all right if I call you Slapper?"

"I guess so," said M.D. "Just don't tell anyone why, okay? And, not in front of Carly."

"Okay, honey. It just seems to go together with Slocum so well, and I don't mean any harm."

April waited.

"Bring him one of them pralines. That'll pep him up," said Moochie.

They sat down and Slapper leaned across the table, all the time tapping his jaw. "Moochie, I'm in deep trouble. Carly has left me. I haven't been able to make the payment on my building for the last two months. Right now I'm living in the back of the store." He shuddered and tears came to his eyes. "I'm sorry. I'm such a failure. I can't last much longer. You're the only one I can talk to." He leaned back and dropped his chin.

Moochie leaned forward and spoke softly, but forcefully. "Raise your head up, Slapper, and look at me." She smiled, "Now---You ain't done by a long shot. Do you hear me?"

"Yes, ma'am." He glanced into Moochie's eyes, then down at the praline. He grabbed it and took a bite, avoiding her eyes.

"Look at me," she demanded as she laid her hand on his. His shaking ceased as he gazed into her face.

"First of all, let's deal with your economic situation. Bud and I are going to pay your back payments and one month in advance. You'll be eating at the restaurant free of charge until you get on your feet."

"But, Moochie---."

"No buts about it. Now listen. I want you to contact Bill Stryker. He makes signs and T-shirts. He'll make T-shirts for you and sell them to you wholesale. He and I have already talked about doing this, but I want you to do it. Have him make some T-shirts, a hundred to start with. My picture will be on the front, and on the back it will say, 'I survived a Moochie hug.' I'll have Bud write down a list of how to survive a Moochie hug which you'll hand out with each shirt. Got it? Then, set a table outside your store so people will see them, and we'll send people over. I'll take one dollar from each sale. The rest of the profit is yours. Does that sound fair?"

"Yes, ma'am, but how am I gonna pay for them?"

"Don't worry, I'll pay for the first batch. After all, this is going to help publicize our restaurant. Like my Bud would say, 'It's one of them mass communication techniques." Moochie leaned back, picked up one of her donuts, and took a meaningful bite. She sipped her coffee. "Go ahead, honey, eat the rest of you praline. It'll recharge your battery."

Slapper did just that, washed it down with coffee, then leaned back and smiled for the first time.

Moochie leaned forward again confidentially. "Now, I want to ask you something. Why in the hell do you slap yourself all the time? I thought at first it was a tic or something, but you do it on purpose, don't you?"

Slapper was embarrassed, but jumped at the chance to tell someone who might understand about his need to be slapped. "It's about my mother, Moochie. I know she loved me, but she always slapped me when I did something wrong." He went on to tell her the whole story.

"Why, Lord-a-mercy, honey, that's the damndest story I've ever heard. Don't you know that everyone makes mistakes? How else do you think we learn? That's why the good Lord put us here on this earth, to make mistakes and then learn from them. See?"

"Yes ma'am, but---."

"No buts about it. Now, the next time you make a mistake just say, 'Thank you, Lord for the lesson and move on. Got it?"

*****

46

Later, Moochie explained to Bud the arrangement she had made with M.D. or Slapper as she now called him.

"Are you crazy, big mama? Bud yelled over the din of the kitchen. "Have you looked at the stack of bills in the back room? We can't afford to be paying for T-shirts or letting people eat free right now."

"I know, love, but I can't stand to see people in great need like that without doing something. It just ain't right. Besides, I'm hoping it'll pay off in the long run, help us pay the bills."

Bud dropped and shook his head. "I hope you're right. Otherwise, we're in deep trouble. By the way, remember the directions I wrote about how to survive a Moochie hug? Give Slapper a copy. Maybe that will help with the sales."

"Okay, love. I already told him about the rules, and don't you worry. I have a feeling this will work out just fine."

*****

They always had a large crowd at lunch time. Moochie stood at her station by the door, across from Pretty Boy. Bud had hung a bell from the ceiling with a sign: "If you want a hug, ring the bell." Word always spread back through the line, "If you ring that bell, be prepared: make sure you hold your head up and squeeze back."

Pretty Boy could sense when the hugging was about to commence. He strutted back and forth in his cage making comments: "Gawk, welcome to Moochie's," "Gawk, call a medic," "Gawk, heads Up," and "Gawk, I love you."

Moochie would shout, "Shut up, dirty bird," but it never did any good.

The people could hear Bud and Brad in the kitchen, working like dogs and singing as loud as they could along with the songs on the jukebox: "I love this bar---come as you are---;" "I want you, I need you, I loooove you;" and "The wayward wind---is a restless wind---." More often than not, the

47

customers joined in the singing, between bites. Pretty Boy helped out when he could, "Gawk, I looove you."

One afternoon after the lunch crowd had cleared out a bit, a fiftyish looking man whom Moochie had seen there often, came to the counter. "Hi, Moochie. I don't know if you remember me, but my name is Grady Lakes."

"Why, I sure do, honey. I see you in here all the time, and Bud and I appreciate it."

"Well, I have a little radio talk program called '*Lay it on Grady*.' It's on WGRB, 97.2, Wednesday night at seven o'clock. People call in and ask me questions. I understand that you give advice to people from time to time. I want you to be a guest on my show."

Moochie's eyes widened, "Gosh, Grady, I don't know about that. I ain't never been on radio. What would I say?"

"Oh, don't worry about that. I'll just have you tell us about your life. Then, people will call in and ask questions about problems they're having. All you have to do is be honest. Just tell it like you see it."

Moochie said, "Hold on just a minute and I'll go consult with Bud."

Bud was cleaning counters and putting food away while Brad was up to his elbows in dirty dishes when Moochie burst through the doors. "Bud! There's this man out here, Grady Lakes, wants me to be on his radio program. What do you think?"

Bud wiped a chili splatter off the counter and turned to face his bride. He laid his finger beside his nose and looked at her.

"Well---?" Moochie said.

"I'm thinking---I'm thinking," he said. "The more people we make contact with, the better our business will be. It's another one of them mass communication principles I was reading about."

"Is that a yes, sweetie?" Moochie said impatiently.

"I say, go for it, big mama. Maybe they'll even pay you for doing it. We sure could use it for the loan payment."

Brad grinned as he started the dishwasher.

CHAPTER NINE

How to Survive a Moochie Hug
by
Bud Arrington

One: Hold your head up. When the air leaves your lungs, it's very important that there be a route by which it can return. Otherwise, you might become seriously dead. If you are not tall enough to breathe from the top, try for a spot under her arm.

Two: Reach around her as far as you can and squeeze with all your might. This helps to tighten your muscles and rib cage, preparing them for the expected assault. If you fail to do this in time, then it's important that you completely relax your muscles and go limp. That way she'll think you fainted and let up.

Three: Do not try to keep your feet on the floor unless you are over six feet tall. It will be impossible and will waste energy which might be needed later. Just be aware of where your feet are at all times so that when she lets go, you'll be able to catch yourself. It's best if your feet touch down shoulder width apart. It will give you more stability.

Four: When you land it's important to suck in as much air as possible to replace that which has been squeezed out.

Five: Immediately look around for something or someone to grab onto. It is possible that you will be disorientated, dizzy or just plain stupified. It will hurt if you fall face down on the floor.

Six: It might help if you have something to sip on while you recover: sweet tea, a Coca Cola or a Bud Light, my favorite.

Seven: Also, recite the Twenty-third Psalm, but not if you're having my favorite above. That wouldn't be respectful and things might backfire on you.

If you do all of the above, I'm pretty sure that you will survive, but not certain. So keep your bone doctor's number handy.

It's been said that a hug by my sweet Moochie can cure anything. I don't believe that because a friend of mine got a hug when he had foot fungus and he's still got it.

Anyhow, if you follow my instructions and are lucky you can proudly say: I SURVIVED A MOOCHIE HUG!

P.S. This is to be given to anyone who buys a Moochie T-shirt or does not have a written will.

P.P.S. I like to kid my Moochie about her hugs. Really, she's the most gentle person you'd ever want to meet. She would never hurt anyone, unless, of course, she's real angry or overly excited.

CHAPTER TEN

The next day, Pretty Boy greeted Ron Harris, an inspector for the Environmental Health Section. "Gawk! Welcome to Moochie's."

One corner of Mr. Harris' mouth angled into a grin before he brought it under control. He walked directly to the counter and asked for a private word with Moochie and Bud in the kitchen.

Moochie recognized him immediately as the man who gave the restaurant an excellent grade before they opened. He often came in for lunch, but today had a worried look on his face. Mr. Harris was a stocky man of about fifty, with gray and black speckled hair. Most people kindly referred to his nose as noble. It was large but at least it was straight. His mouth curled up as though to speak even in his quiet moments.

He motioned Moochie who was wearing a moo moo featuring red, yellow and blue flowers, and Bud to one corner of the kitchen while Brad continued preparations for the noon meal.

He spoke in a low voice. "Mr. and Mrs. Moochie, we have a problem. Yep,yep,yep. Sure do. Someone lodged a complaint with Environmental Health about you having a bird on the premises. Sure did. Yep,yep,yep. That's a violation of Food Service Regulations, section 290-5-14-08 which states that 'Live animals, including birds and turtles, shall be excluded from the food service area.' Yep, that's right, excluded."

Moochie's ears perked up. "Just who is this 'someone?'" she asked. "Was it one of our customers?"

"No, no, no, no, no. Nope. Not one of your customers. Nope. Noooo."

"Well, who was it?" asked Bud as he lifted his shoulders and glanced up at Mr. Harris.

"Can't tell you that," stammered Mr. Harris. "No, no, no. Nope. Can't do it."

Moochie piped in, "Does he own a restaurant, and are his initials W.L.?"

"Why---How did you---? No, no, no, no. Nope. Noooooo. Can't say. No, no, no, can't say."

Moochie said, "That's all right, Mr. Harris, you don't have to tell us. Did you know our Pretty Boy is famous? He's more than a big mouth. Did you know that he was once on the *Tonight Show* with Johnny Carson?"

"No, no, no. Nope. I didn't know that, but Mr. Carson didn't serve food. Anyway, he can't be in the restaurant." Mr. Harris' upper lip stiffened and twitched.

Bud said, "Why not?"

"Well, Mr. Moochie, because birds can carry diseases and they poop, if you'll excuse the expression. Yeah, Yeah, yep, yep, yep. They poop."

Moochie loomed over Mr. Harris and glared down at him. "Well, everybody poops, including you and your dog. You do have a dog, don't you, Mr. Harris?"

"Yeah, yeah, yeah, yeah, oh yeah. I sure do. I have a dog."

"Does he poop?" asked Moochie.

"Yeah, yeah, yeah, yeah, oh yeah. Yep. He does poop. Don't get me wrong, I like Pretty Boy as well as anyone, but we had a complaint and the law says he can't be inside the restaurant. Maybe you could move him outside. Yeah, yeah, yeah. Move him outside."

Bud cast his hound dog eyes upward. "But, he's a big part of the atmosphere in our place. Gives it character. It's one of them business principles that you'd only know if you was a proprietor. Besides, he don't like it outside."

"I'm sorry, Mr. and Mrs. Moochie. I truly am, yep, yep, yep---sorry. The law is the law. You have seventy-two hours to comply. Yep, yep, yep---seventy-two hours."

As he walked out the kitchen door, he gave an apologetic wave. When he reached the front door he avoided Pretty Boy's eyes. Pretty Boy said, "Gawk! I love you."

*****

At three-thirty that afternoon, a young man whom Moochie recognized, walked in and sat in the booth next to the juke box. As usual, he had a *Wall Street Journal* in his hand. She learned earlier that he had recently passed the State Bar exams and been hired by Williams, Cummings, Favre and Stackhouse, a prestigious law firm in Athens.

Moochie waved Peola off before she could take the man's order for black coffee and a piece of apple pie. She walked over as nonchalantly as she could, being Moochie. "Hello, there," she said. "I'm Moochie Dunlop, owner of this here fine eating establishment. I'm sorry, I didn't catch your name before."

"Steve Phelps. I'm pleased to meet you. I'll just have my usual order of coffee and apple pie."

Moochie smiled and patted his hand, "That's fine Mr. Phelps. Say, have you ever seen my office?"

"No, Miss Moochie, I can't say that I have." Steve tried to look as lawyerly and distinguished as possible for a twenty-eight year old, who looked about eighteen.

"Well, come with me, honey. You're about to enter Moochie's world. Hey, Peola, please bring Mr. Phelps' order to my booth. Add a Twinkie on the side."

Steve straightened his tie and grabbed the newspaper, thinking this must be something important. He was about Moochie's height with sandy, blond hair and a cow-lick behind his part. He kept it cut short, probably hoping it wouldn't be noticed, but that contributed to making him look even younger.

His right eyebrow seemed permanently arched making people wonder if he was surprised or just didn't believe what they were saying.

Moochie guided him by the elbow into his side of her booth. "There now, don't that feel good? This booth was 'specially made for me by Bud and Uncle Billy. Do you know my husband, Bud? Hey, April, tell Bud to step out here a minute and meet our new lawyer."

Steve looked surprised, realizing that he had just been hired. But, hey, a client is a client, he thought. He only had two other cases that had been thrown his way by partner Favre. He spent most of his days reading law books and trying to look important.

Bud threw his shoulders back and reached out his hand as he approached the booth. "Hello, there. I'm William Arrington the Third, but ever' body calls me Bud."

Steve stood up as far as the booth would allow, and shook Bud's hand. Realizing Bud wouldn't fit on the other side with Moochie, he slid over to make room.

Peola brought Steve's order. He had a sudden urge to grab the Twinkie and gobble every morsel, but instead reached for the coffee cup.

"I'll have my usual," said Moochie. "What about you, my sweet little man?"

"I'll just have black coffee." Bud glanced at Moochie. "I have to watch my figure, you know."

"Lord-a-mercy, honey. That man's gonna waste away to nothing," said Moochie. Bud grinned, having gotten the expected response from his bride.

Moochie turned her attention to Mr. Phelps as Peola set a large bowl in front of her. It was loaded with two Twinkies, three scoops of vanilla ice cream, and covered with strawberries.

"I have to have something to tide me over 'til dinner," remarked Moochie. "Now, Mr. Phelps---."

"Please call me Steve."

"Okay, Steve, We have us a real serious problem here which may involve the Bill of Rights in the Constitution of the United States of America. It don't get no bigger than that, honey. You see what I mean?"

Steve took a sip of coffee, looking as grave as possible. "Yes, ma'am, it sounds very serious. Tell me about it."

Moochie put a tablespoon full of ice cream and cake into her mouth, taking a minute to move it around so it wouldn't cause a case of brain freeze. "Well, these environmental health people, Mr. Harris, to be specific, told us Pretty Boy can't be in the restaurant anymore. We have to move him outside. Now, ain't that something?"

Steve bit into the Twinkie, leaving a bit of cream filling clinging to the right corner of his mouth, and leaned forward.

Moochie continued, "Surely the Bill of Rights covers birds too, don't it? I mean birds have been around almost as long as we have. The Bald Eagle is the symbol of these United States. They have a right to be where they want to, just like us. He's talking about them birds carrying diseases and so forth. Why, hell, human beings carry diseases too. Ain't that right? Then, he brings up the idea that birds poop. Well, I told him that all living things poop, even him. I told him that. Didn't I Bud?"

"You sure did, sweetie," Bud replied as he warmed his hands on the coffee mug. He loved it when she went on a rampage.

Steve listened in amazement, thankful that he wasn't a judge listening to Moochie argue a case in court.

Moochie continued, "Now, listen, counselor, this tops it off. They're doing all this without giving Pretty Boy a fair trial. Have you ever heard of such a thing? It's a travesty of justice and a violation of his rights if I've ever seen such a thing. Why, we ought to take it straight to the Supreme Court, let the big boys decide. Ain't that right, sweetie?

Bud nodded.

Steve's mind was boggled. Thoughtfully, he finished chewing the last bite of apple pie. Finally, he decided to try and establish his credentials. "Well, Moochie, Bud, I can certainly see why you all are concerned. When I was a student at the University of Colorado, I was president of an animal rights group on campus that tried to protect animals from abuse, et cetera. So, I know where you're coming from. Let me look into this matter, and see what I can come up with. I would like to represent Pretty Boy directly, but the law won't allow that. So, officially, I'll be representing you and Bud. Hopefully, the public impression will be that Pretty Boy alone is the injured party. We'll need as much sympathy as we can get. I'll get right on it. In the meantime, you'd better comply with the law."

Bud and Moochie walked Steve to the door, and formally introduced him to Pretty Boy.

Steve slowly opened the cage door and slid his hand inside, fully expecting to get his finger pecked. Instead, Pretty Boy sensed the importance of this occasion, and hopped onto his finger. "Gawk! Let's make love."

Steve smiled and said, "I like my new client. I think we'll work well together."

*****

As soon as Steve left, deep in thought about how he would defend his first self-generated client. Bud returned to the kitchen and Moochie to her office. Peola approached and asked to speak to Moochie. Moochie was not surprised, having noticed in the last few days that Peola was distracted and even more nervous than usual. Her already-shrill voice had risen a couple of octaves. Yesterday, one of the football players, Winslow Harris, had asked Moochie if Peola was okay.

Moochie said, "Before you sit down, child, I can tell that you need a good hug. Come here to Moochie." The only things still visible about Peola during the hug were her two arms clutching Moochie's sides, and two spindly legs dangling two inches above the floor. When she emerged, her cheeks were wet with tears, not from pain, but knowing that someone loved and cared about her. Typically, her right hand covered the birthmark below her right ear.

"Sit down, child, and tell ole Moochie what's bothering you. Before you do that, though, I want you to know that you are a beautiful person. Did anyone ever tell you that?"

"No, ma'am," said Peola as she dried her tears with a napkin.

"Do you know why I say that, child?"

"No, ma'am."

Moochie took her hand, "Because I can look into your dark brown eyes and see your soul. You can't hide from ole Moochie if I can look into your eyes. Now, as far as that birthmark on your neck is concerned, it only adds to your beauty. It's a sign of God's blessing and to let you know that He loves you. Move your hand from your neck, and remember what I said. Now, tell me what's on your mind."

What Moochie said about her being beautiful set Peola to reaching for more napkins.

Moochie yelled, "April, bring this child a praline before she disappears all together."

Peola looked up with a faint smile and began, "Miss Moochie, I hate to bother you with all this, but I don't know what else to do. My mama lost her job three weeks ago. She signed up for unemployment benefits which keeps us fed, but that's about it. She's looked all over for a job, but no one will hire her, because--. Well, they just won't."

"All right, girl, you're gonna have to be honest with ole Moochie. Why not?"

Peola looked down, "Well, because---because she's too fat. People won't say it, but I know that's the reason. Besides, she's got bruises all over her face where her boy friend has beat her. She's afraid to get rid of him, because he pays part of the bills. And, Miss Moochie, I'm thankful to have this job, but both of us just can't live on what I make."

Moochie put a tablespoon full of Twinkie and melted ice cream into her mouth. Food always helped her think better. She reached across and took both of Peola's hands. "All right, now, listen to me. Ole Moochie's not gonna help a sorry boyfriend. You tell your mama---what's her name?"

"Pinkstaff Rose. Pinkie, for short."

"Is she related to Garcia Rose, our sign maker?"

"Nope."

"Tell Pinkie to fire that boyfriend, and get herself in here tomorrow morning at seven o'clock. She'll be working in the kitchen with Bud and Brad." She raised her voice so April could hear. "And, starting tomorrow, you, April and Brad will be getting a dollar per hour raise. Now, let's get back to work."

Peola jumped to her feet with a big smile on her face and began straightening chairs and buffing tables. April chuckled, ending in a mild snort. There was new vigor in her step behind the counter. Moochie sat back and smiled like a mother lion. Dean Martin sang "That's Amore" and the aroma of simmering barbeque sauce floated through the kitchen door.

CHAPTER ELEVEN

With Grady Lakes' directions spread out on the passenger seat, Moochie made her way to the WGRB studio at 1241 Prince Avenue. She followed the driveway beside the old Victorian house which had been converted to a radio station and offices for a string of stations in Northeast Georgia. She walked up a ramp, through the back door, and followed the dark hallway to the front of the house.

These old houses usually have wide hallways, she thought, wide enough to accommodate hefty people like me. They must have narrowed it when they converted to a radio station. Hell, if two people my size met in this chute, one of us would have to stop and back up.

When Moochie entered the waiting room/old parlor, Grady was surprised and quickly set the shot glass on the table. "Moochie! Hello. You're a little early. I was just relaxing a bit before we go on the air. Would you like a drink---coffee, soda?"

"Well, honey, I might have a cup of coffee, plenty of cream and sugar." Grady rushed to the refreshment table and began pouring the coffee.

Moochie frowned at his back, "You aren't drunk are you Grady?"

Grady, embarrassed, said over his shoulder, "No, not at all, Moochie. Honestly, I only have one drink before the show, that's all. Just to relax me before I meet my fans. You'd think I wouldn't get nervous before each show after all these years. I'm really an introvert, but I'm fine once I'm on the air."

"Okay, honey. I just want you to know, I'm not going to work with no drunk."

Grady, dressed in a dark blue sports coat, white shirt and blue tie with a pattern of small sailboats, set Moochie's coffee on the end table next to the couch. He brushed a hand through his wavy, dark brown hair, streaked with gray. His right eye appeared larger than his left and seemed to draw your attention when face-to-face. "I understand, Moochie. Please believe me. I'm not drunk."

He waved his hand toward the couch and said, "Please--- have a seat."

Moochie sat primly next to the coffee and took a cautious sip. "You call that sweet, honey? Hand me another couple of sugars."

Grady complied, saying, "We'll get started in about fifteen minutes. Do you have any questions?"

Moochie peered over the rim of her coffee cup, "Yes, why are you dressed up like a lawyer when I'm the only one who's going to lay eyes on you?"

"I know this may sound silly, but it's my way of showing respect to the people out there who put their trust in me. They have provided a career and a living for me over the years."

"Okay. Now, I understand. At first, I thought your biscuit hadn't been buttered on both sides."

Moochie gulped her now cooler coffee and asked, "Who's going to be hearing all this, and what kind of questions do they ask?"

Grady smiled and leaned back on the other end of the couch. "My show is broadcast throughout Northeast Georgia. I have a broad range of listeners, from homebound folks who play their radios all day long to high school kids getting a kick out of other people's problems. I must tell you, Moochie, I take my program very seriously, even though I joke and kid around. There are a lot of people out there who need help; advice on all sorts of things. Some of them have no other place to turn, at least, none that they know of. I try to be honest, give them the best advice I can. I tell them who else they might talk to---a preacher, counselor, lawyer, et cetera."

Grady glanced at the clock, straightened his tie and continued. "I've even had a few who were contemplating suicide. I try to guide them to some help. Sometimes all they need is to talk out their problems. Some are just lonely. They have no one else to talk to. I may be their only contact with the outside world. What they are really looking for is love. That's so sad, Moochie. I try to remain lighthearted and lift their spirits. At times, when I'm making jokes and playing the fool, my heart is breaking on the inside. The only way I can survive in this job, my friend, is to be happy and try to make them happy." A mist formed in Grady's eyes.

Suddenly, he jumped to his feet. "Time to go into the studio and get ready. Come on, Moochie. Just remember to be yourself and things will turn out fine."

Moochie followed with new-found respect for Grady Lakes, the radio personality.

They entered a small room with equipment, microphones, books, magazines and papers everywhere. Even the walls were covered with notes and directions.

Moochie looked at Grady with disbelief. "Lord-a-mercy, honey. All of you radio people must be skinny as a piece of pine straw. How am I supposed to fit in here?" A smell of burned wires permeated the room.

Grady quickly kicked things out of the way and dragged a sturdy wooden chair next to one of the microphones. He briefed Moochie about how the show worked, and explained how to adjust the headphones.

At seven o'clock he flipped the switch and the ON AIR light came on. A recorded introduction blared: "This is the *Lay it on Grady Show* coming to you from WGRB in Athens, Georgia, 97.2 on your radio dial," as "Happy Days Are Here Again," played in the background.

"Hello out there all of you northeasterners------. Northeast Georgia, that is. This is your old friend, Grady Lakes, and I can't wait to hear what you're going to lay on me tonight. Grady's got an answer for alllll your problems, no matter how large or how small, and if I don't have an answer, I'll make one up. Ho, Ho, Ho--- Just kidding folks. You won't believe who I've got as our guest tonight. She's the owner and operator of the most famous restaurant in Athens, Georgia----Moochie's Place. If you haven't been there to eat and get a hug from this lady, you are just not hip. Ladies, gentlemen, boys and girls, I give you---(drum roll in the background) Moochie Dunlop, restaurateur, counselor, friend, and heavyweight hugger of the world." "Happy Days Are Here Again," struck up once more.

"Now, Ms. Moochie, tell us about your pretty self."

"Why, Lord-a-mercy, Grady, you make me sound like some kind of superstar, which I ain't. I'm just Moochie, honey, and I tell it like it is."

"There you have it, folks. That's why I like this wonderful, warm-hearted woman. She tells it like it is. No punches are pulled! How did you get into giving people advice, Moochie?"

"Well, it just happened gradual like. I've seen a lot of life, mostly from the underside. So, if any of you out there are having troubles, worried, feeling sad, I know where you're coming from, honey. Ole Moochie's been there. In spite of everything that's happened to me, I still love and like to help people. I guess people sense that and come to me for advice."

"All right, my friends, this is your big chance to lay it on Grady, and our special guest, Moochie Dunlop. Let's get started with our first caller. Hello, who's calling please?"

There was a throat clearing, then a female voice, "Hello---hello. Am I on the air?"

"You're on the air, ma'am. This is Grady Lakes. Do you have a question for Ms. Dunlop?"

"Yes. This is Viola. Oops, I better not say my name. This is my question for Moochie: I just found out my husband's been cheating on me. He denies it, but I found a pair of panties under the front seat of his pickup. I knowed they weren't mine, 'cause they'as too small to fit over my big toe. He says one of his friends must'a' planted them there as a joke, but I know better. This ain't the first time. By the way, I don't have no children and don't want none by this S.O.B."

Moochie leaned toward the microphone. "Well, honey, it sounds like you've got the goods on him. Here's what I would do. Make sure you contact a divorce lawyer first, and arrange to have all of your things moved out the following day. Then, at a time of your choosing, wait 'til he falls asleep, and tie the corners of the bed sheet down good and tight. Then, take a broom handle and whip his sorry ass. Tell him you've been liberated, and you ain't taking it any more."

"What if he gets loose and comes after me?" asked Viola.

"If he's a little twerp, stand your ground. If he's bigger than you are, grab the truck keys on your way out. Drive his truck close to your mother's house and walk from there."

"What if he comes to my mama's house?"

"Call the police and tell them there's a prowler outside that you're about to shoot. They'll come a-running. The next day get a restraining order against him and the rest of his gene pool."

Grady smiled and patted Moochie on the shoulder.

The next caller was a lawyer from Toccoa. "Hello, Mr. Lakes. I can't believe you have this woman on your show. She's not a lawyer or doctor. What does she know about giving advice to people? Does she have a degree?"

Grady glanced at Moochie and noticed that she already had her mouth formed with and answer.

"Honey, I'm your worst nightmare. It don't take a degree to tell people like it is. They don't need to pay no fancy fee to hear the truth from ole Moochie. You crawl back into your hole or try to figure out how to get justice for these people, instead of how to line your pockets with their money. Love your people, honey---serve them---help them, and be thankful for that opportunity."

The lawyer sputtered and spewed a bunch of cuss words before they heard a loud click.

Grady leaned over and whispered, "Want me to take the next one?"

"Hell no, honey. I'm just getting warmed up."

A wife called in, wondering if her husband still loved her.

Moochie responded, "Hell, honey, don't worry about him loving you. Give him all the love you got. Hug him. Kiss him every chance you get. Tell him you love him. I can almost guarantee you, he'll return your love. If he don't, his pilot lights done gone out. Get rid of his sorry ass."

Grady smiled and winked at Moochie.

The switchboard lit up with more calls. Grady and Moochie answered as many as they could before time ran out.

Grady signed off. "Well, my friends, our time has flown by. Moochie, thanks for being here. I hope you'll come back. You tell it like it is, and that's what people want to hear. Ladies and gentlemen, we welcome your cards and letters, telling us what you think of our show. Send them to the *Lay it on Grady Show*, WGRB, 1241 Prince Avenue, Athens, Georgia, 30605. You may also contact us by e-mail at layitongrady@bellsouth.net. Good luck and God bless until the next time."

CHAPTER TWELVE

Moochie called Restaurant Inspector Harris on Wednesday afternoon. "Mr. Harris, this is Moochie from Moochie's Place. Remember me?"

"Yeah, yeah, yeah, yeah, oh yeah. Yep, yep, yep. Sure do---Moochie. Please, call me Ron. Yeah, yeah, yeah---Ron."

Moochie, having moved the phone away from her ear, now held it closer. "Okay, Ron it is. The other day, I forgot to ask you about Pretty Boy's sleeping arrangements. We've been keeping him in a back room at night. Is that all right?"

"Is it a separate room and does it have its own bathroom?"

"That's a yes to both questions, but may I ask what in the ----. Excuse me. What does a bathroom have to do with it? I can't quite picture a parrot using what's built for humans. Can you?"

Mr. Harris sputtered, "Nope, no, nope, nooooooooo, not for the bird himself. No ma'am. Just so there are facilities to clean and take care of the birdcage. See?"

"Yeah. I reckon so, Ron. Bud will be glad he doesn't have to sit and wait for Pretty Boy to ---. Well, you know what I mean. Anyway, the room does have a bath."

"Separate room and bath. Yep, yep, yep, yep---that's okay. Yep, yep, yep, yeah, yeah---no problem."

"Okay. I want you to know that we are going to move Pretty Boy outside during the day. But, you should also know that Pretty Boy now has a lawyer. He's decided to fight for his rights under the Constitution of the United States of America.

I'll see you tomorrow at lunch. Bud's gonna have some fried okra and cornbread dressing."

"Lawyer? No, no,no. Don't need a lawyer. Nope. No lawyer. Yep, yep, yep---see you tomorrow. Cornbread dressing ---yeah, yeah, yeah, yeah, oh yeah."

*****

Since the restaurant opened, their lives had been in high gear. Now, it seemed to shift into overdrive. The business was booming and now they wondered how they might expand. Moochie was pleased, but worried about whether she and Bud could keep up. Pretty Boy's expulsion was just an added distraction.

Moochie could tell that Bud dreaded what had to be done when they arrived on Thursday at six-thirty. He had been brooding since Mr. Harris' first visit.

Moochie said, "Don't worry, sweetie. I'll move him outside."

Bud raised his head and threw his shoulders back, "No, I can do it. It's my job to take care of him."

When he walked into the back room, Pretty Boy came alive, "Gawk! Welcome to Moochie's."

Bud cleaned the cage, filled the food and water dishes and put them back in place, ready to move the cage outside.

When he picked up the cage, Pretty Boy sensed change. "Gawk! Here's trouble."

Bud brought Pretty Boy up to eye level, "You're right, old pal. You have to stay outside today. Sorry about that, but we've got your lawyer working on it."

"Gawk! I love you," brought a tear to Bud's eye. When he brought Pretty Boy through the front door, he saw the Venetian blind in the restaurant across the street drawn all the way up with Wilson Lumkin standing in the middle. He pumped his fist once, then stood with arms folded, a big smile on his face.

Bud couldn't help flipping a bird at Wilson.

Pretty Boy said, "Gawk! Up yours, punk."

When he turned to go inside, Bud saw a Leaders Real Estate agent putting a for sale sign in front of the consignment clothing store between their place and Slapper's. He knew they'd had trouble competing with the likes of Wal-Mart and big box shopping centers.

When Bud opened the front door Pretty Boy said, "Gawk! The party's over."

Bud felt sorry for his friend and thought, if parrots could cry, Pretty Boy would be awash in tears. He soothed, "It'll be all right, Boy."

Moochie stood with her back to him, making coffee when he walked between the counters and into the kitchen. He didn't slow down, but commented over his shoulder, "The place next door is for sale."

She didn't look up, but the seed had been planted as she turned the coffee maker on. She had worried for weeks about turning people away, especially at lunch time.

*****

At quarter to seven Peola Rae walked in holding the hand of what appeared to be Moochie's twin, except that she was black. Pinkstaff Rose had about the same dimensions as Moochie and wore an orange colored moo moo with white trim around the collar. She carried a large pocketbook and Moochie noticed an oversized Baby Ruth bar sticking out of a side pocket. Her face was plastered with what appeared to be a permanent smile, revealing the whitest teeth Moochie had ever seen. If it weren't for the obvious difference, you would swear Pinkie was the sister Moochie had always longed for, but never had.

Moochie's face lit up as she came from behind the counter. "Well, hello, Peola. Don't tell me this is your mother. There's no way she could have a child as puny as you are."

Peola smiled, "Miss Moochie, this is my first mom. You're my second mom and I love you both."

Pinkie and Moochie shook hands warmly, unable to reach around each other for a hug.

Moochie put her arm on Pinky's shoulder and said, "Come on back here to the kitchen, honey, and let me introduce you to Bud and Brad. You'll be working with them, and believe me they can use all the help they can get. By the way, did you get rid of the boyfriend?"

"Yes'um. I sure did, now. I told that no good man to hit the bricks last night. He didn't like it none, but I told him we wuz through; that he's done hit me for the last time."

Moochie introduced her to Bud, who immediately found himself in a Moochie-like embrace, once again fighting for his life. Instinctively, he used the same survival tactics that he had learned well, having lived with his big woman so long. When his feet hit the floor, he introduced Pinkie to Brad who got the same treatment. Moochie nodded approval of this addition to the kitchen crew.

*****

Promptly at seven-thirty Amy and Rube walked in for breakfast.

"Hey, Amy, Rube. How's it going? Have you two cured the world yet?" said Moochie.

"No," said Rube, "there are still a few souls out there that we haven't reached yet. But, more and more doctors of all disciplines are beginning to listen." Amy put her hand on his shoulder and kissed his cheek. Amy is leggy like a New York model. She has a clear, smooth complexion with small features. There was a touch of rouge on her cheeks. Men would definitely find her attractive.

"What'll you all have this morning?" said Moochie.

Chipper and decisive as ever, Amy said, "I'll have my usual, one egg and whole-wheat toast." She tossed her long auburn hair over her shoulder and smiled at Moochie.

"Bring me two eggs, bacon and biscuits, girlfriend, but add a small dish of milk gravy on the side. I just got the lab report on my cholesterol and it's fine, so I'm celebrating. By the way, what's our favorite feathered friend doing outside?"

"Well, honey, the food police have done ordered us to ban our rainbow boy to the outdoors. But, I'll tell you right now, me and Bud aren't going to stand for it. We're prepared to fight it all the way to the Supreme Court." She paused and took a sip of coffee. "Say, Rube, Bud tells me the building next door is for sale. Know anything about it?" Without waiting, she stepped to the kitchen door, "Bud, Amy and Rube will have the usual with a side of gravy for Rube."

Rube said, "I noticed the sign as we came in. If you're interested, I'll have my accountant check it out."

"Well, honey, we're doing so well, and I sure hate to turn people away at lunch time. I just don't know if we can afford it."

Rube smiled and answered, "Sweetheart, you and Bud have been making triple payments on this building. There's no question that you can afford to make payments on the place next door. We'll check it out. If the price is reasonable, should I make an offer for you?"

When Bud brought their orders, Moochie put her arm around him and pulled him close. "Buddy Boy, Rube was saying he thought it might be a good idea to buy the place next door. What do you think?" There was a loud crash in the kitchen as Pinkie dropped a pan. She and Brad were helping Aretha Franklin and the jukebox finish, "What a friend we have in Jesus---."

Bud set the plates down, "Hey, April, please bring some silverware." He scratched his head, reached into his shirt pocket and drew out a plug of Redman. He pondered over it, then slowly pinched off a piece and put it in his jaw.

Moochie waited and tapped her finger on the counter. Finally, she said, "Sweetie, I hate to rush you, but 2008 only has so many days. It's June now and Christmas is just around the corner---."

"All right, already---I'm thinking. Now, if we have too many people to fit into this place, it seems like we need more space. It's one of them business principles."

"One Day at a Time," sung by Johnny Cash played on the jukebox.

"Is that a yes, sweetie?" asked Moochie.

Bud nodded.

April who was waiting on a customer down the counter, burst out with a laugh that ended in a loud snort. The man she was serving, went from surprised to embarrassed, and ended with an amused look on his face. Others, scattered around the room, accustomed to April's unusual laugh, barely glanced her way.

*****

At lunch time people lined up on the sidewalk outside of Moochie's Place, chatting among themselves and laughing when Pretty Boy said such things as, "Gawk. Not tonight dear. I have a headache." The wait was brief while Peola and April led people to their tables. Moochie stood aside and gave hugs to those in need.

Wilson Lumkin surveyed the crowd from across the street, then counted the four people sitting in his beautifully furnished dining room. Deciding that his manager and three waitresses could handle things, he retreated to the private and elaborately furnished office next to the grand entrance to the restaurant and slammed the door. He banged his fist on the desk, then held his head in both hands while his thoughts raced.

"Damn, damn, damn. They're making a fool of me in my own town. I know people are talking about it behind my back. And, even though my father hasn't said anything, I know he's wondering about my mettle. Looks like something drastic is going to have to happen to the low-life invaders across the street." His right eye began to twitch wildly.

Rather than sit around an empty restaurant, he stormed out and got into his black, BMW convertible, laying rubber as he pulled away from the curb. Heads from across the street jerked around, and he gave them the finger. Their resounding laughter infuriated him even more.

As his car approached the old Lumkin home place on Prince Avenue, he suddenly wheeled into the driveway, causing an oncoming driver to stand on his brakes.

Lumkin vaulted out, bounded onto the front porch, then realized he didn't have his key. He kicked the solid oak front door and flung himself down on the top step of the porch.

He sat for a long time staring blindly at the front lawn, unaware of the traffic flying by. He tried to think rationally. "Why am I so worried? I have all the money I'll ever need." But, rage pushed its way from the bottom of his gut and he shouted, "There will never be enough money. I'm addicted to the pursuit of the green stuff, and anyone who gets in my way is dead meat." Confused and scared by his expressed thoughts, he wept.

Greed and wealth were family traits, the legacy of his great grandfather, Steven Wilson Lumkin. The old man had been smart, too smart in the end, since he took his clever secret to the grave with him, puzzling the entire family for all these years.

Visualizing the painting that hung over the fireplace, Wilson pictured his great-grandfather. People always told him that he was just like the old man. He remembered staring at the painting as a young boy, wondering if it were true. He had admired Steven Lumkin all his life, but he hated him for what he had done to the family. He closed his eyes and said over and over, "Where is the money, Grandfather? Where did you hide your fortune?" At some level not understood, a spirit-to-spirit connection was made. The word "buildings" popped into

Wilson's head. Suddenly, there was a small explosion of light in his brain. "My great-grandfather was a builder, he was in charge of constructing some of the buildings downtown. In fact, he built Moochie's Place and one or two other stores along there. What does that have to do with the treasure?" Finally, he hit his head with the palm of his hand. "Why didn't someone think of that before? The old man hid the treasure somewhere in those buildings! It's so simple! I can't believe it! My God, I've got to have those buildings."

He jumped in his Beamer and raced toward his restaurant. He snatched the cell phone from its cradle and dialed Leader's Realty. "Hello, this is Wilson Lumkin, I want to make an offer on the building you have listed on Clayton street."

"Hold on just a minute, Mr. Lumkin, I'll pull up the information on that." There was a pause as Wilson rubbed his neck, suddenly struck by a headache.

The agent came back on the line, "I'm sorry, Mr. Lumkin, that property is under contract. We had an offer this morning and it was accepted by the owner. Sorry about that---we have some other properties downtown---."

"Who made the offer?"

Caught off guard, the agent said, "The restaurant owners next door. Why?"

"Never mind," said Wilson, slamming the phone down.

*****

Slapper peeked around the corner and through the plate glass window. Seeing that Moochie was not busy, he stepped back, then made a beeline for the front door and entered. He walked directly to his usual counter seat, and silently nodded in the direction of Moochie's office. Moochie casually squeezed behind April and in front of the coffee machine. "Hold down the fort," she whispered.

Slapper leaned against the wall on his side of the booth with his left leg slung across the seat, and nonchalantly looked around the room.

Moochie slipped in and whispered, "Don't tell me. You're now working for the CIA, and Osama Bin Laden is hiding somewhere in the restaurant."

Slapper laughed in spite of himself, and ran his hand over the top of his thinning hair. "No. No," he said, as he slid an envelope across the table to Moochie. "Here's the money I owe you for the last batch of shirts. So far, we've sold more than two thousand. Bill and I set up a web site, and we're getting orders from all over Georgia, especially the Atlanta area. It's hard for Bill to keep up with production." He grabbed Moochie's hand and kissed it. "You saved my life. I'm thankful and more than happy to pay you a dollar a shirt. The 'I Survived a Moochie Hug' shirt was a great idea."

"Hey, Peola, bring us some coffee and Twinkies with strawberries on top." She paused and turned Slapper's face with her hand. "Well, I see the bruises have just about healed. No reason to keep slapping yourself. Good for you, honey. I knew you could do it."

They sat eating their Twinkies, sipping coffee, and basking in their economic success. Linda Hopkins sang "Let The Good Times Roll."

*****

Grady Lakes came in early for lunch. Moochie met him at the door. He had a big smile on his face. "Moochie, you wouldn't believe it. The calls started last night, and I've been on the phone all morning. People are demanding that you come back on the show. They loved it. Please be on the show again. In fact, I want you to consider being on the show every week; a permanent guest. What do you say?"

Moochie laughed and grabbed him in a bear hug. When she set him down, his smile was gone and he was gasping for air. "Lord-a-mercy, honey, I thought I'd done insulted some folks, and never would be asked back. As for being on your show, I'll have to talk it over with Bud, see if I can get an answer from him."

Pretty Boy said, "Gawk! Moochie Superstar." Moochie waved her hand at him, "Oh, shut up motor mouth, before I tie your beak together."

Moochie motioned for Peola to take Grady to a table. While still at the front door greeting other customers, a stranger walked up and handed her a sealed envelope with her name on it. "A man asked me to give you this," he said.

When things settled down a bit, and she was back behind the counter, she opened the envelope. Inside was a brief note: "Whatever you paid for your building and the one next door, I will pay you double that amount. Wilson Lumkin. 548-0501." She smiled and stuffed the note back into her pocket. She would discuss it with Bud later.

CHAPTER THIRTEEN

"Pretty Boy Banned," screamed the headline in the *Athens Banner-Herald* the next morning. Moochie and Bud wondered how the paper got the story so soon. Bud suspected Lawyer Phelps had sprung a leak. Moochie said, "Hard to tell. Lots of folks from the newspaper eat lunch here."

Five minutes later the receiver rang. "Hello. Moochie's Place. Moochie speaking."

"Miss Moochie, this is Arch Cameron with the *Banner-Herald*. I guess you saw the headline this morning."

"Yep. I sure did, honey, and I'm curious how you all got the story so fast."

"Well, I can't reveal our source. Let's just say I have 20/20 hearing. I called to ask if I might interview you and your husband sometime today, preferably this morning."

"Hold on ..." She covered the phone and yelled at the kitchen door, "Hey, Bud! There's a reporter on the phone; wants an interview with us this morning."

Bud yelled back, "No later than ten o'clock; have to get everything ready for lunch."

By the time Reporter Cameron arrived, The *Atlanta Journal Constitution* and an animal rights group also had called. Numerous customers, especially students, asked about Pretty Boy's plight.

Arch Cameron walked in and up to the counter at ten sharp. He appeared tense, his dark brown eyes shaded by bushy, overhanging eyebrows, his mouth drawn in a tight line.

His ears and shoulders curved forward, ready to receive any information that might be offered.

"I'm Arch Cameron and this is Larry Shropshire, my cameraman." Shropshire, a man in his forties with graying hair at the temples and a camera slung over his shoulder, said nothing and stood behind the reporter. He had an amused look on his face.

Moochie smiled, turned her head and yelled, "Hey Bud, the press is here."

Looking at the two men she said, "What can I get you gentlemen to eat?"

"We don't need anything to eat," said Cameron.

"Well, it don't look that way to me. You're both skinny as a number 2 pencil. Hell, if a strong wind came up we'd have to pluck you out of the air with a net. It ain't healthy being skinny." With that she called to April, "Please get these two a praline sundae, bring Bud a coffee and me a praline and two Twinkies with coffee." She came around the counter, slung her arm over Cameron's shoulder and said, "Don't mind me. I'm just funning with you a little bit, but I do want you to try our sundaes." She led the two to her office booth.

Bud came out wiping his hands on his apron. When introduced, he shook hands, "Hello, Mr. Cameron, Mr. Shropshire," then dragged a chair from the nearest table.

When the food came, Cameron pushed his aside.

"May we begin the interview? By the way, you may call me Arch."

"Okay, Arch. Now, you eat your dessert like a good little boy or at least try it." She grinned. "Then, the interview will begin. I don't want you fainting away once we commence," said Moochie.

The cameraman grinned and dug in. Arch shrugged his shoulders and pulled his bowl back.

Bud sipped his coffee and eyed the two as they finished the sundaes.

Arch licked his lips and wiped his mouth with a napkin. "Miss Moochie or Bud, please tell us what happened yesterday and what caused Pretty Boy to be banned from the restaurant."

Moochie nodded at Bud who was in the midst of sipping his coffee. He held up a finger while completing the swallowing process, coughed twice and wiped a dribble from the corner of his mouth. "Well, Arch, Mr. Shropshire, being a businessman, a proprietor if you will, there are certain business principles that must be followed. First, you must have good food, like them praline sundaes you just wolfed down. Then, you've got to have atmosphere; a place where people like to be. Do you follow me?" He waited for both to nod.

"Now, Pretty Boy is part of the atmosphere. See? People like him. He makes them laugh. He's an important part of this business. Besides, he's family to us. Wellll, here comes this Mr. Harris from Environmental Health and tells us Pretty Boy can't be inside anymore. We've got to banish his pretty self out into the weather. It just ain't right." Bud glanced at Moochie.

Moochie wiped a bit of chocolate from her lower lip. "It's a violation of the Constitution if you ask me," she said, trying to give Arch the big picture. "All living things have rights, just like you and me. Now, what if they was to tell you that you had to stand outside the door of the *Banner-Herald* everyday. How would you like that? I think you get my drift, don't you, Arch?"

The reporter nodded, waiting.

"Me and Bud, we hired Pretty Boy a lawyer to stand up for him, and he's a good one too, although they just now let him outta one of them lawyer schools. His name's Steve Phelps. You'll have to ask him about anything pertaining to that legal mumbo-jumbo."

Arch looked up while jotting notes and holding one ear forward with the other hand. "All right, Miss Moochie, I'll do that. I wanted to ask you about the problem of birds carrying disease. Is that an issue with Pretty Boy?"

Moochie sipped her coffee, then leaned forward and put her elbows on the table. "The people down at the Environmental Health Department, especially Mr. Harris, have been very nice, and I know they're just trying to do their job, but the law just ain't right. Now, I ain't no doctor, but people carry disease too. Ain't that right? What if they was to ban people from restaurants? Why, we'd have to close this place down, and half the women in this town would have to learn how to cook dinner again."

Mr. Shropshire snickered, then frowned when Arch glanced his way.

Arch, trying to hold on to his professional manner, said, "There's also the question of cleanliness with birds and other animals. Wouldn't that be a problem, having Pretty Boy's cage inside?"

Moochie shook her head. "All I can tell you, Arch, is that all living things poop. Can you name me one person or animal that doesn't poop?"

One of Mr. Cameron's eye brows shot up and the right corner of his mouth inched upward before he brought it under control. He shook his head, waiting.

"All right, then. Why would they discriminate against birds and turtles? Why are they singled out? Maybe you need to go ask one of them professors over at the university. Get them to explain the facts of life to you. Did you know that some restaurants keep aquariums with fish swimming around, and there's one well-known place that keeps lobsters. My question to you is, what's the difference between floating poop and poop that lies at the bottom of a cage on part of the *Banner-Herald*, after we've read it, of course? Is it easier to get that stuff out of water, or just remove the newspaper and throw it away?"

Mr. Shropshire turned sideways in the booth and clamped his hand over his mouth to keep from bursting out in a full laughing spasm.

Arch bent his head down and rubbed his brow, having no ready answer, and no intention of stating it even if he did.

"Could I get a cup of coffee?" he said, buying time to figure out who was the interviewer, and who was the interviewee.

"Hey April, bring Mr. Cameron a cup of hot java," yelled Moochie over strains of "Be-Bop-a-Lula" issuing from the jukebox.

When the coffee arrived, Arch said, "Shropshire, why don't you get some pictures of Moochie, Bud, Pretty Boy and the restaurant? And, if it's all right with you all, I'll interview a few of your customers."

"That's fine, honey. Make sure you both get a hug from ole Moochie before you leave."

*****

That afternoon, Steve Phelps, Pretty Boy's attorney, arrived at the front door. He paused for a minute to say hello to his client. Pretty Boy sidled up to the cage door and waited for Steve to stroke his back. "Gawk! Who's your daddy?" asked the bird.

Steve laughed. "You are, Pretty Boy, as long as you keep paying the bills."

"Gawk! Highway robbery. Call the sheriff," said Pretty Boy.

Steve walked on in to the strains of "The Battle of New Orleans" by Johnny Horton. Passing the counter, he waved at Moochie and April who grabbed a slice of apple pie from the case and began pouring his coffee. Moochie stuck her head over the swinging doors, "Pretty Boy's mouthpiece is here, sweetie."

Brad yelled, "Okay. This is sweetie. I'll be right there."

Pinkstaff Rose shook her head, "Lause-a-mercy, Miss Moochie, I don't know how you put up with these crazy boys. They's always full of devilment. I'm about to run 'em both through the dishwasher and see if that won't help."

Moochie cackled, "Hang in there, Pinkie, I'm going to take one off your hands for awhile. Send that sweet little old man out here." Bud had been taking it all in while pouring barbeque sauce over a pan of ribs. He slid the pan into the oven and began cleaning his hands.

April had already torn the wrappers off two pralines and two Twinkies by the time Moochie reached the office. Moochie greeted Steve, but noticed his eyes were on April. Aware of his gaze, April chuckled, snorting mildly. Bud picked up the coffee next to April on his way along the counter.

As Moochie and Bud sat down, Steve said, "Things are rolling. I've asked Judge Crocker for a temporary restraining order while we're waiting for our case to come up. He said he'll let me know tomorrow. You saw the headline this morning, didn't you?"

Moochie said, "We sure did, honey. In fact, Bud and me have already been interviewed. So, I suspect there will be another article tomorrow."

"That's good," said Steve. "I'll be honest with you. I think that's the only way we'll win. That is, if we have public opinion strongly on our side. In the meantime, I've been busy writing up our case, looking up precedents, et cetera. I've even visited some of the restaurants in town that have animals inside. One has fish and another has lobsters. You won't believe what I'm finding out about lobsters. But, I'll save that for court."

Bud spoke up. "Is there anything we can do to help?"

Steve nodded. "There sure is. You can keep talking it up with your customers; grant interview requests. Moochie you could mention it on the radio program. It would help if we had someone to make signs."

"I bet I could get Brad to do that," said Bud. "He is very upset about what they're doing to Pretty Boy."

Moochie said, "I wonder if I could get Clint Eastwood to write a letter of support for Pretty Boy."

"That would be great. Oh, and there's one other thing we've got to do," said Steve. "One of you will have to take Pretty Boy to a veterinarian and have him examined and tested.

We've got to make sure he doesn't have a disease. If he does, there is no case, and the whole thing becomes a joke."

Moochie said, "I'll call the Small Animal Hospital at the Vet School and make an appointment. Can you take him, sweetie?"

Bud nodded.

*****

By late afternoon a group of students paraded back and forth in front of the famous entrance to the university with signs reading: "Free Pretty Boy;" "Parrots Have Rights, Too;" and "Don't Poop on Pretty Boy." The story was picked up by the news services and carried by several Atlanta television stations at six o'clock, with promises of more coverage at eleven.

By the next day, reporters who were covering the presidential race were amused and latched onto Pretty Boy's plight. At every stop, the candidates were pelted with questions. Both candidates agreed that they were for parrots' rights as long as no Republicans or Democrats would get sick and be unable to vote. The Republican Senator wondered how much Pretty Boy had contributed to his campaign. The Democratic Senator wanted to know if Pretty Boy would be able to vote on the new computer voting systems.

The Senator from Arizona mused: "Does he pay taxes? Maybe I could give him a tax break."

A reporter asked the Senator from Illinois if this might indicate a serious problem of unemployment among parrots. He replied, "I do not like to see people, or parrots unemployed. I think they need to find a way to salvage Pretty Boy's job as a greeter." He grinned and said, "At least it's not the type of job that can be outsourced."

CHAPTER FOURTEEN

Wilson Lumkin was excited when he opened the front door of his restaurant and saw a note flutter to the floor. His offer had been overly generous, to make sure they could not refuse. He grabbed the paper and unfolded it.

Dear Mr. Lumkin,

Thank you for your offer to buy the buildings, but we must refuse. We're thankful for the success of our place so far and hope it will continue. We mean you no harm, and wish to live in peace with all of our neighbors.

Sincerely,

Moochie Dunlop and Bud Arrington

Lumkin crushed the paper in his hand and threw it to the floor. "Son-of-a-bitch! Those bastards must be crazy. How can they turn down a chance to double their money?" He bent over as though punched in the stomach. "What will Daddy think of me?" He remembered the time his daddy had scorned him for a week because he'd let another kid beat him up. He'd spent his whole life trying to please his father. If he found the family's lost fortune, that debt would be paid forever. His life would be his own.

He thought of his son, Billy, a senior at the university, majoring in business and moaned, "Billy, I love you, son. I've tried so hard to be a good example, but I've been a miserable failure. Someday I want to turn the Lumkin Café over to you and I want it to be the best in Athens, something we can both be proud of. Now, our restaurant is almost empty and we're losing money every day. I've got to do something." He sobbed into his hands.

He lifted the phone and dialed a recently changed cell phone number and asked to speak to Rondell, a new name that had been passed on to him. The group was expensive, but did a good job.

*****

When Moochie and Bud arrived at the restaurant the next morning, Moochie shuddered for no apparent reason. She grabbed Bud's shoulder to steady herself. When they stepped in the door they were met by an eerie silence.

Bud grabbed Moochie's arm, and stood very still, listening. "Shhh, I don't hear Pretty Boy," he said.

He ran toward the back room, followed by Moochie. Entering the hall leading to Pretty Boy's room he found the back door standing open; lock broken. Bud's heart leaped in his chest as he dashed to Pretty Boy's door. "Lord, no, no ---." He pushed the door open, and saw the television set on the floor, screen smashed. The table where Pretty Boy's cage sat was empty. He turned to his left and found the battered cage with the door hanging open. It had been thrown against the wall. "No!" he screamed. "Pretty Boy, where are you? Speak to me, Boy." Moochie grabbed Bud and held him tight.

The pull-down steps to the attic had been left down, and there was a big hole in the back wall. They began examining the room inch by inch. Bud cried, "Somebody's done stole our bird, Moochie."

"Now, don't worry, sweetie, we'll find him," Moochie soothed as she peered into the closet.

Bud got down on his knees and raised the bed spread so he could see under the spare bed that he sometimes rested on in the afternoon before getting ready for the evening meal. He saw a lump against the back wall. "Pretty Boy! Is that you?" he cooed as he crawled under the bed. He gently touched his friend, then picked him up and placed him in his other hand. "He's alive! I can feel him shaking."

Moochie had managed to get down on her hands and knees as Bud slid out, holding Pretty Boy in front of him. They sat on the floor, holding and soothing him. They carefully examined the bird, and found no obvious wounds.

Bud said, "I'd better take him on to the vet; make sure he's okay. Can you and Brad handle things here?"

"Sure, sweetie. You just go on and take care of our fine feathered friend."

*****

An hour later Bud called, "He's okay, Moochie. The doctor says he received a pretty good jolt when thrown against the wall, and that he was in shock. I know he's better though, he's sitting on his perch and just said "Let's make love," to the doctor.

Moochie laughed, then hung up and told the rest of the crew.

The police had already been there and left. Moochie told them all that she knew. She said to Officer Waddell, "I know who's behind this, honey, and I want you to go straight across the street and arrest his sorry ass."

Waddell said, "I understand how you feel, Miss Moochie, but we can't just go arresting people without proof, especially important people like Mr. Lumkin. We'd have to have a lot more evidence. We need to find out why the wall was busted in, and the attic steps down."

Moochie said, "He was obviously looking for something, honey. And, I'd like to know what."

*****

At two o'clock Lawyer Phelps walked up to Pretty Boy's cage and was met by silence. His client lay in one corner, his head against the bars. Phelps snatched the restaurant door open, looking for someone to ask about Pretty Boy. April was standing at the end of the bar, talking to ex-mobster, Tony Colosimo. She looked up and smiled as Steve approached.

"Where's Moochie? What happened to Mr. Boy?" he asked.

"Moochie's in the kitchen. Have a seat and I'll tell you what happened," she said while turning to get his slice of apple pie.

Colosimo turned away and began reading the *New York Times*. He didn't trust these lawyers, any lawyer.

April set the pie and a cup of coffee in front of Steve. She touched his hand lightly and said, "There was a break-in last night. Someone busted a hole in the back wall, broke the television set and tried to kill Pretty Boy. He was in shock for awhile and is still scared; won't say much, which is unusual for him."

"I'll say! I've never seen him like that." Steve wanted to ask April out, but couldn't with Colosimo listening in.

The swinging doors to the kitchen burst open and Moochie entered with a tray full of coffee cups. She set them down and waved at Colosimo. "Hey, Tony. How's my big city boy? I'll be down to talk in a minute."

She turned to Phelps. "Well, now, how's the legal business?"

"Fine. April just told me what happened to my client and I don't like it one little bit. I wonder if they were trying to shut him up to keep him from testifying in court. If I ever find out who did it, I'll bring a suit big enough to make us all rich."

"I don't know why they would attack our bird, except he's got a big mouth. Maybe they were just taking out their frustration over not being able to find what they were looking for; whatever that could be."

"Hmmmm. You don't keep any cash here, do you?" said Steve.

"Nope. Always drop it off at the bank. Bud says they might have been looking for the recipe for his ribs."

"Pshaw, that ain't likely," said April.

"I don't know what they were looking for, but they'd better leave Mr. Boy alone. How about a deadbolt lock?" said Steve.

"Bud's already called a locksmith to have one put on today. Hopefully, the policemen will keep an eye on the place, too."

"By the way, Miss Moochie, Judge Crocker denied a temporary restraining order. So, Mr. Boy will have to stay outside for now."

"Well, Lord-a-mercy, honey. These judges ought to learn a little common sense. It ain't right having Birdbrain sit out in the weather like that."

Colosimo looked up from the paper long enough to say "Amen." Then, walked over and put coins in the jukebox.

Lawyer Phelps finished his pie while listening to Johnny Cash singing "Folsom Prison Blues."

*****

Moochie met Grady at the radio station at seven-thirty to prepare the *Lay it on Grady Show* which would air at eight. Grady had his usual shot glass in hand to calm his nerves, and Moochie had a cup of coffee.

Grady leaned back on the couch and smiled. "Moochie, do you realize that our listeners have quadrupled since you joined the program?"

"Lord help me God! There are more crazy people out there than I thought. Who would think that many people would tune in and listen to two nuts like us?"

Grady laughed and ran his hand through his thick, wavy brown hair. "I don't know, babe, but I can tell you right now that we're making a connection at some level with these people. That tells me that the need for advice, sympathy, understanding or love is far greater than I thought. The other thing that has happened, in my opinion, is that we have established trust among these people. They believe in us; maybe because we're on their same level and understand what they're going through. That's a sobering thought, Moochie. It's almost like they depend on us for help. In fact, we may be the only ones they can depend on. I take that very seriously, and I know you do too."

Moochie stared at Grady's larger right eye to see his genuine concern. "I sure do, honey. Sometimes I can feel their pain, and I'll do everything I can to help them. I just hope I don't give someone bad advice."

"We've just got to do the best we can. That's all we can do." Grady set his empty shot glass on the table and turned back to Moochie.

"There's one other thing I wanted to talk to you about." He paused. "I think we should syndicate our program and go nationwide. What do you think?"

"Why Lord-a-mercy, sakes alive, Heaven help our mortal souls! You're talking about the whole United States of America. Why, Grady Lakes, you ought to go get one of them cat scans on your brain. We can't do something like that."

"Yes we can. It would be quite simple, really. It would be the same program. I can handle all the technical stuff. It would just be that we would receive calls from all over the country; wherever the stations are that buy our show."

Moochie studied Grady's face and decided that he was serious. "Grady, if you think there are that many people who need us, and you can handle the paper work, far be it from ole Moochie to turn her back and walk away. Let's do it."

Grady flipped the switch at eight o'clock and the show began, "This is the *Lay it on Grady Show* coming to you from WGRB in Athens, Georgia, 97.2 on your radio dial."

After Grady's introduction the first call came in from a peach farmer in Oconee County, who identified himself as Robby Gober.

"Hello, Robby, this is Grady. Whatever your question is, lay it on us."

"Well, sir, I'm a little hacked off at them food policemen for putting Pretty Boy outside, and wanted to ask Moochie what I might do to help."

Moochie pulled her mike closer. "Thank you for asking, Robby, and thank you for your concern. One of the things you could do is contact every politician that you know and tell them they need to pass laws to protect the rights of all animals, especially parrots. You might mention to them that there are thousands, maybe millions of parrot lovers out there who would most likely vote for them if they did that."

"Okay, Miss Moochie, I'll do just that. I'm also gonna bring you and Pretty Boy a bushel of the best Georgia grown peaches that you've ever tasted."

The next call was a young mother.

"Hello, you're on the air. Do you have a question for me or Moochie?"

"Hello. My name is Lorella. I have a question for both of you. My son is in the sixth grade and he's being bullied by one of his classmates. The boy calls him all kinds of names, and sometimes he'll just come up behind my son and punch him in the back. What should I do?"

"First," said Grady, "have your son talk to his teacher about it. If he won't do it, or it doesn't help, you'll have to call the teacher. If that doesn't help, call the principal and ask him to speak to the bully and his parents. That will usually solve the problem. Moochie do you have anything to add?"

"Yes, If none of what Grady told you helps, have a talk with your son. Tell him he's going to have to stand up for himself. Have him walk up to the bully without warning and punch him in the nose as hard as he can. He'll be suspended for a while, but you'll stand behind him. That'll be better than being afraid all the time. I don't like violence, but sometimes that's all you can do. Good luck, honey."

Grady cringed, but answered the next call. "Hello. Yes this is Grady. What can you lay on me tonight?"

A man's voice said, "Grady, this here's Tommy over in Banks County. I need some advice about this woman I married. She don't work and we don't have no children. I go off to work ever' day, and I work hard, too. When I get home, the dishes are piled up in the sink, the bed's not made and the house is a mess. I ask her why she didn't clean up and she says she didn't have time. Says she 'as too busy keeping up with her programs on T.V. I go to the fridge and notice that the six pack of Budweiser I brought home last night is gone. What do I do?"

Grady glanced at Moochie and pointed at the microphone. She smiled and leaned closer.

"Tommy , sounds like you went to the wedding and came home empty handed. I'll tell you what I'd do. First, if you have to have a beer, drink it before you get home. But, don't bring any extras. Tomorrow morning, tell your wife that when you get home, you expect the bed to be made, the dishes washed and the house clean. If that's not done, you will personally pack her bags and escort her back to her mama's house for further training. Be fair, live up to your part of the wedding vows, but be a man."

There were many other calls, some with problems, some just thanking Grady and Moochie for their advice and how well it worked. Grady signed off and finally, "Send your cards and letters to the *Lay it on Grady Show*, WGRB, 1241 Prince Avenue, Athens, Georgia, 30605. You may also contact us at layitongrady@bellsouth.net."

CHAPTER FIFTEEN

The popularity of the *Lay it on Grady Show* continued to grow in Georgia. Moochie and Grady Lakes developed a partnership. Moochie with her lively manner provided the personality and the punch, while Grady, the professional, had the technical knowledge. He planned the programs and acted as business manager. After the broadcast company he worked for aired them on every station they owned, Grady pursued his idea to syndicate. Before long, and much to their surprise, contracts for the show were picked up nationally.

One evening a girl called the show from Lawrenceburg, Tennessee. She spoke so softly that Grady could barely hear her. "Hello, young lady, this is Grady Lakes and I want you to lay it on us, but first, I want you to speak up so everyone will be able to hear you. Okay?"

"Yes, sir."

"Is your question for Miss Moochie or me?"

"Miss Moochie."

"Good. Now, please give us your name and state your question. Miss Moochie will be happy to answer."

"I sure will, sweetie. Just go ahead and spit it out," said Moochie.

"My name is Gracie and what I want to know---I mean, what I would like to ask, is why does everyone hate me? I don't understand. I try to be nice to everyone, but no one will talk to me in school. If I walk up to a group of girls, they just giggle and drift away. None of the boys have ever spoken to me except to call me names like fatty, lump-head, gross face, pimple face and ugly. I feel so bad and I know I'm fat and ugly and have skin problems, but these things hurt me so deep inside that I don't know how I'll ever make it in school. I'm in the tenth grade now and have been begging my mother to let me drop out."

Moochie grabbed Grady's hand, trying to get a grip on her emotions before she spoke. "Please don't drop out, sweetie, and don't believe for a minute what they say about you. We can't see you from this studio, but I can tell you right now from listening to you talk, that you are one of the most beautiful people I've ever met. Ain't that right, Grady? Can't you hear it in her voice?"

"I sure can, Moochie. Why, if I was a few years younger, I'd ask her to go to the prom with me," said Grady, trying to help, but not knowing what to say.

"Listen to me, Gracie. I know this will be hard to under-stand right now, but they can only hurt you if you let them. Believe in yourself. Know that you are a beautiful person in your own mind and that's what you will become. I know, sweetie. Ole Moochie has been there and I've never let their words hold me back. I let it roll off my back and keep on believing in myself and moving ahead. See?"

"Yes, ma'am. I'll try."

"No, sweetie, don't try. Do it! Okay?"

"Okay. I will. Miss Moochie, may I send you a poem I wrote?"

"Of course you can. I'd be glad to read it. Make sure you have your return address on it so I can get in touch with you. Bye, bye, sweetie. Now, remember what ole Moochie told you."

After the show went national, Moochie was getting ten calls a day for guest appearances at social and civic functions as far away as Greenville, South Carolina. Everywhere she went, folks asked for her autograph. She said to Bud, "Lord-a-mercy, sakes alive, I can't be running all over the country and keep our restaurant going. They must think I'm Wonder Woman or something."

*****

Sam, Rube Winters' fourteen-year-old son, was secretly writing down what he called "Moochieisms." One day he decided to show the list to Bud. Such things as: "It ain't healthy being skinny, honey; If you're still skinny after having one of my desserts, you better see your doctor about lipo-injections; His pilot light's done gone out; Calories, what's that?; You're skinny as a rail, honey; Eat your dessert before I slap your jaws; Food is one of the greatest pleasures in life; Eat up and enjoy while you're still healthy enough; Hug someone and heal the world; and, Get rid of his sorry ass." There were about five pages of sayings young Sam had collected over the years while he was being raised by Moochie. Bud posted all of them on the bulletin board in the kitchen. Then, being into mass communications, he decided that other people ought to see them. He built a magnetic, drop down sign below Moochie's Place out front with a smiley face on the side. Every week he had April or Peola put up a new saying. The editor of the *Athens Banner-Herald*, who often ate lunch at Moochie's, liked the sayings so much that he asked if he could put one in the paper once a week except the one about "his sorry ass."

One afternoon, Slapper sneaked into the restaurant and, all serious like, beckoned Moochie over. His eyes darted around the room as he motioned for her to lean forward.

Moochie who loved all manner of intrigue, whispered, "Let me guess. The CIA wants me to go to Pakistan, sit on Osama Bin Laden and squeeze the life out of him."

Slapper couldn't hold his serious look any longer. A smile the size of the Florida Keys broke out on his face and he leaned forward and pounded the counter with his hand. Finally, he said, "Moochie, you crack me up. No, I wanted to ask if I could use your office booth for a half-hour to have a serious business talk with Bud and Sam."

Moochie patted his hand. "Sure, honey, just don't try to recruit them into the CIA. By the way, how are the T-shirt sales going?"

"Like Bud's baby back ribs, Moochie. I'm serious. I've had to hire two students to keep track of all the orders over the internet. Bill has hired three more people at his shop. Don't worry, I'm keeping track of every dollar I owe you. Your radio show has made a big difference. Guess what else?"

Moochie grinned and as was her habit when talking to Slapper, covered her mouth with her hand, playing along with his bent for secrecy, "Don't tell me you're gonna start making T-shirts for animals like dogs, parrots, and so forth."

Slapper said, "Hey, I hadn't thought of that, not a bad idea though. No, Carly, my wife, wants to come back to me; said she still loves me. I love her, Moochie, but it makes me wonder if she's just coming back because of my financial success with the T-shirts."

"I don't know what to tell you about that, Slapper. You'll have to use your own judgment. Maybe when the next bump in the road comes along, you'll be able to tell. What do you want to talk to Sam and Bud about?"

"I want to ask them if they will allow me to print up a little book with your sayings in it. I know they are your sayings, but thought it might boost Sam's ego a little and it was Bud's idea to put up the sign. Is that all right with you?"

"Sure, honey. It'll be good for my two boys to decide. That's fine with me."

"Great. Send them on out and I'll make my business proposition to them."

"Okay. Hang on just a minute, honey. I'll round them up for you."

When they came out of the kitchen, Sam had a root beer in his hand, and Bud grabbed a cup of coffee as he went by.

Slapper had already carried his coffee to the office and was sitting there spying on the other customers.

When they sat down, Slapper leaned forward, "Sam, Bud, I've got a business deal for you. I want to publish Sam's 'Moochieisms.' I could put them in a nicely designed little booklet, and sell them alongside the T-shirts. What do you think? Sam, of course, would be given credit as the editor, and I would give him half of any profit we make. Sure, Moochie would have to approve, and, Sam, you would have to get permission from your dad."

Sam was wide-eyed. "Me, an editor? Wow! What's an editor?"

"That means you compiled the information."

"That's cool. Let's do it, Uncle Bud."

Bud grabbed his coffee cup with both hands, took a long sip, his eyes on Slapper all the time. He leaned back, took his chaw out of one side of his mouth and wrapped it in a paper napkin. He reached in his pocket for his Redman, pinched off a new chunk and tucked it into the other jaw.

He turned and looked at Sam. "Sam-son, we don't want to rush into anything. This is an important decision, Mr. Slapper. Give us a day or so to think about it."

"But, Uncle Bud ---."

As soon as Bud went back to the kitchen, Sam went to Moochie with the news. Moochie grabbed Sam and kissed him on the forehead. "That's wonderful, Sam. Maybe some day you'll be famous. Now, don't you worry about your Uncle Bud; he's no dummy. He just likes to ponder things. Make sure you ask your dad."

*****

Politicians are attracted to publicity like a compass to the North Pole. Local, state and national campaigns were being waged, and all nooks, crannies and alleys were explored to gain an edge against opponents. Also, politics is not just for politicians. Other leaders have agendas to push like companies, unions, and even colleges.

Ms. Emma Kilpatrick, Mayor of Athens-Clarke County, stopped by to meet Moochie and Bud in July. It was mid-morning and Moochie was resting on her stool behind the counter. April was at the other end of the counter serving a cup of coffee to former member of the Mafia, Tony Colosimo. Tony had just told a joke, coaxing a laugh and snort from April.

Peola finished clearing the tables and was carrying the dirty dishes into the kitchen for Pinkie or Brad to wash. She joined in with Bud, Brad and Pinkie who were singing along with the juke box, "I've got friends in low places---."

The mayor approached the counter with a smile, holding out her hand. "Hello, Miss Moochie. I know it's you because I've seen your picture on so many T-shirts. You've become one of our most famous citizens, and I wanted to meet you. I hope you don't mind."

Moochie stood up and shook hands. "No, Mayor Kilpatrick, I don't mind at all. It's my pleasure and an honor to have you here."

"Please call me Emma; I'm not into titles. I'm sorry to bother you. Just wanted to say hello; chat for a few minutes and see if there's anything I can do for you. I listen to your radio program and thought you might have some advice about how our local government should be run."

As Moochie came around the counter, the mayor said, "I'm a little embarrassed to ask, but might I get one of your famous hugs. If you've read the paper, you know I'm under a lot of stress from the Chamber of Commerce dispute, the smoking ban, et cetera."

"Why, of course, Emma, I'd be glad to hug you. I hug Democrats, Republicans, Independents, Protestants, Jews, Catholics. In fact I hug all of God's children. Have you read the instructions on how to survive?"

"My secretary showed me a copy before I came over," said the Mayor.

"Well don't worry, honey. I know just how much to squeeze and when to stop. I like to think of it as a healing hug. Take your glasses off first."

The Mayor was thin, and almost disappeared when Moochie engulfed her. Being tall, she was able to hold her head up for air, and touch the floor with her toes. When Moochie let go, she swooned and grabbed onto Moochie's arm for support. "Wow!" said Emma. "That was awesome. I've never been hugged like that, even by a fellow democrat."

"What do you drink, Emma?"

"Well, I like orange juice."

"Hey, Peola, darlin', please bring the Mayor a big glass of orange juice, a piece of apple pie with a double scoop of ice cream on it. I'll have coffee and a praline sundae."

"But, I ---," said Emma as Moochie led her to the office.

"Sit down there, honey, and relax. You'll be safe here. This is neutral ground like one of them European countries."

"Switzerland?"

"Yeah. That's it. Switzerland."

Peola set juice and coffee on the table. Emma grabbed the glass and took a sip.

"Drink up, girl. You're skinny as a bean pole. The first thing we got to do is put some meat on your bones."

Emma took a full swallow and smiled, "I've heard that you're straightforward, Moochie. I love it. I haven't been talked to that way since my grandmother died."

Moochie added three creams and three spoons of sugar to her coffee. "That's what ole Moochie is here for, Emma, to tell it like it is. What you need to do is take each issue, face it squarely, and decide what is best for the people of Athens-Clarke County. Decide that honestly. Make your decision, then move on to the next issue. It's your job to serve the people of this county in the best possible way, and that includes all of the people who work for you. Make it clear that it's their job also to serve the people. Those employees need to just go out and do it with no excuses. If they don't do that, sincerely, fire their sorry ass. Now, eat your pie. Apples are one of the healthiest things you can eat."

A newspaper reporter three booths down overheard the exchange between Moochie and Emma. The next day, there was a second page article about the encounter in the local paper. The title was "Moochie Flattens and Fattens Mayor."

Around one o'clock, while Moochie was in the kitchen talking to Bud, William Harriston, President of the University, came in for a late lunch. With him was a curvaceous, dark haired woman. She looked as though she had been poured into her green, tight knit dress, which ended just above the knee. Her perfectly manicured nails with French tips tapped on the table while she picked at her salad and watched Harriston wolf down his Moochieburger and fries. After they finished eating, President Harriston called Peola over. "Please ask Mrs. Dunlop if she is available to speak to us for a moment."

Peola went to the kitchen where Moochie was standing and screeched in her ear, "Miss Moochie, it's the president of the university! He wants to talk to you."

"All right, honey. Show them to my office and bring them a round of praline sundaes. I'll just have a cup of coffee and three pralines; I don't want to overdo it."

Peola pranced back over to them, and shrilled, "Miss Moochie will see you in her office. Please follow me."

The President couldn't believe he was being asked to move. Oh well, he thought, sometimes these yokels have strange ways. He followed Peola, and the woman in green wiggled along behind him.

After they were seated, Moochie waddled over and squeezed in. "Hello. Welcome to Moochie's. We're glad to have you here."

President Harriston half rose, "Mrs. Dunlop, I'm William Harriston and this is Debbie Schettenhelm, my assistant."

Moochie reached across and shook hands with the President then nodded and extended her hand to Miss Shettenhelm. "It's nice to meet you both. Please call me Moochie. We're not too formal around here. I'll call you Bill." Peola set the two sundaes in front of them. The sundaes consisted of two scoops of vanilla ice cream with pralines inserted on each side. The whole thing was covered with chocolate and a mound of whipped cream. A bright red Maraschino cherry sat proudly on top.

"Why, I ---. We didn't ---. "

"Never mind, Bill. They're on the house and besides, cherries are good for you. You can use the nourishment, and your secretary is skinny as a telephone pole except in certain places. Just remember, I don't have no money to donate to the university, not yet anyway."

"Why ---. No---. I didn't come here for that. I just wanted to get your take on what's going on at our fine university. You know, get a feel for what the townspeople are thinking," said President Harriston.

Moochie took half a praline in one bite, "Well, honey, you're in the right place. I'm about as down to earth as they come. My opinion is that you ought to lighten up. Relax. Everyone says they hired you to be a fundraiser. Well, that was their mistake. They should have hired you to be President of this university, just like your title says. If you're a good president, the money raising will take care of itself. Find out what the students need to be the best they can in their field. Then, find out what the faculty needs to do the best job they can. Get to know the faculty and students. Bring them into your plans. You all need to be a team working together to make this the best school it can be. That's what I think, honey. Now, ain't that the best sundae you've ever had?"

Debbie and Bill were about to finish their sundaes and looked tempted to lick the dish. Bill, a little embarrassed at how quickly the sundae had disappeared, said, "Well," cough, "that was delicious, Moochie; I've never tasted better. I appreciate your views on the university and I will definitely take what you said under consideration."

"Okay, honey. Now, you all stand up here. You're not leaving without a Moochie hug."

Bill and Debbie staggered out, holding each other up, wishing they had been more prepared for what they encountered. But strangely enough they left with a feeling of serenity, calmness and yet energized. The President couldn't decide if it was the hug or praline sundae.

After that, there was a steady trickle of political candidates and leaders, seeking Moochie's advice, or, at least to have their picture taken with her.

CHAPTER SIXTEEN

On Friday, Moochie picked up Sam at Hilman Middle School. She could see that he was grinning all over his face before he jumped into the front seat.

"Lord-a-mercy, Sam, I know this is Friday, but I'd say by that grin that you just won the lottery."

Sam reached across and gave her a kiss on the cheek. "No, ma'am, but I've got a surprise for you and Uncle Bud."

"Well, for Heaven's sake, what is it?"

"Can't tell yet. You'll have to wait 'til we get to the restaurant so Uncle Bud can see it too."

*****

Sam dragged Moochie into the kitchen where Bud was up to his elbows making barbeque sauce. He turned around, reached up and scratched his ear leaving a dab of sauce dangling like ketchup off a French fry. He moved in front of the sink to wash his hands. Moochie handed him a paper towel.

"All right, Mama Moochie, Uncle Bud, I've got a surprise for you. Close your eyes and don't open 'til I tell you."

He reached into his book bag and removed his note book. Finding the sheet of paper he wanted, "Okay, open up," he said.

"Since I'm a published editor with 'Moochie's Sayings', and you know how I've always wanted to be a writer, well, here's my first song. My teacher, Mrs. Adler, is a big country music fan and she helped me a lot while I was writing it. I know you both like all kinds of music, and your favorite is

101

country. So, that's what I wrote. It's for both of you because I love you."

Bud grabbed the song and began looking it over while Moochie gave the boy a hug.

Bud turned his head to hide his misty eyes. "Here, Moochie, why don't you read it to us?" By this time Brad, Pinkie, Peola and April had gathered around.

Moochie read:

Dixie Guitar Band
by
Sam Winters

When I die, don't bury me in the sand
Just lean me against the jukebox
Put a quarter in my hand
And play me some country music
By a Dixie Guitar Band.

I've been in ever' bar in Georgia
And some in Tennessee
Glad to spend my paycheck
On any redneck girl I see
But I always save a quarter in my shoe
Cause I know I'll end up sittin'
By the jukebox missin' you. So---.

When I die, don't bury me in the sand
Just lean me against the jukebox
Put a quarter in my hand
And play me some country music
By a Dixie Guitar Band.

I done you wrong and I'm sorry as can be
Cause you're married to another
Who's where I'd like to be

Now I can't shake these barroom blues
And here I sit by the jukebox
Cryin' over you. So---.

When I die, don't bury me in the sand
Just lean me against the jukebox
Put a quarter in my hand
And play me some country music
By a Dixie Guitar Band.

That's why I'll defend my music
Just like I would this land
So come on all you rock and roll bands
And we'll see just where you stand
When you walk into this bar
And hear a Dixie Guitar Band.

I'll be standin' here with my quarter
And a beer in the other hand
Waitin' to shove a quarter in
And hear a Dixie Guitar Band.

When I die, don't bury me in the sand
Just lean me against the jukebox
Put a quarter in my hand
And play me some country music
By a Dixie Guitar Band.

Just play me some country music
By a Dixie Guitar Band.

When she finished all six stood there teary-eyed and
smiling at the same time, mostly because they could see how
proud Sam was of his song. Noticing the smell of burning
sauce, Bud turned the burner off.

Sam said, "I don't know how to write music yet. I'm gonna ask Dad if he knows anyone who could write the music part, or maybe Mr. Slapper would know someone."

Bud used his plaid handkerchief to wipe a tear, then put his arm around Sam. He coughed to let everyone know he was about to speak. "Well, Sam-son, that's the most beautiful thing I've ever heard. Now, I'm not saying I know much about music, understand, but it's got all the ingredients of a great country song, like death, Dixie, beer, women, love lost, and 'specially a jukebox. Why, if Johnny Cash was standing here right now, he'd grab it and start singing, pretty as you please." Sam stood there smiling while the others slapped him on the back or tousled his hair. They could hear the strains of "Baby's Got Her Bluejeans On," vibrating through the swinging doors.

Moochie said, "Sugar, I wondered why you were spending all that time writing down the words of songs you heard on the jukebox. Why, I thought you were just wasting time. Now, I know different. Do you mind if I send this off to a friend in the radio business in Nashville? It's a shot in the dark, but who knows, we could get lucky."

Sam grabbed her by the arm, "Mama Moochie, do you think there's a chance?"

"Now, baby, don't get your hopes up. But, there's always a chance, even if it's slim."

*****

At four o'clock a lady called and asked for Bud.

Moochie yelled, "Hey, sweetie, there's a woman on the phone for you. Grab the line in the kitchen."

Bud quickly washed his hands and picked up the phone. "Bud here, maker of the best ribs in town."

In what sounded like a pain or drug-induced whisper a voice said, "Is this William Arrington?"

"Yes, ma'am. What can I do for you?"

"This is Clara Harper, Florence Harper's mother. I know you'll remember Florence, she is the crazy one in our family. Your wife mentioned your name on her radio program the other night and I knew what I had to do."

"No, Mrs. Harper, I can't rightly say that I know your daughter. Is she from around here?"

There was a long silence. Then, a cough. "She was from Mississippi, but I don't know where she is now. I ain't seen her for years, thirteen years to be exact. She just dropped the baby off here, said she'd be back in a couple of hours. That's the last I saw or heard of her. Young people just don't have no respect for their parents anymore. It's a downright shame."

"Yes, ma'am. That's right, but I don't see what that has to do with me."

"Why, you're the father. At least that's what Florence told me."

"Wait a minute---father? I don't know what you mean. I've never been a father. There must be some mistake. I --- " Bud was shaking. Pinkie rushed over and stood by his side to make sure he didn't fall.

"You used to live in Meridian, Mississippi didn't you?"

"Yes, ma'am, but,---."

"And, you frequented the Hanky Pank Bar?"

"Yes, if it's a bar in Meridian, I've been there. See, I had a drinking problem in those days, so I went to all the bars. Now, I'm shed of that monkey. Thank God."

"My daughter worked at the Hanky Pank," and she told me you and her had an affair, said you was the one who fathered her baby. After the baby was born and released from the hospital, she dropped her off here. That's the last time I seen her."

"But, why didn't someone let me know? I would have taken care of the child."

"Two reasons, Mr. Arrington. I'd heard the type of person you were at that time. Second, I fell in love with that precious little girl. I've taken care of her ever since. Now, things are different. Ginger is having trouble in school; hanging out with the wrong crowd. I'm not able to take care of her anymore." There was a long pause. A coughing fit.

"The doctor tells me I have lung cancer. I won't be here much longer. Please come and get Ginger as soon as possible. I couldn't bear to see her go into an orphanage. My address is 151 Elkington Road, Meridian, Mississippi. Please hurry."

Bud stood as though rooted to the floor, phone at his ear, even after the line was dead. Brad brought a chair and Pinkie helped Bud sit down. She removed the phone from his hand and hung it on the wall. Pinkie stood beside him and patted his back while Brad rushed around trying to get things ready for the dinner crowd.

*****

They worked all afternoon without a word about what happened. That evening when they climbed into bed, Moochie took his hand. "Sweet thing, you're going to have to tell ole Moochie what you found out on the phone so I can help you. Whatever it is, we can work it out. Remember, I love you, and I'm here to take care of you."

Bud squeezed her hand and began, "I've never told you about my life in Mississippi. I was born in Peck, a crossroads outside of Meridian. When I began attending the county middle school, I was kidded unmercifully about my ragged clothes and where I was from. You know how they call people from New York a New Yorker? Well, you can guess what they called me.

"It was not pretty and I've always been ashamed of my life. I guess that's one reason I turned to alcohol. My mother was a prostitute. I only saw my father one time, if it was who my lying mother said he was. He wouldn't even look at me, much less take an interest. I was a nuisance to my mother; always in the way. So, I found places to hide, make myself scarce both physically and emotionally. When I discovered

106

alcohol, it was a blessing; it helped me forget about the loneliness.

"After that, much of my life was a blur. I worked just enough to keep a roof over my head and buy my drinks. I had only one friend, Roger, and many acquaintances. Roger was the type who could drink a lot and still stay under control; what might be called a functioning alcoholic. We went to many bars and picked up whatever women were available. It didn't matter to us in those days. One day, Roger asked me to go back to Monroe, Georgia with him, his home town. Not having any ties, I agreed."

"I understand, and I'm sorry about all that, my little man. Now, what about the phone call?"

Bud, told her the details of the call from Clara Harper. Then, "I've been thinking about it all day, love, and I've decided that if Ginger is really my daughter, then I have to find a way to take care of her. I hate to drag you into this, but I don't know what else to do."

Moochie put her arm around his shoulders, pulled him in and squished his face against her bosom. "Now, don't you worry, sweetie. This is all going to work out. First thing in the morning, we'll call Lawyer Phelps and get his take on it. Then, we'll get you on a plane to Meridian so you can decide if she's your daughter. If you think she is, then make arrangements to bring her back here. We'll take care of her. Just call our lawyer if there are any legal questions. Also, make sure Mrs. Harper is taken care of."

"That's what I'd like to do, love, but how can we afford it?"

"Hell, we can't worry about money when family's involved. We've got to take care of our own. Let Athens First Bank worry about covering the bills. Them fees we pay has got to go for something."

"Moochie, you're a wonder. You know that? I don't know what I'd do without you. Just think. I might be a daddy." He fell asleep in Moochie's arms. She gently laid him over on his pillow.

*****

The next afternoon Bud was on the economy flight to Meridian. He thought of his life there and wondered if he would remember how to find his way around. His mother had died a year before he left for Georgia. Bud, was too drunk to attend the funeral. He wondered about his father, but had no desire to find out what had happened to him.

He rented a Ford Mustang and drove around the town, recognizing a street name here and there. He stopped at a convenience store and asked where he might find Elkington Road. He found it with little trouble and followed the numbers to 151. He continued past the house and drove around, trying to decide what he would say to Mrs. Harper, much less the little girl.

Finally, he turned into the driveway of the run-down little house. There was no other car there, the yard was uncut and paint was peeling from the once white wood siding. All the windows were open and one green shutter hung awkwardly. Bud knocked on the door and waited. There was no sound. He knocked again. The faceless door opened a crack. "We're not buying anything. What do you want?" said a young, sullen voice.

"I'm Bud Arrington. I talked to your grandmother and she asked me to come."

The door opened wider and his curious gaze fell on a girl of thirteen or fourteen in cut-off jeans and a dirty T-shirt. Her straw blond hair straggled down each side of her tear streaked face. Her frightened blue eyes reminded Bud of a fawn caught in the headlights of a speeding car. He wanted to rush in, grab her in his arms and just hold her, comfort her, but knew better.

"I'm sorry. I don't mean to frighten you. I'm just here to help you and your grandmother. May I come in?"

"I guess so," she said hesitantly as she backed away from the door. When Bud entered, the girl retreated to the bedroom.

From the living room, he could see dirty dishes in the sink, and smell the mustiness of an unkempt house.

As he turned into the tiny hall, he saw a grouping of family pictures. One was of a woman who looked vaguely familiar to him. Was that Florence, Ginger's mother?

When he entered the bedroom, he was overwhelmed with the smell, feel and sound of death. Clara's hair was matted down, her eyes sunk into her head and every breath introduced a desperate struggle for the next. Bud had never seen death before. Alarmed, he rushed to her side and bent over. "Ginger, we've got to get your grandmother to a hospital."

Clara touched his hand. "There's no need for that. There's nothing they can do. Besides, we have no money, no car and they took the telephone out this morning."

"But, I can get you there. I'll pay for everything."

"Never mind," she whispered. "Just listen. Thank God you're here. My sweet little girl needs your help. I've been afraid to go and leave her. The rent has not been paid for months, but the landlord let's us stay on. There is no food in the house. The heat has been stifling this summer without a fan. But, my sweetheart has taken care of me. Refused to leave my side. She's a good girl." Clara coughed into a bloodstained handkerchief and struggled to catch her breath.

"Don't you worry about Ginger, Mrs. Harper," said Bud through misty eyes. "I promise you I'll take care of her from now on."

"Thank you God," said Clara as she put both hands to her mouth. "I've told her everything, Mr. Arrington. How you and Florence loved each other very much and had a wonderful life together. How you were torn apart by different careers, but still loved each other. How you both loved her, but decided it was best if she stayed with me."

"I see---. Yes, of course---we loved her very much."

"I also called Children Services yesterday and gave them all the information. I told them I want you to adopt Ginger, if that's even necessary. They want you to come and talk to them." A long coughing spell ensued.

Bud patted her hand, "Don't worry, I'll take care of that. You just get some rest now."

"I'll get plenty of rest shortly. Thank you for coming. God bless you." She turned to Ginger. "He's a good man, Ginger. You can trust him. Remember, you will always be my precious girl. I love you." She looked up and smiled, then her chin dropped.

Ginger pressed against the bed then collapsed and laid across her, crying, "Grandma, don't leave me! Don't leave! I love you."

Bud, moved to a depth of sadness he had never known, could only pat Ginger on the back.

*****

During the next four days Bud made funeral arrangements, talked to Children Services, called Mr. Phelps ten times and Moochie about every hour. Moochie and the staff were worried sick over Mr. Bud. Even Pretty Boy seemed down in the dumps.

Ginger had not talked since her grandmother's death. Nor would she leave Bud's side. She was unable to eat at first, but gradually regained her appetite. Bud rented two rooms at the Holiday Inn, but she refused to stay alone.

Finally, through the efforts of Lawyer Phelps, and because no one else from the handful of people who came to the funeral wanted her, Bud was granted temporary custody. Bud and Ginger were given DNA tests for the record. Results were to be sent to lawyer Phelps.

Bud hated airplanes because the take off and landing made him queasy, and he missed his chew of tobacco. Ginger had never flown. She reached over and took Bud's hand when the wheels left the ground. He squeezed her hand and re-assured her even though he didn't feel so good himself. Just before they reached the Atlanta Airport, Ginger looked at Bud and said, "Are you my daddy?"

Surprised, Bud thought for a minute. "Yes, sweetie, I am your father no matter what the records or tests show. I will always take care of you just like I promised your grandmother. You were meant to be my daughter. I can feel it deep in my soul."

Ginger smiled for the first time and rested her head on his shoulder.

CHAPTER SEVENTEEN

As they drove to Athens, Bud told Ginger about the city and the university. Then, he gave her a quick sketch of all the people she would meet, starting with Moochie. "She's the kindest, most loving person you'll ever know."

He reached into the back seat, then handed her a Moochie T-shirt with instructions on how to survive the inevitable hug.

Moochie had kept the staff and regular customers up to date on Bud's adventure. Pinkie, April and Peola decided that a welcome home party was in order. They decorated the restaurant, and many of the customers brought gifts of clothing, shoes and jewelry they hoped would be fitting for a thirteen-year-old. Moochie baked chocolate and lemon cakes.

When Bud and Ginger walked in the front door, everyone cheered and shouted, "Welcome home Bud and Ginger!" Then, a quartet comprised of April, Peola, Brad and Pinkie sang "You Are So Beautiful---to me." Ginger and Bud were reduced to Jell-O; all they could do was hold onto each other and cry. Ginger had an instant family and Bud's pride overflowed and followed him around for days.

*****

Booker Cleveland was tall for his age, some would say gangly. His chestnut-brown skin contrasted with his dark eyes that were large and innocent no matter how hard he tried to look tough. He wore his tight, curly hair short because Grammy said so, besides it was easier to take care of. He had been visiting a friend near Cobbham and was on his way back to Peter Street where he lived with his grandmother. It was eleven-thirty at night, but it didn't matter. He was grown up now and Grammy Wheeler had just about given up on trying to keep track of him. He felt sorry for Grammy sometimes, but not sorry enough to keep from skipping school, hanging out all night, drinking beer, and stealing a few things from the merchants downtown. Hell, he was fourteen years old and able to take care of himself.

Walking east on Clayton Street, he crossed College Avenue, paying no attention to the red light since there was no traffic coming. In the middle of the block he saw what appeared to be a bum leaning against a building with one foot propped up. He had on old tennis shoes, with baggy pants and his shirt hanging out. His head was bent down, and his face was covered by a black, slouchy hat. Oh shit, Booker thought, it's one of them homeless dudes. He's gonna ask me for a handout. Shit, man, I don't have any more money than you do.

As Booker drew even, the stranger said, "Hey, kid, how would you like to make two hundred dollars?"

Booker stopped in his tracks, and eyed the man who slowly raised his head, revealing a ski mask. Booker blurted, "What the hell you talking about, man? You ain't got no two hundred G.W.'s."

"Sure do, kid," as he held up two one hundred dollar bills. "It's yours if you do something for me."

"Shit, man, I ain't killing nobody for you," Booker said, as he backed up a step.

"No. No. It's nothing like that. All you have to do is steal a bird. That's all. Just steal the bird, and I don't care what you do with him; just don't give him back."

"What bird, man? What you talking about?"

The stranger pointed to where the bird would be, and told him the best time would be mid-morning when no one is looking. "All you have to do is take the bird off the hook, and walk away. It should be a snap." While waving the two-hundred in front of Booker, the boy's eyes were drawn to the biggest diamond ring he'd ever seen and it was surrounded by green stones.

Booker grabbed the bills and stuffed them in his pocket.

Before he walked away, he heard, "I know where you and your grandmother live on Peter Street. Make sure you do the job."

*****

The next morning found Booker sitting on a bench across the street and one block away. He watched the front of Moochie's Place, waiting for the right moment. After an hour of this, his nerves were on edge. He kept thinking, I wish I had never said I would do this. What If I get caught?

Finally, he decided it was now or never; got up and walked toward Moochie's. As he approached the restaurant, he stayed as close to the front of the buildings as possible. Two doors before Moochie's he saw a man inside folding T-shirts. He quickly looked away. He paused for a moment, then pulled his Braves cap down, and walked casually toward the cage.

Pretty Boy was standing on his swing singing, "Fly me to the moon ---."

When Booker reached up to snatch the cage, Pretty Boy said, "Gawk! Here's trouble," and tried to peck Booker through the wires.

Booker bent over slightly, holding the cage below window level and crept forward. When he got past the restaurant, he straightened up and began walking as fast as he could. By the time he reached the end of the block, he was running. Pretty Boy hunkered down in one corner of the cage. Booker went by the Civic Center, crossed over Foundry Street and on down to the river. He stopped at a spot concealed by heavy undergrowth. Two feet away lay a large rock. He took Pretty Boy out of the cage, squeezing him tightly to keep from getting pecked or scratched by Pretty Boy's sharp claws, and reached for the rock. He held Pretty Boy on the ground and raised the rock above his head. Pretty Boy said, "Gawk! Go ahead, punk. Make my day." Booker couldn't help but laugh. He threw the rock as far as he could into the river. He shoved Pretty Boy back into the cage. "I'll take care of you later, you little smart ass."

"Gawk! Smart ass," said Pretty Boy.

A few minutes later, Tony Colosimo was leaving the restaurant. When he stepped out the door, something was missing. Where's Pretty Boy, he thought. He stuck his head back in the door, "Hey, what did you guys do with Pretty Boy?"

Moochie looked up. "What do you mean? He's right there."

"No he's not. He's gone."

Moochie rushed to the front door and looked around. "What the---?" She saw Slapper getting his table ready for the lunch crowd. "Hey, Slapper, have you seen Pretty Boy?"

"No, ma'am. I just came outside."

"Lord-a-mercy, somebody's done kidnapped Pretty Boy. This'll kill Bud. Call the police. Call the police!"

Tony took out his phone, made the call, and quickly disappeared.

*****

A lone policeman arrived a few minutes later to find Moochie's restaurant emptied onto the sidewalk.

April was crying and snorting occasionally when she took in a breath. Bud was frantic, standing there wringing his hands, worried sick over his missing friend. He was telling Brad how excited Pretty Boy was last night because his favorite Clint Eastwood movie was on. "We always leave the television on for him at night so he won't get lonely. He loves old movies, and the *David Letterman Show*."

Brad said, "Hang in there, Bud. We'll find him. I'm gonna go walk around, see if I see any sign of him."

Pinkie had her arm around her daughter, Peola, trying to comfort her. Peola, whose voice rose in pitch when she got excited, was hanging onto her mother. When she opened her mouth, only a squeak came out.

Moochie was busy hugging everyone in sight, even the policeman found himself engulfed by her embrace, all the time worried about his official dignity. Unfortunately, for him at least, there was already a reporter on site.

The policeman backed off and took his pad out, "Now, Miss Moochie, if you don't mind, I need to write my report on this alleged crime."

"Alleged, hell," said Moochie, "Our boy's been kidnapped."

Moochie explained everything she knew, then said, "Now, Officer Waddell, we expect you all to do everything you can to find Pretty Boy. Call in the FBI, and the CIA, and even the National Guard, if you have to. That bird may have a big mouth, but we still love him."

Bud, Moochie and the rest of the crew carried on bravely, but it was not the same without Pretty Boy. Brad organized a group of college students who spent the afternoon and into the evening looking for their friend. Ginger, Sam and a couple of his friends joined the searchers in the afternoon. A steady stream of calls came into the restaurant asking about him. The kidnapping was reported on the radio and television news. The next day, the headline read, "Pretty Boy Birdnapped." One subtitle read, "Volunteers Work Through the Night to Find Parrot." There was a picture of Moochie hugging Officer Waddell. There wasn't much left of the officer to see. The only real evidence was his cap lying on the ground next to him.

At ten o'clock that morning, Booker Cleveland came walking into Police Headquarters. His head was down, and he was carrying Pretty Boy in his cage.

Officer Waddell was called. The first thing he said was, "Call Moochie's Place. Tell them we have Pretty Boy, and he's okay."

Booker was hustled into a back room where he was grilled by Officer Waddell and another officer after his rights were read. They came out with a signed confession. He told them about trying to kill Pretty Boy at the river, then, again when he got to his room in Grammy's house. "Shit, man, that's the most talkative bird I've ever seen. He never shuts up. He just about drove me crazy. The second time I tried to kill his ass, he said, 'Gawk! I love you.' Shit, man, how can you kill a bird who says that to you? To tell the truth, man, I began to like him. I don't think I could have ever killed him. He's the only one besides Grandmother who ever told me he loved me. When Grammy found out I had him, she told me to turn myself in, or she would. So, here I am, man, ready to take my punishment." He thought for a minute, then reached into his pocket and pulled out the money. "Here's the two hundred G.W.'s. Shit, man, hell, I tried to give it to Grammy, but she wouldn't touch it."

"We'll keep it as evidence for now. Maybe you can give it to her later," said Waddell.

The officers got as much information about the masked stranger as they could, and that wasn't much. The only thing that might be helpful was that Booker remembered him wearing a diamond ring surrounded by small emeralds.

Booker asked Officer Waddell, "What are ya'll goin' to do to protect me and Grammy? Hell, man, shit, he said he knows where I live."

Waddell said, "You won't have to worry about that right now because you're going to be in the Youth Detention Center, at least until a judge deals with your case. We'll keep an eye on your grandmother's house. Most of the time, a threat like that is just to get you to do what they want. I hope you've learned a lesson, kid. By the way, knowing a lot of swear words doesn't make you a man. Doing the right thing like you did this morning is what does that."

Booker's eyes, still wide over going to the detention center, said, "Shit, I mean, yes officer. I ain't havin' nothin' else to do with them homeless bums."

*****

At one o'clock that afternoon, California time, Clint Eastwood walked into his Carmel home, after spending the morning playing golf with his producer. He grabbed a sandwich and beer from the kitchen and plopped in front of the large screen television in the den. CNN happened to be on, and the announcer was reporting about a kidnapped parrot in Athens, Georgia. It caught Clint's attention because several years ago, a parrot from Georgia had been considered for a part in one of his movies. Now he remembered, the parrot had pooped on someone's head at a wedding.

The announcer was saying, " --- and when the perpetrator drew back a rock to kill the bird, he said, 'Go ahead punk. Make my day.' And, now here's our reporter in Athens, Georgia, Lawrence Swazy. Are you there, Lawrence?"

"Yes, I'm here, Phil, with one of the owners of Pretty Boy, the parrot who was kidnapped. Now, Mr. Arrington, are you the owner of the bird?"

Bud threw his shoulders back, and shifted his tobacco from one jaw to the other. He tapped the microphone, moved his mouth up against it and whispered to Lawrence, "Is this damn thing on? Are we on national television?"

Lawrence grabbed the microphone, "Mr. Arrington, we are on television and we have time constraints. Could you please just answer the question?"

Bud coughed, spraying the mike with tobacco juice, "Why sure Lawrence, I guess you could say I'm one of his guardians. Sam's his other guardian."

"What is your relationship, Mr. Arrington?"

"Well, Sam's just my young friend; he was raised by my wife, Moochie."

"No, no, no. I mean your relationship with the parrot."

"Oh," said Bud. "Well, he's my friend. I feed him, and clean up after him, you might say."

"Mr. Arrington, you mentioned earlier that Pretty Boy likes to watch movies. Who's his favorite movie star?"

Bud switched his chew back to the original side.

"Well, his favorite is Clint Eastwood, but he likes Catherine Zeta Jones a lot. Can't blame him for that."

"Phil, that's it from Athens, Georgia. This is Lawrence Swazy reporting." The camera shifted to a picture of Pretty Boy, back in his cage in front of Moochie's.

"Thank you Lawrence. Another day in the life of a reporter," said Phil with a big smile on his face.

Clint was cracking up, slapping the arm of the chair. He took a big swallow of beer, and reached for the phone.

"This is Moochie's Place, honey. What can I do for you?"

"Hello, Moochie. This is Clint Eastwood. May I speak to Pretty Boy?"

Moochie felt faint. "You're kidding, right? Rube, is that you?"

"No. This is really Clint Eastwood. I just heard about the kidnapping and wanted to say hello to my fan, Pretty Boy."

Moochie held her hand over the phone, "Hey everybody, it's Clint Eastwood on the phone. I mean it---it's really him!"

She brought the phone back to her ear, "Sorry, honey, it's not everyday we get a celebrity calling here. Just a minute, I'll walk the phone out to Pretty Boy."

Moochie held the phone up to the cage, "Pretty Boy, it's Clint Eastwood."

Pretty Boy bobbed his head and straightened up. He jumped from one foot to the other, then back. "Gawk! Welcome to Moochie's."

Clint smiled. "Hello, Pretty Boy. I just wanted to thank you for being a fan. I appreciate it."

"Gawk! I love you."

"I love you too, Pretty Boy. Could you say, 'Go ahead, punk. Make my day?"

Pretty Boy jumped to a higher perch, and said, "Gawk! Go ahead, punk. Make my day."

Clint laughed, "Very good, Pretty Boy. I like your version better than mine. You just made my day."

"Gawk! Let's make love."

Moochie yanked the phone back. "Sorry about that, honey. He has a one track mind sometimes."

"No problem. Does Pretty Boy have a DVD player?"

"No, no. All he has is a T. V. set."

"Okay, here's what I want to do, if it's okay with you. I'll send Pretty Boy a DVD player and a copy of every movie I've ever made, to let him know how much I appreciate his fanship. I'm sorry about his ordeal. If you ever get to California, bring him to see me."

"Thank you Mr. Eastwood. We would love to. If you ever get to Georgia, come by Moochie's Place for a slab of Bud's ribs."

*****

Things had calmed down by three-thirty that afternoon. Moochie was sitting on her stool sorting through the mail when she noticed a return address from Lawrenceburg, TN. She was puzzled briefly, then remembered Gracie, the high school girl with no friends who had called in to the *Lay It On Grady Show*. Moochie ran her finger under the partially sealed flap and removed a single sheet of lined paper. She read:

Dear Miss Moochie,

Thank you for listening the other night. Now I wish I had never called because some kids from school heard everything and they have been teasing me ever since, calling me a fat whiner among other things. Thanks anyway. Here's the poem I told you about.

Please Help Me Stay
By
Gracie Ledbetter

Have you ever been alone
Without a friend to call your own?
At school I walk among them all
Without someone that I can call
A friend.
I reach out to them and smile the best I can
But no one seems to care.
They walk away or shun me
As if I'm not even there.
All I want is someone to be with or talk to,
A friend.
Should it matter that I'm not good looking,
A gifted student or athlete?
I'm plain and dull in many ways
But my heart still feels the pain
When I lie awake at night
And pray that I might gain
A friend.
Or at least someone who will talk to me
And not just face away.
I want to belong somewhere
Or else I can not stay.
Love,
Gracie

Moochie bent forward on the counter and covered her eyes. Her shoulders began to shudder as she remembered how she had been ridiculed because of her weight and looks. April who was making a new pot of coffee, glanced her way. She motioned to Peola and pointed at Moochie. They both hurried to Moochie's side and put their hands on her shoulders. Moochie pushed the letter away from her and motioned for them to read it. They did and fell against Mama Moochie, sobbing.

There were only three customers in the restaurant at this time and they stared at the trio, sure that there had been a disaster somewhere in the world. The English professor at the end of the counter dropped his fork and asked, "What's wrong, Miss Moochie?"

Moochie, realizing they were scaring the customers half to death raised up and tried to reassure them that everything was all right. "It's a letter from a friend of mine who's having some trouble and it just made me sad. But, don't worry, I'm gonna help her and everything will be okay." Peola and April wiped away their tears and went to see if there was anything the customers needed.

CHAPTER EIGHTEEN

The next day Steve Phelps walked in at his usual time. Instead of the *Wall Street Journal*, however, he had a briefcase in hand. As he passed by, Pretty Boy said, "Gawk! Watch your wallet." Steve smiled and patted the cage.

"I'll talk to you about my fee, later. Right now I'm just glad to see you back at home, safe and sound." He waved at Moochie behind the counter. "Miss Moochie, may I speak to you and Bud in your office?"

His eyes were drawn to April's well-rounded, enticing breasts. He briefly wondered if the nipples protruding from the knit sweater were real. When she looked at him and smiled, he glanced away and said, "Good morning Miss Southgate." He hoped she had noticed his briefcase and how lawyerly he looked.

Moochie yelled into the kitchen, "Hey, Buddy Boy, our lawyer's here. Looks like he's got a plan." She squeezed past April. "Please bring Mr. Phelps his usual, bring Bud some hot java and I'll take a moochieburger with fries and a Coke."

Bud emerged from the kitchen trailing a wake of aromatic barbeque sauce. He was drying his hands with a paper towel and swaying to "Think Twice," by Celine Dion, one of his favorites, as it played on the juke box.

Steve savored a bite of the rich, sweet apple pie with a hint of cinnamon, then pushed it aside. This was his first "real" case and he was primed.

"Bud, I don't mind telling you I was ticked when I heard about the kidnapping of my client. I can't believe that someone would do that to a defenseless animal. The first thing I did was call the Humane Society. They had already heard about the birdnapping and were as upset as I was. They also agreed with us that Pretty Boy should not be forced to be outside in the weather while confined to a cage. I think they'll testify for us in court. Actually, this whole thing might work in our favor; help us gain public sympathy."

Peola came by and topped off the coffee cups and Moochie's Coke. Bud fished in his pocket and pulled out some quarters. "Peola, sweety, go find us some music to fit the mood. From the look in our lawyer's eyes, this is total war."

"Here's what I think we should do," Steve continued. "I'm going to be representing Pretty Boy even though in reality you are his legal guardians. Our contention is that he has rights, just like a human being. So, we're going to treat him like one. I've drawn up the necessary documents for Pretty Boy to sign and file this challenge to the Food Service Rules and Regulations. Let's go ahead and get that formality out of the way. Come with me. You and the other people here can be witnesses."

Moochie said, "Steve, honey, I hate to throw cold water on your plans, and I know Pretty Boy is the smartest bird on the planet, but as far as I know, birds can't write." She grinned and took a swig of her fountain Coke.

"Yeah," said Bud.

Steve smiled. "Have no fear, my friends. I've already thought of that. It's legal for people to sign with their mark, an X. Why can't a bird sign with his mark, a peck?"

Bud threw his shoulders back and shifted his chew to the other side of his jaw, "Hummm. I never thought of that. You lawyers sure are smart."

"I'm mad as hell, and I ... ," blasted from the music machine. Peola stood next to it with a satisfied smile. When Bud, Moochie and Steve arose from the office, she raised her arm and said, "Power to the people." Behind the counter, April laugh-snorted and raised her arm.

As he led Moochie and Bud outside, Steve said, "Anyone else who wants to be a witness to this historic event, come with us." All of those sitting at the counter and in the booths followed, curious about what was going on. April called Pinkie and Brad from the kitchen.

When they got outside, Steve said, "All right, everyone, you are, indeed, a lucky group of people. This is going to be a first in the annals of American history." He glanced at April to see if she was watching him. She smiled shyly confirming her approval, then frowned when she remembered how bored she was in history class. He continued, "Someday, June the fourth will stand along side July fourth as important dates in the continuing development of this great nation. You can say that you were there at the beginning."

Moochie said, "Lord-a-mercy, honey, get on with it. We're not going to war over it. I've got to go fetch Sam and Ginger from their friend's house in a minute."

Steve, deflated momentarily, said, "Okay, Bud, bring Mr. Boy out of his cage so he can sign these papers."

Bud said, "His name is Pretty Boy."

"I know, but if he's going to be a full blown citizen, we have to show respect."

Bud perched Pretty Boy on his arm, next to Steve.

Pretty Boy said, "Gawk! Who's your daddy?"

April laughed with the crowd, and said, "You are, sexy bird."

Moochie said, "Lord-a-mercy, there's no telling what that bird's gonna say after being with these students outside, and watching television all the time."

Pretty Boy's mouthpiece tried to re-establish a modicum of control over the event. "Now, Pretty Boy, when we get in court, you're going to have to watch what you say. The judge might throw us out on our ears. This document grants me your power of attorney. I must point out that if we win this case, and there are ever future suits, I will receive thirty percent. Of course, thirty percent of nothing does not help feed my dog,

Beauregard. See where I've made this X down at the bottom? Now, I'm going to hold this up, and put a little dab of ink on your beak. Then, I want you to peck right next to the X."

Pretty Boy said, "Gawk! Highway robbery," and playfully pecked Steve's thumb.

"Ouch. Damn," said Steve as he stuck his thumb in his mouth. "All right, we'll make it twenty five percent." He put the form in front of Pretty Boy again; this time holding it at the top. The bird waited patiently for the dab of ink, then pecked on the dotted line.

"All right, now, the second document challenges section 290-5-14-.08 of the Food Service Regulations that excludes birds and turtles from eating establishments, as being unconstitutional based on the 'equal protection of the law' clause." April was duly impressed by Steve's pronouncement, but wondered what in the world turtles had to do with anything.

Pretty Boy glanced at the paper, said "Gawk! Equal protection," and pecked his mark.

*****

Across the street, Wilson Lumkin glared out the window of his cold, dark, formal restaurant. His face was beet-red as he slammed his fist into his hand. He turned, walked into his office and slammed the door. He sat at his desk brooding and scheming about how he might get even with the vermin across the street. At times like this, he liked to hold the gun his father had given him on his twenty-first birthday. He grabbed his keys from the desk, turned and unlocked the safe. When he reached for the gun he noticed the distinctive ring on his finger which had been passed down from his great grandfather, S. Wilson Lumkin. Did I have this on the other night when I hired that black kid? How stupid of me. Surely he would notice a ring with a diamond that big, surrounded by emeralds. Just in case, he took it off and placed it in the safe.

*****

Peola and April led the group from the restaurant and the curiosity seekers who had gathered on the sidewalk, in a cheer. "Hooray for Pretty Boy! Parrots have rights, too!"

Steve guided the crowd inside, saying, "Now, we need to have a strategy session."

"Whoops. Almost forgot about the kids," said Moochie. "Bud, would you mind going to pick them up?"

"Be glad to." He untied his apron and headed for the door.

"Sorry about that, Steve. Bud's a new man since Ginger arrived. Have you noticed the sparkle in his eyes? He loves that little girl better than tobacco. He'll be right back," she said, humming along as John Denver sang "Sunshine on My Shoulders."

"Now, ain't that something that that song would be playing on the jukebox? Ginger is truly the sunshine on Bud's shoulders."

"Oh, that reminds me, Moochie," said Steve. "I'm still waiting for the results of the DNA test." He lowered his voice. "What if It shows that Ginger is not his biological daughter?"

"Let's just keep our fingers crossed, honey. He's so proud of that girl. No matter. We'll go ahead with the adoption in any case."

*****

Sam and Ginger led Bud through the door and flew across the room for their Moochie hugs. She grabbed them both and lifted them off the floor.

Sam was the same age, but slightly taller. He fell naturally into taking care of Ginger, introducing her at school and watching out for her. His quiet, confident manner had a calming effect on the more outgoing, impetuous Ginger. Her blond ponytail was never still.

Moochie had been with Sam from the day he was born, in fact she had helped deliver him. In her heart, he would always be her son. Now, Bud could revel in that special love for his own child. When Ginger was around, he stood tall, glowing with pride. Sam went into the kitchen to help Pinkie and Brad prepare for the dinner crowd. Ginger flitted around the dining room, helping Peola clear dishes and straighten chairs.

Lawyer Phelps became restless, anxious to get down to business. While Moochie motioned for Peola and Ginger to bring coffee, he began. "Folks, let's face it, there's only one way this case will ever be won. I hate to use this tactic, but I think we must first try this case in the court of public opinion. We've got to get the people with us; draw attention to Pretty Boy's plight and let them feel pressure from the people through the media."

Moochie nodded, "I see what you mean, honey. I'll put out the word on my radio program."

Bud held his cup with both hands and looked across the rim at Steve. Steve and Moochie recognized the signal, so they waited while he took a second sip, and shifted his chew. "I reckon I could put up a sign outside by Pretty Boy's cage---something like, 'Support Parrot Rights,' and maybe Brad could get a group of students together for the cause."

"Good idea," said Steve. "All right, this is a good start. I'll present the documents and file the case tomorrow."

The sounds of "Wasting away in Margaritaville" followed Steve out the door. Moochie touched Bud's hand and asked him to stay for a moment after Steve left.

*****

Bud was so worried about Pretty Boy that Moochie decided not to tell him about Gracie Ledbetter the day before, but she had been brooding about it since receiving the poem. Now, it was time to ask his advice. She reached into the pocket of her yellow and white striped A-line jumper, worn over a bright yellow blouse, and pulled out the verse. She briefly told him of the call-in to the *Lay It on Grady Show* and read the poem to him.

Bud agreed that it was the saddest thing he had ever heard. "It's too bad that kind of thing is allowed to go on in our schools, but it's not our job to run them, Moochie. The only thing we can do is forgive those bullies, hope they learn their lesson and move on"

"Forgive, hell! These people need to be taught a lesson. The only thing people like that will understand is a fist upside their head. I can't stand seeing anyone pushed around like I was at that age. I feel like I need to do something; protect that little girl."

"Why don't you call Grady and talk to him about it?"

"Good idea, my sweet little man. I'll do that right now."

Moochie heard "Happy Days Are Here Again," then, "Hello, this is Grady."

"Grady, this is Moochie. Remember the call we got the other night from the little girl, Gracie? You know, the one being bullied?"

"Yeah, I thought you handled that pretty well, Moochie."

"Well, guess what. I received the poem that she promised to send me. Here, let me read it to you." She read to Grady as Bud excused himself and returned to the kitchen.

"Damn! You don't reckon she would actually kill herself, do you?"

"I hope not, honey. But, it sounds like we need to see if there is someway we can help. Do you suppose we could afford to fly over there and broadcast our show from Lawrenceburg? We could invite Gracie, her mother, a teacher, the principal and maybe even one or two of the bullies and their parents to be on the show."

"I don't know about that. The local station over there in Lawrenceburg is run by a friend of mine, Frank Murdock. I'll see if he thinks it can be arranged. Something like that might be interesting and a good way to help a lot of these kids. I'll get back to you after I talk to Frank."

"Okay, Grady. But, in the meantime, I'm going to give that poor girl a call. See if I can't cheer her up a bit. At least she'll know we care and she has someone to talk to."

CHAPTER NINTEEN

Brian, an eighth grade student at Hilbert Middle School in Redford Township, a suburb of Detroit, Michigan, turned in a paper for his social studies class entitled "Moochie for President." His uncle had given him a Moochie T-shirt for his birthday, and he began tuning in to WMTR, the local station that carried the *Lay It on Grady Show*, starring Grady Lakes and Moochie Dunlop. Mrs. Glenn, his teacher, was struck by the maturity of the young boy's thoughts and asked him to read it in class.

Brian was outgoing, yet still bashful in front of his peers. He shuffled his feet, then covered his face and turned away from the class. One of his friends yelled, "Come on girly-boy and tell us what you wrote." Brian laughed, turned around and hooked both thumbs in his jeans. He looked up at the ceiling to avoid their eyes, then down at the paper on the podium and began to read.

"I think there's too much hatred in the world: the Palestinians and Israelis hate each other, the Muslims and Christians hate each other, the Irish and English hate each other, Koreans hate themselves, and it seems like everyone hates Americans. Even in our own country, Democrats and Republicans hate each other, Liberals and Conservatives hate each other, some blacks and whites hate each other, some southerners still hate the North, and the haves and have-nots don't trust each other, neither.

"It seems to me like if we're ever going to have peace in this world, we're going to have to love each other. My Sunday school teacher says that 'We're all God's children, so why can't we get along?'

"That's why I think everyone in our class should write to Mrs. Moochie Dunlop and ask her to run for President. Mrs. Dunlop is a good person and she likes to hug people. That's how she shows others that she loves them. Besides that, she's funny. It might help to have a politician in office that has a sense of humor.

"If we could elect Mrs. Dunlop president, we could send her on a worldwide trip and have her hug everyone. That would make them happy and then maybe they would get along."

Mrs. Glenn sent his paper to the editor of the *Detroit Free Press* where it spawned a grassroots campaign to elect Moochie. The national media picked up the amusing story and 'Moochie for President' Clubs sprang up throughout the country. Everyone understood the effort was just for fun, but it provided relief from the tension of the campaign.

Jay Leno said, "Sounds like a good idea to me. The only problem is, she might break some ribs and cause an international incident." David Letterman thought the oval office would be a perfect fit for Moochie, "But, Air Force One would need to have larger seats installed."

The democratic and republican presidential candidates were peppered with questions at every stop:

Q: Senator, are you concerned that Moochie might siphon off most of the fat vote?

A: No, because my tax cut was for overweight people as well as skinny people.

Q: Senator, if you are elected, would you consider Moochie for a cabinet position?

A: Most definitely. In fact, I would make her both Secretary of State and Defense. That way, she could hug our friends and flatten our enemies.

Both candidates enjoyed the banter. It helped to lighten the vicious campaign.

As for Moochie she laughed along with the rest of the country.

Reporters called the restaurant for quotes. "Why didn't you run for Congress first, instead of jumping right into a presidential campaign?"

"Well, honey, if I'm going to get into politics, why not start at the top?"

A reporter from the *Washington Post* asked, "Are you a republican or democrat?"

"I ain't neither one, honey. I don't lie to the American people. I tell it like it is. If somebody don't like it, tell 'em to come to Moochie's Place. Once I feed them a chocolate covered praline sundae, they'll agree with everything I say."

One morning Peola answered the phone in a normal tone of voice, "Moochie's Place, Peola speaking."

"Peola? Did you say Peola?"

"Yes, that's my name. Don't wear it out. Who is this, anyway?"

"I'm the producer of the *60 Minutes* television show. May I speak to Mrs. Dunlop?"

Peola dropped the phone on the counter and began jumping up and down. She screamed and began screeching, "It's *60 Minutes*! It's *60 Minutes!*" Her voice was so shrill the diners covered their ears.

Pretty Boy squawked from the open door, "Looord haave mercy. Pass out the ear plugs!"

Moochie grabbed Peola and held her tight. "Now, now, girl. Calm down. Take a deep breath. Now, tell ole Moochie who's on the phone."

Peola held her hand to her throat and screeched, "It's *60 Minutes*, you know, the television people!"

Moochie patted her on the back, "All right, sweetie. Now, you go sit down and relax. I'll handle this." She picked up the phone. Soon arrangements were underway for Morley Safer to fly to Athens and interview.

*****

"Happy Days are here again---." Hello, out there in radio land, U.S.A. This is Grady Lakes along with Moochie Dunlop coming to you from WNRV in Lawrenceburg, Tennessee.

"Boy, do we have an unusual show for you this evening. Some of you might remember the call last week from this beautiful little town in the middle of the great State of Tennessee by Gracie Ledbetter, a student at Lawrence County High School. What a brave girl she is. She told Moochie and me about the trouble she's having in school because of her appearance and weight. She's been taunted, kidded and bullied throughout her school life to the point where she was desperate enough and, I might add, brave enough to call in and make her problem public, risking further bullying by her schoolmates. Bullying is a serious problem in schools throughout this country and we decided to bring this before the American public; make them aware of it and see if we can't do something about it. Gracie and her mother are here along with Gracie's English teacher and her principal.

"Also, and you won't believe this folks, we have two of the people who have given Gracie such a hard time. They have agreed to be on the show as long as we do not use their names. We will refer to them as student one and student two. They will each be accompanied by a parent who is just as concerned about this problem as the rest of us. They will be known as parent one and parent two.

"And now, ladies and gentlemen, it is my great pleasure to introduce my partner who is famous for her hugs and for telling it like it is, and whom I understand is now a candidate for President of the United States, Mrs., better known as Miss Moochie Dunlop!"

"Happy Days are here again------" blasted from the sound system. Grady had used this theme song for years in hopes that it might spark a bit of happiness in the hearts of those who had been torn down by the daily burdens of life and turned to his show for advice and relief.

Moochie smiled broadly and said, "Lord-a-mercy, Grady Lakes. You make it sound like this is a meeting of the United Nations in New York City. We're just a group of plain folks here to discuss a serious problem in our schools. Thank each one of you for being here to try and help us understand this kind of behavior and what might be done about it. First, let me read this beautiful, but sad poem written by Gracie. It sums up her feelings and how bullying has affected her life. If it doesn't touch you heart, you heart is made of Georgia granite. No one, in my opinion, would knowingly inflict this kind of pain on a fellow human being." She read the poem and passed it around for others on the panel to see.

She patted Gracie, sitting next to her, on the shoulder and said to the listeners on the radio, "Folks, what we're going to do is take calls from anyone who wants to call in. Please state who you are, make a brief comment and then ask your question."

The phone rang and Grady answered. "Hello, this is the *Lay it on Grady Show*. Thanks for calling. Please state your name, your comment, and your question."

"Hello Grady. This is Ann from San Diego, California. I'm a senior this year and like I'll be going on to college next year, and like I have this friend, Roletta who's like from Mexico and like she doesn't speak good English, you know, and like some of the guys make fun of her, call her a 'wet back' and tell her to go back where she belongs, you know, and I just don't like it, you know."

"What is your question and who is it for, Ann?"

"Well, like I just wanted to know how I can get them to stop doing that to my friend, you know, and like she's a legal citizen."

Grady pointed to the male student who squirmed and cleared his throat. "Ann, I'm a senior this year too and I've seen things like this go on all the time. A lot of times this is just some guys who are kidding around, they think it's funny and are just trying to get a laugh from other students. It's usually not meant to be mean, but it can be. I've done things like that before, just to be funny. I guess if you want to stop it, just don't laugh at that person."

Moochie said, "May I point out that if you are the one being bullied, it's not likely to be funny to you." Looking directly at the male student, she said, "I appreciate you being here to help us understand this problem. Just to put things in perspective, I would like to ask you a question. If the person you were kidding was bigger and stronger that you, would you do that to them?"

The student seemed surprised by the question. He turned dark red, paused, in deep thought for a minute. Then said, "To be honest, I would think twice and I probably wouldn't do it."

Another caller, "This is Allen from Akron, Ohio. That's not my real name. I don't want to give it because someone might know who I am and make it worse for me. My daddy's laid off and hasn't been able to find a job for the last six months. I have four younger brothers and sisters. I work after school at McDonalds to help out. We live in a suburb, but haven't been able to make the payment on our house for the last two months. I wish with all my heart that I could dress cool like the in groups at my school, but I just can't. Some of the kids make fun of the way I dress, and none of the girls will even be around me. It makes me ashamed and so I just stick to myself. I try not to bother anyone, but they still make fun of me. I'm afraid to turn anyone in because I'm afraid they would find out and hurt me."

Grady nodded at the principal, a stern-looking man with a square jaw and steel-gray hair. He leaned toward the microphone. "Allen, you've hit upon one of the greatest problems we face as administrators and teachers. It's the fear that keeps students who are being picked on from coming to us for help. We can't deal with these bullies unless we know who they are and have some kind of proof. We need a way for those being bullied to report them without fear of retaliation. I have some ideas that I will share with you later."

Grady broke in. "Thanks, Allen, for calling and thanks to our principal for that answer. If you don't mind, let's hold off on the calls for a moment and ask Gracie to share with us her feelings about how it affects those who are being bullied. Gracie, could you please share your thoughts with us?"

Gracie reached for Moochie's hand. Moochie whispered, "It's okay, honey. You can do it. You're strong and brave. Just tell it like it is."

Gracie held the microphone tightly with both hands. "I'm sorry if my voice shakes, but I'll do the best I can. I'm scared, but relieved at the same time that this has all come out. I was at the point where I didn't know what to do, but knew I had to do something. I couldn't go on with the way things were. I've tried and tried over the years to find ways to deal with the comments and humiliation. I wish I was pretty like most of the other girls and I wish I had a nice figure, but I just don't. Diets don't seem to work for me, at least not very well. It's a constant struggle and worry. I have no friends except my mother and now, Miss Moochie. I have no one my age to talk to. If I just had someone to share my thoughts with, it would help. That's why I've thought about suicide many times, but I've never reached the point where I would try it. I guess I'm just scared to do it."

Moochie looked toward the female student and said, "Honey, may I ask you why you bully other students like Gracie? What do you get out of it?"

The girl looked at Moochie, but not Gracie. She felt her father's withering stare which said, look what you've done to embarrass me. She stammered, "Well, it's just the 'in' thing to do. If you want to be included in the popular groups or asked out on dates, you have to go along with these things. If not, you're considered a 'dork' and you might be next on the list to be bullied. I don't always want to do it and sometimes I feel sorry for Gracie and others, but feel like I have to."

"In other words, you are too scared to stand up to the bullies so you join them. Is that right, honey?"

"Yes, ma'am, I guess so." The girl closed her eyes and covered her face with her hands.

The phone rang again and Grady answered.

"This is Christine from Rochester, Minnesota. I have five kids and I home school them all and what you're discussing is one of the reasons. I don't want them involved in the whole school scene, especially the bullying. My question is for the parents of the bullies. You are responsible for your own kids. Why haven't you done something about their behavior?"

The girl student's father looked at the boy bully's mother and motioned for her to answer, not having a ready reply himself, since this was the first time he was aware of a bullying problem. He was away on business most of the time and besides, his daughter never confided in him anyway.

The mother leaned close to her son's ear and whispered. "Okay, big boy, you are grounded from now on 'til you turn twenty-one or get married and move out of my house." She turned back to the microphone in front of her and smiled broadly, not realizing that the show was only being broadcast and not televised. "Well, it's so nice of you to invite me here this evening to discuss this important matter. I wish my son had kept me better informed about what has been going on at school(she shot a searing glance at her son who was folding a paper airplane using the sheet of unread instructions given to him by Grady when he first came into the studio, and wishing he was home watching *America's Got Talent* on television). I can't believe that my son was involved in something like this. We've tried to raise him right. How he could be that insensitive to other people's feelings, I'll never know. I wish one of his teachers, the school or someone had let us know about this teasing. We would have certainly put a stop to it if we had known."

Another caller. "Hello, this is Gus Gossage from Charlotte, North Carolina. I been listening in to your radio program and wanted to ask you all about this new problem we been having with this here so-called internet. I don't have one of them machines in my house, but they tell me down at the barber shop that there's a problem with these here bullies gettin' on the internet with these here e-mails and text messages using their fast little thumbs to send threats and all kinds of things to kids. Why, they're not safe from bullies even when they're home."

"Who are you directing you question to?" said Grady.

"Why, who ever knows about this here Ethernet with all them messages flying all over the place through the air and up to them satellites and so forth and so on."

Grady glanced around the room, his eyes landing on the teacher. She shrugged and cleared her throat. "Mr. Gossage, I'll try to answer your question the best I can. We've discussed this problem to some degree at our PTA meetings. The law enforcement people tell us one of the best ways to avoid that kind of thing is to make sure the computer is in a public place in the home so the parents will be aware of what is going on over the internet. Also, our counselors have been active in telling our students how to recognize cyber-bullying and how to avoid it. But, it's still a problem that we will have to deal with in the future."

"Thanks to our teacher and thank you Mr. Gossage for your question. Now, let's take some time to discuss how we might deal with the problem of bullying. How can we stop it?"

The Principal raised his right index finger.

Grady filled the air time by chatting about how hospitable Lawrenceburg and the school had been while the principal took a sip from the water glass in front of him and dabbed his forehead with the neatly folded handkerchief from his back pocket.

"We've been trying to find a way to deal with this problem for a long time and there doesn't seem to be an easy solution because of social intimidation and fear. I asked Ms. Dunlop to meet with our administrative personnel and teachers and share with us her experiences with bullying while she was in school. She also suggested that in order for any plan to work there must be consequences for those who bully. We have come up with a plan that we hope will eliminate this problem from our school. It will require the cooperation of all parents and students. A letter will be given to all students and mailed to all parents informing them of the problem. Then, a pledge form will be presented to every student and copies will be sent to all parents. We will ask each student to sign the pledge forms that will be kept in their files. The pledge will say:

'I am now fully aware of the harm that bullying can do to my fellow students at Lawrence County High School. I do not want to hurt them in any way. I therefore, make the following pledge: I _____ will not harass, tease, make fun of or bully my fellow students in any way. I will strive to be kind to and friends with all that I meet. Knowing of the deep hurt that can be caused by my words and deeds, I pledge that I will take every opportunity to help rather than hurt my fellow students. If I break this pledge, I will willingly accept the consequences as established by my parents, teacher or principal.

Signed: _____.'

"Each pledge will be signed by one or both parents. We believe that if we can get all students and parents behind this effort we will eliminate bullying from our school. The school board is fully behind this effort and has established the following rules: If a student violates this pledge, he or she will be suspended for one day and the parents will be called in for conference. The second offense calls for a three day suspension and if a third offense occurs, the student will be suspended for the remainder of the semester." The male bully looked up from the paper airplane and raised his eyebrows as if to say, are you talking to me, dude?

"I have some of these pledge forms with me today and I ask our courageous student, Gracie Ledbetter and her mother to be the first to sign, followed by the other students and parents.

"Also, in answer to Allen's question, I want to inform all of our students who are afraid to turn bullies in that I now have a private line in my office that you may use at any time. No one else will know that you called."

After the signing was done, Grady said, "Thank each one of you for participating this evening in the *Lay it on Grady Show*, and we thank all of you who laid it on us tonight. We'll keep you informed about this effort at Lawrence County High School. We hope other schools will follow suit. This is Grady Lakes and Moochie Dunlop signing off from WNRV in Lawrenceburg, Tennessee.

After they were off the air, the male student crumpled his airplane and with the tearful female student, came over to Gracie and apologized. Gracie said to them, "Don't worry, it'll be all right."

CHAPTER TWENTY

Moochie, standing next to the phone, grabbed it on the first ring. "Moochie's Place. Moochie speaking."

"Hello, Moochie Speaking. How's my favorite girlfriend?"

"Hi Rube. I'm doing fine, honey. If I was any better, they'd have to invent a new category."

"I just wanted to remind you that the closing on your new building is tomorrow morning at ten o'clock at Phelps' office. By the way, what does Pretty Boy think about you using his attorney?"

Moochie giggled. "Listen, honey, he better not object after all he's done to me, or I'll tie his beak together with dental floss."

Rube laughed. "Okay, make sure you bring your co-proprietor with you, and your check book."

Moochie laughed nervously. "Buddy Boy will be there. As for the check book---I'll bring it up to date tonight. Honestly, Rube, I have no idea how much money we have. All I know is we've never bounced a check. I hope the banker doesn't laugh too hard when I explain my round-off book keeping system. I can't imagine them agreeing to lend us three hundred and fifty thousand."

"I told you not to worry about it, Moochie. You have equity built up in the present building, and excellent credit with your suppliers. Besides, I'll be glad to co-sign if necessary."

"All right, honey, if you say so. Are you coming for lunch? Bud's got some good vegetables cooking; cabbage, baby carrots, black-eyed peas---. "

"Yep, Amy and I will be there. See you then."

*****

In spite of Moochie's concern, the real estate closing went fine. Rube suggested they go back to the new building, this time with the idea of deciding what must be done to combine the old with the new, and how to decorate it. Rube said, "If you wish, I can call Garcia Rose who does my publicity work, and invite him to meet us there. He's an artist at heart. Also, if it's all right with you, Bud, I'll call Billy Bob Jackson, the man who remodeled my office building. He'll be able to give us some ideas."

Bud pulled his ear, squeezed his chin, and reached into his pocket and dragged out his plug of tobacco. He deliberately tore off a chunk and placed it into his right jaw. He chewed twice and waited for the nicotine to kick in.

Moochie tapped her foot and rolled her eyes. "Well, Buddy Boy, the universe is getting older as we speak or don't speak. What do you think?"

Bud shifted his chew to the left jaw. "Just a minute, big mama, business decisions need to be pondered. We don't want to rush into anything."

"Well, Lord-a-mercy, honey. All he asked was if we should invite Billy Bob to join us and give us ideas."

Bud rolled his shoulders back and looked up at Rube.

"Sure. That sounds like a good idea. But, I want you both to know that I'm going to ask Uncle Billy to be my assistant on this project."

Rube smiled at Moochie. "Sounds like a great idea to me."

Moochie said, "Well, let's see, this is 2008. Maybe we'll be able to move in by 2025." She smiled, grabbed Bud and pulled him to her side.

*****

As they stood in the building next door, Rube suggested to Bud that he hire Billy Bob and his crew to help with the hard stuff, especially structural matters. As Rube put it, "After all, we don't want the place to fall down around us. Besides, you're working full time at the restaurant, and I worry about you overdoing it, making yourself sick."

Bud agreed, but wanted to do as much as he could to save money. Besides, he enjoyed doing that kind of work, and didn't want to feel left out.

"Don't worry," said Rube, "you'll still be the one in charge. You and Moochie have final say on all matters."

Billy Bob Jackson who was called "Hammertoe," or simply "Toe" by his friends and workers examined both buildings and found that the only real structural problem was connecting the two buildings. He explained to Bud that an opening would have to be cut in the walls and a door constructed to allow the movement of workers and customers. Hammertoe wore a red Georgia baseball cap to keep a mop of black, unruly hair under control. One of his gray eyes was bright and cheerful and made you want to smile, the other eye appeared to be sad and on the verge of falling asleep. This was confusing to Bud at first until he decided to just look at the cheerful side. Hammertoe showed him where he thought the door should go and how it should be done. "First, you'll have to remove the two booths just past the jukebox. There are no electrical wires in that area, as far as I can tell, but you'll still need to be careful. Call me on my cell if you run into a problem. I suggest you start from the new building side so as not to mess up the restaurant any longer than necessary."

"All right, then," said Bud, "we'll knock a hole where you tell us. Then, your crew can construct the door frame. How does that sound to you, Uncle Billy?"

Uncle Billy lifted his Texas Ranger cap back and scratched his head. "Sounds wonderful, just wonderful. It shouldn't be a problem for two smart carpenters like you and me."

*****

That Saturday afternoon Uncle Billy and Bud brought their tools, a small radio so they could listen to the Braves game against the Chicago Cubs, and a coffee pot, loaded and ready to plug in.

While arranging their tools, they saw a head pop around the corner and peer through the window. A few minutes later, Slapper Slocum propped the door open with one foot and slid three folding chairs inside. He reached back outside, looked both ways, then grabbed a sack filled with Krispy Kream donuts.

Slapper grinned and said, "I thought you two might need some advice from a real pro."

As soon as the coffee was ready, the three sat down with a mug in one hand, donut in the other, and pondered what must be done. Slapper said, "The door ought to be domed. It would look more sophisticated."

Uncle Billy left a gap in his donut, and said, "Yeah, that would be wonderful, just wonderful. It would put a little mystique in the place."

Bud finished chewing part of his donut, took a swig of his coffee and set it on the floor. "Well, gentlemen, and I use that term loosely, I hate to disagree but me and Moochie just ain't the sophisticated kind. In fact, most would put us in the square category, so I guess the door's gonna be square."

Uncle Billy said, "Well, all righty then. Anyway, who cares about mystique?"

Moochie, leaving the restaurant for the day, noticed them in the coffee klatch. She shook her head, peeked in and said, "Now ain't ya'll a sight; sitting there with all that work staring you in the face. If I was paying you, I'd fire you on the spot."

All three grinned sheepishly. Bud said, "Now, love, we're just trying to figure this out. We don't want to jump into this thing too fast."

Moochie shooshed him away with her hand. "Lord-a--mercy, honey, there ain't no chance of that. There will be peace in the world, and love in every heart before that happens. I tell you what I'm going to do. I'll bring Pretty Boy over here to supervise ya'll. He gets lonely in his room watching TV all the time. Besides, it might raise the IQ level a bit. I'll be right back."

While she was gone, Brad walked by carrying an armload of signs. He was returning from The Arches, symbolic entrance to the university, after leading a demonstration for Pretty Boy's rights.

He peeked in, "Hey, Bud, is it all right if I store these signs in this building?"

"Sure, it's a mess, anyway. Stack them back in the corner."

Brad laid the signs down and shook hands around. He helped himself to a cup of coffee. "Hey, Bud, you'll never guess who was at the demonstration."

"Some of the football players?"

"Yep. They were there, but that's not who I mean."

"Wilson Lumkin?"

"Nope, but he rode by and flipped us the bird. It was Booker Cleveland. Remember him, the kid who birdnapped P.B.?"

"No kidding?"

"Yep. Said he was out of the detention center and wanted to show his support for Mr. Boy."

When Moochie got back, Slapper and Brad had left and Bud and Billy were knocking holes in the wall. Pretty Boy said, "Lord-a- mercy. Gawk! What a mess."

Bud smiled, pleased to have his feathered buddy around.

Moochie waved goodbye. "Say hello to Lucille for me, Uncle Billy."

*****

The plaster was brittle and smashed into a million pieces. The wire mesh behind it was a different matter. The nails had to be pulled before it could be torn from the studs.

As Uncle Billy ripped a section loose from the two by fours, he saw two large canvas bags stuffed in the wall. "Hey, Bud. Look at this. What in the world ---?"

Bud reached in and pulled one of the bags onto the floor. It was tied at the top with a leather string.

He used his pocket knife to work the knot loose. He reached his hand in and pulled out a crumpled piece of newspaper. "Damn! Workers were bad in the 'good ole days,' too," he said. "Hiding their trash in a wall."

Bud grabbed both bags and threw them into the pile of debris in the middle of the floor. "I'll haul all that away later," he said.

Uncle Billy said, "I have to leave at six. I promised to take Lucille to the mall and on out to dinner. You know how these women are about shopping."

"Yeah, I understand. Before you leave, though, come on over to the other building and help me get the booths loose from the wall. I want to have this place so Billy Bob can get his crew in here on Monday and frame the door in."

When they finished next door Uncle Billy said, "All right, old pal, I'll meet you here tomorrow after lunch so we can finish up."

Bud continued to work until dusk. Finally, he swept the floor of the restaurant, and put Pretty Boy in his room. Before leaving he flipped the television on, and switched the channel to sixty-two where an old James Cagney movie was in midstream, "You, you dirty rat---." Bud said, "Oh shit, now we'll hear that all day tomorrow." He smiled as he cut off a tiny piece from his tobacco plug and placed it in Pretty Boy's cage. He had started this a few weeks back and found out that the bird liked it. "Now, remember, pal, if you tell anyone about this, it's all over. So keep your beak shut. Understand?"

"Gawk! All over," said Pretty Boy.

147

Bud got his pickup from the parking lot. Luckily, he found a parking space close to the front of the new building. He held up traffic while he backed in.

He grabbed the opened canvas bag and flung it close to the front door. A greenback flew out of the bag and floated to the floor. Bud had already picked up the other bag. He paused, then set it down slowly. He walked over and stared down at a hundred dollar bill. He stooped down and picked it up. "Hmmm," he said as he scratched his head. His eyes flew to the bag. He snatched it to him. Opening the bag wide, he peered in, then pulled out a handful of twenties, hundreds and even thousand dollar bills. He mumbled, "Damnnnn!" His eyes closed, giving his brain a chance to catch up with his pounding heart.

Not taking time to open the other bag, he loaded them into the cab of his truck.

Bud was unaware of the stocky man glaring through binoculars from his office window across the street. Wilson couldn't see what was in the bags, but knew what it was in his heart. Hatred flashed from his eyes and envy poured from every cell of his body. "Those bastards," he mumbled as he opened the safe, snatched his 38 Special and stuffed it in his pocket. Outside the back door he jumped into his Dodge Ram 150 sitting next to his BMW and scrambled to intercept Bud.

Bud, unaware that he was being followed, headed home while trying to think of some way to tell Moochie about the money without getting squeezed to death. He was singing "Fly me to the moon and let me play among the stars---." He rolled his window down a crack and enjoyed the soft breeze flowing over the bald spot on the back of his head. It doesn't get any better than this, he thought.

Wilson lagged back until they reached a section of Tallassee Road with an open field and a shallow ditch on the right side. He lowered the right side window and pulled a black stocking mask down from his broad-brimmed hat. The truck lurched forward when he slammed the pedal to the floor and pulled even with Bud.

Bud glanced to the left, saw the gun, twisted his head to the right and hit the brake. The bullet shattered the glass, driving bits of glass and torn plastic into Bud's neck and head as it blew past his left ear. The tires tore through the soft shoulder, and the truck plowed into three small trees which lifted it over the ditch and threw it on its side. Bud's body flew violently forward, then to the right, into the canvas bags. Bud lay deathly still, left wheels of his truck still spinning.

The black Dodge Ram turned around in a driveway and hurried back toward the accident. Approaching, Lumkin saw a white Toyota on the side of the road. The woman in the car was talking into a cell phone. "Oh shit!" he screamed and slammed his fist against the seat. He drove on to wait for another day.

CHAPTER TWENTY ONE

There was no motion from the driver as the emergency medical technicians worked feverishly to get him out. The technician in charge shook his head as minutes slipped by. "He's in shock and bleeding profusely. I don't see how he can make it."

With the truck lying on its right side, they were able to open the left door, but it was impossible to lift him out. "Charles, knock the rest of that windshield out and let's see if we can get him out that way, or at least get hold of him and lift him up. Hurry up, man!"

They finally pulled him out and laid him on a stretcher. One checked his pulse while another tried to stop the bleeding. "I've got a pulse! Let's get him across that ditch and into the ambulance. Be careful, he can't stand anymore trauma."

The EMT called the emergency room doctor as their vehicle screamed through the intersections, weaving around stopped cars. "His blood pressure is a hundred over fifty."

"All right. Did you start him on fluids yet?"

"Yes, sir."

"Get him here as soon as you can."

"Will do."

*****

Bud came to while the doctor was stitching the glass cuts. "Where am I? What happened?"

Doctor Dean looked up from his work. "You were in an accident. You're at Athens Regional. What caused the glass to shatter and cut you like this? Hell, man, you're lucky to be alive." Dr. Dean was gruff, outspoken, and swore like a sailor taking up golf for the first time, but the best at what he did. Perspiration soaked his scrubs as he motioned with his head for the nurse to wipe his forehead.

Bud closed his eyes and muttered, "I guess it must have been the bullet..."

"Bullet! What in the hell are you talking about, man?" Dr. Dean grumbled to the nurse, "The trauma must have made him a little whacko or he's on the sauce."

Bud mumbled, "Someone shot at me --- caused me to go off the road."

Dr. Dean finished cleaning and sewing a wound and looked up, "Damn! He's serious. Serena, get the head nurse in here, now! Nurse Shelby, get the rest of these wounds cleaned up."

Bud's eyes opened. "Where's my tobacco?"

Removing his gloves, Dr. Dean turned his head toward Bud. "Damn, man. Don't you realize that you could have died from this? If that glass had cut a major artery or if you hadn't landed on those canvas bags... The medical technicians said those trash bags probably saved your ass. And, all you can think about is tobacco. That's the craziest thing I've ever heard of. Damn!"

Bud's eyes widened with worry at mention of the bags. "I need to call my wife---right now. Can you get me a phone?"

Just then the head nurse popped her curly-headed pertness into the room. "I called the police. They'll have an officer here shortly. Anything else, Dr. Dean?"

"Yeah. Our patient is having a nicotine fit, but don't any of you dare give him any 'til all our tests are done. Also, he needs to call his wife. Bring a phone in here and plug it in. I'm out of here."

Before the nurse got back with the phone, Moochie burst into the room, and rushed to Bud's side. She put her hand on his head, leaned over and kissed him. Tears filled her eyes. "Lord-a-mercy, my sweet little man, are you all right? What happened? The police called, but wouldn't tell me anything."

Moochie began to settle down when Bud looked into her eyes and gave a weak smile, "I'm okay, love. Shaken up a little. That's all."

"Well, what about all them cuts and bruises ---?" Moochie blubbered.

"It's okay, sweetie. Those are from the glass."

He looked over at the nurse. "Would it be all right if I speak to my wife in private for a minute?"

The two nurses, caught up in the touching scene, glanced at each other, nodded and stepped out of the room.

Bud took his wife's hand. "Moochie, listen carefully, and just do what I tell you to do. This is very important. You must get to my truck right away."

"Well, for goodness sake, are you sure you're all right?"

"I'm a little woozy, kind of weak, but I'll be fine. Now, listen. There are two big bags of money in the cab of my truck." Bud closed his eyes, trying to regain his strength.

Moochie's eyes widened, "Lord, have mercy. He's done gone delirious. Nurse!"

Bud squeezed her hand and put his other finger over his lips. "Shhh. Listen to me. I found the money in the wall when we busted it open. You've got to get it before someone else finds it. Understand?"

She nodded and stifled a question.

"You've got to be strong, love. You saw my truck when you drove in, didn't you?"

"I sure did, honey, and it's a mess. Scared me to death."

Bud closed his eyes for a second then looked at Moochie. "I hate to tell you this, sweetie, but someone shot at me."

"Shot at you? Who? Who would do that?"

"Don't know. Couldn't see. Hard to focus when you're dodging a bullet."

"Maybe it was about the money. Do you reckon it was that worm across the street? Maybe that's why he broke into our place---looking for that money."

"Could be," said Bud. "The police are looking into it."

Moochie, eyes blazing, said, "Wait 'til I get my hands on that little pip-squeak."

Bud patted her hand. "Calm down, baby, there's something more important right now. I want you to get the money out of my truck and take it to our house. You stay there and count it. Get the forty-five out of the top drawer of the dresser and lay it beside you. Then, we'll have to decide what to do with the money. If the police are still at the scene, tell them it's some dirty laundry I was bringing home."

Moochie patted his head. "Lord-a-mercy, I hope I don't faint. They'd have a time getting me in one of these little beds."

"You'll be all right, sweetie. Just do what I told you."

*****

It was dark when Moochie got back to the site of the accident. The policemen were gone. She got out of the car and looked across the shallow ditch at the dark mass that used to be Bud's truck. She thought, my God, how did my little man survive? The moon was bright orange and seemed so close that she could touch it. Realizing there was no choice, she removed her orthopedic shoes and lifted her skirt above her knees. Stepping into the shallow water, feet sinking into the muddy bottom, she pushed the brush and broken limbs out of the way and made her way to the truck. Exhausted, she leaned against the turned up tailgate. Thinking, how in the world am I going to get those bags out of this mess, she steadied herself against the vehicle and inched along the side. When she reached the broken windshield, she peered in and saw the bags. Using a broken limb she smashed the remnants of glass still in the windshield and got down on her knees so she could reach the bags. Dragging them out she threw one over each shoulder to balance herself and waded back across the ditch. She sat on one of the bags to rest for a minute, saw headlights approaching, got up and threw the bags into the trunk of her car.

When she went to the side of her car to get in, a black truck with tinted windows, pulled off the road about twenty feet behind her and sat silently. Foolishly, Moochie motioned for the person to get out and come forward. She wanted to see who had shot at her husband. There was no response. She walked toward the truck and the truck backed slowly away. Suddenly, the truck roared and lurched toward her. With no choice, she dove into the ditch and came up sputtering dirty water. The truck swerved to miss her car and sped away.

*****

Moochie shuddered and shook as she drove home. She was wet, cold and scared. She carried the bags inside, locked the doors and turned the lights off. She got Bud's handgun from the bedroom and laid it on the cabinet while she took a shower and got dressed.

Now, what do I do? she thought. If I call the police, I'll have to tell them about the money. What if they take it away? If I don't call the police, will Lumkin or whoever this is, come here?

She decided to count the money first, then decide what to do. She took the canvas bags away from the windows to the inside bathroom and picked up the first one hundred dollar bill. After counting several thousand dollars, she threw up her hands and said, "Lord-a-mercy, there must be over a million, maybe two million dollars here. It would take me all night to count it." She held her head between her hands and sobbed. Suddenly she thought, why in the world are you crying, honey? You've got more money than you ever dreamed of. She began to laugh and pace back and forth through the house singing "Happy Days are here Again." She wondered what her high school principal would think of her now. Then, she thought of Bud and lunged for the phone on the kitchen wall.

"Hello," said Bud, groggy from medication.

"Hey, Buddy Boy, you're rich. Guess how much was in the bags. Go ahead, guess."

"I don't know---maybe a hundred thousand."

"Wrong! I hope your bed pan is nearby. I don't know exactly. It was too much to count, but I would say it's well over a million, maybe two million. Can you believe it? Sweetie, we are rich!"

"Moochie, Dr. Dean won't let them give me my tobacco. If I felt better, I'd challenge him to an arm wrestling contest. Then he'd know who he's dealing with."

"Lord-a-mercy. Save my soul. Is that all you can think about after I've told you we're rich?"

"Well, I guess I'm just hooked on that stuff. Besides, I don't know what it feels like to be rich. I'm just happy being a proprietor with you."

Moochie's voice broke as she said, "I love you too, honey." She didn't tell him about the attempt on her life.

She cradled the phone, and with her hand still on it, she thought, we need help. She dialed Rube's home number, gave him most of the details and asked if he could come and babysit the money while she went to stay with Bud at the hospital.

*****

Lumkin knew that Moochie had probably taken the money home, but things were too hot right now to do anything about it. That fat bitch most likely called the police, and they'll be on the alert. He spent all day Sunday brooding and plotting how he could get it back. If she leaves the money in the house it shouldn't be hard to break in while they're at work. What if she takes it with her to the restaurant or turns it over to the police? I guess I'll just have to wait for my chance.

He liked money of any kind, but this money was special. For over a hundred years it had been the focal point of his entire family to an obsessive degree. He couldn't let it slip away.

*****

It was five a.m. Sunday morning as Moochie drove home from the hospital. Traces of sunlight filtered up from the far horizon. Bud had been in a drugged stupor throughout the night. She didn't have the heart to wake him and discuss the new-found fortune. She and Rube would have to come up with a plan for now.

Rube was already awake and dressed when she got there. The money was under the bed. The gun lay on the kitchen table in front of him. He stood up when Moochie came in the back door, stretched and ran his fingers through his thick, blond hair.

"How's Bud?"

"He's pretty good, honey. Drowsy from the drugs and mighty sore. But, all the tests were negative. Dr. Dean talks like he'll let him go home sometime tomorrow."

Rube nodded. "Good."

Moochie headed for the kitchen. "I'll start the coffee. Then, I'm gonna take a shower. Be thinking about what we should do with the cash."

"That's what I've been doing all night, Mooch. I've got some ideas we can talk about over breakfast."

When Moochie got back to the kitchen Rube was frying eggs. A pitcher of orange juice was on the table. "How many eggs would you like?" said Rube. "They're small."

"Five or six should be gracious plenty," said Moochie. "I'll fix us some toast with peanut butter and jelly." She started the toast and poured two glasses of orange juice.

They ate and settled down with their coffee; Rube with a cup, Moochie with a pint-size, plastic, frequent customer cup she had gotten from McDonald's in 1999.

"I don't think the money would be safe here at the house with us working. Do you?" said Moochie.

"You're right. This place would be easy to break into. You have a spare tire compartment under the trunk of your car, don't you?"

"Sure do."

"Are your tires in good condition?"

"They're about four months old. But, I'm not worried about my tires, honey. It's having all this cash around that bothers me."

"Here's my idea. I'll take the spare tire out of your trunk and put it in the garage. We'll stash the money bags under the floor of the trunk. You'll rest this morning. This afternoon, drive to the hospital and park on the ground floor of the parking deck. Ask the security guard to keep an eye on your car. You're afraid someone will steal it. See?"

"Lord-a-mercy, who would want that thing?"

"He'll think the same thing, but that will make him more aware that he needs to watch it."

"I guess so, but I'll still worry about it. What about tomorrow morning when I go to work?"

Rube sipped his coffee and smiled. "Park right in front of the restaurant. You're legal for two hours. After that, if the parking cop catches you, she'll give you a ticket. But, heck, what's a little fine to a millionaire?"

"Yeah. I keep forgetting that I'm rich." Moochie tore open a chocolate covered praline. "One thing I've been wondering about is whose money is this? I mean according to the law."

Rube pulled his right ear lobe. "I don't really know for sure. I could call Lawyer Phelps tomorrow and have him do some research for me on a hypothetical question. See whether it belongs to the person who put it there or the ones who found it in a building that belongs to them."

"Sounds like a good plan to me," said Moochie. "Let me get Bud on the phone and run it by him."

When the phone rang Bud had already been awakened by Nurse Serena to take vital signs. His tobacco pouch lay on the swivel table beside his bed.

Moochie gave him the plan. There was a long pause and she could hear the tobacco pouch being opened.

She waited. Still, no answer.

"Bud? Are you there? What in tarnation is going on?"

She looked at Rube. "Maybe I better hang up and call the nurse's station. He might have passed out or something. "Bud, this is Houston calling. Are you there?"

There was a cough, then, "Just a minute, love. I'm thinking."

"Well, shoot, Buddy Boy, I'd like a decision before the first frost. Besides, the cream in my coffee is beginning to curdle."

Rube who had been smiling, laughed out loud, spitting coffee back into his cup.

"All right," said Bud, "sounds like a good plan. Now, if you don't mind, this pretty nurse needs my attention."

CHAPTER TWENTY TWO

Moochie called the workers on Sunday to tell them Bud was in the hospital. Brad Leaptrott came to visit him that afternoon just as officer Waddell was leaving. He was shocked by Bud's appearance. "Do they know who did it, boss?"

Bud grimaced as he spoke. "Not yet, and I couldn't tell them much. I was too busy trying to survive."

"I just came by to make sure you're okay. And, I don't want you to worry. Me and Pinkie will handle the kitchen. We'll just work a little harder, that's all." Brad shuffled his size twelve feet, having no way to show his affection for his friend.

"I know you all can do it, son. But, I'll be there as soon as mean old Doctor Dean takes the shackles off my legs," Bud joked. "He said it might be tomorrow morning or at least sometime tomorrow."

*****

Brad arrived only minutes after Moochie opened the restaurant on Monday morning. "Who do you reckon shot at Bud?" he asked.

"I know exactly who it was--- worm-face across the street. I ought to go over there right now and squeeze him 'til his eyeballs pop out."

"Don't do that. He'll get his sooner or later. Someone that desperate and hateful always makes a mistake. When that time comes, I'll take care of him myself. I'll change today's quotation on the sign outside." He checked the list they had

159

given to the *Banner-Herald*. The saying was "It ain't healthy being skinny."

The phone rang. "Hello, Ms. Moochie?"

"Yes."

"This is Officer Waddell. Just wanted to bring you up to date and see if you have any more information for us."

"All I know is, somebody tried to kill my husband, and I know who it is. Have you arrested jerk-face yet?"

"You mean Mr. Lumkin? Why, he's one of the most respected people in this town. Generous. Always gives to the Police Fund. We can't go around arresting someone like that without evidence."

"Well, looks to me like you all need to get busy. What about fingerprints, the gun, the bullet?"

"There were no fingerprints. We found the bullet and figure it was fired from a .38 Special, Smith and Wesson. That's all we know at this time. Do you know of any reason why someone may be trying to kill your husband?"

Moochie paused, not wanting to tell anyone else about the money until they found out who it belonged to. "Lord, I don't know why anyone would want to kill that sweet little man. He's never done nothing to nobody."

"All right, let me know if you hear anything that might help us. By the way, how is Mr. Bud doing?"

"Dr. Dean tells me he's a lucky man. Says if the glass had cut one of them main arteries he would be dead now. He still hurts and is sore all over, but they say he's going to be okay. He might come home this afternoon. Say, why don't you stop by at lunch and have some of Pinkie's cornbread; make your stomach happy?

"Might do that. Call me if you learn anything else about who attacked Mr. Bud."

*****

Moochie went to the back room to check on Pretty Boy and clean his cage. "Hey, birdwit. What did you watch last night----some porno movie?"

"Gawk! I'm singin' in the rain."

"Oh, no, now we'll hear that all day long."

"Gawk! Hello, Buddy Boy."

"Sorry, boy. Your pal is hurt. He's not here this morning."

"Let's make love," squawked Pretty Boy.

"Oh, shut up, featherhead."

As Moochie hung Pretty Boy's cage outside, Rube pulled his Acura into a parking space, got out and waved. "Hey, Mooch, I talked to Bud; says he's doing better, real sore."

"Yep. That little man is tough as nails. Stubborn too--- that'll get you through a lot."

Rube walked past the cage, "Hey, P.B. How are they hanging?"

"Gawk! I'm singin' in the rain---."

Rube sat down for eggs, biscuits and gravy, and a cup of freshly brewed coffee. He loved the smell of coffee in the morning. It held the promise of a new day; a new beginning.

Moochie wore her leaf-green chiffon moo moo and had splashed on an ample amount of Jessica Simpson fragrance this morning. It made her feel slimmer somehow. She walked over, leaned in close and said, "The 'you-know-what' is still in my car out front."

Rube stopped chewing. "Okay. I think we should only leave it there for today. If it's there too long, it becomes suspicious. You usually park in the parking deck. We'll have to find a new place to hide the cash. I'll call Lawyer Phelps when I get to the office. I won't give the details, but he'll probably know I'm talking about you and Bud. We'll have a meeting after we know more about who owns it. When's Bud getting out of the hospital?"

"Early this afternoon it sounds like. As soon as his doctor sees him and gives the okay. He insists on coming here. Says he can't be sitting around the house."

Tony Colosimo walked in, waved at Moochie and April, went to the jukebox, put in two quarters and made his selections. He strolled to the counter to the strains of "Are You Lonesome Tonight." The song fit his mood perfectly with his wife being in New York.

April set coffee in front of him. "How was your week-end?"

"Boring--- ," said Tony as he blew on his coffee. "Nothing against Athens, but it's not like the Big Apple where there's always plenty of action."

April bent forward and spoke softly, "Did you hear about Bud?"

"No. What happened?"

"He was in a bad accident. Someone shot at him. Ran him off the road."

"Who was it?"

"Don't know for sure. Bud didn't see anything. Moochie thinks it's the creep across the street. Lumkin."

Colosimo's jaw tightened and April saw a flash of anger in his eyes. "I don't know how you deal with someone like that here, but in New York he'd be wearing cement shoes at the bottom of the Hudson River."

April laugh-snorted nervously. "This ain't New York. What can I get you for breakfast?"

"The usual. Make sure the bacon is crisp." He slid his coffee closer as April went to place his order. Tony was especially down today. Living alone, far from home with no one to share his feelings with, was beginning to wear on his psyche. He thought of his first wife, Caresse, and their towheaded son. He still didn't understand exactly what had happened in Louisiana that summer. Being young and idealistic he fell head over heels in love with the sensual Caresse and her wild love-making. Finding out that he was going to be a father lit a fire in his heart that he had never felt before. He, along with all of his large Italian family were dark skinned with black hair. Caresse's hair was naturally auburn albeit with highlights.

When the blond, almost white haired son came into the world, Tony was confused at first, tried to figure out how that could happen, then he became suspicious and finally furious. He never even confronted Caresse, just packed his belongings and drove back to New York. He never discussed it with anyone, certainly not Gail, his present wife back in New York.

Slapper Slocum's head and right eye slowly peered around the edge of the picture window, then disappeared. A few minutes later, he walked to the front door, grasped the knob and looked both ways before entering.

Pretty Boy hummed the theme song from "Pink Panther."

When Slapper got to the counter, Moochie had coffee and a glazed donut waiting. "Morning, Slapper. Who's following you?"

"No one, I hope, but you can't be too careful now days. I heard on the radio what happened to Bud. I hate to sound like Barney Fife, but there are bad people all over the place out there."

Moochie nodded. "Yep. I guess so. Bud's better. He'll be here this afternoon. How's business?"

"Couldn't be better. Since the syndication of the radio show and your campaign for President, sales have gone out of sight. Bill's had to find some other companies to help make the T-shirts. I've got four girls working to ship all the orders. Carly's thinking about quitting her job to help out in the store." His teeth left a half-circle gap in the donut. "By the way, Moochie, I have another idea. Why don't we start producing 'Moochie for President' T-shirts?"

Moochie laughed, "Why, Lord-a-mercy, Slapper. That ain't no serious campaign. Poor people can't run for President in this country. Don't you know that?"

"Course I do. But, that shouldn't stop us from making a little money while it lasts."

"Well, go ahead, honey. Just remember to keep track of my share."

"I'll do that," said Slapper. "By the way, the Pretty Boy T-shirts are printed up and ready to go. Got his picture on the front, it says 'Free Pretty Boy' on the back."

"Good," said Moochie, "maybe that'll help our case. Say, seems like Carly is happy to be back together with you."

Slapper finished the donut and grinned. "Yep. I guess money makes a happy marriage." He motioned Moochie to lean closer. "Did you notice anything different about me?"

"I sure did, honey. You're not slapping yourself silly anymore. The bruises are gone. Is that from the money too?"

"I reckon. That, and I've learned to forgive myself like you told me to do."

*****

Early in the afternoon Bud arrived holding onto Moochie's arm.

Pinkie had a chair set up in the kitchen. "Now, Mr. Bud, you sit yourself down and don't be up here messin' with me and Brad. Don't you worry none. We can handle it. Can't we, white boy?"

Brad shouted over the din of flying pots and pans, and moochieburgers sizzling on the grill, "You bet, big mama. Bud, you can sit there and behave yourself, or go out there and show those footballers who's boss."

It wasn't five minutes before Bud became restless. "Think I'll mosey out and check on the whippersnappers."

With all the cuts and bruises added to his arthritis, he walked and looked like he'd fallen off a pickup and been dragged a hundred feet. When the football players saw him, they were shocked. Then, began to clap and cheer. "Way to go, champ!"

Bud was peppered with comments from around the tables: "You look like the Tennessee Volunteers after we got through with 'em last year;" "Hey, Winslow, you might be able to beat the old man now;" and "Hey, Bud, you must have taken a switch to the knife fight."

Bud grinned on both sides of his mouth, loving every minute of it. "All right, mama's boys. You're all still wet behind the ears. Wait 'til I get back in shape. I'll take on two of you; one with each arm."

Moochie followed Bud, to make sure he didn't fall. She noticed an older man with brown, wavy hair sitting among the boys. "Well, now, looks like you all brought a babysitter with you today."

Still laughing, the man got to his feet. "Hi, I'm Coach Vance Segren." He offered his hand to Bud who shook it gingerly. He then held out his hand to Moochie.

She grabbed him with both hands, pulled him to her, lifted him off his feet and swung him around. When she let go, Taylor and Winslow were there to catch him. They set him back in his chair and waited for him to catch his breath. "There," said Moochie, "now ain't that better than a handshake?"

The players loved it. They purposely hadn't prepared coach for the encounter.

Coach coughed, then smiled. "That's definitely not like a handshake. It's more like a body shake. I need you to come to practice sometime and teach my linemen and linebackers how to do that."

"I'd be glad to, honey. My thinking is, if they can't breathe, they can't run."

She put her arm around Bud. "I don't know if you read about it in the paper, but me and Buddy Boy are being interviewed on *60 Minutes* tomorrow. Morley Safer himself will be here. Wants to question us about this presidential race. It's the craziest thing I've ever heard of. Why, I couldn't be and don't want to be President. But, you know how these media people are, always looking for someway to add color to their news reporting. If you don't have a class or something, stop by Moochie's Place about ten o'clock."

*****

That afternoon when Lawyer Phelps stopped by Moochie's Place, he noticed the front door propped open.

He tapped on the cage, "Hi, Mr. Boy. How's my favorite client?"

"Gawk! Guard your credit cards."

"Now, Mr. Boy, you need to show more respect. I'm trying to get the judge to let you back inside. Don't forget, my fee is thirty percent."

"Gawk! Twenty-five."

"All right, twenty-five, in cash." Phelps was laughing when he walked inside. He waved at Moochie. "Hi, Moochie. Why's the front door open?"

"We decided to keep it open during busy times when the weather's nice so Birdbrain won't feel left out."

"Please don't use that term when you talk about my client. His name is Mr. Boy." He winked at Moochie, then moved on down the counter, sitting in front of April so he could get a better view. He just recently got up the courage to move from a booth to be closer to April at the counter.

He yelled back at Moochie, "Judge Crocker still hasn't put us on the docket. Has Mr. Boy had his exam yet?"

"Nope," she said. "His appointment's next Monday."

"Have you heard anything from Clint Eastwood yet?" He peeked at April when she turned around to get his pie.

"Not yet," smiled Moochie. "I left a message. Expect he'll call any day now."

*****

Bud, Moochie and Ginger arrived home late that evening and found the side door wide open. Every cabinet and drawer in the kitchen had been yanked open and the floor was covered with broken glasses, silverware, pots and pans. Even the refrigerator was standing open. Bud winced every step he took, but managed to walk around the rest of the house. It was in similar disarray. He made his way to the phone and called the police.

Moochie plopped down on the couch and covered her face. "Why is this happening to us, Bud? We're just plain people, busting our butts to make a life. We're not hurting nobody. Why can't they let us alone?"

"I don't know, love. But, It'll be all right. You just sit there and rest while me and Ginger get this place cleaned up."

"You're in no shape to do that. Never-mind, I'm okay." She got up and began helping Ginger clean up the mess.

Two policemen came and interviewed Moochie and Bud while a technician dusted for prints and took photographs.

*****

They couldn't go to sleep; worried about what to do with the money and whether the burglar would return. They decided to bring it inside after Ginger went to sleep. Finally, Moochie said, "Bud, I think we should at least put all that cash in new containers, something less suspicious than canvas bags. Maybe suitcases or better yet, duffle bags that would be flexible and more easily stored. What do you think?"

Bud scratched his head, got up from the couch and went into the kitchen. Moochie threw up her hands, then reached for a copy of *Hollywood Scandals.* Somehow it seemed to sooth her own problems; reading about those of others.

Bud came back with a re-heated cup of coffee and sat down.

"Well, I'm glad to see you back. Thought you didn't hear me, or decided to forget the whole thing; go to India and become a Hindu Monk."

"No, love, just thinking. I'll go to Wal-Mart, get some bags and rope. After we've re-packed the money, you drop me off on Jackson Street by the alley. I'll go in the back way and hide the money. You'll come back in an hour and pick me up. How does that sound?"

"Sounds good except that we don't have a well or tunnel under the restaurant to put it in. What about Ginger?"

"Don't worry, I've got a good place in mind. I'll tell you later. First, let's see if it works. I hate to do it, but I'll go wake Ginger and have her get dressed. We'll have to promise to explain to her about the bags as soon as we can, and take her with us. I don't see any other choice. We can't leave her here."

CHAPTER TWENTY THREE

The Moochie saying in the newspaper the next morning was "Eating is My Favorite Pastime, Honey."

Rube backed his Chevy Silverado as close to the front door as he could. When he walked past Pretty Boy, he gave his usual greeting. "Hey, P.B. How're they hangin'?"

"Gawk! You, you dirty rat."

"Morning Rube. What are you up to? Where's that sweet wife of yours?" said Moochie.

"She's going over some public relations strategies with Uncle Billy and Garcia Rose. She'll be in later. I had this old safe sitting there in my office with almost nothing in it, and thought it might come in handy for you and Bud."

"Great, we can keep our deposits there before we go to the bank." She leaned over and whispered to Rube. "Bud's found a good place to hide the money, at least he thinks so."

Rube gave a thumbs up, walked to the kitchen door and yelled, "Hey, Bud and Brad, I need a hand with this safe."

Bud limped along, mostly to supervise.

As they eased the safe onto the sidewalk and struggled to get the cart under it, Wilson Lumkin peeked through the Venetian blinds across the street. When Bud looked that way, the blinds flopped back in place. He rubbed the stitches that closed the scar on his face and thought, someday your debt to me will have to be paid.

After the safe was in the back room, Rube sat down for breakfast. Moochie told him about the break-in at their home.

"Looks like worm-face is determined to get his hands on that money," she said.

"Yeah. You and Bud be very careful. You never know what someone like that will do. Do you all have a gun?"

"Bud has a pistol of some kind at home. I don't know if he knows how to use it. I certainly don't."

"I talked to Lawyer Phelps. He's researching the laws and court rulings on found money. Says he'll call me back."

"Okay, honey. By the way, our boy Sam has been a big help to us with Ginger. He watches over her like a big brother, sees that she's taken care of at school, and has introduced her to all of his friends. She loves it here."

"Good. A man couldn't ask for a better son. And, it's mostly due to the way you raised him. I'll always be grateful to you for that."

"Ah, pshaw, I can't take credit for that. It must be them genes you gave him."

*****

A short time after Rube left, the television crew practically took over the restaurant. Morley Safer insisted that the interview take place in Moochie's office booth even though the space was limited. They agreed to do the interview in mid-morning when there would be fewer customers. The make-up crew hadn't been told that Bud was injured and sewed together like ripped overalls. Bud explained that it was nothing serious, but still sore. He was amazed when they got through and he looked in the mirror they held up for him. All the cuts, scratches and bruises appeared to be gone. "Feels like my face has been plastered, but it sure does look good," he remarked. Moochie went through the same procedure with more emphasis around the eyes and a royal red, glossy lipstick. "Lord-a-mercy, I ain't looked this good since the sixth grade."

When the star, Morley Safer, and his entourage made their grand appearance at the front door, Moochie and Bud were there to greet them. Moochie asked, "Do you want one of my healing hugs, Mr. Safer?"

Morley said, "I sure do. My staff's been coaching me all morning on what to do." He winked and said, "Just remember, I'm fifty-nine years old."

Moochie scooped him into her arms and gave him one of her best efforts. When she let go, Morley's normal grin appeared to be crooked, and the chrysanthemum in his lapel was crushed. He blinked his eyes, staggered back and was caught by one of his aides. He was speechless for one of the first times in his life.

Moochie grabbed his arm and said, "Step over here, Morley. There's someone I want you to meet." She motioned toward the bird cage. "This is Pretty Boy. He's been on the *Tonight Show* with Johnny Carson, and he's a good friend of Clint Eastwood."

"Oh," said Morley, "I didn't realize you had a celebrity bird. I'll have to interview him sometime. I interviewed Mr. Eastwood once. Seems like a nice man."

Pretty Boy said, "Gawk! Do you feel lucky, punk?"

The gathering crowd, primarily students, broke out in laughter and gave a loud cheer, "Go Pretty Boy!"

Morley stepped back, not knowing what to say.

Moochie said, "Lord-a-mercy, honey. We never know what Birdbrain's going to come out with. He's been hanging around these students too long."

Another cheer went up.

When the show began, Moochie's Place was packed. People stood five deep hoping to see through the front windows, and another two hundred spilled along the sidewalk and into the street. Two policemen controlled the crowd.

Inside, the jukebox blared, "I was country when country wasn't cooool. Yeah, I was country when country wasn't cooool." Customers lucky enough to be inside, sang along until the director pulled the plug.

Moochie insisted that Morley have a cup of coffee and a praline before they got started. She imagined he was a little nervous, even though he had done thousands of interviews in his lifetime. She reached across the table and took his hand. "Now, Morley, you just relax, everything's gonna be all right. If you get in trouble, ole Moochie will come to the rescue."

Morley smiled, but quickly withdrew his hand before any of the staff saw what had happened. After all, he was the one in charge.

Moochie sat across from Morley. Bud eased into a chair at the end of the table, mindful of his soreness from the accident. The technicians arranged the cameras so his left side would not be seen. The director said, "When you see the light come on, you're on the air."

Morley had cut a brief introduction to the Moochie story prior to coming to Athens, and when the light came on he got down to business. "Moochie, please tell our audience why you are running for the Office of President."

"Well, honey, it wasn't my idea to run. It's just that some nice people thought I would be a good one. I guess they were tired of the same old tune; each candidate trying to out-promise and out-spend the other. I think the people sense that something is seriously wrong with the way things are being done right now. Why don't you have a bite of your praline before you faint?"

Without thinking, Morley picked up the candy and took a bite, then immediately regretted it as he tried to chew and ask the next question. "What do you mean," cough, cough, "by the way things are being done?"

"What I mean is that only the rich can make a serious run for the Office of President anymore. Even they have to depend on donations from other rich people. That ain't a democracy if you ask me. Companies and groups are spending millions of dollars in every election to buy influence. They deny it and so do the politicians who receive it. But, the people know, and they don't like it. Let's be honest, it's out and out bribery. And, who's supposed to fix this problem? I'll tell you who---the very ones who get all the money, our President and Congress. There's just not enough courage in Washington to stand up against the money boys."

Morley looked a little wired from the sugar rush of the praline. He turned to Bud. "What do you think of what your wife just said?"

Bud pulled his left ear down and leaned forward, "Well, Morley, most politicians are like the rest of us, if you hold enough money in front of them, they'll follow you anywhere."

"What do you think of Moochie's campaign?"

Bud threw his shoulders back, grinning on one side of his face and said, "She's somethin', ain't she? I love her to death. She's the best thing that ever happened to me. She loves me too, and I've got the cracked ribs to prove it. Her hugs can last up to two months. You have to be a man to take that kind of lovin'."

"Yes, well ---," Morley stammered, anxious to change the subject. "Mr. Bud, what's your job at the restaurant? What do you do?"

Bud looked up, straightened his clip-on tie and said, "Well, sir, as you may or may not know, I'm half-owner of Moochie's Place. I'm in charge of the kitchen; seeing that the food is cooked just right; hiring; greeting the customers and what have you."

"You mentioned hiring, Bud, what about firing; do you do that too?"

"No, no. I ain't never fired nobody in my life, and I ain't about to start; Moochie would have to do that. 'Course, there ain't been no need for that yet."

"Do you ever give advice to people like Moochie does?"

"Well, I don't know if you'd call it advice. I just tell people about my life; tell 'em how I was saved from the clutches of alcohol. Then, I pat them on the back and let 'em know they can succeed in life just like me--- no matter what their problem is. All most people need is a little love and encouragement---you know? By the way, do you drink, Morley?"

Morley was stunned for an instant, but recovered quickly. "Now, Bud, let's get back to the election. What would you do if Moochie is elected and you become First Gentleman?"

Bud laid his finger beside his nose and said, "Hmmm. I ain't never been called a gentleman before. I guess the first thing I'd do is take over the kitchen at the White House and teach them folks how to cook ribs so we could feed all them ambassadors and such."

"I see. Do you ever give advice at the national and international level?"

"Oh, no. I just work at the local level. Moochie takes care of the rest of the world."

Moochie reached over and patted him on the hand. "You tell 'em, sweet thing."

Morley turned to Moochie just as she crammed half a Twinkie in her mouth. She still had a bit of cream filling on her lip. "Moochie, what do you think we ought to do about Congress?"

"Well, sweetie, I've thought about that a lot, and I've decided that we ought to throw the whole bunch out: Republicans, Democrats and Independents alike, and elect us a new batch, sort of like throwing out a spoiled bowl of potato salad. You know what I mean?"

"I get your point," smiled Morley. "What's your take on the stock market, Ms. Moochie?"

Bud frantically motioned for Moochie to wipe the cream filling off her lip. Nonplussed, she complied.

"Well, it seems like we ought to have something more stable than the stock market. Why, it just keeps going up and down. It never stays the same. Why would I put my money into something like that, honey? Hell, I want to know that my money's still going to be there tomorrow when I wake up. I ain't never seen the likes of them people up there on the floor of the Stock Exchange --- throwing their arms up in the air, hollering and screaming like they been shot. They ain't getting my money, honey. I'm putting mine into something safe, like food. You see what I mean, Morley? People are always gonna be needing food. Ain't that right, sweet thing?" Bud nodded his head and grinned.

"I see. One more question Miss Moochie. What is the first thing you would do if you're elected and sworn in as President?"

"Morley, I know there are a lot of important issues that would need to be dealt with, but as soon as I could get around to it, I would have the U. S. Department of Agriculture change the food and nutrition pyramid and put chocolate at the very base of the pyramid followed by fruits and vegetables, et cetera. Chocolate has been given a bad name over the years and now them experts are saying it's good for you. I've always known that. Anything that tastes that good has got to be good for you. See what I mean, Morley?"

"I have to agree with you that it does taste good. I think most people would agree."

Morley glanced at his producer and got the "wrap-it-up signal."

"All right, Moochie, Bud. Thank you for talking to us. Good luck on your campaign." Morley picked up the rest of his praline and shoved it into his coat pocket.

*****

Lawyer Phelps enjoyed coming to Moochie's Place in the early afternoon for two reasons. It was quieter and he could read the *Wall Street Journal*. More importantly, he had a chance to see April. He had rehearsed many times how he would ask her out. So far, he had lost his nerve at the last minute. This might be the day. April no longer took his order, just brought coffee with two creams, sugar, and apple pie. As she leaned near with the coffee, the faint smell of the Betty Boop lotion she had spread on her hands and arms in the morning caused the hair on the back of Phelp's neck to stand up and his hands to quiver.

Today he wore a dark blue, silk tie with a solitary diamond stick pin. When she brought the pie, her emerald eyes glanced down at the diamond as it shimmered in the glare from the florescent lights. "My, don't you look spiffy today. You must be seeing an important client. Either that or you're trying to impress the judge."

"No. It's just that an important firm like mine expects us to look our best." He fingered the Cubic Zirconium on his hand and sniffed the coffee before adding cream. "Anything special you want to hear on the jukebox?"

"Yeah, one of my favorites is 'You Can't Hide Your Lyin' Eyes."

Steve, embarrassed by his attempt to impress April, walked over, put his quarters in and selected April's favorite, plus several others.

When Steve got back to the counter he said, "I see Billy Bob's carpenters just about have the new door framed in."

April smiled and said, "Yep. Won't be long before we open the other building." She paused. "You know, for a lawyer, you sure are having a time coming up with the words to ask me out."

Steve set his fork-full of apple pie down and grinned. "You're right. I'm such a klutz. I'm sorry. Will you have dinner with me and go see the Athens Symphony this Saturday?"

April giggle-snorted. "Sure. I would like that very much. Just remember, you don't have to impress me. Just be honest with me."

CHAPTER TWENTY FOUR

The Moochieism of the day read: "I'd Rather be Fat Than Ugly."

After the breakfast crowd left, Bud went out to sit with Pretty Boy. He enjoyed the time alone with his hook-billed friend. Taking his favorite UGA coffee mug, filled to the brim, he sat on the bench next to Pretty Boy's cage. The cage hung from an extended hook next to the door so he could greet each customer. It was made of heavy metal wire, painted white and had a multi-colored rope which extended across the center of the cage. In one corner was a swing and the other corner held a perch next to a mirror so his friend could sit and admire his pretty self. Wall attachments included holders for water, bird seed and gravel. A circle of spray millet hung next to the seed tray and pine litter covered the floor.

Since the last attack on Pretty Boy, Bud worried about his safety. Tony Colosimo told Bud about a parrot in New York who could fake death. Bud tried it with Pretty Boy, with little success until one day when he spoke angrily to Pretty Boy. The bird dropped to the floor of the cage, stiff legged with eyes closed. Bud was surprised because he had never seen him close his eyes except when asleep. Bud slipped him a pinch of tobacco each time he did it, and worked with him so if someone broke in, he would play dead instead of running his mouth.

Bud was puzzled and even frustrated with Pretty Boy over another matter. He was trying to teach him to sing "God Bless America," and had done so except for one small problem.

Pretty Boy knew all the words to the song, but when he tried to say God Bless America, all that came out was "God Bless Ameri---." That's it. He would not say the last syllable. Bud pondered over it and tried different ways to get him to say it. He closed the door while working with Pretty Boy because it drove Moochie batty when she heard the bird say, "God Bless Ameri---." She would say, "Ca, ca, ca, you dumb bird! Either sing it right or don't sing it at all."

Bud finished his coffee and got up to go inside.

He tapped on the cage, "Remember, my fine feathered friend, it's America. Ca. I want to be proud of you, but it just ain't patriotic to not be able to say America. Think about it."

As Bud walked in, the phone rang. Moochie answered. "It's for you, Buddy Boy. It's Pretty Boy's mouthpiece."

"Hello, Steve. What's up?"

"I called to remind you that Pretty Boy's appointment with the avian specialist is this afternoon at two o'clock. He's to have a complete examination. We'll need the results when we go to court."

"Okay, I know where the University Small Animal Hospital is. Who do I ask for?" Bud set his empty cup on the counter and April snatched it up and put it on a tray to be taken to the kitchen.

April giggle-snorted and said, "Tell Steve I'll see him this afternoon." Bud waved her off.

"Take him to the Exotic Department and ask for Dr. Marquad. They'll tell you what to do. Okay?" said Steve.

"All right. They're not gonna hurt my bird are they?"

"No. No. They'll treat him right. Let me know how it goes."

"Trouble's Back in Town" by the Wilburn Brothers played on the jukebox. Pinkie yelled from the kitchen, "Hey, Mr. Bud, you better get in here and start gettin' them hamburgers ready." She went back to humming along with the music and stacking coffee cups on a tray. Bud was content to be back among the familiar sounds of his kitchen.

*****

The phone behind the counter rang. Moochie snatched a paper towel and wiped the remnants of a chocolate covered praline from her fingers and answered:"You've reached Moochie's Place, honey, home of Bud's famous ribs. If you're not already fat, we'll help you get there."

"Hello, Ms. Dunlop, this is Clint Eastwood. I'm returning your call and wanted to check on my friend Pretty Boy."

"Clint Eastwood! Lord have mercy on my soul. Imagine someone like you returning the call of a crazy woman like me. I wanted to ask you a favor for Birdbrain--- I mean Pretty Boy. He's been banned from the restaurant. They said he might have germs and so on, because he poops. It's the craziest thing you ever heard of. Why, I told them everybody poops from the President on down. Even movie stars do it. That is right ain't it, Mr. Eastwood?"

By this time Clint was nearly falling out of his chair and gasping for breath, his hand over the mouthpiece. Consummate actor that he is, he regained control to say, "You're absolutely right, Ms. Dunlop---."

"Call me Moochie, honey, everybody does."

"Okay, if you'll call me Clint. There's no question that you're right," he said, barely a tremor in his voice. "Even producers and actresses---I won't name names, but they all poop. Please don't quote me on that."

"No problem, Clint. I understand. I'd hate to see that in one of them magazines at the grocery store. They're always revealing y'all's secrets."

Clint scratched his head. "Right. Anyway, I would be glad to write a letter. I doubt if it will do any good, but I'll send it out today if you've got a fax. Otherwise, I'll have to mail it."

Moochie gave him the fax number, then, "Clint, Pretty Boy thanks you for the DVD and movies that you sent. He watches them all the time. I'll call and let you know when the trial is."

"Okay. Let me know if I can help in any other way. My manager mentioned an engagement in Atlanta in the not too distant future. So I might be close by. And, by the way, good luck on your presidential campaign."

"Thanks Clint, but it would take a lot more than luck for this old girl to be elected. Besides, the country needs someone a lot smarter than me."

She hung up laughing and everyone in the place wanted to know what he said. Moochie gave them the details.

She couldn't wait to call Lawyer Phelps with the good news.

*****

Before Bud and Pretty Boy left for the hospital, Moochie said, "See if you can get one of them specialists to twist Birdbrain's beak so he can say America."

When Pretty Boy heard the word he began to sing, "God bless Ameri---, land that I love, stand beside her---."

"Hush, Featherbrain! Your abbreviation is just not right. Say America. Ca! Ca! Ca! Got it?"

"Gawk, ca, ca, ca," said Pretty Boy.

"Now put them together. America!"

"God bless Ameri---, land that I love----."

"Bud, get this unpatriotic bird out of here before I pluck his tail feathers out one at a time." She laughed and shushed him away with her hand.

Bud and Pretty Boy arrived in the Exotic Avian Department of the hospital and Bud set Pretty Boy's cage on the counter.

"Gawk! Who's your daddy?"

The receptionist smiled, "Why, you are, you sexy thing. What can I do for you?"

"We're here to see Dr. Marquad," said Bud.

While they waited, Bud explained to Pretty Boy how important it was that he co-operate and keep his mouth shut.

The bird pecked at the cage door, indicating that he wanted a chew of tobacco.

"No way," said Bud. "That might throw their tests off kilter. I'm sorry I ever started giving you that stuff. It's not good for you."

"Gawk! I love you."

"I don't care. You're not getting any now."

The nurse escorted them to an examination room. It was small, painted bright yellow with a counter and sink on one side, a small examination table in the center and sported that clean, antiseptic smell that reminded Bud of his stay in the hospital.

The first thing Pretty Boy spotted was a picture of a beautiful female parrot on the wall. "Gawk! Hot mama," said Pretty Boy.

"Shhh," said an embarrassed Bud.

Dr. Marquad grinned showing gleaming white teeth against his dark skin, and spoke in a thick accent, "Meister Arrington, today we will be doing a thorough examination of your bird."

"Gawk! Pretty Boy," said Pretty Boy.

"Yes, we will examine Pretty Boy. The nurse will take a case history. I will examine the---Pretty Boy's eyes, nostrils, mouth and skin for insects, sores or other lesions. We will do a blood workup, primarily looking for antibodies to psittacosis or other organisms. I'll take a nasal swab, also checking for psittacosis. Next, I will do a rectal exam, including a rectal swab to check for Salmonella Chlamydiaceae."

"My God," said Bud remembering the last rectal exam he had, "he's only a small bird, not a condor."

"Not to worry, Meister Arrington, we will be using the proper instruments, and Pretty Boy will be sedated."

Bud looked at Pretty Boy who was busy using his beak to search under his left wing for unknown vermin, not having understood a word the doctor said. When Pretty Boy raised his head and saw the look in Bud's eyes, he said, "Lord have mercy."

Bud refused to leave Pretty Boy's side during the examination and suffered much more than his bird. Pretty Boy was oblivious to what went on and came out of his stupor with a dazed look on his face. While they were waiting for Pretty Boy to come around, Dr. Marquad sat down with Bud. "Meister Arrington, he will be drowsy for about an hour. Just let him rest. By the way, are you interested in breeding your bird?"

Bud leaned back and threw one arm over the back of the chair. He wanted a chew of tobacco so bad his jaw twitched. He thought, my pal must get mighty lonely for companionship, sitting in that cage all day. How would I feel, never getting to see my sweet Moochie? "Sounds like a good idea to me," he said.

"I have a client who has three birds that she would like to breed. I will call her and make arrangements."

Bud thought, Lordy, wait 'til Pretty Boy gets the good news. He'll think he's done made it to the pearly gates of bird heaven.

Pretty Boy slept most of the way back. When they got to the restaurant, everyone was concerned about Pretty Boy and curious about the details. Bud filled them in. Moochie was ashamed of scolding Pretty Boy. She stuck her hand inside the cage and caressed his head and neck.

*****

That afternoon Wilson Lumkin displayed two signs in front of his restaurant. One said, "Birds are Dirty and Carry Disease." The other said, "This Restaurant Does Not Allow Birds."

Brad Leaptrott was furious when April told him about the signs. He began contacting his friends and fellow students who were involved in the campaign to re-establish Pretty Boy's right to be inside the restaurant. He also contacted the police department for a permit to demonstrate.

The next day at eleven o'clock Brad and his crowd gathered on the sidewalk in front of the Lumkin Café and marched back and forth carrying signs: "Parrots Have Rights Too" and "Free Pretty Boy."

Wilson Lumkin came out in a rage and screamed at the protestors. He hit one boy in the face and grabbed a girl by the hair and slung her into the street.

Brad stepped in front of him to stop the attack and explain freedom of speech to him. Lumkin was in no mood to listen and punched Brad in the nose, knocking him to the sidewalk. While blood poured from Brad's nose, Lumkin grabbed a stick from one of the signs and beat Brad about the face and head.

Some of the young men pulled him off as the policeman assigned to monitor the demonstration called for backup. One of the officers spoke to Lumkin who was yelling, "He attacked me! He attacked me!"

The officer ordered a halt to the demonstration because they were blocking the sidewalk. He arrested Brad for disorderly conduct and Lumkin for battery.

Lumkin's lawyer met them at the jail and sat in while Lumkin told an irrational story about the demonstrators threatening his customers and claimed that he was protecting his personal property. He was released in a matter of minutes.

Moochie sent Bud to get Brad out of jail. An hour later, bail had been set by the judge. Brad explained what happened and told the judge there were plenty of witnesses. The judge told him that would be good when you get to court, but right now I have to follow procedure.

Bud put up the money and hustled his friend to see Dr. Chisolm about his nose. Brad protested the trip to the doctor. "I don't need a doctor. My nose is fine. Just take me to see that creep, so I can get even."

183

"Don't worry," said Bud. "He's in debt to both of us now. One way or the other, he'll get his just rewards. Right now we're gonna make sure you're okay."

CHAPTER TWENTY FIVE

The saying for the day, "All Living Things Eliminate," obviously was edited by the *Athens Banner-Herald*.

Moochie thought, Lord-a-mercy, honey, they've come up with a new word for poop. Poop is still poop, no matter how you scoop it. She was skimming through the rest of the paper when April came in with a big smile on her face. "Well, aren't you the happy one this morning? Looks like you had a good weekend, honey. How was your date with Pretty Boy's mouthpiece?"

April laugh-snorted. "Great. We ate at the Porterhouse Grill. The music at the concert was great and Steve was a perfect gentleman, doggone it! Just kidding. He's really a nice person when you get to know him and he's not acting like a lawyer."

"Good. I thought so. Ole Moochie has a feel for people, you know. He might be the right man for you if we can put a little weight on him. I've got weeds in my yard at home bigger than that boy."

April got busy putting coffee cups on the shelf and wiping the back counter. Peola and Pinkie came in. Pinkie was smiling ear to ear and humming "Can't help loving that man o' mine."

Peola's greeting was higher pitched than usual when she said, "Hey, Miss Moochie."

"All right, girls, tell ole Moochie what's going on. Something's up. I can see it in your eyes."

"I got me a new man," blurted Pinkie, "and he's a good one this time, Miss Moochie. Got a good job. Got some sense, too, don't he, Peola?"

Peola nodded.

"I done laid down the law to this one, no drinking, no womanizing, and if he lays a finger on me or Peola, I'm gonna knock his head clean off."

"Sounds like a good plan to me. Make sure you don't let him sweet talk you, and make excuses when the rent comes due," said Moochie.

"No, ma'am! He knows I done been set free and I ain't falling for any o' that stuff no more."

Moochie put her arm around Peola. "Now, girl, tell me what's got you wired up this morning."

"Miss Moochie, I'm worried about this new section of the restaurant opening up today. How'm I gonna handle all that plus this side too?"

"Don't worry, honey. Schools out and both Ginger and Sam are here. I'll help on this side if need be. You'll be in charge of the new section. If we need more help, we'll hire someone."

Two of the booths along the west wall of the old restaurant had been removed and the jukebox sat next to the new door that opened into the beautifully refurbished and decorated "Green Room," as Moochie called it. There was a high ceiling, as with most of the older buildings downtown and two glistening chandeliers had been added. The walls were mint green with tastefully framed pictures of outdoor scenes from the Great Smokey Mountains. The forest green booths and tables were covered by white tablecloths trimmed with a green, running leaf design.

Pinkie went into the kitchen to greet Bud, Brad, Sam and Ginger and start her biscuit dough. Ginger was helping Bud clean the grill.

Brad said, "Hey, Pinkie, about time you got here. I thought I was gonna have to make some <u>good</u> biscuits this morning."

"Lord help us. Ain't no white boy in the world can make biscuits like I can. Get outta here now and let me go to work."

Brad laughed and carried a stack of dishes next to the grill.

Bud said to Ginger, "Gingerbread, my pretty little girl, finish this grill then go out and see how Peola plans to use you at lunch time. I've got to get Pretty Boy outside and talk to him about something."

*****

Bud stuck his head inside the back room and yelled, "Damn you, bird!"

Pretty Boy dropped to the bottom of the cage, eyes closed, legs sticking straight out. His feathers were flat and he looked smaller than usual.

Bud laughed to himself, walked over to the cage and said, "Good boy! You're almost as good as Clint Eastwood." He reached in and offered a pinch of Red Man.

Pretty Boy popped to his feet, his feathers fluffed out again. "Gawk! Go ahead Punk, make my day." Bud laughed and stroked his back.

Pretty Boy sat on Bud's shoulder while he cleaned the cage and refilled the water and food containers.

"Boy, remember, I told you that some lady wants you to mate with her female parrots? Well, today's the day. You may not know what this means yet, but believe me, it may turn out to be the best day of your life."

Pretty Boy's head was cocked to one side as he listened. He said, "Gawk! Boy wants a peanut."

Bud grinned, "I think you'll be happy when you see what's in store for you." He put Pretty Boy back in the cage and carried him outside.

While Bud was outside sipping coffee and talking to Pretty Boy, Steve Phelps called.

"Hello, Moochie's Place, Moochie speaking."

"Miss Moochie, Steve. I have some good news."

"Well, if it's good, go ahead and spill it, honey."

"First, the judge has set Mr. Boy's trial for next week, Friday, ten o'clock. Jury's already selected. The judge didn't like it much, but I insisted on a jury trial because I think it's the only way we can win this case."

"Good. Maybe we can get this over with and bring Birdbrain back inside. Have you got all your crib notes in order, as them students say?"

"I hope so, Miss Moochie. We'll need some luck because judges don't like to overturn local laws unless there is good reason. We'll do the best we can."

"Anything else we can do?"

"Nothing right now. There's more good news. I got the results back on the DNA tests for Bud and Ginger.

"Yes."

"Bud is not the father, so he's not obligated."

"Lord have mercy," Moochie exclaimed. "That's not good news, honey. That's terrible. Bud loves that little girl more than life itself. Whatever you do, don't mention this to Bud or anyone else. Just let it lie. I doubt that he'll ever ask but if he does, just tell him the tests were inconclusive or whatever lawyer word you can think of. This ain't no legal matter, Steve. It's a matter of the heart."

"Yes ma'am, I see what you mean. But, if he ever pins me down, I'll have to tell him. It's my responsibility as his lawyer"

*****

The lunch crowd was the largest ever. Both rooms were packed. Sam and Ginger who were to help only if needed, were running wide open and enjoying every minute of it. Bud shouted to Moochie when she came into the kitchen, "It ain't legal working these kids like this."

"I know, honey, but we ain't got much choice. Maybe we can find another worker tomorrow."

Peola's voice reached a frequency never heard by human ear. She was rushing from table to table, scribbling orders and filling tea glasses. Moochie came to help after hugging everyone who rang the bell, leaving the packed counter to April. Pretty Boy kept the crowd outside entertained, singing "God Bless Ameri ---" and imitating Clint Eastwood, James Cagney and Ed McMahon. Bud had installed speakers in the new room and the jukebox was non-stop with old tunes like: "Rocky Mountain High, " "I'm Leaving on a Jet Plane, " "Splish Splash I Was Taking a Bath, " and "Unforgettable. " Most of the people were eating, singing along or trying to do both while basking in the aroma of ribs, chicken and steamed vegetables.

Everyone had a story for Moochie, how her hug had helped Aunt Rose get over the shingles, or freed up Grandpa Willard's frozen shoulder. All were voting for Moochie for President, at least that's what they claimed.

*****

At three-thirty that afternoon Bud and Pretty Boy found the house on Milledge Circle Drive in a genteel neighborhood near Five Points. Most of the homes were occupied by old-line Athenians with roots going back to the early part of the twentieth century. Scattered among the well-preserved homes were a few rental properties occupied by university students.

Bud rang the door bell, then knocked on the door.

A silver-haired lady wearing a beautiful silk dress, white with a sweeping floral design, answered the door. When she opened the screen, Bud was struck by her green, bunny rabbit slippers.

Bud nodded slightly. "Ms. Charmaine, I'm Bud Arrington the Third. This is Pretty Boy, the parrot that Dr. Marquad told you about."

"Yes. Yes. Pretty Bug. Come on in, Rod, and bring that handsome fellow with you."

"Bud, my name is Bud."

"Yes. Of course, Bud. We need to discuss the arrangements. Can I get you a cup of coffee or tea?"

"I would have some coffee if it's not too much trouble."

"No trouble, Rob. Have a seat. You can rest Pretty Bug's cage on the table. I'll be right back."

"Gawk! Let's make love," said Pretty Boy.

"Naughty, naughty, Pretty Bud. We don't discuss things like that in this house," said Charmaine as she left.

After she was out of sight, Bud said, "Now, Pretty Boy, you've got to be on your best behavior. Don't be talking about sex, okay? We might get kicked out on our behinds." He slipped Pretty Boy a bit of Red Man.

Charmaine returned with one of her green bunny rabbit shoes missing. "Here's your tea, Rod. And, I brought Pretty Bud a cracker."

"No. I'm Bud. This is Pretty Boy."

"Ah. How silly of me, I should have brought you a cracker too."

Bud took a sip of the tea instead of the coffee he had asked for, wondering if he should stick out his pinkie.

"Now, Rod, I guess you know that Pretty Bud will have to spend the night. We don't allow any, well, you know, during the day. It's just not the proper thing to do in broad daylight."

"No problem," said Bud. "I brought enough of his food, so he'll be fine through the night."

"Gawk! Make my day," said Pretty Boy.

"My Heavens," said Charmaine. "Maybe this is not a good idea."

"Don't worry, Ms. Charmaine, he's just funning. Things will work out just fine. When do we get to meet the ladies of the house?"

"My, my. I almost forgot. We need to make proper introductions. Every now and then my memory slips. Please excuse me while I go and prepare my precious girls for this important, but delicate undertaking." She got up and padded toward the study with one bare and one green foot.

As they waited, Pretty Boy became restless, jumping from one roost to another, squawking under his breath and searching for vermin under his feathers. Bud was a little wired himself, anxious to get outside and have a chew. He didn't appreciate the antiques covered with doilies, it was just furniture to him. A faint smell of lilacs preceded Ms. Charmaine through the study door.

This time she had both green bunny rabbits on, but on the wrong side. "This way gentlemen," she giggled and motioned them into the room.

A large cage covered half of one wall. Three water dishes clung to one side, three bowls filled with bird seed were on the floor of the cage. Ms. Charmaine stood elegantly, if you didn't look below the ankles, beside the cage. "Pretty Rod and Bug, this is Dolly on the left pedestal, Sugar Plum is in the center and Angel Baby is on the right. They have decided that they will all remain in the same cage tonight. They grew up together and are very close. So, Pretty Rod, I guess that's where you'll stay too."

"Lord have mercy!" said Pretty Boy. He stuck his beak through the bars of his cage and pulled himself as close as he could to the other cage. Then, he stood back and looked wildly at each of his new friends. He jumped from one foot to the other, then, "Gawk! I love you."

"Shush!" said Bud. "I'm sorry, he gets a little carried away."

"Just set his cage next to the girls and let them get acquainted. Tonight, before I go to bed, I'll put them all together."

"Fine," said Bud. He reached his finger inside and rubbed Pretty Boy's head. "I'll pick you up tomorrow morning, pal. Have fun."

For once the bird was speechless as he preened himself.

Ms. Charmaine led Bud to the door. "Mr. Boy, we'll take good care of him. We'll see what the outcome of this is. If there is more than one, you get first pick."

*****

That evening Moochie met Grady at WGRB for the weekly *Lay it on Grady Show.*

While Grady had his usual shot of whiskey, Moochie sipped a coffee loaded with sugar and cream.

"You know Bud's daughter, Ginger, don't you Grady?"

"Well, I met her at the restaurant. Seems like a nice kid. How's she doing?"

"Very good and she's made a new man of Bud. I've never seen him so happy. She and Sam are great friends. It seems that our family circle has been made complete. According to Lawyer Phelps we have a fifty/fifty chance of winning Pretty Boy's case. Lumkin is still our worst problem. We've never seen someone so hateful and obsessed. I guess he's upset because of the success we're having with the restaurant."

"Why don't you get the police to do something about him," asked Grady.

"We've talked to them but they can't, or don't want to do anything about it."

Grady flipped his collar down and completed a Windsor knot in his bright, orange tie. "How's the campaign coming?"

Moochie shook her head. "Lord-a-mercy, honey. People are about to drive me crazy; asking me to speak to this group and that event. Why, I can't do all that and still run a restaurant. If they want me to be President, they'll have to do the campaigning for me."

"Come on partner, we've got to get on the air."

"This is the *Lay it on Grady Show,* coming to you from WGRB in Athens, Georgia, 97.2 on your radio dial." As theme song, *"Happy Days are Here Again, "* neared completion, Grady moved closer to the mike.

"Hello America! This is your old friend, Grady Lakes, along with co-host Moochie Dunlop, that irrepressible, tell it like it is, restaurateur and candidate for President of these United States of America!"

"Hey, folks. Don't mind Grady, he gets carried away sometimes. I'm still Moochie, just like I always was, ready to tell it like it is, at least in my opinion. You can take it or leave it, honey."

Grady leaned in again. "All right, ladies and gentlemen, let's see what you have to lay on Grady tonight. Here's our first caller from Gaylord, Michigan. Hello, who's calling please?"

"Hello, Grady, I have a question for Moochie." There was a loud crash in the background, like a fruit jar hitting the floor, and a "Son-of-a-bitch!" from a female voice.

"Sir, this is Grady, who's calling please?"

"This is Micky Gunderson, hold on ---." They heard a muffled "Damn it, Joyce, shut up. Can't you see I'm on the phone? Hello, Grady, are you still there?"

"Yep, still here, lay it on me, Micky."

"Well, I saw a small article in the *Detroit Free Press* saying that Moochie never graduated from high school and I wondered why."

Moochie grabbed the mike. "Honey, I wonder who put that story out. I've always been ashamed that I never graduated. Never talked about it before. I guess when you're running for office everything becomes public. So be it. Even though it still hurts, maybe if I tell what happened, someone who's being bullied will be helped.

"There was this boy in school, I won't mention his name, but his father was president of the school board. The boy was a hero, played football and basketball, and was a good student, but he was a bully. He picked on me from the time we were in

193

the sixth grade, called me fatso, pig and slob, but his favorite insulting name for me was butterball. Because of him that became my nickname. I did well in classes, but had no friends in high school, never had a date and was never invited to the parties.

"We lived in the country and I had to walk about a mile to and from the bus stop. One day in my senior year, while walking home, the bully pulled along side me in his refurbished 1968 Mustang convertible that had been given to him by his father. Had his girlfriend, Elsa we'll call her, a cheerleader, with him.

"The boy yelled, 'Hey, butterball, how'd you get so fat? I hear your mama's restaurant is going broke because you eat up all the profit'." Elsa laughed.

"I kept walking, trying to ignore him as we approached the bridge over Dead Man's Creek.

"He yelled again, 'Hey, butterball, why don't you come out for the football team. You could play the whole defensive line.'

"Elsa cackled away and laid herself against him, planting her sloppy kisses on his neck.

"I walked a few steps more and he said with a sneering grin on his face, 'Your mama's nothing but a fat, slop-selling whore.'

"When he brought my mother into it, who was working night and day to make ends meet, I lost it. Couldn't help it. I slapped Elsa on the back of her puffy blond head, knocking her into the dash. I came around the car, grabbed a hand full of football hero hair with my right hand and a varsity jacket with my left, lifted him out of the Mustang and dragged him across the road and threw his screaming ass into the ditch. He scrambled up from the ditch and charged like an angry linebacker. When he got close, I reached down to my right knee and came up with an uppercut that straightened him up and stopped him dead in his tracks.

"Then, I grabbed him and threw him into the left, rear fender of the Mustang. Elsa was already out of the car, screaming and running down the road. Hero got up sporting red paint from the car on the leather sleeve of his jacket. He passed Elsa in a dead run. That's the last I saw of those two until the next day.

"Unfortunately, my rage didn't stop there. I put the Mustang into neutral and pushed it over the embankment into Dead Man's Creek.

"Needless to say, I was suspended during that, my senior year and not allowed to graduate."

Grady who had never heard the story, patted Moochie on the back. On the phone, Micky sniffled and said, "Way to go, Moochie! You struck a blow for all of us who were bullied in school. I'm gonna vote for you for sure! Joyce will too, if I can get her to stop canning elderberries long enough."

The next caller was from Decatur, Alabama. "Hello, you're on the air."

"Yeah. This here's Robert Thornton Leon Blanchard, they call me Rabbit for short." There was a clicking sound in the background.

"Yes, Mr. Rabbit. Is your radio turned down? I hear a noise."

"Yeah, the radio's down. That's just me cleanin' ma rifle. Fixin' to go possum huntin' tonight. Got me one o' them phones so's I can talk without the phone stickin' to ma ear."

"What is your question, sir?"

"Well, since Moochie's running for the highest office in the land, I wondered what she's gonna do about this here global warming. Sounds like it might even flood the White House if we don't do something. By the way, thanks for beating up on that bully. He ought to be thrown in prison and left to die."

"Hey, Rabbit. Thanks for calling, honey. You're exactly right about this warming thing. We got us a big problem from what all them scientists are saying. I'd hate to be walking around in my galoshes all the time. The Congress needs to pass a law against all them industries passing gas into the atmosphere. It just ain't right. We got to remember though, it might be some of us common people passing gas by using our cars and them big ole gas guzzlers, called SUV's, to get out to the suburbs. But, if they expect me to start riding a bike with one of them little ole seats, they can forget it. It'll never happen."

Moochie recognized the voice of the next caller before he gave his name to Grady. He directed his statement to her. "Hello, Moochie, this is Mr. Estes, your old high school principal. I wanted to apologize for kicking you out of school during your senior year and not letting you graduate. I hope you understand it was just something I had to do. No choice if I wanted to keep my job. Anyway, I'm so proud of you and your success in spite of what happened. I hope you will be able to forgive me."

"Oh, I understand, Mr. Estes. You know that I was doing something I had to do, too. It wasn't right what you and the school board did. It still bothers me, but I'm not gonna let it hold me back, honey. Thanks for calling."

"I agree with you and want you to know that I'm voting for you for President."

"Thank you, Mr. Estes. I appreciate it. Maybe I can stop dreaming and worrying about that run-in with the football hero now."

Moochie and Grady answered other questions about abortions, stem cells, the war in Iraq, personal problems and where they might call to order a Moochie or Pretty Boy T-shirt.

Then Grady closed the show, "Ladies and gentlemen we're out of time. We appreciate all of your calls and letters. Sorry, we can't answer all of them. Just remember that we love you and God loves us all. Good night and God bless."

Grady walked Moochie to the back door of the station. "I hope we helped a few people out there tonight."

"Me too, honey. There sure are a lot of them hurting. I wish we could help more of them. Maybe we'll find a way."

"Maybe so."

Moochie drove home, wondering what she and Bud should do with the money they had found.

*****

Pretty Boy's coming court battle to establish his rights found a place in the back pages of many newspapers, and the presidential candidates were pelted with questions about parrots' rights. They both were in favor of rights if no democrat or republican would be diseased by the bird and unable to vote. At times, the candidates responded with their own questions. "Did Pretty Boy contribute to my campaign? Will Pretty Boy be able to vote on the computer voting systems?" One candidate suggested that perhaps we should give all parrots a tax break. The other said he did not like to see people, even parrots unemployed. "I think they need to find a way to keep Pretty Boy's job as a greeter."

*****

After closing the next evening, the blinds on the front windows were lowered. Moochie, Bud, Rube and Steve Phelps met in the new room around a center table while the rest of the crew finished chores and listened to the jukebox. Moochie moved the napkins and condiments to another table and pulled up two chairs for herself.

"Sometimes I wish we had never found the money," said Moochie as she removed lipstick from her cosmetic purse and applied the bright red goo to her lips. "Seems like that's all I think about anymore. What in the world are we gonna do with it?" Still looking into the small purse mirror she raked her fingers through her blond curls.

"Don't worry, love. That's why we've got our good friend here and the best lawyer in town. They'll help us figure all this out. That is right, ain't it boys?"

Rube had removed his suit jacket and loosened his tie. He smiled. "We'll do the best we can, Bud. I've found out that money makes life a little easier in some ways, but harder in others. To those who are given much, much is expected. I think I read that somewhere in the Bible."

Steve looked up from his notes, knowing they expected him to have all the answers. "What I've discovered so far is that since you found the money and it was on your property, it belongs to you. However, we must keep in mind that a lot of this is based on common law which is an evolving thing. Also, remember that anyone can bring a lawsuit challenging your ownership. But, they would have to have strong evidence to convince a court that the money is theirs. Obviously, the money had been in the wall a long time, based on the dates. It's very unlikely that someone would show up with documented proof of ownership. I don't think hearsay evidence would do it."

Bud removed his truck key from his pocket and inserted it into his right ear. He worked it around and pulled it out. Finding nothing of immediate interest, he stuck it back into his pants.

Moochie threw him a look of disgust. "Bud, stop it! What if you puncture a hole in there and what's left of your brain spills out?"

Bud ignored her. "Sounds like we've got a good chance of keeping the cash," he said. "Let's say it's ours. What's Uncle Sam gonna have to say about all this?"

Rube sat up and put his elbows on the table. "I can have my accountant look into it, give us all the tax ramifications, if you wish."

"We wish, honey. We don't want any trouble from the feds," said Moochie. "What worries me, is that nutcase across the street. There's no telling what he might do."

"That's a problem," said Steve. "The police can't do much without evidence, even if they wanted to."

"You all need to be very careful," said Rube. "Don't take any chances. Call the police immediately if he shows up at your house again. Bud, you have a permit for your gun, I hope."

"Yep. Sure do. I think if he tries anything else it will be here at the restaurant. He watches us like a hawk, and I'm sure he saw us move the safe in here. That's why I didn't put the money in the safe. But, it's in a good hiding place. I'll call Officer Waddell and see if they will keep a close eye on the place. I might have to start sleeping here myself."

CHAPTER TWENTY SIX

Bud tucked Ginger into bed, kissed her on the forehead and thought, thank you God for helping me find my daughter.

He returned to the master bedroom and found Moochie snoring softly. A half empty glass of milk and a praline wrapper lay on the bedside table. Thinking how lucky he was to have found this kind-hearted woman, he touched her lightly on the shoulder and kissed her cheek. She snuggled deeper into the covers and rolled onto her back causing the mattress springs to squeak in protest. Bud turned off her lamp and tip-toed around to the high side of the bed.

He crawled under the covers and lay on his back. Out of habit he locked his right arm and right leg over the side of the mattress to keep from rolling into Moochie. He had given up trying to sleep on his left side with nothing to hold onto. None of this bothered Bud; he was usually a sound sleeper. Tonight, however, he was worried. Not about the money. He felt it was well hidden. He was concerned about the fate of his fine feathered friend, Pretty Boy. He kept wondering, how would I cope if I were thrown in with three women? Was Miss Charmaine capable of tending four birds?

Even though he was awake, Bud was startled when the phone rang at six o'clock.

"Hello, this is Bud."

"Good morning, Mr. Bug. We've got a serious problem. Hope I didn't wake you, but having a man-bird around has driven my precious little girls crazy. They're acting like common street whores, fighting like cats and dogs over Pretty

Rod. Your bird took up with Sugar Plum and it looked like they got married and had their honeymoon all in a matter of minutes. The other two didn't like it one bit. They attacked Sugar Plum and Pretty Rod. Feathers are flying. Better get over here and pick him up before they kill each other.

Bud let go of the mattress and rolled into Moochie.

"Pretty Boy's in trouble. Got to go get him." He jumped out of bed and slipped into his trousers.

"Lord have mercy on my soul," said Moochie. "That bird's more trouble than he's worth."

When Bud arrived at Five Points he found Miss Charmaine standing at the door. A strand of gray hair fell over her right eye and both eyes were racing wildly. Her black silk housecoat was inside out. One green bunny-rabbit slipper was under her arm. The other was on her right foot, facing right.

She followed as he rushed past her into the study.

Pretty Boy cowered in one corner with a wing thrown up over his head. The three females were pecking at each other on the opposite side of the cage. Bud reached in and rescued his trembling bird. He held him against his neck and cheek. "It's all right, Boy. It's all right." Miss Charmaine kept throwing her hands into the air and shouting, "Is he okay, Mr. Boy? Is he okay?"

Finally, Pretty Boy said, "Gawk! Lord have mercy," and Bud knew things would work out. He reassured Charmaine.

*****

The week before Pretty Boy's trial was hectic, to say the least. Lawyer Phelps had insisted on a jury trial rather than a simple hearing before Judge Crocker. "Our chance will be much better with a jury because, if I'm not mistaken, the public will be on our side."

They had gotten the report of findings from Dr. Marquad that Pretty Boy was free from any disease or condition that might be harmful to the public, and the doctor agreed to testify in court.

Other witnesses for the defense would be a second avian specialist from Duke University, Moochie and Bud, Rube, Sam and possibly Clint Eastwood who was to be in Atlanta and might slip away long enough to drive to Athens. Lawyer Phelps was amazed that Clint would have any interest in a case like this and knew the chance of him attending was slim.

Brad Leaptrott and his covey of animal lovers were primed and ready to go. Their encounter with Wilson Lumkin had fired them to a fever pitch. Demonstrations were staged each day leading up to the trial. They wore Parrot's Rights and Save Pretty Boy T-shirts and carried placards made by Brad, Peola and April. Each day they marched from Moochie's Place on Clayton Street to The Arches; entrance to the University of Georgia. On the way they picked up other students who had an hour or two to spare and were hoping to be distracted from their studies.

Slapper Slocum and his wife, Carly, were busy selling and shipping shirts with Pretty Boy's picture on the front and "Save Pretty Boy," as well as other sayings, on the back. Carly spoke proudly of her role in getting the business started, telling anyone who would listen, "My husband is a smart business man. I always knew we would be successful, it was just a matter of time." Slapper always grinned and looked the other way, remembering how she had warned him against going into business for himself and even separated from him for a while.

Pretty Boy's plight was now a national human interest story, especially for animal lovers. Consequently, reporters from all over the country filled the local hotels. Everyone and his brother in Athens and the surrounding countryside were interviewed, including Pretty Boy. The bird showed off his impressions and sang "God Bless Ameri ---" all week. Bud took him to the back room two or three times a day to get him away from the crowds.

The restaurant was packed most of the time and some even drifted across the street to Lumkin's place. Moochie hired two students as temporary workers. Bud told Moochie, "We're gonna have to stop telling people how good my ribs are, or buy the whole city block and turn it into a restaurant."

Wilson Lumkin was sick with envy. He welcomed the new customers, but spent a lot of time in his office brooding and scheming how he might get the money from the low-lives across the street. One way or the other he would do it. They would not be allowed to keep his family's money.

Lawyer Steve Phelps became an overnight celebrity. The *Banner-Herald* printed his biography, and a long article about him and Pretty Boy in its "Living Section" on Tuesday. He complained of having no time to work on the case because of all the interviews.

Pretty Boy sensed that something special was happening and basked in the spotlight as any good celebrity should. Bud told Moochie, "Pretty Boy seems more content now than he has ever been, having found true love with Sugar Plum. I know he can't wait to become a real daddy just like me."

*****

At ten o'clock on Friday morning, Judge Crocker, a heavy-set man with white hair, slammed his gavel and the trial to determine Pretty Boy's fate as a greeter began. The judge was an impatient man. He constantly tapped his fingers on the ornate mahogany bench in front of him or caressed his gavel; sometimes gripping it as though he would like to throw it at whoever was delaying the procedures of the court. Would Pretty Boy remain outside Moochie's Place or be allowed to come inside and enjoy the warmth and music? More importantly, would the constitutionality of the local law be called into question strongly enough to eventually lead to greater rights for animals? Phelps, realizing that the constitutionality was entirely up to the judge and that this was not a major case, the best he could hope for was to set a precedent for future cases.

Lawyer Ashley Jennings represented the Athens-Clarke County Solicitor's Office. A well-proportioned lady who appeared to be in her middle thirties, she wore a generous amount of Banana Republic fragrance designed to relax the jury and make them feel at peace with the world. It worked for all except the foreman who had suffered from allergies since childhood. His eyes produced copious tears which he transferred by hand to the side of his pants. Thinking he was crying, the female juror next to him reached over and patted his shoulder.

Jennings opened with a statement about the importance of having local control over restaurants and other establishments within the county. She recited a history of how the *Rules and Regulations Food Service* for the Clarke County Health Department were drawn up and adopted by the Athens-Clarke County Unified Government. Then, she read portions of Chapter number 290-5-14 pertaining to the exclusion of live animals from within food service establishments. When finished, she smiled sweetly at the judge and made her way back to her seat. The judge's eyes followed her all the way back to the prosecution table.

Judge Crocker regained his composure, turned to the defense table and said, "Lawyer Phelps, please give your opening statement."

Phelps was still admiring Ms. Jennings when Moochie slapped him on the back. He coughed, turned red because of his thoughts, stood and walked toward the jury. Half way there, he abruptly turned, went back and got his note cards. Some of the six jury members and one alternate snickered. Obviously, this was his first court case. Moochie rolled her eyes as Lawyer Phelps began while Judge Crocker tapped his fingers.

"Your Honor, members of the jury, I believe this trial will go down in history alongside the Scopes Trial of 1925 in Dayton, Tennessee, regarding the relationship between animals and human beings. And further, we will show that animals have rights that are just as important as those that we enjoy.

"As a nation of God-fearing people, we have never been able to come to grips with the right relationship between people and animals, even our fellow mammals. We have slaughtered them by the billions, fed them full of hormones, antibiotics and who knows what else. Why? So that we can fill our bellies and our pockets. Does that sound fair to you?" He looked at each member of the jury individually.

"Our Founding Fathers, when they wrote the Constitution, spoke of the rights of people, but never mentioned animals. Does that mean that animals have no rights, or that they should not be treated humanely? I think not. It means only that those great men expected us to be wise enough to treat the animals fairly. I ask you, ladies and gentlemen of the jury, if you had an animal at home, would you put it outside to suffer in the cold of winter and the withering heat of a Georgia summer? That's what you will be asked to decide and I know that you will take this opportunity to say no to this cruel and inhumane treatment of our fellow creatures. After all, we are all part of God's creation. Ask yourself, what would God have me do?" Steve bowed his head and conjured up a tear that trickled down his cheek. He walked over, sat down and leaned his head against Moochie's shoulder. Moochie reached across, caressed his head and whispered, "Steve, honey, we're trying to get Pretty Boy back in the restaurant, not win an Academy Award."

Ron Harris was the first witness for the prosecution. He did the original inspection of the restaurant, and had handled the complaint of Pretty Boy being kept inside Moochie's Place. Ms. Jennings established his credentials by having him recite his education and the fact that he had served as an inspector for the past fifteen years. He gave his account of what happened when he went to the restaurant to enforce the law.

Lawyer Phelps cross-examined the witness. "Mr. Harris do you own a bird?"

"No, but I have a bird feeder outside my window. Yep, sure do, yeah, yeah, yeah, yep, I have a feeder."

"Do you think birds are pretty?"

"Yes I do. Yep, yep, yep, pretty."

"Is Pretty Boy pretty?"

"Why --- yep, I guess I'd have to say pretty. Yep, yep, yep."

"Would he add to the beauty of a room?"

Pretty Boy, sitting on the other side of Bud, fluffed out his feathers and said, "Gawk! I love you."

The jury laughed and Mr. Harris blushed. "Yes, of course he would. Yep, yep, yep."

Judge Crocker, still grinning, said, "Mr. Phelps, please see that the animal in question remains quiet."

"Yes, Your Honor." He glanced at Bud who put his finger over his lips and stared at Pretty Boy.

Phelps continued the cross examination. "Mr. Harris, would you be afraid to go to Moochie's Place if Mr. Boy was there?"

"Why no, I've been there many times. Yep. Sure have."

"Have you ever known anyone who became sick because of Mr. Boy's presence?"

"Nope. No, no, no. Sure haven't."

"Do you think Mr. Boy is a smart bird?"

Ms. Jennings jumped to her feet, "Your Honor, I object. This line of questioning has nothing to do with the law that says birds are not allowed in restaurants."

"Your Honor, I plan to show that parrots are just as smart as some human beings and, therefore, should have equal rights," said Phelps.

Judge Crocker rubbed his hand across his forehead.

"Objection overruled. You will be allowed to continue for now."

"Now, Mr. Harris, please answer the question."

"Well, yes, he's a smart bird. Sure is."

"Is he as smart as some human beings?"

Mr. Harris thought for a minute and eyed Pretty Boy who jumped from one foot to the other and flapped both wings.

"Smart? You bet," he blurted. The jury laughed and Judge Crocker covered his mouth. "I guess he is smarter than some people. Why, I remember once in high school, Homer Carlisle brought a note that he had to miss school that afternoon because he had to be a ball-bearing in a funeral. Yep. Yep. Yep. Sure did. Yeah, yeah, yeah, yep. Said it was his great, great grandmother who had been dead for twenty years. So, I guess I'd have to agree that he's smarter than some people."

The judge wanted to laugh, but felt his control slipping and put on a stern face. "Mr. Harris, please just answer the question."

"Yes, Your Honor, yep, yep, yep."

"One last question," said Phelps. "How many complaints have you had about Mr. Boy being in the restaurant?"

"Just one by----. Whoops. Can't say. No sir, can't say."

"Can't say or won't say? Mr. Harris, the complaint record from your department is on file with this court and it shows that the complaint was filed by Mr. Wilson Lumkin. Is that correct?"

"Yes, sir. Lumkin, yep, yep, yep. Sure was."

Ms. Jennings called her next witness, Mr. Wilson Lumkin. She asked him about his education, his business, his involvement in the community and charitable events. Through questioning, she established that he was a good, law abiding citizen who was concerned for the health and safety of the people of Athens.

Moochie and Wilson Lumkin glared at each other across the courtroom as Phelps rose to cross examine.

Pretty Boy said, "Gawk! Hereeee's trouble."

Bud said, "Shissh," and slipped Pretty Boy a peanut from his pocket. Lumkin shifted his glare to Pretty Boy.

"Mr. Lumkin, are you a hunter?"

"Yes." He smirked and crossed his arms.

"What do you hunt?"

"Deer, pheasant, quail."

"I see, so you hunt birds. Do you enjoy killing birds, Mr. Lumkin?"

"I love it," said Lumkin as he threw a cold stare at Pretty Boy. The students who had managed to squeeze into the courtroom booed.

"Quiet, or I will clear this courtroom," said Judge Crocker.

"Mr. Lumkin, is there bad blood between you and Mr. Boy?"

"What is this Mr. Boy stuff?" yelled Wilson. "He's not a person. He's just a dumb bird for Christ's sake!"

"I must ask you to refrain from that kind of language and just answer the question," said the judge.

Wilson's blood pressure receded, his red face turned pale and his shoulders relaxed.

"Mr. Lumkin, let me re-phrase the question, have you ever made an obscene gesture toward Mr. Boy?"

"No. I was just using my finger to open the door after Moochie Dunlop slapped my face."

"I see. Did you slap Mrs. Dunlop first?"

"Your Honor, I object. This has nothing to do with this case," said Lawyer Jennings.

"Objection overruled," said Judge Crocker. "Your witness mentioned the slapping and may be cross-examined about it."

"Thank you, Your Honor," said Phelps. "Mr. Lumkin, please answer the question."

"Yes, after she insulted me," sneered Lumkin.

"No further questions," said Phelps.

Lawyer Jennings rested the prosecution's case.

Phelps called Dr. Marquad to the stand to support his office records showing that Pretty Boy was perfectly healthy, and that, in his opinion, no threat to the public.

Dr. Finkbinder from Duke University was the next defense witness. He had done a study showing that parrots on average, have the intellect of three to five year old children. Some were smarter than others.

"Are you saying that a parrot's intellect goes beyond just repeating what they hear?"

"Yes, in my opinion they are able to respond to what people say and even how people feel. This was well established by years of research done by Professor Irene Pepperberg as related in her book, *Alex and Me.*

Steve Phelps called Rube, Sam, Bud and Moochie to establish pretty Boy's character, intelligence and the fact that he was clean.

Moochie created a stir when she was called. Being an un-official candidate for the highest office in the land, she was now a celebrity. There were very few people in Athens who did not know her and most of them had survived a hug.

As she walked to the stand, she waved at and spoke to the members of the jury, calling some of them by name.

Officer Waddel was the security guard in the court room that day. He was standing by the jury box trying to maintain his dignity when Moochie approached.

"Hey, Officer Waddel, how's your sore back? Looks like you might need another healing squeeze."

Before he could react, Moochie engulfed him, lifted him off the floor and gave him a good shake. There was an audible "crack" from his low back. She set him down. "There, now, don't that feel better?"

"Yes, ma'am, sure does. Thanks Miss Moochie."

Rube, a chiropractor, cringed, bent forward and covered his face.

Judge Crocker who had also been hugged by Moochie at one time, tried to maintain the dignity of the court. "Mrs. Dunlop, please take the stand."

"Yes, Your Honor. Say, Judge, I haven't seen you in Moochie's lately. Come on in at lunch time and get you a slab of Bud's ribs."

The judge's mouth watered at the thought, but he said in a solemn manner, "Mr. Phelps, please continue with this witness."

Moochie sat down in the witness chair and tried, unsuccessfully, to cross her legs. She was wearing her new periwinkle blue moo moo and had covered her face and hands with one of her favorite lotions, IMMENSITY, hoping it would be strong enough to capture the attention of the jury.

Phelps sneezed, stepped back and began, "Miss Moochie, please tell us why you are challenging this law."

"Steve, honey, you're the lawyer. You ought to know. If it'll help, I'll tell you again. We think this law is unfair because it keeps Pretty Boy, who's an important part of our business from being inside so he can greet and mingle with our customers. He likes to hear the music and sing along with the rest of us. Sometimes he even dances to a song if it's someone he really enjoys, like Ray Charles. It breaks my heart to see him outside when it's so hot, or cold in the winter."

"Why do you feel this is unfair to birds?"

"Because it bans all animals, but it specifically mentions birds and turtles. That ain't right, honey. It's discrimination if I've ever seen it. And, it allows those mean old lobsters to be in a restaurant. Did you ever see how they have to tape their claws together so they won't kill each other. Seems like they ought to ban them bad boys instead of birds and turtles. Who ever heard of a turtle hurting anyone? Well---maybe the Snapping Turtle."

"Mrs. Dunlop please limit your answers to the question," said Judge Crocker.

"Certainly, Your Honor. It's just that I been reading about them lobsters and how mean they are."

Phelps flattened his hand and motioned downward, hoping Moochie would take the hint. "Miss Moochie, please tell us why you think this law is unconstitutional."

"Well, Steve, honey, as you know them foundering fathers way back there in 1776 said they was tired of them British telling us what to do, so they huddled together in Philadelphia and just told them straight out that we weren't taking it no more. And, them soldiers, they was walking around barefooted, and they was ice all over the ground, and them boys had no shoes. The river was ice cold, but Washington rowed them across and they beat up the British army. That's what gave us the freedom to do what we want to in America. Anyway, that's what they told us in my eleventh grade history class."

When Pretty Boy heard this off-repeated word, he broke out in song, "God bless Ameri--. Land that I love. Stand beside her---." The jury and the audience stood up and sang along. The judge was unsure how to regain control without appearing unpatriotic.

Bud sensed the judge's displeasure, reached in and grabbed Pretty Boy and made a loud "shissshing" sound. He whispered under his breath, "Be quiet, Boy, you're pissing off the judge."

The judge regained his composure. "Ladies and gentlemen, this is the last warning. You must remain silent or I will ask you to leave."

Phelps waited for the hush to settle over the courtroom and continued. "Miss Moochie, why is Mr. Boy important to your business?"

"Why my goodness, Steve---, I mean Mr. Phelps, sometimes I think people come in just to see and talk to Birdbrain---, I mean Mr. Boy. Fact is, some of them have told me just that. Of course, the big thing is Bud's ribs, smothered in his special sauce." Hearing that, Bud's chest popped out and he leaned back in the swivel chair almost tipping over.

Phelps directed Moochie to step down. On their way back to the defense table he whispered to Moochie, "Is Mr. Eastwood here?"

"Don't know. Sam's outside the court room waiting for him."

"Mr. Phelps do you have any other witnesses?" Phelps turned and looked just as Sam stuck his hand in with a thumbs up.

"Yes, Your Honor, I have a special character witness that I wish to call at this time. I call Mr. Clint Eastwood."

It was as though an electric shock had been released in the courtroom. Everyone, including the judge, jury and Lawyer Jennings bolted to their feet as the famous actor strode to the witness stand. There was buzzing like a thousand bees let loose. Clint gave Pretty Boy a mock salute as he went by. Pretty Boy responded with a saying from one of Clint's movies, "Do you feel lucky, punk?" Everyone laughed and Clint couldn't help but smile.

Clint was sworn in by the clerk whose hands were shaking so badly she almost dropped the Bible.

Phelps said, "Mr. Eastwood, I know you are on a tight schedule, so I'll keep my questions to a minimum. Please, just tell us how you met Pretty Boy and why you think he should be allowed in Moochie's Place."

Clint related how he had first read about Pretty Boy disrupting a wedding. Then, he saw the bird on television and later on the *Tonight Show* with Johnny Carson. "My agent called and tried to get Pretty Boy in one of my movies, but it never worked out. So, I've known him for a long time. I heard about him again when he was birdnapped and used one of my lines from *Dirty Harry*. I made contact again, and we've been friends ever since.

"As for why I think Pretty Boy should be allowed in the restaurant, I don't think he would be a threat to anyone and he would be a great asset to the owners. He's a born actor and loves to be around people. I think the rule is unfair in this case."

All of this was irrelevant, but Lawyer Jennings was enthralled by the presence of the great actor and sat silent. She declined to cross examine. Clint was dismissed and cheered out of the room.

Ms. Jennings recovered sufficiently for her closing. Her argument was organized, logical and sound, legally. Basically, she defended the statute in question as an honest effort by the county government to protect the health and welfare of the people of Athens-Clarke County.

Phelps tore his eyes from Ms. Jennings well-proportioned legs extending from her sleek business suit, and rose to his feet, more confident now. He scanned the courtroom to make sure he knew where April was seated. He glanced at his notes and began. "Members of the jury, thank you for being on the jury and serving Clarke County, The State of Georgia and the greatest country in the World, The United States of America."

Moochie rolled her eyes toward the ceiling and whispered to Bud, "He forgot to mention the Universe and the Cosmos." Bud grinned on one side.

Phelps continued, "This case will go down as one of the most important cases in this century concerning the rights of animals." He glanced at April to see if she caught the last statement.

"I think we have proven beyond reasonable doubt that Mr. Boy is healthy, free of disease and no threat to the people who enter Moochie's Place. Further, we have shown that he is well taken care of; his cage is cleaned daily. People are allowed to keep birds and other animals in their homes, even when there are small children present, with no threat to their health. Why not pass a law that requires all animals who are in restaurants to have a periodic physical examination instead of banning them completely. People carry diseases too. Should we ban them from being in restaurants? Finally, I think the way the law is written, singling out birds and turtles, goes against equal protection of the law in the Constitution. That is, if you believe, as I do, that animals have implied rights under our Constitution.

"I ask you, ladies and gentlemen of the jury, to look at Mr. Boy, confined to that cage day in and day out. The owners are forced to put him outside everyday under the sweltering sun, even if the thermometer rises above one hundred degrees." Pretty Boy was not paying attention to his lawyer, but rather pecking in his seed dish. Bud, realizing that Phelps was trying to gain sympathy, leaned over next to Pretty Boy's cage and whispered harshly, "Damn you, Birdbrain!" Pretty Boy immediately keeled over, his feathers slicked back and his feet sticking straight up in the air. There was a gasp from those in the court room who were watching Pretty Boy. Moochie who had not been told of the new trick Pretty Boy had been taught, jumped to her feet and screamed, "Lord have mercy, you've done killed our bird! Pretty Boy, please don't go! I take back all the bad things I've said about you."

The jury members turned to see what had happened and were horrified by the apparent demise of the defendant whose fate they were charged to decide.

The judge was totally flabbergasted. He motioned his law clerk to his side and whispered, "What in the hell are we supposed to do now? I've never had a defendant die in my court before. If we call 911, they'll think it's a joke. I can just see the EMTs trying to revive a bird. Damn!"

Bud was holding his head, asking himself why he had done such a stupid thing. There was only one thing to do now. He leaned next to the cage, said, "Good boy," and slipped a peanut next to Pretty Boy.

Pretty Boy miraculously came back to life, pecked at the peanut, gave a wolf-whistle and said, "Let's make love."

Phelps paused to allow the full impact of Pretty Boy's acting ability to impress the jury.

"Would you have this poor, almost human, creature continue to suffer? It's a wonder that his poor little brain has not already been cooked. Then, in the winter I've seen him standing outside, huddled against the metal bars, trying to keep from freezing to death." Pretty Boy jumped from one foot to the other, tilted his head to one side while looking at Phelps, then tilted his head to the other side, all the while chirping softly. Bud was caught up in Phelp's contrived and exaggerated fantasy, and half the jury had tears in their eyes. Moochie covered her mouth with her hand to keep from laughing.

Phelps appeared to collapse and caught himself on the railing which separated him from the jury. His cheeks were wet with tears. He took out his handkerchief and blew his nose, softly so as not to offend the jury.

"Your Honor, members of the jury, I rest my case."

He stumbled back to his chair and laid his head on the table. Bud reached across and patted his hand. Moochie leaned toward Phelps and whispered, "Suck it up Steve, they don't give Emmys to lawyers."

Judge Crocker instructed the jury and sent them out to deliberate.

CHAPTER TWENTY SEVEN

"I'm worried," said Bud.

"What are you worried about? We just won the case for Pretty Boy, or at least we'll get another look by the Mayor and County Commission. The judge says we have to obey the law, but he strongly recommends that the Commission consider making an exception in Pretty Boy's case. Besides that, we've got more money than we know what to do with. What more could you want?" asked Moochie as she handed him the cash box for the next day.

"Did you see the look on Lumkin's face at the trial? I've never seen such hate. When you add hate to a nut like that, there's no telling what might happen. I'm afraid he might break in here again; maybe hurt Pretty Boy."

"The police know we're suspicious about the creep. Maybe they'll keep an eye on the place. I'll call them right now."

"Okay, love, but, they can't keep an eye on every place in town. I think I'll stay here tonight, just to make sure."

"Suit yourself. Ginger and I will be safe at home. Make sure you call if anything happens." Moochie grabbed Bud with one arm and pulled him to her side. She rubbed his shoulder and kissed him on the cheek. "Don't worry, it'll be all right. I love you."

She plucked her jacket from the counter and yelled over her shoulder, "Come on, gingerbread girl, let's get on home."

The back room was fourteen by twenty-four with a twelve foot ceiling and drop-down stairs. The back walls were brick, framed and covered with drywall, painted sunflower yellow. The cinnamon brown, tiled floor sparkled like a new penny. A single door opened into a hallway. Immediately to the right was the outside door. The hallway to the left led to the kitchen door and on into the main part of the restaurant.

Bud cleaned Pretty Boy's cage and turned the television to channel sixty-two. *From Here to Eternity,* starring Burt Lancaster, Montgomery Cliff and Frank Sinatra was playing. Burt was lying on the beach with Deborah Kerr. "Gawk! Hot mama," said Pretty Boy.

Bud laughed. "Cool down, pal. I'm going to take a shower."

Bud came out of the restroom and settled down on the cot, head propped up on three pillows. Pretty Boy hopped down to the food dish and began pecking at his food. He then settled down on the lowest perch to watch Frank Sinatra die in his friend's arms. Being a TV addict, he had never liked a cover over his cage.

"Okay, pal, time to get some sleep," said Bud as he turned the sound down. He picked up the phone and dialed home.

"Hey, sweets. Just checking in on you all. How's that pretty little girl of mine?"

"She's just fine, honey. In her room and already sleeping, I think. We both miss you, Buddy Boy. Ginger's as smart as a whip. She gets her home work done in a flash so she can read her book."

"Takes after her old man," said Bud. "Genes will show every time."

"In that case, honey, I hope she never takes up that nasty tobacco chewing habit that you have. How's Birdbrain doing?"

"Fine, a new movie just started, starring Groucho Marks, so we'll probably hear that all day tomorrow."

"Any sign of trouble?"

"Not yet. I'm gonna try to get some sleep now. I'll call if anything happens. I love you and that little girl."

"Bud, she's thirteen years old now. You're gonna have to stop treating her like a child."

"I know, I know, but I love her so much, I want her to stay just like she is."

"Won't happen."

"I know, love. Call me if you need to."

Bud got up and checked the back door one last time. He lay on his back and said a prayer for the Lord to bless his family, even his sorry father who had abandoned him so many years ago. He laid his .38 Special under the cot within easy reach. The 45 cal. was at home with Moochie. He looked at Pretty Boy and said, "Goodnight, pal." Turning on his side, he went to sleep.

*****

At three-thirty, two figures dressed in black were dropped off on Thomas Street. They quickly faded into the shadows of the surrounding buildings. Within minutes they were behind Moochie's Place and found the phone line. The two locks on the back door were a push-over for professionals like them. They were there to get this job done and be out of town within minutes. Their instructions were simple. Find the two bags of money that Lumkin felt belonged to his family and bring them back to the pick-up point on Thomas Street. From there they would be driven to the location just outside of Bogart where they had parked their car. At that point they would be well paid, in cash, for the job.

If they could not find the money, they were to burn the place to the ground. If that happened, they knew Lumkin would be monitoring the police band radio. All they had to do was be at the pick-up point and be taken back to their car. Easy in, easy out and get paid well for it.

They entered the outside back door, took two steps to Pretty Boy's room and cracked the unlocked door. In the glow of the television they saw the cage and someone asleep on the cot. They pulled their .9 millimeter Berettas and motioned which direction each would take. They didn't account for Pretty Boy's acute hearing. At the first creak of the door, his head rotated and cocked to the left. As the thieves circled the room, he said, "Gawk! Lord have mercy!"

Bud sat straight up on the cot, but it was too late. Both of the men were on him with guns pointed at his head.

"Don't move. Don't even twitch or I'll blow your head off," said the taller thief.

Bud was paralyzed by surprise and fear, his hands clutching the thin blanket around him.

"Gawk! Heeere's trouble," said Pretty Boy.

"Shut that bird up!"

"Right," said his short, stocky helper as he lunged for the cage. He grabbed it with his gloved fingers wrapped around the metal spindles. Pretty Boy reacted quickly, striking hard with his black, curved beak. When the crook saw the hole and felt the blood seeping into his glove, he picked the cage up with both hands and slammed it into the television screen. Pretty Boy had dropped to the bottom of the cage in his "play-dead" mode. The screen exploded and the television died as Groucho was saying, "Well, Madam, don't get fresh with me, unless you want to of course." The spindles of the cage were bent and broken. Pretty Boy spilled onto the tile floor and lay still, stunned by the impact.

Bud was aghast and wanted to rush over and get Pretty Boy, but knew that would mean sudden death. "Please, please, mister, don't hurt my bird." Bud wasn't sure if Pretty Boy was hurt or playing dead.

"Forget the bird. We're here for the money. Where is it?"

"There ain't no money here," said Bud.

"Open the safe, right now, before I send a bullet through your brain."

"Honest, mister. I'll open it, but there ain't no money in it."

The tall one grabbed Bud by the pajamas and dragged him to the safe. "Open it and make it fast before I stomp the life out of your bird."

Bud, his brain trying desperately to remember the code for the safe, reached for the dial. Two-six-one-eight-three. Nothing happened.

"Hurry up, old man! We don't have all night. You better get it right this time or your bird is through." He motioned for his helper to get ready to stomp Pretty Boy who was beginning to come out of his act and recover from the shock of the impact.

"Please don't do that. I'll get it right this time. I promise!" Bud couldn't control his hands. He wrapped them around his body and held them tight under each arm pit. He prayed silently, Lord please help me. Calm my hands and give me the numbers.

He found the dial and held tightly to prevent the shaking. He said aloud, "Two-six-one-eight, no, seven, it's seven, not eight."

"Hurry up, fool. My patience is running thin."

"Okay! I've got it now. Two-six-one-seven-three." Please open, he prayed, placing his hands under his chin.

"Click." He pulled the handle and the door opened.

The tall man in command slapped Bud out of the way and stooped down to examine the safe. He yanked the nearly empty cash box out and spilled it on the floor. "Damn! What's this? I thought we were talking about real money. What did you do with the rest?"

He walked over to where Bud had been knocked to the floor and stood over him. "I ought to shoot you between the eyes right now."

Bud, holding his left hand in front of his face, said, "Please don't do that, mister. All we keep in there is change for the restaurant business tomorrow."

"Damn you," said the boss, as he slammed Bud's head with the Beretta. Bud collapsed, unconscious, blood pouring down his face. "Get the gasoline and douse this place down."

A few minutes later, his sidekick reported. "This place is ready for the torch. Let's do it and get the hell out of here! We still get paid whether we have the money or not."

"Right. Get ready, man. When I light this match, this old place will go up in a hurry. We'll need to move fast."

They got to the outside door before he lit the match and tossed it over his shoulder.

Pretty Boy hopped up on Bud's chest. "Gawk! I love you." The bird cocked his head from one side to the other and rotated it wildly as he watched the flames grow bigger. Not knowing what else to do, he spread his wings and lay flat against Bud's chest. Bud moaned and rolled his head back and forth, blood running into his left ear and to the floor. He felt Pretty Boy on his chest and reached up with his right hand as he opened his eyes to see if his friend was okay. He held onto Pretty Boy and rolled to his left side, propped onto his left elbow. The acrid smoke was already filling his lungs and he knew they only had minutes to get out. Staying low, he crawled toward the back door, cupping the bird in his right arm.

*****

Thirty minutes earlier Moochie had awakened suddenly. She turned on her side and tried to go back to sleep. She had drifted off to sleep thinking about Bud and Pretty Boy and they were still on her mind. Should I call him? She thought. I'd hate to wake him if he's sleeping soundly. Finally she sat up on the side of the bed. She shook her head. Something's wrong. She picked up the phone and dialed. Nothing happened. No ring. "What tha ---? No ring. No service. What's wrong? The line's been cut!"

She screamed, "Ginger, get up! Something's wrong. We've got to go check on your daddy."

*****

Two Georgia students, one being supported by the other, were walking to their loft after a party. "Look at that, man. There's smoke coming out of that building." He leaned his friend against a building, took out his cell phone and dialed 911.

"Hey, ma'am, there's a fire over here on Clayton Street."

"Thanks for calling. Please give me your exact location," said the operator.

"Let's see, we're on Clayton Street, just a minute, let me look. Yeah, we're on Clayton Street, near Jackson Street. Better hurry, looks like a bad one."

"Could you please give me your name?"

"Can't do it, ma'am. Had a couple drinks, might get in trouble." He slapped the cell phone shut.

*****

"Don't worry, Boy," coughed Bud, "we'll make it to the back door and get some air," as he half crawled and dragged himself along the floor. He held Pretty Boy close to his chest.

When they reached the metal back door it was engulfed in flames and too hot to touch. "Oh, no!" said Bud. He thought, I've got to get Pretty Boy some air or he'll never make it. "Lord, please help us," he pleaded. Looking through the haze over his right shoulder, he saw the clothes dryer. He crawled toward the dryer, moving Pretty Boy on the floor beside him. His friend was limp by now.

"It'll be all right, Boy. Don't you worry none. I'll get you outta here. I've got an idea."

He laid Pretty Boy on the floor, out of the way. He raised up, grabbed hold of the dryer and yanked it away from the wall. He tore at the clamp holding the flexible vent pipe to the dryer. Finally, it gave way. Bud grabbed Pretty Boy and pushed him, head first into the pipe. He reached in as far as his arm would stretch, trying to get Pretty Boy outside. "Go, Boy, go. Keep going. Get on outta here."

Bud looked, but could no longer see the door. He lunged toward where the door should be and crawled as fast as he could on the hot floor. I've got to get to the kitchen, get some water and douse myself down, he thought.

*****

When they reached the city limits, Moochie and Ginger heard a siren. "No! No! Please Lord, don't let it be the restaurant."

Ginger, in her pajamas, was curled up in the passenger seat, crying softly. "Are they going to be all right, Miss Moochie?"

"I hope so, honey. We'll be there in just a few minutes."

When they arrived in front of the restaurant, a fire crew was already there with their equipment in place. As Moochie and Ginger approached the front door, a fire fighter emerged from the building, coughing and holding his throat. "Can't get in there, Captain, too hot, too much smoke. Probably nobody in there."

*****

Bud made it to the kitchen sink. He turned the tap on and stuck his head under the cool water. He turned his head to the side and gulped, trying to get some air. Unable to open his eyes, he tore the drawers open searching for a towel. Finding one, he soaked it and threw it over his head. The flames were leaping at his pajamas. Chunks of flaming debris were dropping from the ceiling. He turned to make a dash for the front entrance, but his lungs had all they could take. He dropped to the floor on his knees and went into a coughing and choking spasm, clawing at his throat. He tried to crawl forward, but fell on his face and lost consciousness again.

*****

"My husband and Pretty Boy are in there. You've got to get them out."

The captain came over and shouted over the din, "Can't do it Miss Moochie. Too much heat and smoke. Can't risk a man's life. It would be almost certain death to send someone into that inferno."

"Then, I'll have to go in myself," said Moochie.

"Sorry, Moochie. I know how you feel, but I just can't allow it. You'd never make it."

"Well, honey, I don't care whether you allow it or not. Buddy Boy's in there and I'm going in. Gingerbread, you stay here and wait for us."

Captain Strock motioned for three of his firefighters to stand in front of the door as he pleaded with Moochie. "Please, please, don't make us have to keep you out by force. I don't want to do that, but it's just too risky. Don't you see?"

"Captain, you can move them boys out of the way or I'll go through them."

The three men didn't want to be there any more than Moochie wanted them there, and they cringed when she made her move. The first one stepped in front of her and she swiped him out of the way with her left arm. The other two grabbed her by the arms and tried to hold her back. She brought her arms together and they crumpled to the sidewalk.

Moochie grabbed an oxygen mask from the fireman who had already been inside and pulled it over her head. She moved quickly across the smoked-filled dining room, knowing exactly where the door was to Pretty Boy's room. The smoke was so thick she could see nothing, but she felt her way along the wall to the door. She pushed the mask up and screamed, "Bud! Where are you?" She could hear only the crackling of the fire and feel the heat through her shoes. Knowing she couldn't last long, she held her breath and pulled the mask down. She moved across the room to the cot. No Bud. She turned and stumbled back to the door.

The kitchen! They have to be in the kitchen, she thought. She began to cough violently and lifted the mask. Moving to the kitchen door, all she could manage was a whisper. "Bud?" She heard the water running over the crackling of the fire and staggered to the sink. She pulled the mask back down.

Her foot struck something. She fell to her knees and felt with her hands. "Bud!" she yelled into the mask. Working her arms under him, she stood up. She staggered against the sink and slid to the floor. Still holding Bud, she rolled onto her knees, ready to make another attempt to stand up. She stood again, but could feel herself losing consciousness. She stumbled once and caught herself. Things were swirling around in her head. Her massive body began to sway. She took two unsteady steps forward and felt her legs give way.

She fell into the arms of two of the firefighters she had knocked down. They caught her under each arm and half-carried, half-dragged them out. When they reached the front door, another fireman took Bud and slapped an oxygen mask on his face. Another helped put him onto a stretcher.

The captain who was holding a mask over Moochie's face, called for three others to help him get her to a stretcher.

After about five minutes Moochie came to and snatched the oxygen mask off. "Where's Bud? Is he all right?" She raised up and saw Ginger bent over Bud, crying. She rushed to their side. Bud lay unconscious with a blue tinge to his skin.

"Come on, honey. You can make it. Come on, Buddy Boy. I love you. Is he breathing? Tell me he's breathing."

"Yes, ma'am, he's breathing. It's shallow, but at least he's breathing. We need to get both of you on to the hospital, now."

"I'm all right, honey. Just take care of my sweet little man."

Moochie turned to Captain Strock and screamed, "Where's Pretty Boy!? Where's our bird? He's still in there! I've got to get him out."

She rushed the front door, but there were six firemen this time. They grabbed her and held her until she slumped to the ground. The young fireman who was holding her head up, brushed tears from his face.

CHAPTER TWENTY EIGHT

Bud woke up under the oxygen tent with a throbbing headache. Seeing the IV in his left arm, he reached across with his right hand and felt the bandage over his left eye. He moved one leg, then the other. His nose was dry and sore. When he turned his head to the right he saw Ginger asleep in the recliner. He tried to speak, but nothing came out. He closed his parched mouth and remembered the fire. He tried again. "Ginger," he whispered.

Ginger's eyes popped open and she jumped to her feet, her blonde pony tail flipping wildly. "Daddy, you're awake! Are you all right? I've been so worried about you. I must have fallen asleep. How do you feel?"

Bud whispered, "Not so good, sweetie. Where's Moochie?"

"She's in a room down the hall and doing really cool for all that she went through."

"What do you mean, all that she went through? What happened?"

Ginger took Bud's hand and squeezed it. "She saved your life, Daddy. You're not going to believe what she did."

"What's her room number? I want to go see her."

"You can't, Daddy. You just got out of intensive care this morning. Besides, the nurse told me you have to stay under the oxygen tent until you get better. I can take her a message if you want."

"Okay, babe. What happened?"

Ginger reached into the tent and handed him an ice chip, then pulled the straight-backed chair close to the bed. "Let me see, the first thing I remember is Mama Moochie screaming that we'd better go to the restaurant and check on you. She had tried to call and couldn't get through. We heard the sirens as we drove into town. The firefighters were already there. One of them had gone in to try and get you out and---." Ginger began to cry. "I was so scared, Daddy. I didn't know what to do. But Mama Moochie just knocked the firemen down and went into the fire to get you. I just knew I'd never see her or you again." She bent over and sobbed.

Tears formed in Bud's swollen eyes as he thought of Moochie's love for him; that she risked her life to save him. "Was she hurt bad?"

"No, sir. Nurse Jane says she'll be all right. Her throat and lungs may be damaged some, and she's got burns on her hands, arms and knees. But, she's awake and threatening to make trouble if they don't let her see you."

"Where's Pretty Boy?" asked Bud.

Ginger had already been asked that question by Moochie and knew it was coming. She said, "I don't know. He's missing. No one has seen him yet. Was he in the kitchen with you?"

Bud turned his head and tried to shake the fog from his brain. "No, baby, he wasn't in the kitchen." He re-ran what had happened before he passed out. "I remember holding Pretty Boy and crawling to the door, but it was too hot to open. I knew I had to get him out quickly. I---. I was trying to think of a way---. Oh! I know. I pushed him into the dryer vent, hoping he could get out. I've got to get outta here and go look for him."

"You can't, Daddy. You've got to be on the oxygen right now."

"Hand me that phone, little girl."

Bud took the phone and dialed Brad's cell phone.

"Brad here."

Bud whispered, "Pal, I need your help."

"Bud! Is that you? Where are you? Are you all right?"

"Yeah. I'll be okay. I'm at St Mary's and can't leave. The reason I called is I want you to do something for me. Pretty Boy's missing and I want you to find him." Bud coughed. Ginger spooned another ice chip into his mouth.

"Sure, boss. I came to work at six and found the burned-out building. They told me what happened. Can't believe it. Can't believe it. The fire is pretty much out. They're still dousing down the wall of the second building. Looks like it'll be okay. Where's Miss Moochie? Is she okay?"

"She'll be fine, they say," Bud said in a raspy voice. A fit of coughing overwhelmed him. It hurt so bad he had to stop speaking. Brad held the phone patiently while Bud recovered and whispered, "Can't talk much. Go to the back door. Just past the back door where the dryer vent comes out of the wall. Look for him in the vent first, but I hope he made it outside. Call me as soon as you can. Room 212."

*****

The entire scene was taped off by the police. Brad couldn't get through the burned out rubble of the building to the back door and had to go a short distance to the end of the block, then down the alley to where the door once stood. How in the world could that little bird survive something like this? He got as close as he could and looked around, then sat down on his haunches and prayed. "Lord, please help me find the words to tell Bud about Pretty Boy." He rose and looked again at the wispy smoke still rising from the remains of the building. He climbed over the debris, lifting partially burned boards and wet drywall, knowing full well that if he found the bird, he would be dead. He called out in desperation, "Pretty Boy, where are you? Come on Boy, speak to me," not really expecting a reply. Finally, he made his way back to the alley. He turned and looked once more before plodding back up the alley. He reached for his phone and began dialing the hospital number, thinking Lord, what am I gonna say to Bud?

As he passed two trash containers loaded with beer cans from the night before, he heard a rustling sound. He hesitated, then closed the phone and stuck it back into his pocket. Probably just a rat, he thought, but listened some more. He heard a scratching sound and a weak, "Peep." He pushed one of the garbage cans to the side and found Pretty Boy hunched down, wet and shivering.

"Boy! I can't believe it. You're alive!" He grabbed Pretty Boy and huddled him into the crook of his arm, warming him as he began walking, then running back to the front of the building. In front he saw Peola, Pinky and April holding each other and crying. He yelled, "Call the Animal Hospital. Boy's alive! I'm taking him in to be checked." As he pushed by them, April was on the phone calling as he had directed. "Peola, you call Bud at St Mary's, room 212. Tell him I've got Pretty Boy and am taking him to the hospital." He rushed on toward his car.

*****

Moochie's doctor, concerned about the stress on her heart, ordered an echocardiogram and stress test. To his surprise, she passed with flying colors and was released in three days with prescriptions for cough medicine and antibiotics. Bud stayed for a week. Ginger wouldn't leave the hospital and slept in Bud's room. Moochie brought her food and clothes, and either Peola, Pinky, April or Brad were there with her most of the time.

As Bud improved, he shared his suspicion about Lumkin with Brad. Bud said, "He wasn't with the two who did the job, but I don't doubt that he was behind it." He had given the police a description of the two crooks as well as he could remember, and told them the pair was looking for money. He didn't tell the police or Brad about the found money. It might have burned up in the fire, and that might not be a bad thing.

"That S.O.B!" said Brad. "How can someone do something like that? How can they let him get away with this? If I had my way, I'd---he curled his right hand into a fist and pounded it into his left palm."

"I feel the same way, my boy, but we can't go flying off the handle and get ourselves in trouble. Don't worry. He'll get his comeuppance, one way or the other."

Tony Colosimo called Moochie to see if he could help.

"Well, honey, I guess there's nothing anyone can do right now. We have insurance and we'll just have to rebuild. In the meantime, I worry about all of our good customers like you. All of ya'll will be skinny little creatures with knobby knees and elbows by the time we get things up and running again."

"Don't worry about us, we'll be fine. Just get yourself well. Who was behind this, Miss Moochie?"

"I don't have no proof, but I'm betting it was that Lumkin fella across the street."

"In New York we don't put up with people like him. He'd better be careful or he might find himself face to face with Jimmy Hoffa," said Colosimo.

"No, honey, we don't want something like that. We'll just have to hope the police can come up with some proof."

*****

Moochie called Rube to ask his advice, and to thank him for insisting that they insure the buildings. Rube assured her that he would help her through rebuilding an even better restaurant.

Although the fire was being investigated by the police and the State Insurance Commissioner as arson, there was little evidence and no eyewitnesses stepped forward.

The people of Athens and, indeed, people from all over the country were stunned and outraged over what had happened. They demanded that something be done, and the Police Department took a lot of heat. The reward from the state, added to the money offered by the people, amounted to thirty thousand dollars for information leading to an arrest.

*****

Brad told Moochie, "Don't you worry about Pretty Boy. The avian vet said he would keep him about three more days. I'll pick him up and bring him home. I know he'll require a new cage, just tell me what else he needs and I'll get it."

"Thanks Brad. Just try and find a cage like the one he had. I'll ask Sam to help me find the food and other things for our precious bird." Moochie insisted that the employees continue to receive their pay, just as though nothing had happened. She asked Brad to pass it on to the rest of the crew.

*****

Clint Eastwood called, "If you and Bud or Pretty Boy need anything, and I mean anything, just let me know."

"Clint, honey, you're a sweetheart. You've done so much for us already. You're a true friend and we love you. I promise to let you know if there's anything you can do."

Moochie missed the weekly *Lay it on Grady Show*, and the phone lines were flooded with offers to help. Grady assured his audience that the great lady was doing okay and would be back soon. He told them of her heroic effort to save Bud and said, "There is no way you're going to keep someone like that down. Believe me, Moochie will be back. All she wants is your prayers."

*****

Aides of the other two presidential candidates called to express their concern. Moochie told them, "Honey, you tell your boss not to worry about me. Just tell him to be concerned about this country and what needs to be done."

*****

Brad called the employees together and they decided to continue working, but now they would be cleaning and repairing the second building, getting it ready to re-open.

The inside of the original building was pretty much destroyed by the fire or water damage. All drywall and/or plaster and the floors had to be redone. The electric and heating and air systems would have to be replaced. All cabinets, booths, including Moochie's office, were too far gone to save. Whoever they hired to rebuild would have to deal with the Historic Preservation Society about those things.

Sadly, the jukebox was damaged, perhaps beyond repair and most of the old records were melted or warped. So far, no one had told Bud the bad news about his beloved jukebox and he was afraid to ask.

*****

Rube met with Moochie and Bud. "The first thing you need to decide," said Rube, "is whether you want to rebuild or move to another location."

"There ain't no doubt about that, honey. We want to stay there. We're not going to desert our people. Ain't that right, sweetie?"

Bud cleared his ear with his little finger while reaching for his tobacco with his other hand. He took a pinch and placed it behind his lip.

"Well, Lord-a-mercy," said Moochie, "hold the presses, the grand proprietor is about to speak." She gave him a friendly slap on the back causing him to cough, almost swallowing the tobacco.

Bud recovered and grinned on one side, leaning back in his chair. "As I see it, from a business man's point of view, our restaurant was a big success in the present location, so why change it?"

"Hallelujah!" said Moochie. "Now, the world can go back to its normal pace. I suppose you and Uncle Billy will want to be supervising the whole thing."

"That's right. Someone with good sense and experience has got to be in charge."

Rube laughed. "All right, I'll get an architect to draw up the plans and we'll get started as soon as possible. In the meantime, what do you want to do, just rest?"

"Hell no, we've already had too much rest. Ain't that right, my sweet little man?"

"That's right. All I need is a stove and we'll be back in business."

"I know a good re-modeler who can probably build you a temporary kitchen in the back of the second building. He knows how to comply with all of the fire and health codes. Of course, you wouldn't have as much space to serve people, but you could keep things going. Want me to look into that?"

"I think I can speak for both of us, honey. That's a big hell yes!" said Moochie.

"Okay, will do." Rube paused and looked at both of them.

"Yes---what's on your mind, honey? Spit it out."

"I just wondered about the money. Did the crooks get away with it? Did it survive the fire?"

Bud looked at Moochie, then back to Rube. "Yep. The money is fine, I think," said Bud. "I'll have to look and make sure as soon as I'm able, but the wall where the money is located was undamaged and was declared stable by the building inspector. We've talked about it and wondered if you could check into fixing us some kind of foundation or something like that?"

"I'll talk to my accountant and lawyer Phelps about it; see what they have to say. I'll get Phelps to look into it. What would you like to use the money for?"

Moochie and Bud looked at each other. She put her arm around her husband and said, "We're so proud of Bud's recovery from alcoholism that we would like to help that cause in some way. Also, it has been such a struggle for us trying to start a new business, we thought it would be nice to help others who have the courage to step out on their own. Ain't that right, Buddy Boy?"

Bud nodded.

CHAPTER TWENTY NINE

The night before Bud came home from the hospital, Moochie visited. Ginger was there. Moochie kissed Bud on the cheek and sat down on the front half of the recliner, being unable to slide all the way back. Ginger pulled up the chair from the corner.

"I hate hospitals," said Moochie. "There are too many sick people in here."

Ginger looked at her with a dumbfounded look on her face. "Duhhh. Mama Moochie, where else would you expect them to go?"

"I guess you have a point there, honey. But there are so many of them. They ought to organize themselves and demand more fun things to do, like playing cards, dancing or something like that. And, they ought to do something about the smell--- smells like everything has been sprayed with Lysol. You know what I mean?"

Ginger thought about rebutting, but just shrugged her shoulders. Bud grinned and took a sip of water. "I'll be glad to get home tomorrow. Getting tired of just laying around."

"Well, little man, we'll be glad to get you home, but there's not much to do there either. We need to talk about something. Is it all right if Ginger hears about the you-know-what that's hidden?"

Bud turned on his side and looked at them both. "I don't see why not, can't keep it from her forever."

Moochie stretched her legs out in front and crossed her ankles. "Want me to tell her, or you?"

"What's the big secret? Somebody tell me."

"I'll tell her, love. Come up here little girl and hold my hand."

Ginger ignored his reference to little girl and complied with a puzzled look on her face. "What's got into you two? What's this all about?"

"Now, I don't want you to get too excited; start screaming or anything. Just relax and I'll tell you. First, you can not tell anyone else. Don't ever mention it, even to us unless you're sure we're alone. Okay?" Ginger nodded.

"A while back we found some money hidden in the walls of the restaurant. A lot of money in canvas bags. So we hid it."

"Why? How much was it and why did you hide it?"

"Because we didn't know what to do with it or who it belonged to. So we decided to stash it until we could figure all that out. Come to find out, it probably belongs to us."

"Super!" said Ginger. "Why don't we go to the Mall of Georgia and spend some of it?"

"It's not quite that simple, honey," said Moochie. "There's a problem. Bonehead, across the street, better known as Mr. Lumkin to some, feels like the money belongs to him. At least that's what we hear through the grapevine."

"Why?"

"Claims his granddaddy put the money there many years ago," said Bud.

"Did he?"

"Don't know. No way to tell for sure. No way to prove it one way or the other. So, our thinking is, it belongs to us since we found it. See? It was clear that the two arsonists had clear instructions to burn the building if they couldn't find the money. That's how bitter he is."

"Yes. Why don't you just tell him that the money belongs to you?"

"He probably knows that, since we own both buildings. But, he's obsessed with finding that money. Seems like he'd do anything to get it, fact, we think he's the one who ran me off the road and almost killed me, and he's already broken into the restaurant before." Bud reached up and felt the bandage on his head.

"Is he the one who started the fire?" asked Ginger.

Moochie uncrossed her ankles and shifted her weight in Ginger's direction as the chair groaned. "Don't know for sure, sugar, but our guess is he's responsible. He might have paid someone else to do it."

"Well, like why don't the police lock him up?"

"Not quite that easy I'm afraid. The police are looking into it, but they have to have proof. If not, their hands are tied," said Bud.

Moochie said, "Anyway, right now we've got to find the money, see if it was damaged by the fire. I guess we'll have to bring it home since the construction people will be all over the place. What do you think, Buddy Boy?"

Bud turned onto his back and fluffed the pillows under his head. He reached for and took a drink of water. "I guess that's about all we can do. Should be okay since one of us will be home all the time. At least for now."

"Do you think he would come to the house to try and get the money?" asked Ginger.

"Don't know what this guy might do. He's a nut, but don't you worry. I'll have my gun handy," said Bud.

"You never told me how much money there is."

"Hold your hat, girl, it's a little over two million," said Moochie.

"Whoa! You're kidding!"

"Nope. Two million," said Bud. "It's been more trouble than it's worth, really. That's why we decided to put it to good use; set up a foundation."

"What do you mean, good use. Why, it won't be but a couple of years before I'll need a car. And like some of the girls at school have nicer clothes than I do. I could help you spend that money."

Bud grinned and looked at Moochie. "Better explain what we're going to do with it, love."

When she finished they sat in silence for a moment. Bud said, "I don't see how either your mama or me would be able to see if that money is still where I put it, or burned up in the fire."

"You're right about that, honey. I sure couldn't get up in that attic."

Ginger broke in, "Well, where in the world did you hide it? I can climb up in the attic. Just tell me what to do."

"Don't know about that. Might be too dangerous for my little girl," said Bud. "It would have to be done at night when there are no people."

"I bet we could get Rube to help. He already knows about the money," said Moochie.

"Good idea," said Bud. "We can call him when I get home, talk things over, see what he thinks we should do."

"Okay. I'll call him tonight."

*****

Rube didn't mind. He took Ginger with him. Bud had given strict instructions about the location, where the rope was tied and how to pull the money up. Bud and Moochie waited in the car.

Ginger was in charge of the flashlight. As they pulled the steps down to the attic Rube said, "Wait 'til we get into the attic before you turn the light on so we don't attract attention from the outside."

Bud had laid down plywood on the joists around the opening. From there they would be on their own.

"Okay, Ginger, turn the light on. We have to be very careful so we don't fall through the ceiling. Hold onto the rafters or braces, whatever you can reach. We'll have to go slow."

Young Ginger began to shake and the flashlight jumped around.

"What's wrong? Are you all right?"

"I'm scared, Mr. Rube. I can't help it."

"That's okay, girlie girl. Don't worry about it. Just sit back here on the plywood and shine the light in front of me. In fact, that might be better. We won't get in each others' way."

Ginger sat and crossed her legs. She braced one hand with the other to hold the light steady.

Rube made his way forward and to the right side of the attic, as directed by Bud. It was a flat roof so there was plenty of headroom. At times he had to bend over and make his way under a support. Concentrating on where his feet went, he didn't see the nail that had been driven all the way through a two by four. When he grabbed for the board, the nail dug into the palm of his hand. He yelped "Ouch!" jerked his hand away and began to fall. He thrust his left foot out and stepped on the next joist, but there was nothing to grab onto and steady himself. He fell forward into the insulation, but was able to spread both arms out and catch himself on the joists so he didn't fall through the ceiling and into the restaurant below.

Ginger screamed, "Mr. Rube, are you all right?"

Rube got his hands on both joists and raised himself up, placing one foot on each side. He sputtered, trying to spit the insulation from his mouth. He reached for the brace again, avoiding the nail this time. "I'll be all right," he affirmed as he wiped his face with a shirt sleeve. After a minute, "Okay, I'm ready, shine the light out front."

He made his way to the side of the attic where he found the rope tied to a brace. He loosened the knot and gave a hard tug. There was little resistance and he called out, "Doesn't feel like there's anything attached." He peered into the opening of the wall. "Hey, girlie girl, pitch me that flashlight." Ginger did as told and the flashlight hit Rube on the leg and fell into the insulation. He dug around and found it, then shined the light into the opening.

Ginger yelled, "Can you see the bags?"

"Yeah, looks like two big lumps."

"Well, like that must be the money Papa Bud talked about?"

"Maybe so. I'll give it another try." He grabbed the rope and pulled the slack out, then felt the full weight of whatever was attached. When he got it to the top, he opened one bag to make sure. "Hey, girlie girl. Looks like it's all here and there are no burn marks. I'll bring one bag at a time across to the opening. You can help me haul it to the car."

When they got home, Ginger helped Bud and Moochie stuff the money bags under their bed and Bud placed his pistol on the nightstand within easy reach.

CHAPTER THIRTY

In two weeks every inch of the remaining building had been swept, mopped, dusted and cleaned. Peola, Pinky, Brad and April had never worked so hard nor enjoyed it so much. Each one loved and felt obligated to Moochie and Bud in one way or another. Getting the undamaged building ready to open was an opportunity to express their appreciation. They became bonded as never before, through their unspoken feelings for their heroic bosses.

Brad brought his music box in and set it up in the corner. They were accustomed to working with music, and it made them more comfortable. Still, it was not the same as having the jukebox going full blast. "I hate to admit it, but let's be honest," said Brad. "We all fell in love with the music Bud likes so much."

April laughed hard, then snorted like a hog thrown an ear of corn. "Yeah, I guess we did. We knew every word of most of those songs."

Moochie and Bud hobbled in from time to time to check on the place. Bud couldn't wait to get back and lord over the building of the new temporary kitchen, as well as the reconstruction of the original building. On one occasion he remarked, "Damn, it's like a tomb in here with no 'real' music. What are we gonna do about that?" He still couldn't bring himself to go next door and look at the remains of the old jukebox. Moochie felt sad because she didn't have an answer for him.

Slapper Slocum came in one day, looked around and sat down to watch them work. He chose the corner so no one would be able to sneak up behind him.

Pinky said, "Lord-a-mercy, Mr. Slapper, what in the world are you doing sitting in that corner, slapping your jaw?"

"Sorry, Miss Pinky, the fire has made me so nervous I must have reverted back to my old habits. I miss the old place so much. It was one of the few places, besides my own store where I felt safe. I miss seeing my good friends, Moochie and Bud. They've been so kind to me. In fact, Moochie saved my life and my marriage."

"Shucks, Mr. Slapper, I know what you mean about them two. They saved my fat and sassy self too. Sure did. Gave me a job and everything. I love 'em to death. Now, you get over here and pour yourself a cup of this fresh coffee and grab one of them float-on-a-cloud biscuits. They's some grape jelly right next to 'em. Slather some of that on and you'll be back on top of this old world. See if you ain't."

Slapper covered up a smile and sauntered over to the newly-built counter, glancing at the street to make sure there were no spies or terrorists outside. "Can't be too careful now days," he said, to no one in particular.

*****

In the afternoon, Tony Colosimo came in for coffee, and looking for someone to talk to. April was bent over cleaning the coffee counter, swaying back and forth to the strains of "You've got Cheating on Your Mind." She wore a Banana Republic shirt, tucked into tight jeans, secured by a web leather belt. Tony watched for a moment, then said, "Hello, April, we could use someone like you back in New York, to keep things tidied up I mean."

She raised up and smiled broadly. "Sorry, I'm not going anywhere where they don't have grits with butter and sugar in the morning."

"How's Bud and Moochie? I know they need some time off after what they went through, but was hoping I might see them today."

"Shoot! Those two are doing just fine. You couldn't hog tie them and keep them down. Bud says he'll be back in here on Monday cooking ribs and moochieburgers."

"I hope so. I miss the way it was. This is my home away from home. I still miss the Big Apple though. Nothing like the streets of New York."

"Not for me. I'm not a big city girl. Maybe Arizona, New Mexico or some place like that. How's your wife and kids?"

Tony picked up his coffee cup and leaned forward. "April, please don't mention this to anyone else. I got word from my wife that she wants a divorce. Says she can't take it anymore, living alone, taking care of the kids, working. She's met another man and wants to move on with her life. Can't say that I blame her. It's been so long and if I go back up there, I'd be dead in a matter of days."

April reached and patted his hand. "You poor thing. I'm sorry. Sounds like you need a new start in life, a new beginning. You lost your first wife too, didn't you?"

"Yeah. That was a disaster. I was young and in way over my head. I couldn't keep up with that one. Then, she had a son with blond hair. She has dark brown and I have black hair. There's never been a blonde in my family. Something didn't add up, so I just picked up, left Louisiana and went back to New York. I still don't know what the whole story was about that."

"Have you seen her or the baby since then?"

"Nope. Never have, but I do wonder what happened to them."

April leaned in. "Now might be a good time to find out. Looks like you're gonna be free. Just for your information, I read in *Good Housekeeping* that two dark-haired people can have a child with blonde hair. Something to do with genes."

Tony pushed his cup forward. "Fill her about half full." His eyes glazed over briefly as his mind considered what April had said. What if---? "I don't know, April. Guess I'll need time to think. Maybe there is a chance."

She thought it best to change the subject. "Me and Steve are still going out, but for a lawyer, he sure is shy. He's a nice guy, but I don't want to push him. What do you think?"

"I don't know much about lawyers, although I've been in the courtroom with a few, but if he's like most men, he needs some space. Let him make up his own mind. Things will work out better that way. That's just a little advice from someone who grew up on the streets of New York, for what it's worth."

"Maybe you're right, but I can't wait around forever." She smiled, turned and walked to the coffee maker while Tony visualized wild bedroom scenes with Caresse, his first wife.

*****

Sam spent a lot of time at Moochie's house for several reasons. One being Mama Moochie had raised him and they were bonded like mother and son. Bud was fun to be around and they both liked country music. When his father, Rube, and stepmother, Amy, weren't traveling for the business, they came to see Moochie and Bud often, knowing that Sam was likely to be there. It gave Sam more than his allotted time each week to spend with his dad and stepmother whom he loved a lot. But, the overriding reason was that he and Ginger were good friends, they went to school together, listened to music together and really enjoyed each other's company. Each fourteen, they confided in each other about things that adults might not understand.

One day Moochie picked Ginger and Sam up from school. Returning to the house, she pulled alongside the mailbox. She snatched the mail and pitched it to Sam, "Bring that in for me, honey."

Sam browsed through the envelopes as they drove up the driveway. One caught his eye. The return address said Station KRLG, Nashville, TN. "Mama Moochie! Here's a letter from Nashville. Can I open it? Maybe it's about my song! Can I?"

Moochie coughed and said, "Sure, sweetie, give a look, but don't get your hopes up."

Sam tore it open. "Ginger! Mama Moochie! Listen to this. Your friend at KRLG, Chris, says he's sending the song on to Ben Wade. Who's that?"

"Isn't that the new, young country singer, the one who sings *'Ain't You Ever Gonna Love Me?*" said Ginger.

"Says he has no idea whether Wade will like it, but thinks there's a chance. Wouldn't it be great if he did?"

"Cool down, Sam Boy. We'll just have to wait and see," said Moochie. She knew it was difficult to get a song published and didn't want Sam to be hurt.

*****

Moochie felt much better. She still coughed a lot and her hands and knees were sore. Dr. Carr said her lungs and throat were healing just fine. She told Grady she would be able to resume the radio program next week. The listeners were clamoring for her return.

She had pretty much forgotten about the political campaign since the fire. But, she couldn't get away from the flood of mail from her fans and supporters seeking any way they could help and urging her on. Moochie knew there was no way to win and she had treated the campaign as a joke. As she read the mail, she realized there were many people out there who were dead serious about her being elected president. It was sad to Moochie knowing they were looking for a hero that didn't exist. Some of the letters touched her heart with their hope against all odds. "How can I let them down and dash their hopes?" she asked Bud. Feeling guilty she explained to Bud, "Honey, I've grown to love these people even though I've never laid eyes on them. They've been so good to me and I just can't ignore them. I know that doesn't make sense; that they are just an audience, but, shoot, I don't know how to explain it. Do you see what I mean?"

"I think so, love, but I worry about you trying to do too much. You've been through a lot and we need to spend our energy on re-building the restaurant and all."

"I know, sweetie, but these poor souls have found hope, and ole' Moochie is gonna try not to let them down. That's why I need to get back on the airwaves as soon as I can." She thought, Oh no, I'm beginning to sound like Grady Lake, feeling like I owe something to all them poor people out there.

"What do you think we should do with the money?" said Bud, his feet propped on the coffee table.

"I been pondering about that a lot," said Moochie. "I'm tired of worrying about it all the time, hiding it. I think we should put it in the bank, a separate account, and let the chips fall where they may. Let Lawyer Phelps deal with it; do whatever has to be done, tax-wise and otherwise."

"Yeah, well, whatever's left of it will go into the foundation that Rube and Phelps talked about. Maybe it'll help some folks and they tell me we won't have to pay taxes on it."

"Yeah and that way the Lumpster across the street won't be able to get his hands on it." Moochie reached over and moved Bud's feet off the table and threw a warning glance.

"I'll call Steve right now and tell him what we're gonna do." She reached for the phone.

The receptionist signaled Steve. "Hello, Miss Moochie, how's Mr. Boy, my most famous client?"

"He's doing fine, honey. Still as sassy as ever. We're hoping the commission will revise the law or make an exception, allowing him to come back inside. Say, Steve, I want to tell you our plan and see what you think."

"Fire away, Miss Moochie. My very first clients take precedence over everything else."

Moochie finished and Phelps gave a sigh of relief. "Moochie, I have to apologize to you and Bud. That's what I should have advised you to do in the beginning. I don't know what I was thinking. I wasn't thinking really. That's the only thing to do and it sure would have saved us all a lot of worry. There's one other thing. I think we should set aside a certain amount of the money as a contingency fund in case you need it to meet your bills each month. Is that all right?"

"Okay, honey. That will be fine. I know Bud will feel a lot safer that way. The money's been nothing but trouble and I'll be glad to get it taken care of."

*****

Bud was still sulking around the house. Moochie knew what was bothering him. He was worried about his music machine. One day she said, "Well, Lord-a-mercy, Buddy Boy, why don't you snap out of it. I miss the music too, but we have to move on. See what I mean?" Then, she got an idea.

She went to the kitchen counter and picked up the phone. "What was the name of that dump in Monroe where you found the jukebox?"

"It was called Precious Memories, but that was the only one she had. No need to call."

"Won't hurt to try. Information please." The phone rang and Moochie handed it to Bud.

"Precious Memories, Mildred speaking."

"Miss Precious, this here's Bud Arrington. Remember me, I'm the one who bought the jukebox from you?"

"Why, I sure do. It was you and that other nice gentleman who liked my wart so much."

"That's right; Uncle Billy. Well, you might of heard about the fire we had over here in Athens. Burned part of our restaurant down and also got the jukebox. Just about broke my heart."

"Sorry to hear that."

"Just curious about whether you might have another jukebox in your place. I sure would like to find one."

"No, sir. I can't rightly say that I do. Howsomever, I might know where you can find one. Let me do some checking around. I'll give you a ring if I find anything."

"Okay, Miss Precious, I'd be much obliged if you can." Bud hung up.

"Well?" said Moochie, hands on hips.

"She's gonna look around for one. Sounds like she may have something in mind."

"There now, ain't that better than sitting here moping?"

That evening Bud called Uncle Billy with the hopeful news.

*****

The next morning, Precious called. "I think I found a nickelodeon fer ye. Took me all night to convince him to let her go, but I think we got a deal fer ye. Better get on over here while he's still in a daze."

Bud called Uncle Billy immediately and went by to pick him up.

When they arrived at Precious Memories, Precious was standing out front in her high top tennis shoes and sweater buttoned to the top, even though it was a warm day.

As soon as Billy got out of the truck, she smiled and pointed at the wart in the middle of her forehead. Billy grinned and gave her a knowing wink.

"What did you find me?" asked Bud.

"I found you a beaut, but we got to strike while the iron is hot. This sometime boyfriend of mine, Willard Wuepper, has one that he's agreed to sell. He's fascinated by my wart, likes to just sit and stare at it. So, we agreed on a price for him, then, I'll add my ten percent finder's fee and you'll have a jukebox. Come on, let's go take a look at her."

They climbed back in the truck with Precious sitting in the middle, clutching the front of her sweater with her hand in case Uncle Billy got any ideas.

Willard was a burly man with a brush cut and dark tan from working outside. He reached his hand with its short stubby fingers for Bud to shake, all the time looking at the wart on Precious' forehead. "Come on into the house," he said in a low, scratchy voice. "The box is right here in the living room."

Bud and Billy walked to the jukebox and looked it over from top to bottom. Precious pointed out that it was two years younger than the one Bud had bought before. All the while, Willard stared at the wart with lust in his heart. The wart seemed to grow larger the longer he looked at it. Uncle Billy kept his eyes diverted from the pair.

Finally, Bud coughed and covered his mouth. Not wanting to show his enthusiasm, he mumbled, "How much if you don't mind my asking?"

Precious stepped forward, being the business woman that she was. "Well, seeing as how it's you two fine gents, all we're asking is two hundred measly dollars. That is right, ain't it Will, honey?"

Willard stepped back from the wart and momentarily shook off his dazed look. "Right."

Bud tried to look shocked, but would have gladly paid more. He said, "Well, Miss Precious, that's a lot of money, but we'll take it." He pulled out a roll of bills and pealed off four fifties. "I presume that includes the records too," he said.

"Yep. Sure does, don't it Will, honey?" She turned and looked Willard square in the eyes, giving him a direct view of the pink, marbled-looking wart.

Willard gulped and said, "Yes ma'am."

CHAPTER THIRTY ONE

Since the fire, Moochie, Bud and Pretty Boy were still reeling from the psychological trauma. But, like Moochie said, "Honey, we got to get up from here and get back to work. We can't be sitting around feeling sorry for ourselves. There's too many people depending on us. Your new kitchen is almost ready and I know you'll feel better when we get back with our people."

Bud coughed to clear his easily irritated throat. "Love, I've been wondering how much more we can take. Nothing is worth losing our lives and I worry about the affect all of this is having on Ginger. In spite of the insurance on the building, the bills just keep pouring in. The law can't or won't do anything. I sure would hate to just give up and close the restaurant."

"I know how you feel. I'd like to go over there and slap both jaws, then pinch his face off. But, don't you see, honey, if we did something like that, he would win. We couldn't survive if we did that. He would win because we would be destroyed. No, we've just got to keep on going; survive; be a success. That's the only way we can win."

"Yeah, I know that in my heart. It's just that it's so hard trying to meet the payments each month. Besides that, I don't know if my old body can take the beating." Bud rubbed his forearm that had been scorched.

"Well, at least the insurance company will pay for the damage and the adjuster says they'll put pressure on the police and insurance commissioner to find out who caused the fire. 'Course, they want to get their money back."

251

*****

The rubble of the original building had been cleared and a new foundation poured. They decided, and the insurance company agreed, that it would be cheaper to start from scratch. The old Moochie's Place sign had been singed on one end but not burned, and was restored by Garcia Rose. Rube found a young architect who met with Bud and Moochie to determine what they wanted in the new building, pointing out to them the building codes and requirements they must meet. The plan was now set, and the builder, "Hammer Toe" Jackson, who specialized in commercial buildings, had already started the framing.

The building next door which had been serving as a large dining area, had some water damage to the floor, but was still sound. This building had been built at the same time as the burned building, with a similar facade; brick and mortar with two large plate glass windows. Hammer Toe's crew and subcontractors were almost finished with remodeling, adding a kitchen, counter and booths. He assured them, it would be ready to open on Monday.

*****

It was a beautiful day in Athens. There were thin, high cirrus clouds and the near white quarter moon was still visible in the Western sky. It was supposed to be hot, but the morning was still pleasantly cool. Passersby knew Pretty Boy. Some waved and smiled at him as they hurried on their way. Others stopped and exchanged pleasantries or quips with the now-famous bird. Pretty Boy still had to be outside the restaurant, so his new cage hung on a hook next to the front door of building two. The door was left open so he could hear the jukebox. His new quarters in the back of the remodeled building were not as spacious, but included a bathroom, a requirement if a bird was to be kept on the premises of an eating establishment. A door opened directly to the alley. Ginger had a new television set in her bedroom at home and Pretty Boy had been assigned her old one. The Athens-Clarke County Commission was to meet tonight to consider the rule regarding parrots and turtles being banned from restaurants. Moochie had already prepared her speech in support of Pretty Boy.

The entire crew was back together for the first time since the fire. Bud still had a bad cough which worried Moochie. She walked with a limp from the fall on her knees. She called them together for a short meeting before the doors opened. April straggled in just as the meeting began. "Sorry, gang, but I was out kinda late last night."

Moochie spoke in a softer voice now. "Me and Bud and Pretty Boy have been through a bad time, facing death and all. I been thinking lately; wondering what would happen to Ginger, Sam and all of you if Bud and I were not around. I don't know what to say, honey. You all have been so good to us. Your love and concern during this time has made us realize what's really important in this old world; friends and family. All the other stuff is just fluff. You've made us realize that we can't let this bump in the road stop us from having the best restaurant in Athens; the kind of place where people can enjoy good food and good friends. We're just gonna go on loving every person who walks through that door. Ain't that right, Buddy Boy?"

Bud looked up in surprise, not expecting to be called on. He sported a new haircut, with enough left to comb back over each ear. Moochie had coaxed him into spraying some of the Michael Jordan cologne she had bought him on his neck. He wore his usual golf shirt, this one was white with a red university insignia on the left breast, which was mostly covered by his sparkling white apron. "Well, love, I guess that's right, but it's gonna be hard for me and Brad and Pinky to love all them people from out in the kitchen. Guess we'll just have to put our love into the food that we send out."

Pinky smiled broadly. "That's right, boss. Them biscuits are gonna have so much love in 'em they'll float outta that oven and float right onto the plate all by themselves."

April laughed-snorted loudly, "I'm doing the best I can to love all the customers, but there's only so many hours in the day or night."

Peola shrilled, "Lord, April, you need to clean up your act. If you're gonna help me out on the floor, you're gonna have to get some rest."

Moochie held up her hand, "All right, honey, let's get ready to serve all them customers. Bud, why don't you get that music box ready to go; put some quarters in and play something to get us in the mood to work?"

Bud smiled broadly as he thought of Precious and her wart, then sauntered toward the jukebox. He dropped two quarters in and made his selections. As he turned toward the kitchen, he saw the *Banner-Herald* fly in the door and heard someone yell, "Paper!" As he bent over to pick it up, he saw the headline, "Pretty Boy's Fate Decided Tonight!" All were anxious about what the Commission might do, but it didn't seem to bother Pretty Boy who was busy welcoming his fans, "Gawk! Welcome to Moochie's," and talking trash with the college students, "Go home to Mama," and "Yo Mama is a Gator fan."

"Lord-a-mercy, them football players have done polluted our bird. Be quiet, Birdwit."

By seven-thirty the restaurant was packed and more customers waited outside. Moochie hugged and listened to each one as they entered: "Are you and Bud all right? I'm sorry about the fire. Who would do something like that? We're so glad you were able to re-open." Arch Cameron from the *Banner-Herald* and his photographer were there snapping pictures and asking questions. The Mayor and three members of the Athens-Clarke Commission showed up. The Mayor whispered to Moochie that she was all for Pretty Boy, but didn't know if they had the votes to get him inside. University

President Harriston brought one of his young secretaries to breakfast. She stood out in the crowd with her red leather jacket, tank shirt and Tommy Hilfiger pants. A Dooney & Bourke bag was slung over her left arm. Even two of the firemen who had been man-handled by Moochie came in. Moochie cried, thanked them profusely and apologized.

Unexpectedly, vans with camera crews from the three major networks drove up and blocked the middle lane of Clayton Street. The crowd swelled and finally the whole block was cordoned off and traffic re-routed. City officials had been caught totally off guard along with everyone else, including Moochie and Bud. Jane and Joan of Foster's Jewelry Store across the street became concerned about security and locked their door. The employees' plastered their faces against the display windows, trying to see what was going on.

While Moochie was being interviewed with several microphones in her face, her cell phone blared out, *"Happy Days Are Here Again."* "Excuse me, honey, but I have to get this call."

"Hello, Mrs. Dunlop? This is Senator Obama from Illinois. I just wanted to call and tell you how sorry I am about the fire, and congratulate you on the re-opening of your restaurant."

"Why, thank you, honey. Why don't you come on down here to the South and have a slab of Bud's ribs sometime? We'd love to have you."

"Thank you, Mrs. Dunlop. I might just do that. Good luck in the race for the White House."

"Thank you, honey. Say hello to all them nice people up there in the windy city, especially Oprah Winfrey."

Five minutes later the phone rang again, "Hi, Mrs. Dunlop. This is the Senator from Arizona. I'm sitting here in the Senate Office Building, having coffee and a sweet roll with my campaign manager. I was glad to hear that you and your husband are doing fine after the fire, and wish I could be there for the opening of the restaurant."

"Well, honey, you need to get on down here and have one of my chocolate covered pralines and a Twinkie Twin Pack with your coffee. Good luck in the election. I hope I don't beat you too bad, honey." She chuckled.

"All right, Mrs. Dunlop. I'll tell my manager what you said so he can be prepared." He was laughing when he hung up.

A lady reporter from CBS asked, "Do you mind telling me who called?"

"That's private, honey. Let's just say it was two of my opponents."

"What did they want? Were they trying to take advantage of your popularity on the radio?"

"Don't know. You'll have to find out who they are and ask them."

That sent the media people scurrying to call their respective networks and find some answers.

*****

Wilson Lumkin stood in his doorway across the street with a disgusted and bewildered look on his face. He thought, what does it take to get rid of those people? I've done everything I can. They're like a plantar wart, they just keep coming back. Why are they so popular? I have more money and influence, I'm better looking, and the food that I serve is much better. It must be the media people. They're not fair, always writing about them, giving them free publicity. If I could, I'd blow them all to pieces. They deserve it. If I could only find that money, I'd be happy. Maybe my old man would be proud of me then. Lumkin went outside and passed out menus to entice people into his restaurant.

*****

Bud was in the kitchen preparing his secret barbecue sauce when he got the call.

"Hello, is this Pretty Bud?"

"Yes'am this is Bud, or what's left of me."

"Mr. Boy, I'm very sorry about what happened to you—the fire and all, but I've got good news. It's been twenty-six days since Sugar Plum and Pretty Bud had----well, you know---got married, and Sugar Plum hatched two precious little eggs yesterday and now we've got two of the prettiest parrots you've ever seen."

Bud lowered his phone hand and yelled, "Brad, go tell Pretty Boy he's a daddy!"

Then, he raised the phone again. "Ms. Charmaine, that's mighty good news. Pretty Boy's gonna be a proud father. You said two, were they boys or girls?"

"One of each, I think. You know it's almost impossible to tell, especially when they're so young, but I have a sixth sense about things like that. The one I think is a boy is a spittin' image of Pretty Bud. So, I think I know which one you'll pick. Remember, I gave you first pick if there was more than one."

"I think you're right, but I guess I'll have to talk it over with Pretty Boy first. When can we pick him up?"

"Oh, Doctor ------, oh, you know, the animal doctor, the one with the foreign sounding name, he says in about two weeks, depending on how things go, but you can bring Pretty Bud over to see them."

"Good," said Bud. "Would two-thirty this afternoon be okay?"

"That'll be fine. I'll make us some hot chocolate."

Brad was grinning when he came back into the kitchen. He'd thought of a way to rib Bud.

Bud looked up. "Well, how did P.B. take the good news?"

"He was okay 'til I mentioned Sugar Plum's name, then his beak turned red and he swooned against the cage door." The corners of Brad's eyes crinkled and his jaws puffed out before he burst out laughing.

"Just a chip off the old block," Bud said. "A sucker for the opposite sex."

"Lord, Miss Moochie, how'm I s'posed to work with two crazy things like this?" Pinky yelled through the swinging doors.

Moochie said, "Lord have mercy, we'll never hear the end of it. We're gonna have another Birdbrain around here. Is it my imagination or is that bird acting more like a human being every day?"

April said, "He's seen so many movies, he thinks he's an actor. Go for it Pretty Boy! Congratulations."

The jukebox blared "Oh Lord, it's hard to be humble---."

"Gawk! Hard to be humble," said Pretty Boy.

*****

At one o'clock most of the lunch crowd had cleared out and the press was gone after wringing every morsel of news value from the story. Bud had been scurrying around all morning, trying to get everything done so when the time came to see Pretty Boy's new family, they wouldn't be late. Moochie said, "Lord-a-mercy, Bud, you beat all I've ever seen. You'd think you were the father of them birds."

As for Pretty Boy, he had been strutting around in his cage all morning, feathers fluffed out like a peacock, talking to everyone who walked by.

*****

At one-fifteen Steve Phelps came in for his apple pie and coffee, and to see if he could impress April enough to get a date. He stopped at the front door to say hello to his former and most famous client, the one who had really put him on the map as a lawyer, and helped make him a full partner. Everyone knew his name when he walked down the street and he was even known nationally, at least among the animal rights people.

"Hey, Mr. Boy. How's my favorite client?" as he tapped on the cage.

"Gawk! Hello, big shot."

"Now, now, Mr. Boy. Remember what I did for you in the courtroom. It was a brilliant performance, even if I do say so. At least I got you a hearing before the Athens-Clarke County Commission. Maybe they'll exempt you from the law."

"Gawk! Where's the money?"

"It's not about money, Mr. Boy. It's the principle of the thing. It's about equal justice under the law. That's what we were after."

"Lord have mercy!" squawked Pretty Boy.

Steve tipped his hat, smiled and walked through the door. As he made his way to the counter, he thought of his conversation with Moochie about the money. The first time he had heard about the money, Moochie swore him to secrecy. A few weeks later he was with April, and tried to impress her by telling her that Moochie and Bud had found a lot of money. Thankfully, he hadn't been told where the money was hidden, so he couldn't tell her that. Still, he felt guilty about violating a client's trust.

He walked over and sat in front of April who was busy making a new pot of coffee. He loved her and had tried to find a way to ask her to marry him. Now, maybe he could come up with the right words.

Steve laid his briefcase and hat on top of the counter. "Hello, angel eyes. How's my girl?" There was a new cockiness about Steve now that he was successful. April didn't like it one little bit.

She turned and said, "Well, now, aren't you the mighty one; a big, successful lawyer. I don't buy it, mister, and I'm not your girl. So get off your high horse and talk like a real person. Otherwise, we're all out of apple pie."

Steve got a sheepish look on his face and bowed his head. Looking up, he said, "I'm sorry, April. I didn't mean it. I guess all this attention just went to my head. I'll do better. I promise."

"All right, now what can I get you, the usual?"

"Yep, and I want to talk to you about something."

April set the coffee and pie in front of him and said, "Well?"

Steve's brain scrambled for words. This was not the right time. He leaned forward so no one else could hear. "April, remember what I told you about the money? Well, it has all been taken care of. We're in the process of setting up a foundation for Moochie and Bud. The money will be well used. You didn't tell anyone about it I hope."

April looked surprised, having expected something else. "Of course not, I wouldn't tell something like that." Privately, she thought, I wish I didn't like wine so much. It goes to my head sometimes. She had been dating around and wondered if she had let something slip. Feeling guilty, she said, "By the way, I'm free tonight if you have anything in mind."

Steve forgot about the money and took a big bite of apple pie.

*****

Bud and Pretty Boy arrived at Miss Charmaine's house at two-twenty-five. She was sitting on the front porch of the well preserved, two story home. The swing hung between two of the large pillars holding the roof. Charmaine wore a red, slouch sun hat, tied under the chin with white straps. A curl of gray hair hung down in front. She wore a bright green, strapless chiffon dress with green shoes. One was a forest green pump. The other was a lime green sneaker. Sitting on the table next to the swing was a pitcher of green liquid and two glasses, filled to the brim and decorated with sprigs of mint. She waved as Bud approached with Pretty Boy in tow.

"Hello, Miss Charmaine. You look so nice with your pretty dress and hat. Did you buy a new outfit?"

"Oh, no, Mr. Pretty Boy. This is the dress that I wore to my high school prom back in ---, well, it was a long time ago. It still fits though. I like to get it out and wear it every now and then. Makes me feel young again. Won't you have some green tea?"

Bud, expecting hot chocolate, had never had green tea before, but didn't want to hurt her feelings. "Sure, I'll give it a try."

Charmaine handed one of the glasses to Bud, who settled into a wicker chair close to the table. He set Pretty Boy's cage on the floor next to him.

"Pretty Boy sure is excited, being a new daddy and all. He can't wait to see his kids and Sugar Plum, of course."

"Of course, Mr. Bud. We'll go see them as soon as we have our tea."

Bud, not wanting to be rude, leaned back in his chair and took a sip. "Uhmm. I like this tea. Was it hard to make?"

"Oh, no, I bought it over at the Earth Fare store. It's only a short walk from here."

Pretty Boy was fit to be tied. He strutted back and forth in the cage, jumping from the rope to one swing and then the other and kept saying, "Who's your daddy?"

After a few minutes, Miss Charmaine rose, saying, "Well, Pretty Bud sure is anxious. Guess I'd better take you on back to see the new babies."

She rose and swayed from side to side until she got her balance, then moved toward the front door. With each step Bud thought she was going to topple over, but she kept her balance by grabbing his arm. They made their way to the back bedroom where Charmaine kept the parrots. She had moved Sugar Plum and the two babies to a separate cage. She explained, "Dolly and Angel Baby are still very jealous of Sugar Plum, so I had to separate them to keep them from killing each other." She smiled and waved her finger at the birds, "You naughty, naughty birds. Now, be nice. We have visitors."

The two grown female parrots in the large cage went wild when Pretty Boy entered the room. They began squawking and flying back and forth. Sugar Plum cringed in the corner and covered her babies.

When Pretty Boy saw Sugar Plum and the babies, his feathers puffed out and his beak turned red. He reached through the spindles of the cage and clawed at the air, trying to get to his family. Bud said, "Calm down, Boy. It'll be all right."

Bud asked, "Will it be okay if I put him in to see them for a little while?"

Charmaine nodded nervously and stumbled toward Sugar Plum's cage. "All right, just take Bug out and put him in when I open the door."

Bud did as told, and for the first time saw the scared, shy part of Pretty Boy take over. He laid low on his feet and pulled his feathers tightly together. He gradually inched his way toward the corner where his family was cuddled together. Sugar Plum laid back, still mainly interested in protecting her babies. Pretty Boy inched closer and finally reached out and touched Sugar Plum with his beak. She relaxed and finally allowed Pretty Boy to move closer. Then, she reached over with her beak and pushed the little ones toward Pretty Boy who nuzzled them and covered them with his wings. Miss Charmaine was crying and Bud had tears in his eyes.

When they got back to the restaurant, Bud told everyone what had happened and there were shouts of joy and a few more tears. Bud finally said, "All right everyone, now we have to decide what to name Pretty Boy's son. Miss Charmaine will have to choose one for his daughter. Think about it and let me know what you think we should call him. I'm presuming that Miss Charmaine is right, that it's a boy. Remember, tomorrow night we go to City Hall to see if we can get them to let Pretty Boy and his son be inside Moochie's Place..

CHAPTER THIRTY TWO

Closing the restaurant was left to Brad and the rest of the crew. Moochie peeked in her purse to make sure the speech was still there. She was exhausted from being on her feet all day, what with the stress of re-opening Moochie's Place, and the excitement of Pretty Boy's new family. Nevertheless, she knew if they were to get their parrot back into the restaurant, she had to be at this City-County Commission meeting. It was a personal matter for her and Bud.

This was the big test. One vote on the Board could make the difference. There were rumors that Lumkin had at least one of the commissioners in his back pocket.

As she and Bud walked to the meeting, Moochie re-marked, "It's a shame that money has so much influence on politics these days. It just ain't fair. It's like trying to run for President with no financial backing. Shoot, I wouldn't make a serious run at it, even if I had the money. So, I don't know why I'm complaining. I guess it's because I'd like to see our democracy work, but right now it's only a dream, honey."

"I know, love. That's the way it is, though. All we can do is tell people about it; let them know what's going on; keep standing up for our rights. You'll do fine. Just tell it like it is. Maybe they'll listen." Bud grabbed her hand to let her know that everything would be all right.

They arrived at City Hall and found a crowd waiting. The six o'clock news had said Moochie was going to speak tonight when they reported the story about the re-opening of Moochie's Place. Most of the people wanted a hug, and she tried to oblige, leaving a couple of folks staggering around trying to regain their equilibrium.

Those who were seated inside stood and cheered as Moochie and Bud took their seats. Two ladies and a man on the back row eagerly moved over to give them room. Madam Mayor gaveled the meeting to order.

The preliminaries were taken care of efficiently, and the first item on the agenda was considered. It involved a request by the police department for funds to put surveillance cameras at the intersection of Broad and North Milledge. Only one man spoke against it, saying the cameras cause drivers to slow down too much because of fear they'll be caught. A representative from the Sheriff's office described how the camera system worked, the cost and the likely income from fines.

While all of this was taking place, Moochie reviewed her speech one last time. Bored, Bud leaned back and scanned around the meeting room. It reminded him of a church in many ways, with its high ceiling and pew-like benches. All of the woodwork, including the spindled railings were glossy white. The mayor sat at a large desk in the middle and elevated above where the choir loft would have been. The clerk sat at another desk directly in front of and below the mayor. Long tables with microphones in front of each chair ran down each side on the same level as the clerk. The distinguished members of the Athens-Clarke County Commission sat behind the tables in their swivel chairs, most with a serious expression and a few trying to give the cameras a flattering, profile view.

Finally, a motion was made and seconded on item one. There was discussion and the vote was called. Bud noted that the motion was approved seven to two and decided to be more careful at that intersection.

He laid his hand on Moochie's shoulder as item two, the one concerning Pretty Boy, was announced and read into the record. Mayor Kilpatrick, wearing a light green jacket falling just below her waist with a white satin shirt, collar turned out, called for citizen comments. A man rose from the second row on the left and approached the podium.

Moochie and Bud looked at each other. Moochie leaned toward Bud and said, "Oh no! It's the Lumpster. He has a lot of nerve showing his face here after all he's done to us."

"I know, love, but he has the right to speak. Let's see what he has to say."

Lumkin looked the part of an important business man with his navy blue, pin-striped suit, white shirt and maroon Ruffini tie. Their nemesis began, "I'm Wilson Lumkin, 132 Clayton Street. I'm the owner and operator of the Lumkin Café, one of the finest places to dine in Athens since the fifties. It was started by my father and we have served this community in many ways. I also own other businesses in this city, and am President of the Chamber of Commerce. I was born and raised here and have only the best interest of Athens at heart." He glanced to his right as one of his business friends said, "We appreciate that, Mr. Lumkin."

"I'm here to speak against changing the ordinance for food service in Athens-Clarke County. These rules were made to protect the people from dangerous diseases, and I fully support them. There are people sitting in this room tonight, who willingly disobey these rules, putting customers' lives in grave danger." He turned and looked squarely at Moochie and Bud, leaving no doubt who he was referring to. "I won't call names, but you know exactly who I mean. I've done everything I can, legally, to stop them. They've been able to get away with it because of public sympathy created by the media, which they have shamelessly manipulated. Personally, I wish there was some way to keep this kind of people out of our business community." He nodded toward the mayor and commission, then turned and glared at Moochie and Bud as he returned to his seat.

"Does anyone else wish to speak before we discuss this item?" said the mayor. Bud squeezed Moochie's hand. She rose, her stomach brushing the perfectly coifed head of hair in front of her. The woman leaned away, then glared over her shoulder. When she saw Moochie, her countenance softened. She returned Moochie's nod of apology. Moochie sucked in her breath and gingerly worked her way to the center aisle. When she approached the first row, she spotted Ron Harris, the man who had inspected the restaurant and put Pretty Boy on the skids to the outside. He was a regular patron of Moochie's Place. His favorite was ribs and fried green tomatoes. When she reached his side, she grabbed him by the shoulder and stood him on his feet. "Hey, Mr. Harris, how've you been? You're looking a little peaked, honey. Maybe you need a good hug from ole Moochie. Get you back on the right track."

"Hi, Moochie. Maybe I do, yep, yep, yep, yeah, maybe so. Hug, yeah, yeah, yeah."

Before he finished, Moochie already had him in her embrace. She genuinely liked Mr. Harris, even though he had kicked Pretty Boy out. Being a little hyped up, she put one of her best hugs on him. When she let go, Mr. Harris staggered to his left and fell into the lap of Shelba Young, wife of the president of one of the local banks who was sitting on the second row. She put Mr. Harris on his feet immediately and guided him back to his front row seat. Some in the audience were laughing and chatting back and forth, forgetting where they were.

Moochie moved to the left, in front of the podium as Mayor Kilpatrick gaveled the audience back to order. Moochie leaned forward and grabbed the microphone. She cleared her throat right into it, surprising herself and the crowd with a mighty rumbling sound that reverberated throughout the room. A hush fell over the place.

"I'm Moochie Dunlop, co-owner of Moochie's Place, 133 Clayton Street, Athens, Georgia. I'm also a write-in candidate for President of these United States of America. God bless America!"

The crowd erupted with laughter and applause. One man stood on his feet and shouted, "God bless America!" before the mayor glared him down.

Moochie purposely cleared her throat again and everyone fell silent. She removed her handkerchief from the front pocket of her moo moo and wiped the mike. "Thank you, folks. I appreciate your kind attention. I just want to say a few words about changing this discriminating rule that them folks over at the Health Department have. Now, I don't blame them folks, especially Mr. Harris. They're just trying to do their job, see? But, I'm here to tell you that the rule just ain't fair.

"Let me read you what it says on page twenty-eight of them rules and regulations. Says in section K: 'Live animals, including birds and turtles, shall be excluded from within the food service. This exclusion does not apply to edible fish, crustacea, shellfish or to fish in aquariums. Patrol dogs accompanying security or police officers or guide/service dogs accompanying handicapped persons or trainers of such dogs, shall be permitted in dining areas or other public access areas.'

"Now, I'm not here to speak for them turtles, honey, but somebody needs to. They're so slow and have to carry them heavy shells around all day. How would you like to walk around all day with your head sticking out from under that shell. It don't seem fair."

Lumkin said so most people in the room could hear, "Why don't you have gastric by-pass surgery, fatso?" A hush fell over the room as Moochie slowly turned to face him.

She lazered Lumkin with her eyes, but managed to keep control of her voice. "I don't have surgery, Lumphead, because I enjoy being fat. We all have to make choices in life, and that's my choice, just like you choose to be ugly. Plastic surgery might help your face, and it would certainly help those of us who have to look at you sometimes, but I don't know that there's anything that would help your ugly heart. Now, if you don't mind, I'd like to finish my speech." There were titters of laughter and a few handclaps as Lumkin turned red and looked as though he might explode. Moochie turned back to the mike.

The mayor suppressed a smile and pounded the gavel. "Please, members of the audience, respect other's right to speak and remain silent. Also, Miss Moochie and all others, I must remind you that you are to speak only to members of the Board and no one else. Also, remember that you are limited to ten minutes."

Moochie resumed, "Thank you Mayor. I apologize. The reason I'm here tonight is to speak on behalf of our bird and loyal friend, Pretty Boy. He could be here and speak for himself, but *Sands of Iwo Jima* is on early tonight and he wanted to watch it." There were a few muffled laughs before the audience remembered what the mayor had said.

"There are just a few things that I wanted to say about that rule. First, it seems to be unfair to birds and turtles. I mean why do they have to be singled out? America is about being fair, and we ought to be fair to animals as well as human beings. At least that's how I see it. Some say animals are just dumb creatures and we can do whatever we want with them, but that ain't right. Pretty Boy is very smart, maybe even smarter than some people in this room. Why, Dr. Marquad says he's the smartest bird he's ever seen. He's even done tests on him and says he's at least as smart as a five-year-old, maybe smarter. Says he even has emotions just like us.

"I know some of them health people are concerned about disease and what have you, but I want you to know that we keep Pretty Boy as clean as a whistle. Clean his cage every day, sometimes twice a day. The other thing I want you to know is that Pretty Boy is important to our business. Why, some people come there just to see and talk to him. He's important to this town too. Why, I'll have you know, he's personal friends with Clint Eastwood. That ought to tell you something. Another thing you might not know is that Pretty Boy is now a father. That's right. He now has a son without a name at this time. And, I can't bear the thought of that sweet, little baby being out in the weather, especially when it's so hot in the summer or cold in the winter. How'd you like to stand outside in a cage with that Georgia sun beating down on your head, even if it is covered by an awning?

"We had Pretty Boy checked over completely by Dr. Marquad, and he says there's nothing wrong with him, no disease, no bacteria or viruses that he could pass on to humans. All this is written down for you right here in this paper the doctor gave to us." She passed it to the Clerk.

"What we would like to see you do is change the ordinance to say that any animal allowed in a restaurant must be clean and be examined by a veterinarian every six months and certified to be healthy. That way, the public would be protected and Pretty Boy could be back in the restaurant, and equal protection under the laws of the *Constitution* of the United States of America would be satisfied. Don't that sound fair? That's all I have to say, Your Honor." She turned and made her way to the back row, taking high fives and "Way to go, Moochie!" shouts from the crowd.

Mr. Harris testified for the Health Department and explained the concerns behind the rules, ending with "Yep, yep, yeah, that's the rule. Parrots and turtles must stay outside because they might carry disease. Yep, yep, yeah, oh yeah.......yep. But, personally, I want you to know that I like Pretty Boy and hate to see him out in the weather."

A motion was made and seconded to strike "including birds and turtles" from the rule and to insert a sentence stating that any animal in a restaurant, besides those excepted, must be certified by a licensed veterinarian to be free from disease that might be harmful to the public.

The Commission discussed the motion which was strongly opposed by one member, and it was eventually passed by a six to three vote. Mr. Lumkin stomped down the aisle and out, giving Moochie and Bud the finger as he went. The vein on his neck was a bulging, dark blue cord. His head was jerking wildly about in anger.

CHAPTER THIRTY THREE

That night as Moochie and Bud lay in bed, Bud clutching his side of the mattress and Moochie reviewing the events of the day, she said, "Bud, I've been thinking about something. Want to know what it is?"

"Sure, love, what's been running around that pretty head of yours?"

"Well, it's about our safety and Ginger's too. She's here alone, at least part of the time, and we need to make sure she's safe, see what I mean?"

"Yeah, I know, I worry about that too."

"You saw Lumkin's face tonight, there's no telling what that nut might do. I'm gonna talk to Rube tomorrow, see if he has any ideas about what we should do."

"Good idea, love." Bud let go of his side of the bed and rolled into Moochie. He raised up and kissed her on the lips. "Good night. See you in the morning." He climbed back up the slope, anchored himself with an arm, and quickly fell asleep.

At two-thirty Bud woke up in a cold sweat, shaking and mumbling incoherently. Moochie reached over and pulled him close. "What's wrong, honey, bad dream?" Bud said nothing, but his trembling finally stopped.

"Tell me about it, Bud. What happened?"

"It's nothing, love, just a dream."

"Buddy Boy, I've never seen you that upset. What's bothering you? Is it Lumkin? Are you worried about him?"

"I guess you got me to thinking about his hate. I've seen folks like that before and it always means violence. It means folks have lost control and there's no telling what they will do."

"It'll be okay, sweetie. Don't you worry none. We'll just stay alert and protect each other. Okay? Now, turn over and I'll rub your back." Moochie eventually fell asleep and her hand dropped away. Bud was awake most of the night, haunted by knife fights he'd seen in Mississippi juke joints.

*****

The next morning, Moochie sat on her stool sipping coffee, reading the paper and waiting for Rube and Amy. They usually came in about seven-thirty. The headline read: "Pretty Boy Wins." A picture of him ran on the first page with an article that quoted most of Moochie's speech. There was a picture of Bud and Moochie on page three.

Moochie looked up at Pretty Boy, sitting inside the door now, munching on his breakfast seed. "Hey, Birdbrain, I didn't hear any thanks yet for all I did for you last night."

Pretty Boy cocked his head to the right. "Gawk! I love you."

"All right, that's better. I was wondering if you'd even noticed the difference of being inside."

"Gawk! Inside."

Slapper Slocum peeked around the corner of the window to see who was there. Moochie ignored him. A minute later he walked briskly to the door and entered, glancing over his shoulder to make sure he wasn't being followed. He nodded at Pretty Boy and said, "Good morning my fine feathered friend." He looked at Moochie to see if she noticed his happy attitude. She finished her coffee and waited for him to sit on the stool in front of her.

"Well, Slapper, you're looking mighty chipper. Someone must have bought a box of T-shirts this morning."

"Nope. I'm just being my usual happy self. Carly is finally beginning to recognize what a brilliant business mind I have. She loves me as long as the money's rolling in. Here's a check for your share of this month's income. The Pretty Boy T-shirts are selling as fast as Mr. Stryker can make them."

"Good. This will help us pay the rent this month." She shoved the newspaper over to Slapper.

Rube and Amy entered, hand in hand, right on time. They ordered their present usual, and Moochie yelled to the kitchen, "Two over light, wheat toast. Pancakes and small juice!" Amy was strikingly sexy in her grey, low cut blouse with puffy short sleeves trimmed in red and her red pencil skirt. There was a fruity scent about her that Moochie didn't recognize.

Rube walked to the newly acquired juke box and dropped in a quarter, "I Didn't Know God made Honky Tonk Angels" began as Rube returned and kissed Amy on the cheek. "Remember the first time you heard that song?"

"I sure do," said Amy. "It was right after you asked me to marry you. How could I forget?"

Moochie cleared her throat and set a coffee and small juice in front of them. "Rube, I been meaning to ask you something. You know all the trouble we've been having with the dummy across the street. Well, me and Bud are concerned about our safety, and especially Ginger. What do you think we should do? Do you know anyone in the security business that might help us?"

"Sure, Lock Tight Security installed my system at the office and at home. I'll call Larry Tucker, better known as Tightlip, and ask him to call you today. They did a good job for me."

"Can they install cameras and sound systems too? Seems like that's the only way we're ever going to catch these hoodlums in the act."

"Yep, they do all that."

*****

272

Tightlip walked in at one o'clock with his clipboard, ready to inspect the place for trouble spots and camera locations. He wore a blue felt hat, pulled down in front, and dark glasses. Bud accompanied him as he looked over, around and under everything, especially the doors and windows. Finally, he whispered to Bud with his hand cupped around the unused side of his mouth, "Do you want to go with me to your home or lend me a key?"

Bud lowered his voice, "Can't leave the restaurant now. Here's a key that'll get you in the back door."

"All right, I'll call you with any questions. Say, you don't have a cup of hot java I could take with me, do you?" he said in a hushed voice after looking over his shoulder.

"Sure do." Bud walked over and whispered to April, "Please fix Tightlip a cup of coffee to go."

"Why are you whispering?" inquired April.

He gave her a blank stare, not realizing that he was mimicking Tightlip.

Tightlip grabbed the coffee and waved Bud and Moochie closer, covered his mouth and confided, "I'll lock the key inside and get back to you tomorrow with an estimate."

Peola put a quarter in the machine. The "Theme from Pink Panther" played as Tightlip left.

*****

Bud picked up Sam and Ginger from Hilsman Middle School at 3:30 and drove to Five Points and Miss Charmaine's house to get Pretty Boy's son. They found Miss Charmaine sitting on the front porch with her right foot propped on a chair. Her ankle was wrapped with an ace bandage.

"This is my daughter, Ginger, and my might-as-well-be-son, Sam. They came to help me get Pretty Boy's baby."

"Pleased to meet you both. I hate to part with that precious little boy. The other one, which I think is a girl, is already spoken for. Sugar Plum certainly will miss them both."

"What happened to your foot?" said Bud.

"Don't know exactly. One of my shoes must have turned over and I toppled into the coffee table. Ruined the table, but I guess it broke my fall. Just sprained my ankle and skinned me up a bit. I'll be all right."

"Miss Charmaine, I hate to bring it up, but don't you think it would help if you wore the same type of shoe on both feet? You'd be more level and less likely to fall."

"Good idea, Mr. Boy. Can't see like I used to. My judgment is a little off too." She reached for her walker and pulled herself to her feet. "Come on, we'll go get that sweet little bird for you. What you gonna name him?"

"Don't know for sure yet, we've talked about it a lot at the restaurant. I guess I'll just have to let the crew vote on it and see which name wins. Maybe I'll do that when we get back."

*****

When they walked into Moochie's Place, the workers, some members of the football team, Steve Phelps and other afternoon customers gathered to see Pretty Boy's son. The proud father with his cage next to the front door, was the first to see them coming. "Gawk! Lord have mercy," he squawked and hopped skittishly from one perch to the other.

Little Jimmy Dickens just happened to be on the jukebox singing, "May the Bird of Paradise fly up your nose."

Bud raised the baby bird's cage high above his head. "All right, everybody, we've got to make a final decision on a name for Pretty Boy's son. Anyone who's here is eligible to vote. April and Peola, will you pass out some paper and a pencil to anyone who wants to vote. Write your choice down and fold the paper. We'll collect the votes and count them."

Different names were bandied about as people wrote their choices: Pretty Boy II, Bud's Bird, Junior Boy, Birdbrain II, Junior Birdbrain, and Sugar Boy. "Moochie brought out a notebook to jot down the names.

"April, call out the votes for me." When all the votes were counted, Moochie held up her hand. "Here's the winner by a small margin over Pretty Boy II. The winner is---Sugar Boy!" That'll be his official name. No matter, to me he'll still be "Junior Birdbrain."

Everyone cheered as Bud took Sugar Boy out of the small cage and put him in with his father.

Uncle Billy who was sitting at the counter said, "All righty then," and raised his cup to offer a toast. "Here's to Sugar Boy, offspring of our beloved Pretty Boy, the brightest and best of all birds. May he grow up to be just like his daddy and bring much pleasure to us all."

Another cheer went up as those assembled lifted whatever they had in their hands. Moochie put her arm around Bud as a tear rolled down his cheek. Slapper Slocum, there for an afternoon coffee break, cheered with the rest as visions of a Sugar Boy T-shirt danced in his head, while the Georgia football players saw this as a good omen for a Sugar Bowl bid.

CHAPTER THIRTY FOUR

On Wednesday evening Moochie met Grady at the WGRB studio for their nationally syndicated radio program, the *Lay it on Grady Show*. Grady was dressed to a T, as usual, in a navy blue sports jacket, and red and blue striped tie. Moochie tried to follow suit out of respect for their listeners. Her meticulously made up pretty, round face glowed from a forest-green Moo Moo, low-cut and accentuated by a mint-green scarf. Grady did the usual introduction and Moochie gave a brief summary about the situation with Pretty Boy and his new son, Sugar Boy, and the Moochie for President campaign.

"Sugar Boy or Junior Birdbrain, as I call him, was given the first name of his mother, Sugar Plum. It was only fair that we do that since she made a considerable contribution to his birth, honey. Pretty Boy did his part, too, but everyone gives him all the credit since he's so well known, and that don't seem fair. By the way, Sugar Boy is a sweet little bird and I don't mean no harm by calling him Birdbrain.

As far as the campaign is concerned, I don't have much to do with it. It's up to the people how they want to vote. And, when you're only a write-in candidate, it makes it harder for them to vote for you, even in those places where they are allowed to write-in. I don't take the campaign seriously. I go around and speak to small groups when I can and try to enjoy it. But I've got too many other things to worry about, honey. Like rebuilding the damaged part of the restaurant and protecting my family. Somebody is out to get us, and I'm not gonna let that happen. Now, Grady, let's see who's calling tonight and what they've got on their minds."

"All right, could we have the first caller. Please state your name and where you are from. Then, ask me or Moochie your question."

"Yes. My name is …." There was a sound like a distant chainsaw.

"Sir. Please turn your radio down and continue."

"Sure. Long pause. My name is Freeze Epting, I'm from Lake Sacajawea, North Dakota. I want to know what you think about this global warming thing. I don't want them glaciers up in Canada melting and sliding down here on top of us."

"Well, honey, I don't want to see that happen either. Now, I'm the farthest thing from a scientist you could find, but most of them fellows seem to think that's what's happening. So, I'll have to go along and figure there's something going on. Whether there is or not, we all need to do more about protecting the place where we live. This ole earth has been good to us for the most part and we ought to protect it. If some of them chemicals we put in the air is hurting us, let's do all we can to stop it, or at least cut back on them. Don't that make sense?"

Freeze coughed real loud into the microphone. "Makes sense to me, Moochie. If I ever get the money, I'll be driving one of those ethanol burners."

"That's the spirit, honey. Do what you can. If they ever make one of them hybrid cars that will carry someone like me, whose weight is slightly above normal, I might buy me one."

"All right, thanks for answering my question."

Grady broke in, "Okay. Thank you, Freeze, for calling. Keep warm up there in North Dakota. Our next caller also has a question for Moochie. Hello, you're on the air."

"Hello, this is Weed Thompson from San Francisco. My question is, if you're elected President, will you have a 'gay' person in your cabinet?"

"Well, honey, I'm not going out and look for any gays, any more than I would for a straight, a woman, man or whatever. See my point, honey? If I was elected, which is very unlikely, I would look for the best people I could find, to help me. I'll tell you one thing, honey. There won't be any sexual goings on of any kind at my cabinet meetings. They can all keep their hands to themselves, if they want to stay working for me. There's too much to be done with all the problems we have in this country and the world to allow time for that kind of thing."

The next question was for Grady. "Hello, this is Evelyn Woodall, that's a fake name 'cause I don't want my in-laws to hear about this. I'm from Oak Ridge, Tennessee. I've got a problem that I need you to help me with."

"Lay it on me," said Grady.

"Well, my husband is over in Iraq for the second time and my old boyfriend has been coming around on a regular basis. I think I'm still in love with him. Should I tell my husband? Oh, by the way, I'm pregnant."

Grady looked at Moochie and shook his head in disgust. He turned to the mike. "First of all, Evelyn, who is the father of the baby?"

"I don't know. My husband went back to Iraq about six months ago and that's when I started seeing Joe, whoops, I mean Sam."

Grady said, "I'm no lawyer, but it seems to me that you have a moral and legal responsibility to your husband. He must be made aware of the situation in my opinion. Your second responsibility is to that baby who will have the right to know who it's father is." He glanced at Moochie and could see that she was about to burst. "Moochie, do you have any advice for Evelyn?"

"Yes I do. Honey, you need to get your act together. The only one you've thought about so far, is your own self. While your husband's been off over there fighting for this country, you've been back here running around and pleasing yourself.

Get real, girl. Don't expect me or this radio audience to feel sorry for you. Start thinking with your head instead of other body parts, about other people, including your husband and that baby, and what your decisions will do to them. You've made your bed and will have to sleep in it, honey. The ones I feel sorry for are the ones you will hurt."

Grady took another call, this time for Moochie. "Yes, sir. Go ahead with your question."

"Mrs. Dunlop, my name is Cliff Crenshaw. I'm a chef here in Washington, D.C. My question is, if you're elected President and Bud becomes first gentleman, what will you serve the Queen of England if she comes to visit the White House?"

"That's a good question, honey. If I know Bud, we'd start by handing her a Bud Light to wet her whistle. The hors d'oeuvre would be Georgia peanuts, shuck your own. The salad would be homemade coleslaw with a wedge of cornbread to push it with. The main dish would be a rack of Bud's ribs slathered with his famous sauce, and extra napkins to protect her evening gown and keep her mouth clean. Dessert would be two Twinkies with a chocolate covered praline gently resting between them. Caramel sauce would be drizzled over the entire thing, then sprinkled with powdered sugar. Now, don't that sound good, honey? Makes my mouth water just thinking about it."

"Mrs. Dunlop, don't you think that might cause an international incident? I mean, she might be insulted."

"Insulted? Why, honey, you can't insult someone by giving them the best-tasting food there is. I think it might improve our relationship."

Grady who was doubled over laughing, pulled himself together. "Well, ladies and gentlemen that's all the questions we have time for tonight. This is Grady and Moochie signing off for now. Take care and God bless."

CHAPTER THIRTY FIVE

Lumkin's daddy, Charles, was a big man with a full head of steel-gray hair and matching eyebrows. For a man of seventy-five, he was in good shape and proud of it. His cold, piercing blue eyes and attitude of the-man-in-charge, made ordinary people shrink and move out of his way. He had no weaknesses that he recognized and tolerated none in others. His mission this morning was to get his son's attention once and for all, wake him up; make him the man he wanted him to be. Charles had always been tough on his son, pushing him, urging him on, telling him never give up, show no quarter, win at any cost. That's the way he had been treated by his own father and it had worked for him. He was one of, if not the most successful man in Athens. He had started one business after another, including the Lumkin Café, which had been the finest and most popular eatery in this part of Georgia. He had served on the City Council for years, was Mayor for four years and finally, served in the Georgia State House of Representatives for three terms. Now all of this was fading away. He had turned his empire over to his only son, and he didn't understand why the boy couldn't live up to the family legacy. As the father and titular head of the Lumkin clan, he was embarrassed when he didn't get proper respect because of his son's failures. People whispered behind his back. Wilson had to do better and he knew just how to make that happen. Bring more pressure.

Lumkin senior walked across the almost empty dining room of the Lumkin Café. There was one man sitting on the far side, biting into a chocolate covered donut. The place used to be packed on Monday mornings. He found Wilson, sitting in his office with coffee, staring out the window.

Even though his father came to check on the business quite often, Wilson, deep in thought, was startled and jumped to his feet, not wanting his father to see him so down.

"Daddy, what's up?"

"I'll tell you what's up. My blood pressure." He glared at Wilson, his face twisted into a frown of contempt. "This is a disgrace. Where are all the customers? What's wrong with you? This place used to be filled. Now look at it. Empty. Look across the street, that's where all the customers are. You are letting those two low-life nobodies over there, who know nothing about restaurants, steal all of our business. And here you sit on your ass, wondering what's up. Get with it, boy, or I'm gonna have to fire my own son and come out of retirement." He turned on his heel and headed for the door.

"But, Daddy---."

Charles Lumkin never looked back and slammed the door as he went out.

Wilson went to the window and closed the curtains. He slumped to his knees and cried like he hadn't done since he was a small child. Finally, seeing no other choice, he got up, locked the office door, went to the safe and dialed the combination. He took out the nine mm Beretta and placed it against his right temple. His hand shook uncontrollably. He lowered the gun to gain control. This is the only way out, he thought, and raised the gun again.

There was a knock at the door. "Mr. Lumkin, there are two men here to see you about a job." It was Luella, his waitress and cashier.

He lowered the gun for the second time and fought to regain control of his thoughts. "Okay, give them breakfast and have them wait."

He sat at his desk and tried to relax by taking deep breaths, with no success. The people across the street had humiliated him in his home town and taken away his business.

Fatso had even slapped his face in public. He could never forgive that or live it down. It didn't seem fair that they were so popular, or that she had become a radio star and been interviewed by *Sixty Minutes.* They didn't have money or political power, and yet politicians flocked to their door. Worst of all, they had found and stolen the family treasure he had searched for all of his life, and just as he had figured out it had to be hidden in the building next to Moochie's Place, they had bought it out from under him.

He had tried everything: broken in to find the money, had their bird kidnapped, and run Bud off the road. He fought them at City Hall, and even burned half their restaurant down. It boiled down to two choices: kill himself, or get the money back. If he got the money, maybe his daddy would cut him some slack and perhaps even love him.

Feeling as though an oppressive weight was pulling his shoulders down, he walked to the door and invited the two shady characters into his office.

*****

On Friday, Moochie picked up Sam and Ginger at the middle school at three-fifteen. When they got to the restaurant, they helped out where needed, mostly in the kitchen. Sam worked until six-thirty when his mother, Kristy, picked him up.

This Friday night was busier than usual with arch-rival Tennessee fans and Georgia tailgaters filling the streets prior to tomorrow's big game. The kitchen was "organized chaos;" Bud yelling orders and waving his sauce-covered hands; Brad sizzling hamburger patties on the grill, and Pinkie filling plates with ribs, Moochieburgers, fries, coleslaw and her special hot biscuits.

Out front, Moochie handled the counter while April and Peola scurried around delivering drinks and taking orders over the din of laughter and constant pounding of the jukebox. A Tennessee fan chose "Rocky Top," and set off a roar of good-natured "boos" from Georgia revelers. April laughed and snorted while Peola's shrill voice played off the walls and ceiling.

Pretty Boy and Sugar Boy's cages sat on either side of the front door. Pretty Boy squawked "Welcome to Moochie's!" with more than usual gusto, as though showing Sugar Boy how it was supposed to be done.

*****

At eight-thirty Ginger tied the four sides of the full plastic bag together and hefted it out of the garbage can. Laying it on the floor, she put a new bag in and stretched it to fit. She lifted the full bag and went out the back door to the dumpster. As she tossed the bag, someone grabbed her from behind and slapped a cloth over her mouth and nose. She struggled briefly then collapsed into a stupor. Her limp body was placed into the trunk of a black Chevy Malibu with dark-tinted glass.

At nine o'clock Bud yelled, "Hey, Brad, go out front and tell Ginger to get on back here. We'll never be out of here by ten if she don't help us finish up."

Brad came back into the kitchen. "She's not out in the dining room. Moochie thought she was back here."

Bud paused from putting sauce in the refrigerator. "Well, where in the world could my girl be? She's sure not back here. Pinkie, have you seen her?"

Pinkie looked up from scraping dough off the mixing table. "Nah, Mr. Bud. Last time I saw her was a while back when she took the garbage out."

"Brad, check outside. See what she's doing out there," said Bud.

Brad opened the door and stepped out. Seeing nothing, he walked to the garbage container then up and down the alley for a short distance. When he approached the dumpster again, he saw a white tennis shoe. Could be Ginger's, he thought. Next to the shoe was a cloth. He picked it up and noticed a strange smell. Worried, he hurried back into the kitchen. "No sign of her outside," he yelled, "but look what I found."

Bud's heart leaped in his chest when he recognized Ginger's shoe and his eyes narrowed as he tried to think where she might be. Grabbing the cloth from Brad, he sniffed it. Turning, he hurried into the dining area.

"Moochie, have you seen Ginger? She's not in the kitchen and she's not outside." He raised his voice, "Hey, gang, anybody seen Ginger?"

The crew went silent, each scanning the dining room, then looking at each other as they considered the question. April said, "I haven't seen her, Mr. Bud." Peola said, "No, Mr. Bud, she hasn't been out here all night."

"Brad found Ginger's shoe outside. Moochie, call the police," said Bud as he leaned across the counter to hang on against the rising fear within.

The crew gathered around and chattered back and forth, trying to think of a reason Ginger would leave without telling anyone. Where in the world would she go? They could think of no possible answers.

The police were there within minutes. They found Moochie and the crew surrounding Bud, praying for Ginger's safety.

Bud handed Lieutenant Edwards the cloth. "Don't know what it is, but Brad found it outside by the dumpster along with Ginger's tennis shoe."

Edwards brought the cloth to his nose. "Smells sweet, could be chloroform. I'll send it to the lab to be tested."

He ordered the two officers with him to look around outside. "Make a thorough search of the whole area; see if anyone is there who might be involved or if there are any other clues, then tape off the back of the building and the alley."

The Lieutenant interviewed everyone. "Do you think she might have gone somewhere on her own?" was his first question.

Moochie said, "She's only fourteen, Lieutenant, and she's never done anything like that. She would have told us if she was going somewhere. Wouldn't she, Bud?"

"No question," mumbled Bud.

"Could she have gone off with a friend, a schoolmate, maybe?"

"She wouldn't do that, not without asking us. That's for sure," said Moochie.

"When and where was she last seen?"

"Pinkie saw her take some trash out the back door about eight-thirty," said Bud.

After a few minutes, one of the officers yelled from the back door, "No sign of her, Lieutenant. Nothing else that might help."

The lieutenant was convinced. He called for a child alert bulletin to be broadcast on all TV and radio stations.

When the interviews were over, Brad suggested, "Why don't we help the police by looking for Ginger? We could cover the downtown area in a hurry and recruit students and anyone else who would help."

"Sounds like a good idea to me, honey. Bud, are you up to it?" said Moochie.

Bud was already headed toward the front door. Brad shouted, "Hold on, one second. Let's go down to Thomas Street. We'll each take a street going west all the way to Pulaski Street, then turn back and look on the other side of the street. Ask people if they've seen a fourteen-year-old girl with blond hair, wearing a green blouse, jeans and one or no shoes. If they want to join the search, bring them with you. We'll blanket downtown first and meet back at the Civic Center on Thomas Street. Okay, let's go!"

While walking the streets, Moochie thought of Sam. He would be devastated. Ginger was his best friend. They did everything together. She took out her phone and dialed. Kristy answered.

"Kristy, Moochie here. I need to talk to you and my boy, Sam. Please ask him to pick up on the other line."

Sam came on. "Hi, Mama Moochie, what's going on?"

"I'm sorry, but I have bad news. Ginger's disappeared, maybe kidnapped. We're out looking for her right now."

Kristy gasped and said, "No!"

"Why? Why would anybody take Ginger?" said Sam.

"I don't know, son. I guess to get at me and Bud. I just thought you all should know."

"All right, Mama Moochie. We'll be right there." He slammed the phone down.

Moochie dialed again, this time to Rube. "Rube, honey, we need your help. Ginger's gone, possibly kidnapped. We're looking for her, but can't find her yet."

"Are the police there?"

"Yeah. They're doing all they can. They've put out a bulletin on TV and radio."

"Okay, Mooch, don't worry, we'll find her. I'll call Angela, have her call all my employees; put them on alert. I'm sure they'll help any way they can. Amy and I'll be at the restaurant in a few minutes."

In the meantime, Lieutenant Edwards called the University Police and asked for their help.

*****

An hour later the searchers reassembled at the Civic Center. No sign of Ginger. Lieutenant Edwards picked up Moochie and Bud and took them back to the restaurant in case there was a ransom call from whoever took the girl. Brad broke the crowd into crews and sent them to canvas the neighborhoods around downtown, all the parks within the bypass, and the university campus closest to downtown.

It was a long, fearful night for everyone. At two-thirty on Saturday morning most of the crews had returned with no word about Ginger. Moochie had made a new pot of coffee, which she served along with eggs and grits, biscuits and whatever else they wanted. The searchers hovered around, some lying on the floor; waiting for directions on what to do next. Brad moved among the crowd, thanking them for helping out. Bud sat at the counter staring at the phone. He refused food, but sipped coffee. Moochie kept track of him with her eyes and came over every now and then to pat him on the shoulder and tell him things would be all right.

The Athens-Clarke County Police Department had been on alert all night and Lieutenant Edwards was still waiting for the ransom call, which was almost certain to come if she had been kidnapped. His technician had arranged for the call to be recorded.

After listening to Moochie and Bud's suspicion of Lumkin's involvement, the Lieutenant called for a stakeout at Lumkin's home in Five Points. Lumkin arrived at nine p.m. There was no sign of life in the house after eleven. No other cars came or went.

They also told him about the money they had found in the restaurant wall and their suspicion that Lumkin's objective was to get the money that he claimed belonged to his family.

"Do you have the money?"

"No. Our lawyer has used it to set up a foundation," said Moochie.

*****

When fourteen-year-old Ginger came to, it was pitch black. She screamed and began to cry. There was no sound around her except for her own sniffling. She stuck her hand straight up and touched metal. She was lying on what felt like coarse carpet as she ran her hand over it. Franticly she reached out on both sides and found that she was confined in a box or a container of some kind. She screamed and sobbed until her throat ached. After a while, she raised her feet and tried to push up. No give. Kicking out on all sides she found no opening. Noticing the faint smell of gasoline, she decided that she was in the trunk of a car. She screamed again, then realized that would do no good. She kept telling herself, calm down, don't panic, relax. That helped some, but she knew she was in deep trouble and was scared for her life. She took turns screaming and praying. Finally, she closed her eyes and thought, my Daddy and Mama Moochie will find me. "Please God!"

*****

The call came at three-fifteen a.m. Bud answered. A gruff and obviously disguised voice said, "Listen carefully. Your daughter is alive and well right now. Drive your pickup truck, alone, and bring all of the money you found in the restaurant. Take highway 441 south to Bishop. On the right hand side you will find The Oconee River Methodist Church. It's a small sign so pay attention. You're only going to get one chance at this. Turn right and drive around behind the church. Place the money under the shelter over the back door. Drive on around the church, turn left and go back to the restaurant.

Bud yelled, "You son-of-a-bitch! If you hurt my daughter, I'll kill you even if it takes the rest of my life. Do you hear me, you bastard?!"

The voice came back calmly, "Don't threaten, Mr. Arrington, just listen. The life of your daughter depends on it. Your daughter is still all right, but if the police become involved in any way, she will be killed instantly. You will be observed as you get in your truck and leave the restaurant and as you arrive at the church. If you make a mistake, you will never see sweet little Ginger again. If you co-operate, she will be released where you can find her. Be there at four o'clock. You have forty-five minutes." Click.

Bud's usual ruddy complexion turned pale. He swayed on the stool and would have fallen if Moochie hadn't been there. "There is no money to take," he muttered. "They'll kill her for sure."

They both looked at Edwards who had his hand over his eyes and was in deep thought. He looked up. "Now, let's not panic. We've got to come up with a plan if we're to have any chance at all. We'll put fake money in bags. We'll have to be there when they pick them up, before they discover what's really in the bags. But how? The church will be locked. Does anyone know about that church, a member, who the preacher is?"

April's eyes lit up. She blurted, "Yeah. I've been there a few times. The preacher was one of my teachers in Oconee County before he started the church. His name is Reverend Horvath, I think his first name is Dickie. At least that's what they called him. He'd be in the phone book."

Moochie grabbed the phone book from under the counter and flipped through the pages. "Here, Horvath, Roger, William, Richard..."

"That's it!" said April. "That's his real name---Richard."

"Says he lives on Windy Hill Drive. Here's his number."

Lt. Edwards dialed. "Hello. Is this Pastor Horvath, Richard Horvath?"

"Yes..." said a kind voice.

"Pastor Horvath, this is Lt. Edwards, Athens-Clarke County Police Department. I hate to bother you, but we need your help." He briefly explained the situation, and asked, "Do you have a member who lives close to the church? We can't risk you driving to the church with a key. They might see you and panic."

The preacher thought for a minute. "Well, the closest ones are two doors down, Bill and Wanda Lockman."

"Do they have a key to the church?"

"Yeah, they sure do. He's on the church board."

"Do you have his number?"

"I have the church directory. Here's the number."

"Thanks Reverend," said Edwards as he slammed the phone down, then picked it up and dialed the new number. It rang several times.

"Hello," said a sleepy voice.

"Mr. Lockman, this is Lt. Edwards, Athens Police. We really need your help. Let me explain what has happened." When he finished, he ask, "There may be some risk involved. Are you willing to help us?"

"Yeah, I guess so. I know the people at Moochie's Place. Been there many times. Nice folks." He paused for a minute. "There's no danger to my family, is there?" His wife caught a deep breath, and clutched his arm.

"No, just keep them inside, and you shouldn't be in any direct danger either. It's just a matter of you opening the church for us and going back to your home. Here's what I want you to do. Put on some jogging clothes and tennis shoes. Make sure you have the church key in your pocket. At exactly two minutes to four o'clock, leave your front door and begin jogging, go past the church and keep going. You will look over your shoulder and watch for a dark blue pickup truck to turn and go behind the church. When that happens, you will turn and slowly jog back toward the church. When directly in front of the church, turn, go to the door and unlock it, turn around and jog back to your home. The timing is critical. Do you understand Mr. Lockman?"

"Yes. Two minutes 'til four o'clock, with the key."

"Oh, one other thing. After Bud's pickup leaves, could you stay out of sight, but watch for another vehicle to turn into the church? If you see one, call me immediately. Write this number down. If you can get the license number of the other vehicle, all the better, but don't let them see you. It might put you in danger."

"Got it."

"I'll call if things change," said Edwards and hung up.

By this time Wanda, Lockman's wife, was in tears. "Who was that?" she blurted.

He took her in his arms. "It's all right," he said. He told her everything Lt. Edwards had said.

"Bill, don't go! It might be dangerous."

"I gave him my word. Besides, if there is some way I can help that little girl, I have to do it. If she is hurt or killed, I'd never forgive myself."

By this time Wanda's jaws had stopped quivering and were firmly set. "That poor girl. I tell you one thing. They better not come into my house or try to hurt my children."

"Don't worry, darling. You just stay inside and everything will be fine. "

*****

Moochie, April, Peola and Pinkie were busy cutting up old papers and magazines, tying them into bundles and stuffing them into plastic bags.

Edwards turned to Bud. "Does your truck have a cover over the back?"

"Yeah---."

"Go get your truck from the parking structure and drive behind the restaurant. Unsnap the cover over the back. We'll load the bags of 'money' into the passenger side of the cab. Three of my officers will slip into the back of your truck."

Bud looked up with his bloodshot eyes. "What if they're seen?"

"We've made a pretty good sweep of this whole area, especially behind the restaurant. The lights will be out and the boys will get in there quickly. We're short of time and we're gonna have to take some chances. I'm sorry, but if we don't catch them at the drop-off, it may be too late for Ginger."

"Okay. I guess there's no choice."

Brad said, "Lieutenant, can I go with him?"

"No. Sorry. They would think you were a policeman."

Bud loaded the fake money while three black-clad officers slipped under the truck bed cover. Bud then returned to the kitchen.

Edwards said, "Set your watch with mine. Time it so you turn into the entrance on the far side of the church at four, on the nose. Pull next to the canopy behind the building and make the drop. Get back in the truck and drive out the exit driveway. When you stop to make the left turn back onto 441, my men will slip out of the truck and enter the front door of the church which should be unlocked. You come back to the restaurant."

"Will Ginger be released then?"

Edwards hesitated. "Don't know. It's more likely they'll let her out somewhere safer for them."

"What if they are parked in back of the church? Should I call you?"

"Not while you're back there. We don't know if they'll be there or drive into the church later for the money. Most likely, they'll wait to make sure it's all clear."

"Where will you be?"

"I'll be in an unmarked car waiting for your call. Our police units are already on alert. I've talked to Sheriff Berry in Oconee County. They'll be on high alert since you'll be in their jurisdiction. I'll let them know as soon as I get your call that you're headed back to the restaurant. We'll all hold back until my officers at the scene attempt the arrest. If they try to escape, we will blanket that whole area with patrol cars. Okay?"

"I guess I'm ready." Bud zipped up his windbreaker. Moochie kissed him lightly on the cheek, then turned away and made herself busy serving the helpers. She didn't want Bud to see the fear and tears in her eyes.

*****

Bud drove fast at first, then checked his watch. He slowed down a bit, unsure of just how long it would take to reach the church. His mind was kept busy checking the time and praying that things would go smoothly and that Ginger would be all right. He had been by the church many times before and knew exactly where it was.

*****

Lockman's wife, Wanda, peppered him with "what if" questions. He tried to soothe her worries and keep things quiet so the children wouldn't be awakened, as he rummaged through the shelves in the closet, looking for his warm-up suit.

Dressed, he waited by the front window, watching the clock on the far wall slowly ticking away the minutes before he was to leave the house. Wanda sat by his side. He put a reassuring arm around her. "I'll be fine, just a little nervous, that's all."

"Don't worry," she said. "I'll be watching out the window. If they try to hurt you, I'll come out and help."

"No, no. Don't do that! Just stay in here and take care of the kids. Okay?"

"Don't worry, I'll take care of my family," she said, a steely tone to her voice.

At exactly three-fifty-eight, he stepped onto the front porch, stretched and looked both ways. His senses were on high alert. The sky was a rich electric midnight blue, the stars sparkled like pure white Christmas tree lights. No cars in sight. He stepped off the porch and began jogging down the sidewalk, south, past the church. He looked straight ahead, afraid to look at the church. Still no cars. After all, it is four o'clock in the morning. Then, he saw a flash of light reflect off the small post office to his right. He glanced over his shoulder. A vehicle approached, but it was too soon to tell who it was. He jogged on, then turned his head to see that it was the blue pickup turning into the church. He stopped, turned, and began jogging toward home. He felt in his pocket to make sure the key was there.

As he approached the church, he saw Wanda come out on the front porch with his camouflage cap jammed down on her head and his shotgun in her hand.

"Oh, my God!" he muttered. "She's become a vigilante." Then, he saw her duck behind the bushes next to the porch.

He turned sharply, went to the front door of the church, and hand shaking wildly, managed to jam the key home and give it a twist. As he turned to make his way back to the sidewalk, he saw Wanda rustling through the shrubbery, the shotgun barrel pointing directly at him. I hope she doesn't shoot me before I make it home, he thought.

When he approached the front porch, he whispered harshly, "Wanda get up and get in the house before you get us all killed."

She complied, but only after scanning the entire area with squinted eyes to make sure no bad guys popped up.

Lockman rolled his eyes as he followed her inside. They both huddled next to the window, waiting to see the pickup exit, then watch carefully to see if another vehicle showed up.

After Bud turned left from the driveway, he drove half a block and suddenly turned left again into a used book store. He turned out his lights and pulled behind the store. He thought, if my daughter is released, I want to be here to pick her up and make sure she's safe. He dialed Lt. Edwards.

"Hello, Bud? How did it go?"

"Fine. There was no car there. No sign of them anywhere. Do you think they'll come later?"

"Don't know. Hope so. We'll have to wait and see. I heard from my officers. They're in the church, positioned by the back door. When the kidnappers show up, they'll be ready."

"What if they don't show up?"

"Then, all we can do is wait to hear from them. Are you on your way back?"

Bud hesitated. "No, Lieutenant, I'm parked a little ways from the church."

"What? Damn! Why? What if they spot you?"

"I'm well hidden behind a store. I just want to be here in case Ginger is let go."

"That's a dangerous thing to do. Not part of the plan. Better stay there now, though. If they see you when they come for the money, they might panic and do something drastic."

Bud slouched down in the truck. He remembered the first time he had seen the daughter he didn't know he had. How frightened she was. When her grandmother died, she was all alone. Bud not only felt sorry for her, but he also fell in love with his daughter. At that instant he knew that he must take care of her, protect her. The feeling of a father for his child had overwhelmed him. Before Moochie, he had never felt a personal responsibility to take care of anyone, even himself. Moochie and Ginger were his heart and soul. Ginger was the only one in this world, besides Moochie, who had ever cared for him. He wished they had kidnapped him instead of his girl. If anything happened to her, his strong desire to make the restaurant a success, his very desire to live would be gone. He knew that.

As Bud reached up and unscrewed the cab light, he thought, I wish I had my thirty- eight with me. He felt like he had to do something; not just sit there. I'll just watch for now and not get involved. But, if Ginger is there, I want to be there to help her. He opened the truck door and slipped into the shadows behind the bookstore. He peeked around the corner of the building. Seeing no car lights in either direction, he sprinted across Price Mill Road. Praying to God that there would be no dogs to announce his presence, he tried to stay in the shadows as he moved across the backyards of the two houses before reaching the church. His breathing was heavy as he crawled under a cluster of privet bushes next to the church parking lot.

The wait began. Bill and Wanda watched the front of the church. Bud lay on the cool, damp ground under the bushes. The pungent smell of greenery and the shrill sound of cicadas engulfed him. At twenty past four Bud heard faint voices coming from the field behind the parking lot. Expecting them to pick up the money by car, he was surprised. He waited. About five minutes later, he saw two figures crouching in the combination of tall weeds and wild wheat next to an old, dilapidated storage building. They raised up slightly. With pistols pointing toward the back of the church, they stepped cautiously into the parking lot. Halting silently for a moment, they moved swiftly toward the back door. Each grabbed a plastic bag filled with fake money, gun in the other hand. As they turned to leave, the door flew open and two of the policemen emerged and slid to either side of the back entrance to the church, guns in firing position. The third policeman, still inside, commanded, "Drop your guns! Now! You're under arrest."

The kidnapper nearest Bud leveled his gun and shot the policeman crouched on the right side of the door, wounding him in the leg. The officer screamed and returned fire, missing his target. The other policeman, left of the door and the officer who emerged from the church, opened fire on the kidnapper who was shooting. The man, hit twice, fell backward, dropping the bag and his gun.

The second kidnapper dropped to one knee and fired wildly at the officers. The officer left of the door fell back against the building clutching a deep wound to the shoulder. The kidnapper turned and ran back into the field. The unwounded officer chased him, stopping to fire a couple of times. Bud heard the kidnapper scream, curse and then saw him continue to retreat into the field. The policeman hesitated, then turned around to help his fellow officers. He snatched the phone from his pocket and yelled, "Two officers down, two officers down! Need emergency help and backup now! Behind Oconee River Methodist Church. One kidnapper down, one wounded, but escaped on foot!"

Bud was horrified. Everything had happened in seconds. Bud's first thought was to go help the policemen. Then, he thought of Ginger. The one who got away will kill her. He turned and carefully crawled into the high weeds of the field to avoid being seen and mistaken for a kidnapper. He rose to his feet and ran, hoping to catch the kidnapper before he reached Ginger.

For a man of forty-five, Bud considered himself in pretty good shape. His lungs hadn't fully recovered from the fire and still burned when he ran, but he had no choice. Bud prayed for stamina and ran full out, but soon realized he would never last at that pace and Ginger would be lost. He slowed and just tried to keep up and follow the trail. The kidnapper also seemed to be slowing down. The crook dropped out of sight. Bud got closer and realized that he had descended into a deep ravine. Glad to be out of the field, where the weeds and briars tore at his legs, Bud paused then followed, half walking, then sliding down the side of the depression.

Breathing hard now, Bud feared the crook might stop and wait to ambush him. I don't have a gun, he thought. Maybe he'll think it's the policeman who's chasing him. I hope so. Either way, Bud knew he couldn't stop, not with Ginger out there.

Bud reached the bottom of the ravine and realized he had stepped into a nearly dry creek bed. He paused and looked up the other bank. He was gaining ground. His prey's left arm was hanging loosely at his side as he made his way up the bank. Bud knew that Price Mill Road couldn't be far away. That must be where the kidnappers had parked. That's where Ginger would be. He had to catch him before he reached the car. Bud stumbled and clawed his way up the creek bank, fighting the lower limbs of spruce and gum trees.

Reaching the top, he looked up in time to see a flash of light and hear a loud boom before he felt a strong tug on the left side of his body. It was as though someone had hit him with a hammer. He reeled backward, landing in a distorted heap in the creek bed. Nearby, a black snake raised its' head, looked, then slowly turned and slithered deeper into the bushes. Water trickled into a small pool, mixing with Bud's blood. The broken limbs and blades of grass didn't seem to mind. Nature returned to normal and life continued on its' eternal way without regret or remorse.

CHAPTER THIRTY SIX

Moochie called Lieutenant Edwards. "Have you heard from Bud? He's not back yet."

"He called a while ago. Decided to wait around by the church to see if the kidnappers showed up with Ginger. Said he wanted to be there if they freed her. Haven't heard from him since. I did get a call from Sergeant Moore. We've two wounded officers on their way to the hospital. One of the kidnappers was killed. The other might have been wounded, but he escaped."

"Well, Lord-a-mercy, where's my Bud?"

"I tried his cell. No answer. The sergeant tells me the kidnappers were on foot and came from behind the church. My men and the Oconee County Sheriff's deputies are combing that whole area, especially the roads behind the church. They must have left a car somewhere back there. Don't worry, we'll find the car and the one who escaped."

"I'm worried about Bud. Where could he be?"

"When he called he was parked behind a used book store, not far from the church. I'm pulling in there right now. There's his truck. No sign of Bud."

"Lord-a-mercy. You don't reckon he went after the kidnapper, do you?"

"Don't know. The officers didn't report seeing him. That's a possibility. I'll alert all the officers to watch for him. We just turned on Price Mill Road. We're gonna check out any likely spots where they could be. I'll let you know."

"Okay, honey. Is there anything we can do here?"

299

"Just pray that we can find them and they're safe. That's all."

*****

The wounded kidnapper staggered to the Malibu, desperate to get away. First, he had to get rid of the girl. Dead witnesses don't talk. He walked to the trunk and opened it. Ginger, still groggy from the chloroform and trembling from fear, cringed as far back in the trunk as she could.

He put the gun in his pocket, reached in with his good arm and dragged Ginger out by the hair. He threw her on the ground and held her down with his foot. He took the forty-five out and pointed it at her head. Ginger screamed, closed her eyes and whimpered, paralyzed with fear.

Bud emerged from the woods, clutching his shoulder and yelled, "Ginger! No!"

The gunman turned and pointed the weapon at Bud. He fired as Bud crouched and made a move toward him. Bud heard the whine of the bullet as it passed his ear.

Ginger scrambled to her feet and ran toward Bud. "Daddy!"

The gunman raised the gun again, pointing at Ginger.

Bud heard a shot ring out and saw the kidnapper fall face down on the grass.

Bud looked up and saw Lieutenant Edward's putting his thirty-eight back in the holster. Bud collapsed from the loss of blood and Ginger slumped on top of him.

Edwards snapped to the officer next to him, "Call the EMT's! Hurry!" He rushed to the side of Bud and Ginger.

Ginger was crying and holding Bud's head in her arms. "Daddy. Daddy! Wake up. Say something. Please Daddy---."

The lieutenant felt for a pulse. "Don't worry, Ginger. He's breathing and he's got a pulse. The EMT's will be here in a minute."

* * * * *

Lumkin hadn't slept all night. At four he got out of bed and went to his home office. He switched the radio to the police band. The men he hired and paid $5,000 were going to call him as soon as they had the money and released the girl on a back road in Oconee County. He would then tell them where to meet him so he could give them the other half of their pay. These men were recommended by the same Atlanta source as the arsonists he had hired, and should know what they were doing. He hoped so, because this might be his last chance to get the family money and save face with his father.

At four-twenty-five he heard the "Officers down" call and knew the plan had gone terribly wrong. For the next forty-five minutes Lumkin wrung his hands, paced back and forth across the small room, but mostly sat with his ear close to the radio. At ten minutes past five, he heard Lt. Edwards speaking to the dispatcher. "The second kidnapper is dead, and the victim's father, Mr. Arrington, is wounded. The girl is free and in good condition. The emergency people just arrived."

"Damn, damn, damn! Seems like nothing can go right for me," Lumkin mumbled. "That Arrington bastard is hard to kill. Both of my men are dead, so they can't talk. At least I won't have to pay the rest of the fee." He groaned and held his head, trying to stop the pounding. I'm still in deep trouble with my father. I'll have to find another way to get the money or it's all over for me. His left eye twitched wildly and he fell back in his chair as a vision of the devil with his father's face loomed over him.

* * * * *

The EMTs stopped the bleeding in Bud's shoulder and inserted an IV. Fluids were started as they drove to St. Mary's Hospital. Ginger was given a sedative and hovered over Bud, her hand resting on his good arm as the ambulance sped east on

441. She cried and prayed for the only father she had ever known, a man who had risked his own life to save her. She shuddered, knowing that she had been only a second away from death.

Moochie and Brad hurried to the emergency room as soon as they got the lieutenant's call and were there when the ambulance arrived. Moochie grabbed Ginger in her arms and held her tight. "Lord, thank you for saving my daughter and husband. What would I ever do without them?"

Moochie touched Bud's arm as they rushed him past her. "Hang in there Buddy Boy. I love you."

The nurse said, "Mrs. Dunlop, we need to examine your daughter also, check her over and make sure she's all right. We'll let you know about them both as soon as we can. Okay?"

"Sure, honey. Do whatever you have to do. Me and Brad will wait out here."

Soon April, Peola, Pinky, Sam and Rube arrived. They all sat in a corner of the waiting room, talking quietly. Peola leaned against Pinky and closed her eyes. Rube reassured Sam that Ginger would be all right.

The doctor who examined Ginger made a brief appearance and called Moochie into a small room next to the admittance station. "The only thing I could find were a few scratches and bruises. Of course, it was a very traumatic experience for a fourteen-year-old. I suggest you take her to your family doctor and discuss with him the likely need of counseling."

Ginger emerged shortly and was grabbed by Moochie. "How's my girl?" The others gathered around.

"The doctor says I'm okay, just stressed. Says it'll take some time to get over it. He gave me a prescription to like help me rest. How's Daddy?"

"Don't know yet. We're still waiting for the doctor's report."

Moochie led Ginger to a couch and held her in her arms to sooth the trembling. It was another hour before they were led to a room and talked to the doctor.

He began. "He should be all right. He lost a lot of blood from the wound in his shoulder. We're in the process of replacing that. The bullet was lodged in the back of his shoulder and damaged the deltoid muscle. We had to go in from the back to remove the bullet, so the entire shoulder will be bandaged. He will be on antibiotics for a few days. He was lucky, though. It didn't fracture the bone nor destroy the tendons and ligaments that hold the shoulder together. It usually takes a lot of therapy to rehabilitate a shoulder muscle, and he will be in some pain for a while. He is conscious now, but sleeping because of the medication. I want to keep him in the intensive care unit for a few hours, just as a precaution. One or two can visit at a time. The nurses have my instructions and will help you in any way they can. Please tell your family doctor to call the hospital and get my full report."

After they took turns visiting, Moochie refused to leave the hospital, but insisted that everyone else go home and rest so they could give her relief later in the day. She turned to Rube. "Rube, honey, can Ginger go home with you. I don't want her to be alone right now."

"Sure. No problem. I'll call Amy so she can get the guest room ready."

Ginger protested but Moochie insisted. "Sweetie, I know you don't want to leave your daddy, but you've just got to get some rest. Okay?"

*****

Moochie was there, hand resting on his forehead, when Bud woke up at eight o'clock.

Moochie smiled. "Hello, love. How's my hero?"

"I'm okay. Ginger! Where's Ginger?"

"She's fine, honey. Couldn't be better. The doctor says she's okay; just traumatized a bit."

"What happened?"

Moochie filled him in on what had happened at the scene and how they were transported to the hospital.

Bud was moved to a regular room shortly thereafter. Between naps, he watched the Georgia-Tennessee game and got excited when Winslow Harris, one of the players he knew from Moochie's Place, threw a block that freed tailback Cobb for a long gain.

Moochie napped in the recliner next to the bed.

*****

Bud went home on Monday with orders to rest. On Tuesday he was back in the restaurant, but unable to do much. Mostly, he sat in the dining area drinking coffee and talking to Rube, Uncle Billy, Slapper and members of the victorious football team who came in, silently proud of their scrapes and bruises from the game. This time Bud's shoulder won the wound war. He was hero of the day. Everyone had heard or read about the kidnapping and Bud's role. He would have enjoyed the adulation a lot more if his shoulder hadn't hurt so bad. He threatened to take on two football players, one with each arm, as soon as his shoulder was well. They laughed and said if they could beat Tennessee, surely they could beat an old geezer, especially a wounded one like Bud.

*****

That evening when Moochie and Bud retired to their bedroom after saying good night to Ginger, Moochie had a serious look on her face that Bud was not accustomed to seeing. She was usually the upbeat one; brushed everything negative aside and plowed straight ahead. Not tonight.

Moochie climbed into bed first and propped herself up against the headboard. The bedsprings made their usual objections, but finally settled down. Bud struggled to get his pajamas on.

Moochie, Bible in hand, looked over her reading glasses and said softly, "Can I help, sugar?"

"No, I can do it. Dr. Springer says I need to go ahead and use the arm as much as I can, just so I'm careful."

He came around and climbed onto the high side of the bed. Picking up *Daily Word*, he thumbed through to find the day's devotion.

Moochie let the Bible drop and sighed.

Bud said, "What's wrong, love? Something's bothering you, isn't it?"

Moochie turned her head toward him. "Yes, I'm really worried about you and Ginger. I've been so hell-bent on making our restaurant a success that I'm afraid I've been unfair to you. Putting you both in danger, just to satisfy my desire to win, to see this through and not give in to Lumkin. See what I mean, love? I don't want to lose you and Ginger, not for anything. You are my life and I'm just asking too much. That's not fair. Ain't that right, honey?"

"I see what you mean, but even though I hung back at first, unsure of whether we could make it financially, now I know we can. It's been a struggle to make the payments, but we've done it. We're probably the most successful restaurant in Athens. I'm proud of that, love. People know me now and speak to me when I walk down the street. I never thought that would happen. I've got the most wonderful wife and daughter that a man could ever have. I'm willing to fight for that, no matter the cost."

"But you've been through so much. You've almost been killed three times. I can't bear to see you suffer like that."

"Don't worry about me, love. I'm tougher than I look. Besides it's more than just about us. What about all the people who depend on us: Brad, Peola, April, Pinky, and Sam. Just think about all the people who love Moochie's Place. What about them? Where would they go? They're like part of our family. We can't let them down."

"I know, honey. But, if anything happened to you or Ginger, I might as well die myself. It's like you say, there's no telling what that nut across the street might do next."

"You're right about that, but I feel a lot safer now that Tightlip has installed security systems here and at the restaurant. Shoot, we've even got cameras and sound systems. The best money can buy. Now, all we have to do is pay for them." He smiled and patted Moochie's hand. Bud knew Lumkin wouldn't give up. A fire and a kidnapping? What would he try next? Unable to hold onto the side of the bed, he snuggled close to Moochie and fell asleep. He dreamed of chasing a man, trying to get a look at his face.

CHAPTER THIRTY SEVEN

Lumkin sat alone in his office at the restaurant, withdrawn, stewing about what he should do now that the kidnapping had failed. He brushed his open hand through his wiry, black hair, then clutched the right corner of his mouth and cheek, annoyed by the recent development of a tic. He was now having episodes when he thought he was another person and that someone was trying to kill him.

His bitterness toward and fear of his father, pushed him over the threshold of rational thought. Wilson hated his father and yet wanted his love more than anything else in this world. That was confusing.

Wilson tried to think of ways to improve the restaurant business, overcome the popularity of Moochie's Place, and avoid being fired by his father. But his mind kept wandering back to how he could get even with Moochie and Bud? Now they were rebuilding the burned part of their place, and it would be even harder to beat them.

His mind turned to the hidden money he had been searching for all his life. He thought, if somehow he could just get the money, everything would be all right. His father would forgive him and maybe even praise him for the first time in his life. That money belongs to me and my family. They deserve to be punished for taking it. They must be made to pay.

What about my son, Billy? He'll soon be ready to take over the business. I can't pass a failed business on to him. And my wife, Delores, has been so good to me. I want her to be proud of me. I can't leave her alone. Why should I kill myself when it's the fault of that couple across the street. It's up to me now. I'll have to take care of it myself. He bent his head forward and massaged his forehead, trying to ease the sudden headache gripping both temples.

*****

The replacement for the burned-out building was under construction and progressing rapidly. The declining housing market around Athens left Hammertoe all the workers and tradesmen he needed to get the job done.

Bud and Uncle Billy toured the building every afternoon, then sat on the bench outside and pondered what should be done next. They offered advice to Hammertoe every chance they got. Bud would call Hammertoe over, offer him a chew which he never accepted, then tear off a chunk and stuff it in his right jaw. He always began, "Now, we don't want to interfere, but---."

Hammertoe finally asked one day, "Mr. Bud, why do you always put your chaw on the right side?"

Bud looked at him like he was from Uzbekistan. "Why? Because I'm right-handed, that's why." Actually, Bud had no idea why, but didn't want to appear stupid.

Bud put the tobacco away and asked, "Toe, do you reckon the floor on that side will be sturdy enough to hold my bride when she sits in her office?"

"Sure it will, Mr. Bud. I'm gonna put double two-by-eights under that part of the floor. That ought to do it."

Uncle Billy piped in with, "Well, all righty then."

Hammertoe always listened kindly to Bud and Uncle Billy, then went about doing his job.

*****

Two weeks after the kidnapping, Ginger was doing well, but afraid to be alone, even in her own room. Bud bought a cot and set it up next to his side of the bed so Ginger could use it if she had a bad dream or was too scared to sleep in her own room. Some nights she fell asleep with Bud holding her hand and soothing her with made up stories about how wonderful her mother was.

Bud got physical therapy on his shoulder three times a week and was improving, but it was sore and hurt at times. He managed to do his job in the kitchen, with Brad doing any heavy lifting.

Things were back to normal in Moochie's Place, at least as normal as possible until the burned building was re-built. There was still a long line for lunch, and some of the downtown businesses staggered their lunch breaks to keep them from being swamped at noon. Moochie and Bud appreciated that, because like Bud said, "No matter the size of the restaurant or how many people come, the lease payments are always the same."

*****

Friday before the Auburn game was especially busy. Auburn fans came to Athens by the bus load and Georgia fans jockeyed for tailgating positions much like the Sooners lined up to homestead Oklahoma Territory. Most of the fans were in a party mood.

Bud and Moochie opened at six-thirty in the morning, knowing they would be worn out by the end of the day. Bud went to the back room to get Pretty Boy and Sugar Boy. He always enjoyed Pretty Boy's greeting, "Welcome to Moochie's."

"Good boy," said Bud. "Now, all you have to do is teach Sugar Boy how to say that."

"Gawk! Say welcome."

Sugar Boy, pecking at his seed bowl, gave a weak "peep."

"Gawk! Who's your daddy?" said Pretty Boy.

"Gawk!" said Sugar Boy.

"It's all right, give the boy a chance. It'll take time," said Bud as he freshened the cages.

"Gawk! Pretty Boy go outside?"

"No, Pal. You're a free man now. You get to stay inside," said Bud.

He carried both cages to the front and placed them on either side of the door.

*****

Tightlip, the security expert, was the first one in the door, arriving even before Brad and the rest of the crew. Sitting on the last stool at the far end of the counter, he glanced around the room, admiring his work to secure the building. Moochie sidled the length of the counter and stood in front of him with a cup of coffee.

"Hey, Tightlip. How's everything in the security business?"

He leaned across and whispered, "Shhh. Careful, Miss Moochie. You never know who's listening. I don't want anyone to know who I am."

"All right, honey. But don't you think you should take off your shirt that says Locktite Security on the back?"

"Hmmm. Never thought of that. By the way, is your home system working okay?"

"Far as I know, honey. It makes Buddy Boy a little nervous, having the cameras in our bedroom. Know what I mean?"

Tightlip grinned and motioned for Moochie to lean in. "I hear you, and I sympathize with Mr. Bud. Just turn it off when you need to. Call me if you have any trouble with the system."

After Tightlip left, the early tailgaters began to pour in, hungry for breakfast and already hyped for the game that was to start at three o'clock. It was obvious that some had begun to celebrate with their favorite beverage long before the kick off. The rest of the morning and through lunch time, was chaotic with the jukebox going non-stop and the workers scurrying around with trays of moochieburgers, fries, ribs, vegetables and fountain drinks. Moochie's Place did not have, and did not want, a liquor license. As Moochie said, "Shoot. Some of these crazy fans are drunk enough already. We don't need to contribute to something like that, honey."

*****

Things had calmed down by two-thirty when Steve Phelps, who hadn't been there for a while, walked in for his pie and coffee. Pretty Boy said, "Gawk! I'm broke."

Steve leaned toward the cage and whispered, "Don't worry, Mr. Boy, I'm not after your money. Just remember who got your feathery ass in out of the cold."

"Gawk! Pretty Boy inside now."

"That's right, Mr. Boy, and don't you forget it." He turned, smiled at Sugar Boy and stuck his finger inside the cage.

Sugar Boy leaped on the finger with both feet, digging his sharp little claws into flesh, drawing a drop of blood.

Steve said, "Ouch! Damn!" under his breath and withdrew the finger. "If you weren't a minor, I'd sue your ass off." He glanced at April to make sure she hadn't heard him.

April had his coffee there as soon as he hit the seat. She smiled, remembering their date two nights ago. "How's my favorite lawyer," she said.

Steve morphed back into his cool, lawyerly demeanor. "I'm fine, April. I've missed you over the past two days and finally couldn't stand it anymore. I just had to see your beautiful face again." Strains of "When You're Hot, You're Hot," by Jerry Reed filled the restaurant.

"Oh, get off of it, Steve. You just wanted some of this fresh apple pie." She reached behind her for the generous slice she had just cut, and placed it before him.

"No. No, my dear. You're better than any pie that's ever been baked, even the lemon pie my mother used to make."

311

April laughed out loud and snorted as the breath returned to her lungs. She leaned toward him, elbows on counter. "So, what's new with my important lawyer today?"

"Nothing special. I do need to talk to Moochie. I've been working on a foundation for Moochie and Bud." He immediately thought, I just violated client confidentiality, but didn't let on.

April's right eye arched. "What kind of foundation?"

"Sorry, April, can't tell you that. I'm not supposed to reveal private matters like that."

"That's all right. I'll get Moochie for you." She thought she already knew what that was all about. She waved her hand at Moochie on the other end of the counter and motioned her over.

Moochie came through the opening in the counter and made her way to where Steve was sitting. As he turned she grabbed him by the shoulders and yanked him off the stool, putting him into one of her best hugs. Being caught off guard, he did not have time to take a deep breath and found himself struggling for air. After what seemed like several minutes, he managed to find breathing room just above her right clavicle. He gulped a lung full of air and wrapped his arms around her waist as far as he could and squeezed with all his might. That seemed to help and Moochie eased up. Finally, she held him at arms length. "Lord-a-mercy, honey, I haven't seen you in a spell. I thought you'd done got too uppity to visit us anymore since you won that case for Pretty Boy. I hear you been getting all kinds of animal rights cases since then."

Moochie let go and Steve fell back onto the stool. He took a couple of deep breaths and regained his voice. "Yes, ma'am. I got a lot of publicity among certain groups in this country. I've been very busy, had to travel a lot, but I miss you all, especially April." He looked at April and grinned.

"I guess she told you about the kidnapping and all that mess. Ginger and Bud almost got killed. Now, don't you go straying off too far. We might need you around here if that nut across the street tries anything else."

"Yes, she filled me in on all that. Please don't do anything rash. Here's my card with my cell and home numbers. Always call me before you do anything. Night or day. Okay?"

"Will do, honey. Now, what was it you wanted to see me about?"

"Oh, I need to talk to you about something. I see your office is open. Can we meet privately for a few minutes?"

"Sure, honey. It's not very busy right now. Come on over and bring your coffee and pie. Ginger, darlin', could you bring me some coffee and my usual? And, tell Bud to join us if he can."

They moved to the over-sized booth on the end and settled in, Moochie on the spacious side. She brushed a blonde curl off her forehead and glanced quickly at her crimson fingernails to make sure she had not damaged one during the struggle with Steve.

Steve forked a stray apple slice that had slid from under the crust. "Here's what I think---. "

"Hold on just a minute, honey. Buddy Boy's not here. Besides, it's hard for me to think when I haven't eaten for two whole hours."

Bud emerged from the swinging doors, wiping hands on the sauce stained apron. He paused at the coffee maker and drew a cup of hot java. "Hard to beat a good cup of coffee," he said to no one in particular.

"Don't know how you stand that black coffee," said April as he passed between her and the counter.

"If I wanted my coffee white, I'd just have a glass of milk," smirked Bud. Then, he looked over his shoulder and smiled. April giggled, followed by a small chain of snorts. She loved to rag Bud, just to hear his response.

Bud set his cup on the table as Steve slid over to make room. Louis Armstrong's version of "A Kiss to Build a Dream

On," played on the jukebox. Bud said, "I love jazz almost as much as I do country music, don't you?"

Steve, from New York and raised on rock music, didn't like country, but he could tolerate jazz. He said, "I like the beat, reminds me of the sounds on the streets of New York."

"New York?! Why, honey, that's straight from the soggy streets of New Orleans," said Moochie.

April arrived with Moochie's latest "usual;" a large bowl with a chocolate covered pralene in the middle, a scoop of strawberry ice cream on either side and Twinkies on the outside. She set it in front of Moochie along with a squeeze bottle of Smucker's chocolate. Moochie proceeded to cover the entire conglomeration with the dark chocolate. Noticing the increasing size of Steve's eyes she said, "I sure do like dark chocolate, honey. It's one of my favorite health foods."

Bud took a sip of coffee and grinned broadly. "My sweet Moochie sure loves to eat. It's sort of like her hobby."

Moochie waved her tablespoon at Bud. "Look at your skinny self, Buddy Boy. If you get any thinner, I'm gonna start using you as a book mark."

Steve laughed out loud, tried to cover it with a cough and almost choked until he was red in the face.

"First time I've ever seen a lawyer unable to speak," said Bud.

Steve finally gained control. He spoke in a low voice to avoid snooping ears. "Moochie, Bud, I think I've set up the kind of foundation you want. Basically, without going through all the legal terms, it will establish a fund to make grants to individuals who want to start their own business. People much like you, who start out with no money and might be a risk for most lending institutions. Of course, they would have to make application and be approved by a committee made up of you two plus anyone else you wish to appoint. I've also set up a college fund for Ginger which will draw interest over the years, and made arrangements for an annual grant to Alcoholics Anonymous. Does that sound like what you're after?"

"Yes, honey, but what if the money runs out?" said Moochie.

"Oh, that'll never happen. The grants will be funded by the interest only. Other contributions can be made to the fund and as it continues to grow, more grant money will be available."

Bud leaned back and locked his fingers behind his head, "Well, now, love, that sounds just like what we need, a fund that never runs out of money."

Moochie shoved a gargantuan spoonful of ice cream into her mouth and rolled it around to keep from freezing her tongue. "Sure does, honey. Wish we'd had that when we started out. Steve, sounds like you've got it all worked out. Go ahead and make application to the feds or whoever. Just bring us whatever we need to sign."

CHAPTER THIRTY EIGHT

The night was overcast, the air heavy as Moochie, Bud and Ginger closed the restaurant that evening. They were tired from the long, busy day.

They dropped the proceeds for the day into the night deposit slot at Main Street Bank, turned left on Thomas Street and made their way to Loop 10 and on to Tallassee Road.

"Daddy, don't forget. I'm spending the night at Carla's."

"Okay, ginger bread girl, we'll drop you off on the way home. Just remember tomorrow is a school day, so don't forget to do your homework. And don't stay up too late."

"Daddy, it's like I'm fourteen and nearly grown up. You all still treat me like I'm a kid. Besides, Carla is good at math and she's gonna help me with my homework."

"Okay, kiddo. I just worry about you."

"You got everything you need?" asked Moochie.

"Yep, I've got my bag right here. Carla's mom will drive us to school in the morning."

Moochie sighed and stretched her legs as far as she could in Bud's extended-cab truck, remembering that she had never been invited to spend the night with anyone when she was growing up. Fat doesn't leave much room for friends, she thought.

"Feels good to be off my feet," said Moochie. "How's your shoulder doing, love?"

"It hurts like the dickens right now. Guess I overdid it today," said Bud.

Ginger, leaning over the seat, put her hand on Bud's shoulder. "Daddy, you need to be more careful. Don't over do it. Let me and Sam do more around there. You think you're the only one who can cook ribs, but Sam's as good as you are."

"You're right, babe. You two have been a big help to us. I guess I'm just particular about my ribs; want to make sure they're done right. Them good-tasting ribs is my contribution to this old world. I'm not much good at anything else. See?"

"Daddy! Don't say that. You're the best dad anyone could have. Sam says the same thing. So, don't be putting yourself down. Isn't that right, Mama Moochie?"

"That's right, honey. No need to beat yourself up. Be more positive. Shoot, you're better than most men I know. I'm so proud of the way you put yourself in danger to save Ginger. That's the bravest thing I've ever seen. You and Ginger both are my pride and joy."

"Thank you, love. It's been a real struggle for all of us, trying to make the restaurant a success and survive all the things that have happened to us. I never realized how hard it would be to start a restaurant, all the repair work, trying to make the payments and meet payroll every week. People don't realize---." His voice trailed off.

"That's right, honey," said Moochie. "There were times when I didn't know if we could hang on, pay our workers and the rent. Even then, we kept the faith, and the money always came. The T-shirt sales by Slapper helped some. Then, my job with the radio station pays pretty well, especially since we went national."

"You're right, Mooch, we've done all right so far. Don't worry about me, I'm just a little down right now, thinking about what happened to Ginger and not knowing what might happen next."

They dropped Ginger off at Carla's on Chadd's Walk Lane. Bud slipped her a ten dollar bill. "Have fun. We'll see you tomorrow."

There was no moon and not even a star could be seen as they turned into the driveway at ten-thirty and pulled into the carport.

Moochie waited patiently behind Bud as he fumbled with the key, trying to remember the code to turn off the alarm when they entered.

A dark figure with a ski mask stepped from the shadows behind the house, grabbed Moochie over the shoulder far enough to reach her mouth and held a pistol to her temple. Her scream was muffled by his gloved hand. "This is the F.B.I. Don't scream, don't move, don't say a word or I'll blow your head off. Understand?"

Moochie, startled, gasped and nodded her head. Bud jerked his head around, then slowly turned his body.

"I mean business and I'm only going to ask you this question one time. Where is the money? You know what money. My agents told me the money wasn't at the restaurant and that's why they set the fire. Tell me now what you did with it or I'll pull this trigger."

"No, no, don't do that. I'll tell you anything you want to know. Just, please let her go."

"I won't ask again," he said and tightened his grip on the gun.

Bud recognized Lumkin because of his build and his voice. He thought, so this is what it's all about. The money. Lumkin wants the money we found; he thinks it belongs to him. Bud started, "Mr. Lumkin, we turned the...."

Lumkin screamed, "I'm not Lumkin. I'm the head of the FBI. I've been keeping track of you two. You took the money and hid it. Now, where is it?"

Bud shuddered and thought, Oh, my God! He's crazy. I'll have to play along or he'll kill Moochie for sure. "The money's in the newer part of the restaurant, the part we're using right now. It wasn't affected by the fire," said Bud, thinking that would give more time to appease Lumkin.

"If you're lying, she dies. Now, get back in your truck. Your wife and I will be sitting in the back seat with Agent

Murphy. Take us to the restaurant. Don't make the mistake of trying anything. Other agents will be following us."

Bud looked around and saw no one else. "Right," he said. "No problem," as he turned toward the truck.

Lumkin loosened his precarious grip over Moochie's shoulder and grabbed a handful of the back of her Moo Moo, pulling it tight around her neck.

Bud could hear Moochie's teeth chattering from fear and wanted to comfort her, but was too scared of what Lumkin might do if he said anything.

Moochie regained control and her jaw tightened as they made their way back downtown. Finally, she decided to try talking some sense into Lumkin. "Mr. F.B.I. man, if you don't mind my asking, what did we do wrong?"

"You took money that didn't belong to you," he snarled. Then, he snickered which morphed into a spate of laughter. "Now, I'm gonna get that money back," he growled. "My daddy will finally be proud of me."

"Oh, is your daddy with the F.B.I. too?"

"No, stupid, my daddy is President. He's the one who ordered us to get the money back."

Oh no, thought Moochie, he's completely off his rocker or he's hallucinating from some drug. Moochie decided it would be better to remain silent and think of some way to get the upper hand on Lumkin without getting shot.

Lumkin still kept the gun pointed at Moochie, but turned his head to the left and said, "Murphy, move your fat ass over, you're crowding us."

Moochie rolled her eyes when Bud looked over his shoulder.

As they approached Moochie's Place, Lumkin said, "Pull around to the alley in back and turn off your lights."

Bud complied.

"Now, me and your wife will get out first. You follow and be very careful. Unlock the back door, go in and turn the alarm off. Murphy, if he tries anything, shoot to kill." Bud did as told.

As they started down the hall, Bud was hoping and praying the parrots wouldn't hear them and start making noise. No such luck.

Pretty Boy and his son were watching a re-run of *The Honeymooners.* As Lumkin passed the parrots' door, Pretty Boy squawked, "One of these days, Alice---."

Sugar Boy added, "Gawk!"

Lumkin's face was twitching badly now and his eyes were darting around wildly inside the mask. His head jerked around. "Murphy! Check that noise. Shoot whoever's there." As they moved on down the hall he said, "Take me to the money."

"The money's in the attic. We'll have to go up the stairs," said Bud, trying to think of what to do when Lumkin found out there was no money.

"You two lead the way," said Lumkin.

Apparently Murphy had returned because Lumkin yelled over his shoulder, "Murphy, cover my back."

When they reached the attic steps, Bud said, "The money's tied to a rope and is down between the walls. You'll have to pull it up."

"No. You go up, get the money and bring it back here. Don't make a mistake or I'll kill her."

Perspiration poured from Moochie's forehead as she clutched her hands together to prevent the shaking. She thought, I wish I could get my hands on that S.O.B. I'd ring his neck.

Bud carefully made his way up the steps and onto the rafters, far enough so that Lumkin couldn't see him, knowing that if he fell through the ceiling, Moochie would be killed.

It was hot in the attic and the air had a dry, musty smell. Bud was sweating profusely. He crouched down and grabbed his head in both hands thinking, what have I done? I'm trapped. What can I do? He raised his head and frantically looked around for a way to keep the charade going. He looked back toward the opening at the top of the steps and saw the box of black trash bags Brad used in the kitchen. He made his way toward the opening.

Lumkin yelled, "What are you doing? Hurry up! Maybe I should go ahead and shoot fat ass and come up there so I can watch you."

"No! Don't do that. I'm just having trouble getting one of the knots loose. I'll do it as fast as I can."

Lumkin's hand was shaking by now and this worried Moochie. "Please be careful with the gun," she said.

"Shut up, bitch, or I'll blow you're head off. Murphy! Get over here. Go up there and see what he's up to."

In the meantime, Bud was hurriedly filling two bags with insulation. Then he saw it, the number ten iron skillet they no longer used in the kitchen. He tucked it into one of the bags, along with papers from a cardboard file where he kept old bills, to make the bags look full.

Bud tied the bags and carried them to the opening. He looked down at Lumkin, standing at the bottom of the stairs. "Here it is," he said, dreading what would happen when Lumkin saw what was in the bags.

"Hurry up and bring it down," shouted Lumkin. "All the money better be there. I don't want my daddy to chew my ass out again."

Bud started down the steps. On the third step, he paused and thought, it's now or never. Maybe I can draw his attention by throwing one of the bags to the side. Then, I can jump him. He heaved the bag with the skillet into the middle of the kitchen.

Lumkin swung the Beretta toward the bag, then back toward Bud. Moochie cringed, then realized Bud was in danger. She swung her right elbow into Lumkin's abdomen. He bent forward, shooting wildly into the floor. Moochie grabbed his gun hand and held on as tight as she could. Lumkin hit Moochie in the back of the head with his other hand knocking them both forward onto the floor. The weapon came loose. Moochie grabbed it and threw it as far as she could into the dining area.

Lumkin screamed, "Murphy! Where the hell are you?!"

Bud jumped off the steps and onto Lumkin's back. The stoutly built man rolled and struck Bud with his left elbow, knocking him into the back wall of the kitchen.

Lumkin rose into a crouch and started for his Beretta, Bud hot on his trail. Lumkin ran through the restaurant, knocking over tables as he went. When he saw the gun, he dove and grabbed at it with his right hand.

Bud landed on top of Lumkin's head, reached and knocked the weapon away.

Lumkin rolled over and threw Bud off, grabbed him by the throat and began choking him.

Moochie struggled to her hands and knees and saw what was happening. A low, growling sound much like the starting of a reluctant motor, rose from her throat as she stood on her feet and yelled, "You bastard! I'm here to eat ice cream or kick ass and I'm all out of ice cream!" When Moochie's three hundred pounds of fury struck him in the back, Lumkin went flying and finally rolled onto his back. The big woman landed face down on top of him. Lumkin made several attempts to push her off, then gave up.

She yelled, "I've got his sorry ass pinned, honey. Go turn the alarm on and call the police.

Bud dialed 911, but couldn't get words out of his bruised throat. He threw the phone down, stumbled down the hall and turned the alarm on. He went back to Moochie's side and helped her hold Lumkin down. They heard the sirens, then collapsed from exhaustion and relief.

Lumkin moaned and mumbled, "Murphy, get lard-ass off me or I'm putting you on report."

Moochie looked at Bud and, with her hand, made a circular motion by her right temple. Bud grinned and gave a weak thumbs up.

CHAPTER THIRTY NINE

Moochie and Bud felt they must be in the restaurant the next day. Pain, lack of sleep, nothing must keep them away. They knew everyone would understand, but they had not missed a day since opening and they didn't want to start now. They felt an obligation to the workers and customers of Moochie's Place. In spite of everything, their spirits were high and there was a great sense of relief. As Moochie said, "Thank God, worm-face is locked up. Maybe our lives can get back to normal now."

Moochie applied makeup to the bruise on her face. She was sore all over, but most of the body bruises were covered by her usual moo moo. She just resolved to resist screaming every time she moved. She splashed some of her Gloria Vanderbilt perfume behind each ear and in the hollow of her neck. That always made her feel rich and Bud liked it; said it turns him on.

Bud could barely move his left arm. Moochie said, "Honey, you better go on and call your doctor about that shoulder, and while you're at it, get him to look at your throat, it's already turning blue."

He agreed. "I'll call the doctor as soon as they open. Brad can manage the kitchen while I'm gone. Right now we'd better go on to the restaurant."

*****

They opened the restaurant and called a meeting of the staff as soon as April came straggling in after another late night with Steve Phelps. They explained what had happened and reassured them they would be all right. Peola and Brad had already heard about it on early morning radio. There were numerous questions and comments. Pinky said, "I hope they lock his mangy hide up and throw away the key."

"They did lock him up, but I don't know how long he'll stay. His daddy will probably have him out before you know it," said Bud.

Pretty Boy and his son were unusually subdued when Bud brought them to their respective hooks by the front door. Pretty Boy said, "Gawk! Bad man." Sugar Boy "Gawked" several times, then curled up in the corner of his cage. Bud, sensing how they felt, said, "I know how you feel, my fine feathered friends, but maybe he'll be out of our hair now. I hope so. Anyway, he's a sick man and we need to forgive him. Remember what Jimmy Carter said, "I never met a man I didn't like." He glanced over his shoulder to see if Moochie was listening.

Moochie said, "Lord-a-mercy, Bud, you and them birds beat all I've ever seen. You'd think they were human beings, the way you talk to them. Besides, it was Will Rogers, not Jimmy Carter."

"I know that, love. Just wanted to see if you were awake this morning. What are we gonna say to the customers?"

"Oh, they'll be asking all day long. We'll just tell it like it was. The truth always outs, don't you know. I can't believe you just said we ought to forgive that creep after all he's done to us. He's almost killed you three times. You're too kind hearted, Buddy Boy. I should have smothered his sorry ass last night when I had the chance."

"Now, babe, don't talk like that. You might upset the boys," as he pointed at Pretty Boy and Sugar Boy.

Moochie crossed her arms and curled her lips up. "Why, sakes alive, them birdbrains don't care about all that mess."

*****

324

At mid-morning, Bud, frustrated because he had to be so careful with his shoulder, came out from the kitchen to have a cup of coffee with Moochie, Uncle Billy, Rube, Amy and Slapper Slocum while April and Peola laughed and joked with Winslow Harris, offensive lineman for the Georgia Bulldogs, at the other end of the counter. Anne Murray caressed her song on the jukebox, "When we're together, it feels so right---." Bud cradled his right arm around his coffee and looked up at Moochie who was standing behind the counter. "Love, ain't that a beautiful song, and she's so right, it sure is nice to be sitting here with our good friends."

"You got that right, honey. We've got the best friends in the world and I could kiss every one of you to pieces. We've got a lot more friends too, Buddy Boy, all over this country, if you want to know the truth. Why, I got a note yesterday from the Governor of California, wishing me well in the election. Says I have a lot more common sense than some of the others running."

Bud smiled broadly. "Yeah, I wish he was here. If it wasn't for my bad shoulder, I'd like to take him on in an arm wrestling contest." He glanced toward the other end of the counter to see if Winslow had heard him.

Winslow laughed out loud and slapped the table. "What you talking about old man? You can't beat the Terminator. I'm the only one might be able to do that."

Bud flexed his right bicep. "Look at that you young whippersnapper. Hush before I come down there and embarrass you in front of them girls."

The big lineman went into a fit of laughter, pointing at Bud's arm. April laughed and snorted while Peola squealed with delight.

Bud jumped to his feet and splashed coffee onto the counter. "Whoops! I almost forgot my doctor's appointment at eleven-thirty." He rushed out the door.

After Bud left, the group scattered and Moochie and the staff began serving lunch.

*****

By one-thirty the crowd had dwindled and Moochie sat on her stool behind the counter replacing her Creme of Crimson lipstick, lost in the process of greeting all the customers. She carefully checked each fingernail and buffed any nicks or scratches as she watched Peola and April clean tables and carry dirty dishes to the kitchen. When the phone rang, she reached under the counter and brought it to her ear. "This is Moochie, honey. How may I help you?"

"This is Charles Lumkin. I'm sure you've heard of me. I want to talk to you about my son. You've been nothing but trouble since you opened that dump across the street. Now you've had him arrested and I want to know why."

"Well, Mister..., now what did you say your name is? Was it Lumkin? Yes, that's right---Lumkin. Listen, buster, don't try to impress me with your name. I don't care what your name is. You're no more important than anyone else. Now, if you want to talk to me, get off your high horse and act like a human being. Understand?"

There was a gasp followed by a fit of coughing, then a long pause. "All right, Mrs. Dunlop---."

"Call me Moochie."

"All right, Moochie."

"Miss Moochie to you."

Another long pause and what sounded like wheezing on the other end of the line. "All right, Miss Moochie. I want to talk to you about my son, Wilson. What did he do to you? Whatever it is, I want to ask you to drop the charges. If it's money you want, I'll see what I can do."

"You know very well what he did, it's on the police record. Besides that, he tried to kill my husband twice, kidnapped our daughter, burned our restaurant to the ground and held a gun to my head last night. Now, you want to buy his way out of jail. Mr. Lumkin, we don't want your money. All we want is justice and to be left alone. You ought to be ashamed of yourself. You should go to church and pray to God as hard as you can that you don't go straight to hell and burn in eternal damnation."

"Why, I'll have you know I go to church every Sunday, I'm a deacon, I pray every night and I've donated several million dollars to my church over the years. I'm known as a good, Christian man."

"You can't buy your way into Heaven, Mr. Lumkin. You need to pray some more and this time stop lying to God. He's not impressed with you anymore than I am, honey. It sounds like you've created yourself in your own image. You better find your real self inside and go to God as that person, not who you think you are. See? That's the only way He's going to listen to you."

"But, Mooch....Miss Moochie, I've tried to raise my son right, given him everything he ever needed, an education, set him up in business."

"Sounds to me like you raised him to be just like you and that ain't good enough by a long shot, honey. You need to get right with God and then get right with your son. Stop browbeating him. Show him a little love. Know what I mean?"

There was no answer, silence, and then a "click."

*****

In the afternoon, Moochie picked up Ginger and Sam from school. As soon as they got in the car they peppered Moochie with questions. "What happened Mama Moochie? We've been hearing rumors all day. Are you and Daddy okay?" said Ginger.

"We're both fine. Don't you worry none. Nobody's gonna keep this woman down for long, and your daddy is as tough as they come. He did hurt his bad shoulder some and had to go to the doctor this morning. The doctor says he'll be all right with time. Got bruises on his throat too. So don't be surprised when you see him. I've got some bruises and scraps but otherwise okay."

"Well, what happened? Was it at home? In the restaurant? Did he have a gun? Tell us," said Sam.

Moochie summarized what had happened, minimizing the danger they were in and how scared they were. She concluded with, "Me and Bud were cool as a glass of ice tea in the summer. We just wrestled the gun away from him and pinned him to the floor. That's all there was to it. No problem for a couple of street fighters like me and Bud."

Ginger sat back and sighed. "When's all this gonna be over, Mama Moochie? I just worry so much about you and Daddy. You both work so hard, never have any time off to enjoy yourselves, and have to worry about all the rest of us. It seems like we ought to do something fun for a change."

Moochie thought for a minute, then smiled. "You're right my pretty girl. We need to do something different, something we would enjoy."

They sat silently for a moment, then Ginger's eyes lit up. She turned to Moochie, "Mama, why don't we have a party? A big party. Invite a lot of people and just have fun."

"Hmmmm. We do have a lot to be thankful for. First, we're still alive and Lumkin is in jail. Our beautiful newly rebuilt and refurbished restaurant needs a formal open house. Besides, this crazy election will soon be over too and we need to celebrate that. I'll be glad to see it end. Shoot, I'll be lucky if I get a handful of write-in votes. That's all right. At least it'll give people another choice. Hey! That's it. Why don't we have a party at the restaurant on election night. Just celebrate."

"Yeah. We could celebrate the good things in our lives. Have each one stand up and tell what they are happy about. How does that sound?" said Ginger.

"Yeah and maybe we'll be celebrating a victory over the Florida Gators. We play them next weekend in Jacksonville, but everyone will be back home by Tuesday. Maybe Coach and some of the players will show up. I'll get a chance to meet them," said Sam enthusiastically.

"Sounds good to me," said Moochie. "Let's run it by Bud. See what he thinks. You'll both have to help me get all the invitations out and everything. No, there won't be time for that. We'll just have to put it in the paper and put a sign up at the restaurant, maybe call a few people."

"No problem, Mama Moochie, and I know everyone else will help. This is gonna be great. I can't wait," said Sam.

When they got back to Moochie's Place, the three of them jumped on Bud like a fruit fly on an over-ripe banana. Finally, he grinned and said, "I been thinking about doing something like that for a long time. It would give us a little publicity, you know. It's one of them mass communication principles that you might not understand, but it works."

Moochie just rolled her eyes and gave a thumbs up to Ginger and Sam.

*****

Word of the party spread through Athens like a wild fire on the West Texas prairie. Grady insisted on talking about it on their syndicated radio show, *Lay it on Grady*. It was picked up by all of the television networks as an amusing side item since Moochie was a write-in candidate for President.

"Lord-a-mercy, heavens to Betsy and sakes alive!" exclaimed Moochie." If that don't beat all I've ever seen. You try and throw a little party and all hell breaks loose. Who knows how many people might show up at our door? Where would we put them all? Lord, we done got ourselves in a mess. What are we gonna do, Bud?"

"Don't worry, babe. Things will work out just fine."

That evening just before closing and while Brad and Pinky were finishing up in the kitchen, Bud stepped out the back door to get a breath of fresh air and rest a few minutes. He reached into his pocket and pulled out his package of Red Man.

As he pinched off a chunk and plugged it into his jaw, he knew it would be harder to quit chewing than it was to quit drinking.

A disheveled form came down the alley in an unsteady gait. Bud thought, must be one of them homeless people. As the man approached, Bud said, "Good evening. How are you?"

The man stopped and looked up, unaccustomed to having people speak to him. "Okay, I guess," he mumbled.

"Did you eat dinner yet?" asked Bud.

"No. Nothing to eat right now. Maybe I can find a job tomorrow."

"You need to eat. Come on in here," said Bud. "Do you like ribs?"

"Yes, sir!" he said and licked his lips.

Bud thought there was something familiar about this man as he held his arm and led him inside. There was a faint smell of body odor mixed with good earth scents that Bud remembered from sleeping in a tent when he was a boy back in Mississippi. "Hey, Brad, get this gentleman a big plate of ribs with all the fixins, and a big slice of apple pie."

This was not the first time Brad had heard that request. In fact, he and Bud had set up a little table in the back corner of the kitchen just for this purpose. Pinky didn't like it one little bit. "Mr. Bud, you must be crazy letting people like that in here. Why, they could pull out a gun, rob us and shoot us all dead before you know it. It just ain't safe, I'm telling you right now."

Bud stepped back outside. He shrugged and leaned back against the building. Looking up into the dark blue, star-studded sky, he thought, that could have been me if I hadn't met my sweet Moochie. He smiled and said, "Thank you, Lord."

He reached over and picked up the can he kept by the back door, spit into it and continued silently, "Lord, I worry about Moochie. She hates Lumkin so much and maybe he deserves it, but it's not good for my bride. It tears her up inside and she's had trouble sleeping lately. Help me find a way to get her past the hate."

The back door cracked open and Moochie yelled, "Come on Buddy Boy, let's go home a little early and rest our beat-up bodies."

Bud stepped back inside, walked up the hall and entered the kitchen just as the man was eating his apple pie. The man had removed his tattered coat and set his sweat stained, broad-brimmed hat on the table next to him. He used his fingers to rake his wavy, white hair back over each ear. He had a thin spot on the back of his head, much like Bud's. His hand was shaky as he lifted his fork with a morsel of pie.

Bud smiled and asked, "How were them ribs?"

The man lowered the fork, looked at Bud, raised his shaky hand a few inches off the table and said, "Very good." He hesitated for a moment, looked again, this time intently at Bud and nodded his head. "If you don't mind, might I have a brief word with you, Mr. Arrington?"

Bud, now curious about this stranger and wondering how he knew his name, said, "Sure. I guess I can sit with you for a minute. Where are you from?"

The man tensed, his face red, and clutched his chest. Then, his face relaxed and he looked at Bud as though trying to figure out who he was. "Right now, I'm living in Tent City; looking for a job. Not many jobs out there."

"You're right about that. By the way, seems like I've met you before. Where were you before Athens?"

"All over the country, but I lived in Meridian, Mississippi most of my life. That's where you're from too, ain't that right?" The man managed a grin on one side of his face.

By this time Bud's brain was in panic mode, trying to figure out who this man was. "How do you know my name? Who are you anyway?"

"I'm ashamed to tell you that. Besides it's not important at this time in our lives. I just felt a great need to see you one last time." He grabbed the table to steady himself and rose to his feet. "Thanks for the food. I have heard that you are a generous man."

By this time Bud's eyes had narrowed and when the man reached for his hat, Bud grabbed his hand. "Wait a minute, you're not leaving here without telling me your name."

The man looked down toward his feet. "I guess there is no other way, and besides, I guess you have the right to know. My name is William Arrington the Second. I'm your father."

Bud was stunned, unable to speak for a long minute as he stared into the man's face, thinking back to all the times he had longed for his father, wondering where he was, and the frequent nightmares he had suffered through, chasing a man but never being able to see his face. This was that face. Anger at the man who had shunned him; wanted nothing to do with him, filled his body and mind as a thousand questions rolled around in his brain. He shouted at his father "What in the hell are you doing here? Why now? What do you want from me?" His voice rose loud enough to turn the heads of Moochie, Brad and Pinky.

His father shrank back, covered his face, and mumbled, "I'm sorry, I'm sorry. I should have never come here. I didn't mean to upset you. I just wanted to see you for the second time in my life."

"What about my life? You sure as hell didn't want to see me the first time, did you? You ignored me as though I didn't exist. You wanted nothing to do with me or my mother. You walked out and I never saw you again until now. Why now!?"

The man looked much older now and feeble. He began to shake uncontrollably. "I wanted to see you because I can't erase you from my mind. Thoughts of you keep coming back to me. I can't shake it. The guilt that I feel. I've tried to get away by bumming around the country, by drinking myself into oblivion, by cheating, lying and stealing. I'm a no good, drunken bum, not worth killing. But, you are still my son and I---I love you and I always will."

"Don't call me your son! I'm not your son, never have been and never will be, so get that out of your head right now. Do you know what it's like to never know your father, to go through life looking for him in every face you see? Always wondering where you are, what you are doing, why you don't love me, why you turned your back on me. I didn't ask to be your son. But, I've always felt guilty somehow, wondering what I did to cause you to hate me, to run away and leave me."

The old man put one arm into his ragged coat and fumbled for the other sleeve. Moochie helped him find it. "I'm sorry. Didn't mean to cause any trouble. I'll get on out of your way now."

"That's right, go on and leave, old man, and don't show your face around here again! If it's money you want, you can forget about it. I don't have any to spare. Now, get on out of here."

The bum hunched over and stumbled to the kitchen door, down the hall and on out into the chilly night air.

Bud, overwhelmed by the pent-up hatred of his father, the trauma of the night before and a heart that was torn apart by his conflicting emotions, fell into the chair, laid his head on the table and cried like he did as a small child when his father left the first time.

Moochie shooed everyone out except Ginger who already had her arm around Bud, tears flooding her eyes. She knew what it was like to be abandoned.

Moochie got them home and finally tucked them into bed: Ginger sleeping on the cot next to her daddy, holding his hand.

CHAPTER FORTY

Bud woke at one-thirty a.m. His heart was filled with conflicting emotions: his father had abandoned him, ignored him all of his life, had never spoken to him or even sent a card, never tried to help. He is a worthless bum by his own admission. I don't owe that son-of-a-bitch anything. And yet, there was something about the old man. If he had not told me his name, I could have liked him, even become his friend, helped him out in some way.

I can't believe how cruel I was to him; the things I said. I don't really know anything about the man; what his life has been like; how he feels. I guess I was just thinking about my own feelings. Maybe that was unfair. I'm always preaching to Moochie about forgiving and I can't even forgive my own father. He began to cry softly so as not to disturb Moochie or Ginger.

Moochie laid her hand gently on top of Bud's and whispered, "It'll be all right, sweetie. I know you'll have to find him. Things will work out just fine. Now, let go of the bed and roll on over here so I can give you my healing touch. He fell asleep in Moochie's arms.

*****

The next morning Bud helped Brad and Pinky through the breakfast crowd, then went to Moochie and whispered, "I have my cell phone with me and I'll call you in two hours so you'll know I'm okay." Moochie nodded and kissed him on the cheek.

334

Bud had never been to Tent City, but knew about where it was. He drove east on Lexington Road and turned into Stryker Tech, a sign company owned by Bill Stryker, a long time business man whose hobby was building airplanes, bicycles and anything else mechanical. He had heard that Mr. Stryker allowed the people from Tent City to take water from the faucet in back of his shop at no charge.

He parked his truck and was met at the door by a middle-age man with mostly gray hair parted on the right side and combed over to cover a bald spot. His eyes were bright with a friendly glow and his right eyebrow arched whenever he spoke as though he was inquiring whether you agreed with what he was saying. He had a cell phone stuck in his left ear and continued to take a sign order as he motioned for Bud to have a seat. He finished the order and looked up with a smile on his face. The shop smelled of ink and paint and Johnny Cash sang "Folsom Prison Blues" in the background. "What can I do for you, sir? Need a sign or maybe some T-shirts?"

"I'm Bud Arrington from Moochie's Place, Moochie's husband and co-proprietor. Remember? She hooked you up with M.D. Slocum, the T-shirt man."

Bill jumped to his feet. "Remember? Why, man alive. Your wife saved me and Slocum from the poor house. My business was about ready to go under before I started getting orders from M.D. or Slapper, as Moochie calls him. What can I do for you? You name it and I'll help you all I can."

"Bill, I wanted to talk to you for a minute about Tent City. I found out last night that my father that I've never known before, is staying there and I'd like to find him. I wanted to ask if I could park my truck here and if you could point me in the right direction. I'm a little scared to go up there if you want to know the truth."

"You're in the right place, Bud. I know several of the people up there quite well. They're mostly good people, just down on their luck. There are a few bad ones that you have to watch out for. Come on, I'll show you the way."

He led Bud to the right of his building about a hundred feet and pointed to a fence with a well-worn path next to it. Bud could see The Loop or By-Pass 10 through the underbrush and a few small trees to the left.

"Follow this path to the city, smile, be friendly and ask if someone can direct you to where your father stays. I'll leave the back window of my shop open. Yell if there's trouble and I'll come running."

Bud made his way along the fence and up the hill toward the tents. It was a damp, dreary day and Bud felt uneasy. It was sort of like walking into someone's home, unannounced. Tall Johnson grass leaned over and brushed his legs as he made the climb, leery of what might be lurking in the thick grass on either side, and what he might find at the top. Would his father even talk to him after last night?

He approached the first tent and saw a man sitting on a stump warming his hands over a small fire. The man wore a Cleveland Indians baseball cap. He had a full beard and long, black hair straggled from under the cap. He looked up expectantly when he heard Bud's footsteps.

"I'm sorry to bother you, sir, but I'm looking for my father and wondered if you might show me where he's staying. His name is William Arrington. Do you know him?"

"Don't know him well, but his tent is about the third one down on the left. You might be a little late."

Bud said, "Thank you," wondering if his dad had pulled up stakes.

Going as directed he found two folding chairs in front, and a tent with one of its flaps open and tied back. Sobbing came from inside. To the right was a lean-to fastened to two small trees. A light-skinned man with a goatee and camouflaged hat pulled down over his brow sat in a battered, aluminum lounge chair.

"Hello," said Bud.

"What do you want up here?"

"Just trying to find someone," said Bud.

"Well, make it quick and don't bother the woman inside."

Bud didn't answer but spoke to the person inside the tent. "Hello. May I speak to you for a minute?"

The crying stopped and shortly an uncombed head of blond hair popped out of the tent. It was a young woman; Bud would guess about twenty-one. She wore a plaid shirt, tucked into jeans and flip-flops. She was about average weight and height with a pretty face even though she wore no make-up. "Hi," she said as she emerged, wiping her cheeks.

"Hello. I'm Bud Arrington and I'm looking for my father, William Arrington. Am I in the right place?"

She started crying again and fell into Bud's arms. She sobbed, "Your daddy's dead. He told me about you last night. I tried to wake him up this morning, but he was gone. I called the police and they came up and contacted the coroner. They took him away about two hours ago. Said he would be at the Athens Regional Morgue. Wanted to know if I knew any of his relatives. I told them all I know is he has a son."

Bud set the girl in one of the chairs, then fell into the other one and covered his face. Too late, he thought. Too late. I'm so sorry. Please forgive me Daddy.

The girl sniffed; took out a handkerchief and wiped her nose. "I'm sorry. Your father was a good man, a good soul. There was something inside of him that made him special. He genuinely cared about people and I hate to be cynical, but it's rare to find someone like that, especially in a place like this. I was lucky to meet him. He found me really; and saved my life."

Bud looked into her striking, emerald green eyes. "I'm the one who should be sorry for you. I never knew my father, but you two apparently had a relationship, and I'm sorry for your loss." Bud felt a strong nicotine urge, felt of his pocket to make sure the tobacco was there, then decided not to chew at a time like this.

"Oh, I guess it was a relationship, but not the kind you're thinking of. It's like he adopted me, unofficially of course, and

I was his daughter. By the way, my name is Brandy, Brandy Culpepper."

"Nice to meet you, Brandy. If you don't mind my asking, how did you meet?"

"On a park bench down on the Oconee River Greenway. My purse had been stolen, even though it had no money in it. I had spent what little I had left on alcohol. I was in nursing school for a while but couldn't afford the tuition, so I dropped out and got a job as a waitress. When the restaurant closed, I couldn't find another job."

"Why didn't you go home?"

"My mother's dead and my father is a crackhead; no job. There was nothing to go home to. I'm sorry to say this, but I was desperate and felt like I had no other choice but to turn to prostitution in order to eat.

"When Bill found me, I was at rock bottom; just lying there on the bench praying that God would let me die.

"Bill got me off the bench, hooked my arm around his neck and half carried me to the near-by Dairy Queen where he used the few dollars he had to buy me food. He brought me to his tent, put me on his cot and covered me with his only blanket. He slept on the ground that night. The next morning he stood outside of Walmart and begged enough money to buy another cot and blanket. I've been here ever since. We were going to the Methodist Church lunch program every day so we would have at least one good meal."

"What are you going to do now?"

"Don't know. I do know that I can't stay here. It's not safe with the creep next door. Your dad always carried a knife and his pistol. He protected me. Now, all I've got is the gun, but I still don't feel safe." She glanced at the man next door, then closed her eyes as though praying.

"When your daddy got home last night, he asked me to write a letter to you. He was shaken and so very sad. He told me what happened and felt like he needed to tell you about his life; said he owed you at least that much. Let's go into the tent and I'll read it to you. Don't know if you can read my handwriting."

As they moved inside, the man next door said, "Don't stay too long. I'll be listening and if things get fishy, I'll drag you out and whip your ass all the way down the hill."

Brandy began to tremble, leaned close to Bud and said, "Don't worry, I've got your dad's pistol and if he tries to come in, I'll shoot his ass. He thinks I belong to him now that Bill is gone. He knows that I'll have to go to sleep at some point and when I do, he'll make his move."

She reached under her cot, brought out the pistol and a folded sheet of paper. She laid the gun beside her and began to read:

"Dear Son,

First, I want to say that I love you. I've always loved you, even in the darkest days of my despair when I was drowning in alcohol, no longer able to reason or take care of myself, trying to blot out the memories of my miserable life. I'm not trying to make an excuse, son. There is no excuse. I just want to explain and maybe someday you'll be able to forgive me.

I was eighteen years old, from a middle to upper-class family and a senior in high school when I met your mother. I mean no disrespect for your mother because she did the best she could, but she was a prostitute. When she became pregnant, I was ashamed, embarrassed and afraid to tell my parents or anyone else. I took the easy way out and just ran away from it all, and I've been running ever since. I thought with time I would forget, but that never happened. The thought of you and what I had done has followed me up to this very minute.

I should never have come to see you tonight, but when I found out you were here in Athens and people told me how kind you were, I was unable to resist. I just had to see you. I had no intention of telling you who I was, but thought if I could just look at you one time, it would ease my shame and the hurt in my heart. Instead, it broke my heart and hurt you at the same time. I'm so very, very sorry. I know you can't accept this now, but in spite of all, I do love you.

Dad"

She brushed a tear and handed the paper to Bud. "His instructions were to deliver this to you if anything happened to him. He was a good man, Bud, and I hope you will be able to forgive him."

Bud took the paper and stuffed it into his pocket. He bowed his head, unable to speak, but knew he loved his father and had already forgiven him.

After a while, Bud said, "Brandy, gather all of your belongings together. You'll be staying with Moochie and me until we can find you a place to live. Also, you are now employed at Moochie's Place as a waitress. As soon as I get back there, I'll make arrangements for my father to have a decent burial."

They stepped outside. Bud glanced to the left and saw the neighbor moving toward them with a broken tree-limb in his hand.

Bud stopped and said to Brandy, "Take all you can carry and run down to the sign shop. You'll be safe there. I'll be along as soon as I can." He turned and faced the man with the goatee.

The man walked up to Bud, face red, eyes bulging. He stuck his face into Bud's and shouted, "I told you to leave her alone! She belongs to me and you're not taking her. Now, I'm gonna have to whip your ass." He drew the stick back and over his head.

Bud raised his right leg and came down as hard as he could on top of the man's foot. He felt the bones break as the man screamed and bent forward. Bud raised up to his full height and came down on the back of the man's neck with his right forearm. The brute fell face down, then rolled onto his back, grabbed his foot and screamed, "You broke my foot, you son-of-a-bitch!"

Bud turned and walked down the hill. When he got to Stryker's, he called Moochie. "I'm okay. Oh, by the way, I just hired us a new waitress. I didn't have time to talk to you about it. Her name is Brandy, and she'll have to live with us for a while. I'll take her on to the house, move her into the spare bedroom and be back to the restaurant as quick as I can."

"Well, sakes alive, honey, are you all right? What in the world happened?"

"I'll explain everything when I get there."

*****

When Bud arrived at the restaurant he walked straight to Moochie's office and motioned for her to follow. As she passed April she whispered, "Please bring us two cups of coffee and see that we're not disturbed." Bud was shaken and she could tell he had been crying. She reached across and took his hands in hers. "Now listen, honey. Just calm down. Whatever happened at Tent City will work out just fine. Ole Moochie will see to that. Just take your time and tell me what happened."

Bud lifted his downcast eyes, "He's dead, Moochie. Died before I got there. I didn't get to see him. Didn't get to say goodbye or tell him that I love him or that I forgive him. Nothing." He turned away, took out his handkerchief and cleared his nose.

Moochie rubbed and patted his hand as April set the cups in front of them and made a quick exit.

Bud reached into his pocket and passed Moochie the letter his father had dictated. She read it while wiping tears with her napkin. There was a long pause as the big woman, thinking I've got to be strong for Bud, regained control. Finally she looked up at her man, who had been through so much, with a weak smile. "I'm sorry, real sorry. It's strange how we can be so connected to someone we didn't even know. I don't understand it, but God knows and understands and that will have to be good enough for us. I'll call Allen Free, the undertaker, today. Remember him, he's one of our best customers. He'll make all the arrangements. Don't you worry none about that. Now, tell me about our new waitress."

Bud explained the whole story, even how they'd escaped, and concluded with, "She seems to be a good person, Moochie. I think you'll like her. We'll have to introduce her to the rest of the crew tomorrow. If I'm not mistaken, she'll fit right in." Bud picked up his cup, took a sip and relaxed. Moochie knew that he would be all right.

CHAPTER FORTY ONE

The week before the big party passed quickly. Although Moochie and Bud felt better physically, Bud's father's funeral was very sad with only the two of them and Brandy to mourn his passing. Reverend Horvath, April's pastor, was kind enough to preside even though Brandy was the only one who could tell him anything about William Arrington II.

Moochie had taken Brandy to buy clothes and to look for an affordable apartment. They decided to take their time since rental prices were high in Athens and Brandy was comfortable living with them.

They heard that Lumkin was released on bail, but ordered to stay home with an ankle monitor until his trial. The judge was assured that he was under a doctor's care and was responding to medication.

*****

Bud awoke at five-thirty a.m., the day the furniture for the rebuilt restaurant would arrive. The next evening they would celebrate the grand opening and the Presidential election results. Bud let go of his side of the bed and let gravity roll him next to Moochie. He gently touched her arm to see if she was awake. Moochie's eyes fluttered and remained closed. She stretched and turned from her left side to her back, dropping her right arm across Bud's chest. The blow knocked the wind out of him. He moaned and crawled up his side to recover, thinking he should know better by now.

Hearing Bud moan, Moochie's eyes popped open. "Morning, honey. What's wrong, you got a cold or something?"

"No, love. I'm fine. Just wanted to see if you were awake. Now that you are, why don't we go on in and see how the restaurant looks?"

"Why not? Give Ginger and Brandy another thirty minutes before you wake them up. We'll drop Ginger off at school a little early. By the way, I'm glad you found Brandy. She fits right in with the rest of the crew, and she's a hard worker too. Works well with Peola out on the floor."

The thought of how he had found Brandy made Bud sad. Moochie heard him sigh and understood. She patted his hand. "I know you still miss him, sweetie."

"Yeah. You're right and I don't understand that. I never even knew him; he played no real part in my life, and yet his death saddens me. I wonder what it would be like if he had lived and we had become friends. Guess I'll never know the answer to that."

"True, love. But, at least you got to meet him. That's worth something. Even if you hadn't met him, there would still be a tie there, a family tie that's beyond our understanding. I have a feeling that you will see him again, just not in this lifetime."

"I hope so. At least I was able to give him a decent burial and say goodbye."

*****

Entering through the front door Moochie was surprised by the openness of the dining area. "Lord-a-mercy, honey, this can't be the same size as the old building."

"Yep. Sure is. We just don't have tables and chairs and all the other stuff in here yet. The furniture company will bring the tables and chairs today at nine o'clock. Brad and me will move the jukebox in here today and hook up the speakers."

Moochie looked around. The new counter to her left ran the full length of the room with a break in the middle and another at the far end, much like the original and exactly as she wanted it. The laminated, white counter top sparkled under recessed lighting in the ceiling. Padded midnight blue barstools would arrive with the rest of the furniture. The walls were sea blue to blend with the navy blue floor tile. Moochie's "Office" sat in the back left corner with the rest of the booths lining the back and right wall. A prominent space was reserved for Bud's jukebox.

"Ain't it a sight?" asked Bud.

She grabbed Bud and pulled him close. "Sure is, my little man. Like a shiny new dime. There's no rat in Clarke County that would dare walk into a place this clean. Remember when we first saw the old building?"

"Sure do. It was a mess." Bud looked around and stood silent for a moment. "All it took, love, was a major fire and almost getting ourselves cooked like a slab of ribs or shot by a lunatic."

Moochie became somber at the thought. "Yeah. I thought we were goners when we went down in the kitchen. Thank God the firemen got to us in time."

"Yep, and that reminds me, the saying of the week is 'Be thankful, honey.' I better go put it up on the sign."

Moochie smiled. "That'll be perfect for our party tomorrow night."

*****

Early Tuesday morning Uncle Billy rested at the counter after finishing his two eggs, over light, with sausage. Moochie kept him company from behind the counter on her reinforced stool, her size ten loafers barely touching the floor. Bud stood beside her with his left hand wrapped around a cup of black coffee. "I love the smell of fresh brewed coffee, don't you?" he said, waving it under his nose.

"I sure do, honey, but I don't see how in the world you can drink it black like that. Shoot, I need a bunch of cream and sugar to cut the edge a little. Uncle Billy drinks his black too."

"Yep," said Billy. "Nothing against cream, mind you, but I'd rather drink it separate. Every now and again I'll add a pinch of sugar to satisfy my sweet tooth. My doctor tells me sugar is bad for my health."

He pushed his Rangers baseball cap to the back of his head and looked at Moochie and Bud. "Well, folks, tonight will be wonderful, just wonderful. It's election time and your party is gonna be the biggest thing happening in Athens this time of year, at least that's what I hear on the TV and radio."

"Lord-a-mercy, honey, I'm a little worried. It never entered my mind that it would get so out of hand. I thought it would just be our gang here and a few other people watching the election returns. My goodness, it's amazing how fast the word spread. I guess we should have made it by invitation only, but I didn't want to keep anyone out. You know what I mean?"

"Yeah, I know," said Bud. "Once again, it's one of them mass communication phenominals. All you have to do is plant the seed and it just grows. I hope they don't all expect to eat. We're just having 'or derves' as them French people say. Once they're gone, that's it."

"Can't feed the whole world," said Moochie. "Sounds like a lot of people might end up outside. We sure can't feed them."

"Oops, spilled my coffee," said Uncle Billy. "April, please hand me a napkin." April complied as she made her way to the jukebox.

"Lucille and I will be here. Let us know if we can help."

"Thanks," said Bud. "We'll just have to wait and see what happens. As Calvin Coolidge once said, 'Damn the torpedoes, full speed ahead.'"

"Wasn't Coolidge," corrected Uncle Billy. "It was some admiral during The Big One when the German Nazis were sinking our ships."

"Whatever," said Bud. "Somebody said it."

"Misery Loves Company," by Jerry Reed blared from the music box. April waited patiently to make her selection.

*****

The Tuesday night dinner crowd was not large and the last couple left by seven o'clock. The whole crew was there and had plenty of time to clean and straighten the old and new dining areas. They set out plates of riblets, corn on the cob, cornbread, cheese and crackers. There was sweet tea and coffee to drink. Moochie insisted they serve apple tarts, chocolate covered pralines and Moochie's special; Twinkies with decadent chocolate drizzled over the top. "Who ever heard of eating without dessert?" she said. At one point Moochie yelled, "Sam and Ginger, stay away from them specials before you have a sugar fit."

The party was to start at nine and all was ready by eight-fifteen. Moochie peeked outside where a crowd was already gathering. "Mercy sakes. There's television crews out there interviewing folks. Can't even have a little get together without all the news hounds."

April was teaching Peola to clog to "Big Daddy's Alabamy Bound," while Brad and Pinky sang along with Jerry Reed. Moochie and Bud clapped their hands and stomped their feet, Bud yelling "Yee Ha!" every now and then. After the dance was over, Peola, having never heard of clogging, concluded that it was the dumbest dance she had ever done.

At five to nine Moochie unlocked and stepped outside the front door of the newly rebuilt side of the restaurant. "Attention please. Thank you all for being here to help us celebrate the opening of our new building. As you'll see when you get inside, Hammertoe and his crew did a fine job. I'm real sorry. We had no idea so many people would be here and the restaurant just won't hold everyone; fire codes you know. We'll turn the sidewalk speakers on so y'all out here can hear what's going on inside. We can only let one camera crew inside for the same reason, so you all will have to share. It would really help if the ones who get inside will look the place over then come back so others have a chance to go in. Thanks for your help." With that she stepped back and people began to file in.

Things moved slowly at first because everyone stopped and spoke to Pretty Boy and Sugar Boy who were near the front door. Bud saw what was happening and moved them to the middle wall next to the jukebox. Pretty Boy kept repeating "Gawk! Welcome to Moochie's," looking expectantly toward Sugar Boy each time. Sugar Boy just said "Gawk!" and jumped back and forth from the swing to the roosting rod in the middle of the cage.

The aroma of barbequed ribs permeated the restaurant and John Denver sang "Sunshine on My Shoulders." Moochie was glowing, perched on her stool behind the counter, with Bud by her side. He had rigged a microphone so all could hear his bride, the mistress of ceremonies. Another sound system was set up in the middle of the room for others who wanted to speak. Television sets were plugged in around the restaurant so those who were caught up in politics could keep an eye on the returns.

Bud saw Miss Precious standing by the jukebox bragging to one of the football players about how she had sold the music machine to him. She wore a new, wine-colored sweater, buttoned to the top, not wanting to incite any lechery. Other players hung around, admiring the large, pink wart in the middle of her forehead.

At ten o'clock Moochie motioned for Brad and April to mute the televisions and turn the jukebox off. She tapped on the mike to make sure it was working. "Sorry to bust in on the fun, honey, but we decided from the beginning to make this a Thanksgiving party. After all, Thanksgiving is only three weeks away. We wanted a chance to tell all of you how thankful we are to you for making our restaurant a success. It has been rocky at times and even scary, but we managed to hang in there and come out on top, even if we are a little less for the wear, if you know what I mean."

There was loud applause and shouts of "Way to go Moochie and Bud! We knew you could do it! We're proud of you!"

Moochie held up her hand. "This man standing next to me has been a rock. He took most of the blows and is still standing. I'm so proud of him there's no way to express it. I just love him to pieces."

The place went wild with the football players leading the cheers. "You're the man, Bud! Show us your muscle, Bud! You're the champ!" They began leading the crowd in cheers and barking like the bulldogs they were: "Woof, woof, woof."

Bud was embarrassed, but held up his good right arm and made a fist. Moochie handed him the microphone.

"Thank you, folks. Don't mind them wimpy football players in the back." He laughed and shook his fist at them. "They think they're hot stuff even though they got beat by the Florida Gators on Saturday. They'll be okay, though. Just hang in there guys."

"Yeah! Go Dawgs!" yelled the crowd.

"Anyway, this party is our way of showing our thanks to everybody who's helped us along the way." He looked at Moochie and put his arm as far around her as he could reach. "Personally, I'm thankful for my sweet bride. She has saved my life in more ways than one. I love Moochie for who she is. She's the most beautiful person in the world to me. Through it all, the strength within her has stood like a mountain and flowed like a river." Moochie reached over and kissed him on the cheek and his speech faltered for a moment.

"I'm also thankful for, and proud of, my daughter, Ginger. She's a gift from God and I love her with all my heart."

He looked at Sam, standing next to Ginger with a big smile on his face, looking like he was about to burst. "Sam is like our own boy. Sorry, Rube and Kristy, but if you ever want to get rid of him, we'll take him in a minute." Kristy, standing in the back, smiled and waved.

Bud bowed his head for a moment. "Me and Moochie say thanks every night for the rest of our family: Brad, Pinky, April and Peola. Our success is in large part because of them. They stood by us through the good, bad and ugly. We'll always be thankful for them. And, Brandy, welcome to the family. We're so glad we found you. Finally, we love you all, every last one of you. Thank you. Thank you." He handed the mike back to Moochie.

Moved, Moochie said in a husky voice, "Anyone who wishes to speak and tell what they are thankful for is welcome to step up to the mike."

There was already a line. Peola announced that she and senior offensive lineman, Winslow Harris, would be getting married in January.

Not to be outdone, April dragged Pretty Boy's mouthpiece, Steve Phelps, to the mike. The football players in the back shouted, "Go for it, April!" She giggled out loud and snorted into the microphone. Startled by her own sound, she held the mike away for a moment, then said, "Steve and I are getting married next month."

Winslow whispered to Peola, "Looks like they got a head start."

Brad Leaptrott said he was thankful to have a job as an entomologist, working as a researcher under a new grant for the university, adding he'd still be working part-time at Moochie's Place.

Pinky Rose told how Moochie and Bud had been so kind and had given her a job at a difficult time in her life.

Others stepped to the microphone such as Slapper Slocum, speaking of his success in the Moochie T-shirt business and announcing his latest creation, a Sugar Boy shirt.

Ron Harris of the Environmental Health Section, who had been forced to ban Pretty Boy from the restaurant, said how sorry he was and how much he liked Pretty Boy, Moochie and Bud.

Grady Lakes told of the success of the *Lay it on Grady* show and reminisced how Moochie had become a radio star.

Grady handed the mike to Brandy. "Mr. Bud's dad, William, saved my life when I was at the lowest point: at the end of my rope, so to speak, with nothing else to hold on to." Unable to control her emotions, she broke down and sobbed. Grady put his arm around her for support. When she regained control she said, "Mr. Bud and Miss Moochie restored my faith in humanity and gave me hope for the future. Thank you both from the bottom of my heart." Her voice quivered. "I…I love you…." She placed the mike back on the stand.

Ginger pushed Sam forward, grabbed the mike and put it in his hand. He coughed and began. "Mama Moochie, Papa Bud, I have an announcement to make. Mama and Daddy already know about it, but I've been saving it as a surprise for you. Guess what. Ben Wade, the famous country singer, is going to record my song, 'Dixie Guitar Band."

Moochie screamed, "Lord-a-mercy, sakes alive, hallelujah and praise the Lord!" Bud jumped to his feet and they both rushed over to congratulate Sam.

The football players gave three cheers for Sam: "Hip, hip, hooray! Hip, hip, hooray! Hip, hip, hooray!"

Arch Cameron, reporter for the *Banner-Herald* and his cameraman, Larry Shropshire, moved in to interview Sam.

When the line of speakers dwindled, Moochie announced the current election results, adding, "I want to thank the young student, Brian Polanski, for nominating me for President. I honor his belief in me. It would be impossible for someone like me to really run for that office much less be elected. Why, honey, you'd have to be a multi-millionaire or have a lot of millionaire friends helping you. That's what's happened to democracy in this country and it's a shame. But, I'm glad that our young people are still able to think and believe in a free and democratic way. Maybe someday they'll lead us back to what our founding fathers wanted for us. Thanks to all who took the time to write in my name on their ballot. Even though the votes won't count, I would be happy to beat Micky Mouse, Homer Simpson, Jefferson Davis and all the other write-ins that represent the frustration of voters.

"Now, let's go back to celebrating all the many things that we have to be thankful for, and that's a lot. Sam and Ginger, turn Bud's music box back on and let's enjoy each other's company."

The place was still packed at ten-thirty. Spirits were high and laughter could be heard all over the restaurant, even above the jukebox. Bud went to check on Pretty Boy and Sugar Boy, knowing it was past their bed time. Pretty Boy was still greeting people and telling some of the football players how ugly their mama was.

Booker Cleveland, Pretty Boy's birdnapper, stood next to Sugar Boy's cage with Police Officer Waddell who had become his mentor. Booker had been taunting the bird all evening, trying to get a rise out of him. Finally, Sugar Boy blurted, "Gawk! Go ahead punk!" Booker started jumping up and down, hugging Waddell and others. "He did it! He did it!" Pretty Boy glanced proudly at his son.

Miss Charmaine stood close by, talking to a lady employed at Foster's Jewelry. She looked up and smiled when Sugar Boy spoke. She nodded his way and said, "He's an offspring of one of my girls, Sugar Plum. Smart bird, just like his mama. Mr. Boy has done a fine job raising him." The lady looked puzzled but decided not to ask who Mr. Boy was.

Also in the group were two ladies who work in the ladies boutique at SteinMart. They were drawn to Charmaine's unusual outfit. She wore white New Balance cross trainer shoes. Her florescent green skirt brushed just below the knees. An orange turtleneck peeked from beneath a pink, knit jacket. More than one head had turned when she walked into the room.

The first boutique lady cupped her mouth and said, "Would you look at that hairdo. Why it could be declared a national bird sanctuary any day now."

The other lady giggled and slapped her on the back. "I sold her the green skirt. Where she got that orange blouse, I'll never know. She's a sartorial train wreck waiting to happen."

Charmaine's escort son stood nearby, chewing on a rib and dripping sauce on his university T-shirt. Bud had never met her son.

Moochie and Bud made their way around the room, giving hugs and talking to well-wishers. Presently, they were engaged in a conversation with Rube and Amy about the restaurant business and how much they appreciated his help in getting them started. Rube looked puzzled when the boisterous crowd outside suddenly quieted.

All heads turned toward the open front door. There were loud gasps and looks of amazement as Wilson Lumkin's wife, Delores, and son, Billy, walked in.

Moochie didn't know what to say for one of the first times in her life. She, Bud and the rest of the crowd stood and stared at the Lumkins. In a moment Delores spoke softly to Billy and patted his arm. They began the long walk toward Moochie and Bud. Delores' eyes were filled with tears as she approached them. Shaking, she reached out to Moochie, who took her hand. Delores leaned forward and said, "Miss Moochie, Mr.Bud, Wilson is under house arrest and under the care of a doctor, as you may know. Billy and I have something to say to you and we wanted to do so publicly."

Moochie's other fist was clinched, her mouth a thin line.

Delores stepped back, supported by her son. "We're sorry--sorry that you have been hurt. My husband is accused of doing some terrible things and if they are true, he will have to pay with time in prison or an institution." Her voice faltered and she paused.

Moochie started to say something, but Bud touched her arm, and held his hand out flat. They waited patiently as Mrs. Lumkin regained control.

"I don't know how you could ever forgive us, but I came tonight to ask you not to hold Wilson's actions against my son.

Billy will be taking over the restaurant and trying to make a go of it. It will be tough on him and me as we try to hold things together while Wilson is gone. I'm sorry. That's all I have to say." She began to turn away. There was complete silence in the room and outside.

Moochie said, "Wait," taking a step forward. "Me and Bud do forgive you and your family, even Mr. Lumkin. That's what it says in the Good Book. Forgive your neighbors, over and over again if you have to." Bud, surprised by Moochie's change of attitude, nodded and stepped up beside her.

She continued, "And don't you worry none about your son and the restaurant. We found some money and set up a foundation to help young people starting out in business. Sounds like Billy might be eligible for that. He'll do just fine. Bud might not admit it, but people get tired of eating ribs every day. We'll send those folks to your restaurant. Won't we, Buddy Boy?"

Bud, stunned by the idea that someone would get tired of his ribs, finally nodded.

Moochie continued, "Now, you just hold on a minute. If it's all right with you, I'd like to give each of you a nice, gentle hug. Is that all right?"

Mrs. Lumkin nodded as they stood in silence, not knowing what to expect. Moochie grabbed each in turn, said "Bless you," and gave them a long hug. The crowd broke into thunderous applause, some crying and laughing at the same time.

Shocked silence fell over the people outside and some began to take cover while others fled the scene. As the lone gunman, waving an AK 47, pushed his way through the door, Pretty Boy pleaded, "Loooord, have mercy!" Some of the women screamed, but there was no place to hide as they cringed and backed as close to the walls as they could.

Lumkin's face was wildly distorted, his temple veins like purple ropes, his head whipping from side to side, his body turning in circles. He fired a burst into the ceiling, scattering debris over the people. Some fainted, others, trying to dial 911, dropped their cell phones.

He approached Moochie, Bud and his own family screaming, "Money! Where's my money? Now---taking my family! Kill! Orders are to kill!" He confronted Moochie and lowered the gun. "Got to kill!"

Deloris screamed, "No, Wilson!" and stepped in front of her husband. Lumkin's finger tightened on the trigger as the front door slammed open again. His head jerked around as Lumkin Senior screamed, "Wilson, son! Stop! Don't do it!"

Lumkin whipped the gun around as his trigger finger convulsed into a spasm. The bullet ripped away part of his daddy's thigh, spinning him violently through the plate glass window and into the crowd outside. Several people, standing by the window, broke his fall as they sprawled onto the sidewalk, some injured by the broken glass.

Bud took two steps toward Lumkin and froze when the madman turned the gun his way. Lumkin's face turned pale when he stared at his wife, standing next to Bud, as though he had just awakened from a nightmare. There was a moment of recognition and surprise. "What are you doing here, Delores? Billy? What happened? Where am I? Delores!! What have I done?" He slowly turned the gun around, stuck it in his mouth and closed his eyes.

Bud lunged at Lumkin, grabbed and yanked the barrel of the rifle, sending a shot into the ceiling. Bud threw the gun away as Lumkin collapsed facedown onto the floor.

Uncle Billy, holding Aunt Lucille tightly next to the back wall bowed his head. "Lord God Almighty, Maker of Heaven and Earth, what have we come to? Have mercy upon our miserable souls."

Pandemonium reigned. Soon the shouts and screams were overwhelmed by police and EMT sirens. Wilson was cuffed and hauled away. Most of the injured were treated on the scene while Wilson's father and others were taken to Athens Regional

Hospital. Those who had not run away initially, huddled in small groups, trying to fathom what had taken place.

The police taped off the scene and interviewed as many as possible.

When things settled down, Moochie, Bud, family and close friends gathered in the other dining room to sort out what had happened and to sooth and reassure each other, especially Moochie and Bud, whose hands were shaking so badly he had to refuse a cup of coffee.

At one a.m. Moochie stood up and took Bud's hand. "Come on, my sweet little man, we're going home and sleep soundly the rest of the night. I have a feeling that a heavy load has been lifted off our shoulders. We didn't win. Nobody wins in something like this. But we did survive and we can be thankful for that. Tomorrow is a new day and we're going to make the best of it. We've got our love and that's all we need. Ain't that right, Buddy Boy?"

Bud, now calm, straightened up and threw his shoulders back. "Yep, that's true my sweet Moochie. As one of them English poets once said, "Hope springs eternal in the human chest."

"Breast. Human breast."

"Right. Breast."

Made in the USA
Las Vegas, NV
14 October 2021